TO: Michael
Be the differ...

MW00323936

The Ark Project

THE CLONE PARADOX

Book 1

J.W. Elliot 2022

J.W. Elliot

Bent Bow
Publishing, LLC

This is a work of fiction. Characters, names, places, and events are the product of the author's imagination or are used fictitiously. Any resemblance to persons, living or dead, historical events, or locations are entirely coincidental.

Copyright © 2021 J.W. Elliot

All rights reserved. No part of this book may be reproduced or transmitted in any form or by any means, electronic or mechanical, including photocopying, recording, or by any information storage and retrieval system except as may be expressly permitted in writing by the publisher.

Bent Bow Publishing, LLC
82 Wendell Ave., STE 100
Pittsfield, MA 01201
USA

ISBN 978-1-953010-08-7

Cover Art by Bruce Rolff and Camil Kuo

Cover Design by Brandi Doane McCann

If you enjoy this book, please consider leaving an honest review on Amazon and sharing on your social media sites.

Please sign up for my newsletter where you can get a free short story and more free content at: www.jwelliot.com

CHAPTER ONE
THE RAVEN FALLS

THE BLUE ORB of the earth dangled in the inky blackness of space. Its startling blueness was marbled with wisps of clouds and patches of brown, like a diseased organism. Kaiden had come to the moon searching for a cure for that disease, but when the cause of the infection was humanity itself, what hope did they have of finding an antidote?

Kaiden shifted his gaze away from where the earth peeked over the gray lunar horizon. The glass dome that covered the landing bay of the Ark Field Station gave a panoramic view of the pitted landscape and the sprawling complex of buildings that comprised the station. It perched on the edge of the lunar Sea of Tranquility, a potent symbol of how humanity was now reaching for the stars.

Their mission was a routine flight to provide security and transport for the delivery to the International Seed Bank of animal and plant tissue, seeds, and DNA. Then they had to pick up half a dozen human test clones for shipment back to their base, called Ararat, in the high deserts of Montana. The docile clones were just lining up on the metal catwalk beside his lunar transport ship.

"They're pitiful," Kaiden said, and he meant it.

The six clones stood in a line watching him with placid, disinterested eyes. Each represented one of the broad ethnic groups of Earth—European, Indian, Asian, African, Australian, and Native

American. They each had the same withered appearance and sunken cheeks. A few of them had blue lips. It might be his job to escort the experimental clones to and from the lunar field station, but he didn't have to like it.

"They drug them before transport," Casey said. "Poor things. What would it be like to be nothing but a lab rat?" Casey was a stocky blonde who was easily the best pilot Kaiden had ever flown with. She wore the standard-issue black security uniform with the red ark symbol of The Ark Project, or TAP, stitched into the left shoulder that everyone on his team wore.

"Do you really think this is the answer?" Kaiden asked. "I mean, look at them. What kind of future is that?"

A shiver of disgust swept through him. The clones gave him the creeps, even while he pitied them. It was like some Frankenstein experiment in which the bodies were normal, but the mind and soul were scarred. If a twisted Frankenstein humanity was the solution to earth's problems, maybe it would be better just to die before it came to that.

"It's a future where we're alive," Casey said.

"I don't call that living," Kaiden responded.

"These are just the prototypes," Casey said. "When they get the bugs worked out, they'll look and behave just like us."

"They better not behave like you," Delano said as he stepped up with the paperwork for the shipment under his arm. He had a lean, handsome look about him. He cast a smile and a wink at Casey, who grinned and tried to act like she hadn't seen.

"Shut up," Casey said. "At least I know how to be responsible."

"Hey," Delano said, "I'm responsible." He held up the paperwork as evidence. "I just don't mind having fun while obeying the rules."

"Rules? You wouldn't know a rule if it climbed into one of your big, flaring nostrils."

"Whoa, that's low," Delano said.

"But deadly accurate," Burl said as he came up behind Delano with his rifle slung casually over one shoulder.

"All right," Kaiden said. He needed to keep the ribbing to a minimum. They weren't a formal military security force, so the rules were more lax for them, but too much of this sort of thing could undermine discipline. As the only African on the team, he'd been teased occasionally for his black skin and short curly hair. Friendly banter was okay, but it could easily get out of hand.

"Let's get 'em loaded," he said. He turned to the ship. "Raven," he yelled. A black head poked out of the bay doors. "They're coming on board."

Raven waved at them to come. Someone coughed behind them, and Kaiden spun around to see a willowy young woman with pale skin, long brown hair, and freckles, wearing a white lab coat, standing with her hands clasped in front of her. She bore an expression of controlled patience.

"Who are you?" Kaiden demanded.

"I'm here to monitor the clones during transport. Permission to board your ship, Captain."

Kaiden snorted and glanced at the clones. "Looks like they need feeding and some rest more than monitoring. What do you people do to them while they're up here?"

"I'm afraid I'm not allowed to share that information," the scientist said with a guarded expression. She glanced up at the window of the control room, and Kaiden was sure she was aware that someone might be recording them.

"What is your name?"

"Willow."

Kaiden smiled. "How appropriate."

Casey cleared her throat and gave him a wide-eyed, it's-time-to-shut-up look.

"Right," he said. "Sorry. Let's get them loaded."

Raven waved at Burl and Delano, who led the six clones up the ramp. The low gravity made the procession comical as they made their way with a slow shuffle. When Raven saw Willow fall in behind them, she gave Kaiden a big wink and a thumbs up. This surprised him because she had been moody during the entire trip.

Kaiden rolled his eyes. His crew were constantly trying to set him up with someone. His best friend, Quill, said it was because they wanted him to ease off their constant training and missions and thought if they could get him interested in a woman, they could enjoy more free time. Well, it wasn't going to work.

Kaiden did the familiar shuffle up the ramp and into the ship before securing the hatch and initiating the pre-flight protocol.

The lunar transport was a medium-sized freighter with plenty of room for the six clones, the five crew, and the scientist. It never landed on earth because it was too large to get back into space cheaply, but the moon's lower gravity allowed it to land directly on the surface and launch from there. The transport had private rooms for the crew, a fully stocked medical ward, and a kitchen. A central corridor connected every area of the ship and terminated in a wide bay at the rear. The journey to the Earth Orbital Space Station was about thirty-six-hours, and once they were on their way, it would be a relaxing trip.

When all the clones were settled, and everything was set, he joined Casey in the cockpit—a long, oval compartment with four seats, two for the pilot and co-pilot and two behind for the navigation and communications officers.

They worked in silence as they executed the lift-off and then obtained orbit in preparation for the slingshot from the moon's gravitational pull toward Earth. When they were well on their way, and the navigation and communications officers left to run through the post-lift-off checklist, Casey leaned back and sighed.

"So, what do you think of that new scientist?" She wiggled her eyebrows. "She's cute."

"Even if I thought she was," Kaiden said, "there's no way you're getting out of the simulation I scheduled."

"Come on," Casey said. "How many times do we have to do that? We've made this trip, what, twenty times this year, and nothing ever goes wrong."

"That's *why* nothing goes wrong," Kaiden said. But he had a funny feeling about this one.

The ship lurched.

"What the…" Casey jumped into action, checking the systems and monitors.

"Did we hit something?" Kaiden asked.

He whirled away from the main controls to check another set of monitors when the explosion ripped through the cockpit with a flash and a bang, followed by a deep, penetrating silence and utter blackness.

Kaiden awoke to the feeling of falling. His arms and legs flailed about in a panicked attempt to catch himself until his brain realized that he was still in the cockpit, twisting lazily in the microgravity environment. He considered the possibility that he had been sucked into the vacuum of space until he realized that he was still breathing. Hissing and beeping rushed into his ears, and he opened his eyes to blink at the flashing alarm lights and the remains of the mangled control console. Droplets of blood revolved and pulsated against the inky backdrop of space, and Kaiden knew the blood was his own. But the lunar transport and his crew and cargo were his first priority.

Smoke billowed from the cockpit controls, turning the air into a thick, black soot that coated the inside of his mouth and burned his eyes. The air stank of burning plastic and hot metal. His head throbbed, and his ears filled with a high-pitched ringing. Kaiden dragged the extinguisher from its holder and unloaded its contents into the ragged hole below the console until the smoke subsided.

Where was Casey? The explosion had been so sudden, so violent. It was a miracle the hull hadn't been compromised. But that explosion was no mechanical or electrical failure. It could only have been a bomb. Yet how could that be? He had ordered Burl and Raven to inspect the ship before they left the orbiting space station, and he hadn't left sight of it while at the lunar station. How could anyone smuggle a bomb on board without his knowledge? Surely, none of the clones could have done it.

Kaiden glanced down at his arm and the crimson bubble of blood that expanded there. He let go of the empty fire extinguisher and let it float away as he grabbed the jagged gash that shone pink against his black skin. Droplets sprayed in every direction as he tried to stem the flow of blood.

He fought against the sense of falling and struggled to focus his mind on what had happened and what needed to be done. He flipped the communication switch while still holding the gash in his arm.

"Delano? Do you copy?"

Static.

"Raven? Burl? What's your status?"

Static crackled again.

Debris and smoke swirled around him in lazy circles. Emergency lights blinked red, and some of the screens had gone black.

"Burl?" he said again. "What's your status?"

No response.

Kaiden dragged himself toward the control panel, careful not to overdo it and propel himself across the room. He had to determine the extent of the damage and make sure the spacecraft was still operational. He reached for the keyboard when a blonde head pushed through the debris and thumped against the panel beside him.

"Casey?"

Kaiden choked on the word. Terror tightened his stomach. He grabbed a bundle of wires hanging from the ceiling and hauled himself around. He reached for Casey, fighting the lightning pains that exploded behind his eyes, the rushing nausea, and the spray of crimson droplets from his arm.

Casey kept rotating, propelled by the propulsion from the blast. Her hair spread out around her like a lion's mane. Her blue eyes stared, vacant and empty. Kaiden grabbed her and shook her. Her arms and legs flopped around in the microgravity environment like some rag doll.

"Please, no," he said.

The door swished open behind him. Kaiden shoved himself around to find Raven floating upright in the doorway. She had one boot hooked under a bar to keep herself from moving. Her dark hair splayed out around her. Her expression was grim, her face pale. She held her service pistol in her hand. It was the Model 9 Rapid Repeater, specially designed for use in space. Behind her, a body in a black uniform twisted in a grotesque circle amid a halo of blood and smoke. Was that Delano?

"Report," Kaiden snapped. "What's going on?" He was relieved to see one of his security team alive and doing her job. He could always depend on Raven.

Raven glared at him. "I warned you not to accept this mission." Her lip lifted in a sneer. Kaiden could barely hear her over the ringing in his ears.

"How's the rest of the ship?" Kaiden yelled.

"I'm sorry," she said. "The clones have to die."

"What?" Kaiden rubbed his ears, trying to dislodge the obnoxious ringing. He must have heard her wrong.

Raven raised the gun and pursed her lips in determination. Their gazes met, and Kaiden read her intention in her dark eyes. Raven meant to kill him.

"Wait!" he yelled. He couldn't believe it. Not Raven. She was his friend. They had trained together. He had picked her for his team because she was so driven, so dependable.

A gunshot rang through the cabin. Raven jerked. A red hole blossomed in her chest. A spray of blood, flesh, and the fragments of an explosive round spit toward him, peppering the console beside him. A crimson balloon wiggled outward from Raven's chest. Her eyes widened, and her gun fired off three rounds as she twitched. The recoil sent her flying into the wall. Kaiden yanked on the dangling wires, desperately seeking to twist himself out of the way of the exploding rounds.

Two bullets zipped past him, but the third grazed his head before smashing into the console with a bang, sending out a shower of plastic fragments. Kaiden struggled to keep his focus through the burst of pain. Raven's eyes stared at him. Someone in a white coat appeared in the doorway behind her. The gun slipped from Raven's grasp to spin leisurely through the air. The red bubble from Raven's chest grew larger, like an inflating balloon. Then the scene swam away into the black oblivion.

CHAPTER TWO
DESTROYING ANGELS

THE MIDDLE-AGED, *black woman watched Kaiden. Her stiff, black hair had been straightened and parted to the side. Her lips were unnaturally red. She still wore the white lab coat that made her black skin seem darker. Kaiden hated the coat. It represented something evil. Something dangerous.*

"You don't understand," she said.

Her voice was soft and melodic. Kaiden remembered how she used to sing to him back when he was too young to understand what she did for work, what she had become.

"Why didn't you save her?" Kaiden accused. "You're supposed to be this great scientist."

The woman swallowed and blinked.

"I tried, honey. I did. But science can't solve everything. There are limitations."

"It should." Kaiden knew he was being belligerent, but he didn't care. "If scientists can make clones, they should be able to save a little girl from an infection."

"It wasn't a normal infection. It was—"

"I don't care!" Kaiden shouted and lunged to his feet, the tears boiling to the surface. The ache inside burned white-hot. "You should have saved her. It's all your fault."

He took pleasure in the shock and hurt on her face. He had wanted to make her hurt like he was hurting, to punish her.

DESTROYING ANGELS

Tears swam in the woman's dark eyes. Her lips trembled. "I know you don't approve of my work," she said. "But you'll see that it's for the best."

Kaiden threw up his hands and stormed from the room, slamming the door behind him.

The peculiar smell of burned plastic, oil, and antiseptic penetrated the blackness and dragged Kaiden back to the light and to the pain. When he opened his eyes, he found himself in the infirmary strapped to the table—the confusing dream or hallucination of the woman he had never seen before still lingered.

He should know who that woman was and why he hated her so much, but the dream had melted into the chaos of his throbbing headache and the murky memories of how he came to be staring up at the white, plastic ceiling of the medical ward. His arms floated over him in the microgravity environment. When he tried to unfasten the straps across his chest and legs, a pale, white hand pressed against his chest.

"Lie still, Captain."

Kaiden rolled his head to the side. The lab tech floated beside him. Her white lab coat was spotted red with an erratic polka dot pattern. Her brown hair was pulled back in a ponytail that couldn't contain the hair without gravity to help it. Her pretty, dark eyes studied him with concern. They were rimmed with red, and a smudged tear still glistened on her cheek where she had wiped it away. Kaiden tried to remember her name. She was the scientist sent to monitor the clones.

"Willow?" he said.

She wiped another tear from her eye and gave him a smile that lit her eyes and brought tiny dimples to her cheeks. She was a white girl who couldn't be more than eighteen or nineteen years old, like many of the people who worked on the project. The best and the brightest, he thought—at least that's what The Ark Project slogan said.

"Glad to see you're awake," she said. "We lost oxygen there for a bit, and your head took quite the beating. You've got a concussion, but you should be fine in a few days."

"Low oxygen?" Kaiden asked. "That didn't affect you?"

Willow shrugged. "It wasn't out long."

Kaiden raised his arm to examine the jagged gash. The pink scar was already forming.

"Those little Internal Nano-Cellular Repair guys work fast," Willow said.

That was one of the benefits of working for TAP. All its employees received an injection of Internal Nano-Cellular Repair particles, or INCR. As his healing wound showed, the nano-organisms that repaired damaged cells worked quickly.

"What happened?" Kaiden asked.

Willow's smile faltered.

"They hit us," she said.

"Who?"

"I think it was the Destroying Angels."

"The terrorist group?" he asked.

Kaiden frowned. He had been briefed on them, but no one had any credible evidence that they even knew about this mission. Commander Rio had assured him that no more than two or three people outside of his crew knew their flight schedule.

Willow nodded. "The ones that have been assassinating political leaders, claiming that they were clones."

Kaiden didn't watch the news because it was usually just propaganda. He relied on his briefings, but he knew about the assassinations.

"Right, so Raven was one of them?" he said. The betrayal burned bitter in his throat.

Willow rubbed a hand over her forehead. "I guess so."

"Is she alive?"

Willow's gaze drifted to the blinking lights over Kaiden's head.

"No," she whispered.

"The rest of the crew?"

Willow shook her head, and her lip trembled.

"All of them?" A knot tightened in Kaiden's chest. He couldn't believe it.

"And the lunar clone prototypes," Willow confirmed in a shaky voice.

Kaiden stared at her. Then, he grasped his head in both hands as he fought to keep in the tears. A warm ache burned in his chest. His entire crew? Casey. Delano. Burl. They were his friends. His responsibility. He blinked at the sudden sting in his eyes.

"What happened?" he demanded.

Willow took a deep breath, brushed at a new tear, and tried to steady herself. "I'm not sure, but there were at least two explosions—one in the cockpit and the other in the engine room."

"Any breach?" The cockpit hadn't been breached, but every compartment in the spacecraft could be sealed and locked down, so he had to check.

"No. The hull wasn't breached, but we lost the engines and the pseudo-gravity generator."

"So, we're floating helpless?"

Willow grinned. "I'm not just a lab tech."

"What?"

"I hacked the system, rebooted the software, and got us moving again on one engine. I was afraid to turn around because you already had the course set, and I don't have any experience with space navigation. If I messed up and we missed, well…" she trailed off. "Anyway, we lost communication when they blew the console, so I couldn't get any help. I think we'll reach the space elevator in another two days." She rubbed the back of her neck. "A bit behind schedule, but, hey, better late than never."

"My entire crew," Kaiden mumbled. "Half my team." He gaped at Willow. "How did she do it? I mean, my people were trained."

Willow picked at a bloodstain on the sleeve of her lab coat but wouldn't look at him. "She just walked up and shot them, I think," she said. "The same way she killed the clones."

"Crap," Kaiden said. "Those clones were important."

The clones had been on the moon for three years with no pseudo-gravity and exposed to radiation and low oxygen environments. If cloned humans could survive and reproduce under those conditions, the door would be opened to space colonization. Their loss was a huge setback. And he had been responsible for their safety. The clones were all between sixteen and nineteen years of age like most active personnel at TAP. And Raven had just shot them down in cold blood.

"Rio got his intel all wrong," Kaiden said, "and he's going to blame me for this."

Willow pursed her lips and pinched her brow together, but she didn't say anything.

"What do these Destroying Angels have against clones, anyway?" Kaiden asked.

"Don't you watch the news?"

Kaiden smirked. "Not unless I have to. I don't need propaganda. I need good solid intel—facts."

"That explains a lot," Willow said. But she didn't give Kaiden a chance to reply. "They're the terror wing of the Sons of God. You've heard of them?"

"Of course." Kaiden didn't go to briefings for nothing. He made sure knew about any potential threat to his crew.

"Well, they're a religious group that thinks science has gone too far. I don't know how they found out about The Ark Project, but they must have someone on the inside."

"Raven was on the inside," Kaiden said.

"True," Willow replied. "But I don't think she was meant to survive. I mean, how would she explain coming back with everyone else dead with bullets in their heads?"

Kaiden scowled. "This is what radical religious bigotry gets you."

Willow's expression darkened. Kaiden had annoyed her. He didn't know her well enough to know why. This was his first mission with her. She seemed unusually well-informed about what was happening and why for a mere medical technician.

"To them, clones are a crime against nature, against God," she said. "Clones represent the greatest arrogance of the human mind, that it can sidestep natural evolution and create superior people."

"I'm not sure what the answer is," Kaiden said. He had long wondered about the efficacy of the cloning program. TAP claimed that since they could perfect humans by manipulating their genetic code, they had a moral obligation to do it—especially when the survival of the human species depended on successful space colonies. He hadn't liked the look of the clones they picked up and wouldn't choose that for himself, but this was his job, and he hoped that it would make a difference.

"TAP says we can," Kaiden said.

Willow frowned. "Maybe. We haven't proved that yet, have we?"

Kaiden snorted. As a captain of security for TAP, it was his duty to follow orders. It was that simple. "Can't do that without clones to test, can we?"

Willow raised her eyebrows. "Indeed," she said.

The way she said this made Kaiden study her. She wasn't telling him something. He yanked at the straps again, suddenly suspicious. Why had she tied him down? Why were they the only survivors?

Willow watched him struggle with a bemused expression on her face. "What are you doing?" she asked.

Kaiden stopped struggling. "Why are you still alive?"

Willow smiled. "I told you, I'm not just a lab tech."

Kaiden eyed her. She had said that already, but what *was* she? He had served with Raven and had known her well. Raven wouldn't do a thing like this.

But this woman was a complete stranger. Why should he believe her? Why was *he* still alive? Why hadn't Willow killed him the way she had killed Raven? Maybe Raven hadn't betrayed them, after all. What proof did he have of Raven having set the bombs and killing the crew and the clones? Maybe it was Willow all along.

He fought with the straps while Willow watched in mild amusement. He cursed in impotent rage.

"Let me out," he said.

Willow undid the straps. Kaiden grabbed the table and pulled himself upright, fighting with the nausea his motion caused. He searched for his weapon, but it wasn't there. She had disarmed him.

"Lost something?" Willow asked.

Kaiden glared at her. "Where's my weapon?"

Willow pointed to the corner where the pistol revolved in the air in leisurely circles. Kaiden pushed off the table and snatched it. He shoved himself around to level the gun at her chest.

"How did you survive when no one else did? Were you in on it with Raven?" he demanded.

Willow stared at him as if this was the last thing she had expected him to say. She scowled, and her brow pinched tight again.

"You're the captain," she said. "What do you think?"

CHAPTER THREE
A CASKET AND A ROSE

WILLOW STARED AT the gun Kaiden leveled at her chest. This had not gone according to plan. She didn't think he would shoot an unarmed woman, but he had sustained a brain injury and lost his crew and cargo. Men had done far crazier things with less provocation— men like her father.

She let go of the table and raised her hands. The movement in the weightless environment pushed her away from Kaiden, but he stared at her with dark, accusing eyes. He was a stocky black man with close-cut hair and dark brown skin. He was handsome and widely regarded as one of TAP's most capable security officers, which was one of the reasons she had chosen him.

The bandage she applied to the wound on his head slipped sideways, revealing the bloody gash where Raven's bullet had grazed him. She pointed at the bandage. "That's going to fall off," she said.

"I asked you a question," he demanded. "Why are you and I the only ones alive?"

Willow put her hand on her throat. "I don't know," she said. "I was just trying to survive."

"How did you know how to use a gun?"

"All you have to do is pull the trigger," she said. "Look. I was just here to monitor the clones, like I said. You can call the field station to verify it."

"I will. But first, I'm going to check on my crew."

The intercom crackled, and a weak, trembling voice came over it.

"Kaiden," the voice said. "The clones….the clones…" The voice crackled and cut off.

A chill swept through Willow. Kaiden would never believe her now.

"Hang on," Kaiden said. "I'm coming."

Willow grabbed the table and dragged herself toward the door to follow him, but he waved her back with the pistol.

"You stay here," he snapped. "If I see you in the corridors, I *will* kill you."

Warm indignation burned in Willow's throat. "I just saved your miserable life."

"So you say. Don't leave this room."

"Fine." Willow folded her arms. Let him run around and see that what she told him was true.

The door swished open as Kaiden pulled himself through and glided into the hallway. When the door closed again, Willow hauled herself to the computer and switched it on. The blue holographic screen crackled to life, and she monitored Kaiden's progress on the onboard cameras. There were gaps in the coverage because the cameras focused only on the most important parts of the ship, like the cockpit, the engine room, and the lab where the clones were kept.

Willow didn't see him until he reached the ward where the clones had been strapped onto their beds after she had given them a sedative. He used one of the microgravity handles to drag himself forward with one hand while holding the pistol in the other. Sedating the clones was a much more humane way to transport them than to let them be aware of what TAP was doing to them.

The door to the lab swished open as Kaiden approached, and he hesitated in the hallway. He holstered his gun and, using the microgravity handles, hauled himself through. Willow switched cameras. Blood splattered the walls and floated in the air. The six clones had holes in their foreheads, but the back of their heads were gone—disappeared into the fabric and cushion of their pillows. Bits of blood and bone floated in the air around their heads like a ghastly halo. Burl was making feeble efforts to reach the clones, dragging his rifle behind him. A long, red trail smeared the floor, showing his progress from the doorway before the gravity generator cut off. Little droplets of blood followed him. Willow clutched at her throat. She had thought he was dead.

"Kaiden," his voice came harsh and crackly over the intercom. "I can't save them. Kaiden."

"I'm here," Kaiden said, yanking his way into the room to collide with Burl. He rolled him over so that he faced him.

At the sight of Burl's ruined chest, the bile rose in Willow's throat. Kaiden cursed and started cutting away the clothing with his knife. That was no normal round Raven had used on Burl or the clones. But, of course, a normal bullet might not have been fatal since the INCR could repair even serious wounds long enough to allow the injured to seek medical attention. But damage like that was beyond repair. It had been an exploding round for sure. Raven hadn't wanted anyone to live.

"Who did this to you?" Kaiden asked.

"Willow," Burl said.

Kaiden stared in horror at his friend's pale face streaked with blood. That hole in his chest was too big. And Burl had just said that Willow had done it.

Rage started in the pit of his stomach. She had lied to him. He was duty-bound to kill her or capture her and deliver her to TAP.

"I'm sorry, Burl," he said. "I can't do anything for you."

"We lost the clones," he gasped. "Raven."

Kaiden scowled. Was Burl confused?

"I thought you said it was Willow."

"Willow and Raven." Burl coughed and grimaced in pain.

Kaiden gripped his hand, struggling to keep the tears in. "Take it easy," he said.

Burl closed his eyes and, for a moment, Kaiden thought he was dead. Then he took another shuddering breath. "Raven came first, then Willow." His hand drifted to where his sidearm should have been. The holster was empty.

"Who shot you?" Kaiden said. He had to know. If Willow was guilty, she might have already tampered with the images from the security cameras while he was unconscious.

"Raven put the gun to their heads and pulled the trigger. One by one. I was too late."

"But who shot you?" Kaiden insisted.

Burl swallowed and gave a long slow blink. "Raven shot me. Willow took my gun."

Kaiden bowed his head over his friend. He had failed them all. And he would have to spend two days with Willow without being able to trust her loyalty. She would have to be restrained. He had no choice. But if Burl was right, Willow hadn't killed them and had only taken the gun to kill Raven, as she said. He would check the footage on the cameras, but for now, he needed to check the rest of his crew.

Burl's hand went limp in his, and Kaiden looked up to see the animation leave Burl's face. His eyes remained still and staring.

The International Space Station loomed large in the cockpit window, its lights dazzling against the devouring blackness of space. Flight training was part of the standard training protocol, and all transport security personnel were expected to be qualified pilots, though not everyone had had a knack for it like Casey.

The proximity alarm beeped, and Kaiden set to running through the pre-landing checklist as best he could with the damaged console. Usually, Casey did this, but she was gone. The bitter pain of it still burned in his throat.

Kaiden had restrained Willow for twenty-four hours while he examined the security footage, snapped photos of the incident, carried all the bodies to the room where the clones had been killed, and drafted a thorough report. He could find no evidence that Willow had done anything other than what she said. The footage showed Raven murdering the clones and the crew, including Delano, as he raced to the cockpit. It seemed to be a clear case of treason and cold-blooded murder. But it made no sense. Why would Raven do such a thing? There was no excuse to keep Willow restrained any longer, so he had let her loose.

"We made it," Willow said. She pulled herself into the seat beside Kaiden and strapped herself down. Her ponytail splayed out behind her. She had exchanged her lab coat for a flight suit.

"Thanks to you," Kaiden said without looking at her. Two days of awkward interaction had proven that she was capable and skilled. It was a ghastly business—one that would haunt him for the rest of his life, to say nothing about what it would do to his career. They would both be suspended, at the very least, and certainly investigated. The terrorists had carried out their worst attack on clones in months—right under his nose and on his own ship.

"I made a full report of how you saved the ship," Kaiden said.

Willow glanced at him. "I didn't do it alone."

"I recommended you for a citation and possible promotion," Kaiden said. He looked at her. "I'm sorry I accused you."

Willow waved him away. "You were in shock. And no one is going to promote me. We'll be lucky if we're not fired and thrown in prison for this."

Kaiden studied her for a moment before turning to peer at the monitor from the co-pilot's seat. The pilot's seat was gone, and the pilot controls were too mangled to be repaired, so he had been forced to rewire much of the console to allow them to fly the spacecraft from the co-pilot's seat. Communication was still down, though as they neared the Space Station, they might be able to make contact with their personal wrist terminals, or WTs, which had a much shorter range.

Guiding the spacecraft toward the space station was always tricky, but it was downright dangerous with compromised controls. He tried to focus on nudging the craft into position, but his mind kept struggling to make sense of the last two days.

It was supposed to be a routine flight, and Kaiden had lost his crew—his friends since cadet school. Raven had meant to kill *him*, and he had failed to protect his own people. He was returning with a cargo of dead clones, each with a single hole in their foreheads, like any nice, clean execution. He should have done something to stop it. He should have recognized Raven's betrayal. He was their captain. He was responsible.

"Here we go," he said as he nudged the controls, steering the craft toward the docking station.

The great, donut-shaped, centrifugal gravity generator of the International Space Station spun in front of him, nearly blocking the view of the blue orb of Earth behind it. The space station stretched out on either side of the donut, like an immense hot dog. Kaiden avoided the spinning gravity generator and maneuvered toward the blinking green lights of the docking station.

This was the secure TAP section of the station, and it was a good thing. Anyone coming in with a cargo of dead bodies would have caused an international sensation, especially if it was known that clones were on board. But TAP worked overtime to keep the lid on things like this. Formally, TAP and its programs didn't exist, and the success of their mission required absolute secrecy. But there would still be hell to pay when he faced Commander Rio, the head of TAP security at Ararat.

Kaiden glanced at Willow. He wanted to trust her, but he had become even more convinced that she was hiding something. It was just a gut feeling, but he had learned to trust his instincts, and they told him something wasn't right with her.

Kaiden coaxed the craft onto the pad.

"I'm sorry about your friends," Willow said.

"Yeah. Thanks." Kaiden didn't want to talk about them. He knew their deaths would go unnoticed by all those billions of people down there—unnoticed and unreported. The Ark Project was top secret. Those who served the project lived inside a world that the masses of natural humans knew nothing about.

This galled him. Good young men and women were giving their lives to save humanity from its own stupidity, and what did they get for it? Nothing but suspicion and indifference. He may not like the idea of cloning humans, but at least they were doing something. Now, they were being murdered by religious fanatics.

Kaiden sighed. None of this self-recrimination was going to help him when he faced Commander Rio and took responsibility for what happened to his ship and crew.

Several hours later, Kaiden and Willow pulled themselves into the space elevator and strapped themselves into their seats before beginning the descent toward Earth. The elevator consisted of two large cargo bays on either side of the cable and half a dozen smaller pressurized passenger compartments between the cargo bays. Kaiden and Willow found themselves alone in one of the passenger compartments.

The descenders whirred into motion as they sped down the nano-fiber carbon tether that was secured to the earth on a huge floating ship near the equator. The Earth Orbital Space Station was attached to the tether at the geostationary altitude far above the earth with a counterweight swinging in space even farther out. The elevator shuddered as it picked up speed. This trip used to take four or five days but had been reduced to twenty-four hours by the new high-speed descenders.

Kaiden settled into his seat to gaze out the window at a world awash in a flood of blue and churning white that could not hide the great scars of humanity. It always surprised him how blue Earth appeared from space. It seemed so inviting with no hint of the burning heat, arid winds, and massive storms that raged across the surface. The only green left on the planet hugged the coastlines or cut through the barren lands—little ribbons of life clinging to dwindling rivers. The rest was a dull brown, like it was diseased and dying. Megacities sprawled out to enfold the desperate natural humans in protective arms of metal and glass.

"She was one of us," Kaiden said.

"What?" Willow turned away from the window and her own musings.

"Raven was one of us," he repeated. "She started a year after I did." He didn't want to believe that Raven could so brazenly murder the people who had trusted her to protect their backs. It was the worst kind of betrayal, but he had seen it for himself in the footage of the security cameras.

When Willow didn't say anything, he glanced at her. She still had her hair drawn back in a ponytail that stood on end.

"I'm sorry," Willow said. "I wish there was something I could do."

Kaiden looked away. Did he want her to do anything? Maybe not. Maybe he just needed someone to understand.

As they fell earthward and began to feel the draw of Earth's gravity, her ponytail slowly assumed a more natural look. Kaiden blinked at the dizziness that spun around in his head as his backside took the weight of his body. The shoulder straps ceased tugging at his shoulders, and he settled more comfortably into the padded seat.

"I never get used to this," Kaiden said.

"Me neither," Willow said.

Kaiden glanced back out the window when pain suddenly flashed behind his eyes. He sagged against the shoulder straps, groaning in pain. *He stared at the blank cover of the coffin. She was in there, her little body so ravaged by disease that they couldn't even cover it up with makeup. Kaiden placed the single rose on the lid. "I'm sorry, Rose," he said. "I'll stop them."*

"Captain?" Willow said. She touched his shoulder.

Kaiden blinked and regained his balance. He massaged his forehead. The pain focused right behind his eyes.

"You all right?" Willow peered closely at him.

Kaiden nodded. "My head," he said, "it feels like my brain is going to explode."

Willow straightened and studied him. She knew something he did not. "You still have a concussion," she said. "You should have seen the doctor at the Space Station, like I told you."

"I'm all right," Kaiden snapped more harshly than he intended. He couldn't afford to see a doctor. He didn't need that kind of scrutiny now—not after having two strange visions in the space of a couple of days. This kind of thing got good security personnel reassigned or discharged.

"Umm, who's Rose?" Willow asked.

"What?" Kaiden glared at her.

"You said, 'I'm sorry, Rose.'"

"I didn't say anything."

Kaiden blinked and ran a hand over his close-shaved head. He was having hallucinations—first the woman and then the coffin. How could he get PTSD from a bomb blast he could barely remember? But he didn't want Willow to report him to Rio. If Rio, or anyone else, got so much as a whiff of an idea that he had PTSD, his career would be over. He would be dismissed from his command and probably retired. TAP didn't mess around with mental disorders of any kind.

"I'm fine," he said.

Kaiden turned to watch as the elevator descended through the clouds, doing his best to appear as if everything was all right. When it burst through the bottom of the cloud canopy, the Pacific's wide blue waters spread out on the western horizon and the dry, rocky coast of the Isthmus of Panama on the eastern. All over the world, sprawling cities swarmed with millions of unhappy people who couldn't care less that his friends had died trying to give humanity a second chance.

Chapter Four
Reprimand

THE BARREN, CRUMBLING landscape that hid TAP passed beneath the airship. Ararat, the extensive complex that housed the top-secret Ark Project labs, couldn't be seen from the air. No one was supposed to know it was there. It had been carved deep into the bedrock—an impregnable and unassailable fortress buried beneath miles of solid stone. It had been Kaiden's home for over ten years. The jagged peaks of the Rocky Mountains stabbed upward to the west. From horizon to horizon, barely a single patch of green could be seen in the vast, barren landscape.

Willow sat beside him in silence. They had boarded a fast airship at the sea base that anchored the space elevator and sped north to a TAP installation in Mexico before switching to a TAP gunship that would take them north to their base at Ararat. Kaiden had tried to sleep, but he hadn't been able to rest. Strange dreams and disturbing emotions boiled inside him. Had he lost control of his own mind?

Ever since the elevator, Willow had given him sideways glances as if she wanted to say something. But Kaiden didn't want to talk. He kept replaying what had happened in his head, searching for the clue he had missed. There must have been signs. All the little details of Raven's strange behavior while on the mission crept into his mind. He should have noticed the way she refused to look at him when they boarded the ship. He should have noticed when she ate alone and refused to socialize with them. Then, she was suddenly friendly when they picked up the clones. She was off, and it had been his responsibility to know. Why did he miss it? Was he so confident in his team's preparations that he had been too willing to give her leeway?

As they entered the docking bay, Kaiden found Commander Rio standing with his hands behind his back, waiting for him. The golden Commander stripes stood out bold on his right sleeve. Rio was a young black man like Kaiden, but he was far more ambitious than Kaiden had ever been. Kaiden had hoped to avoid the confrontation for a little while, at least, but Commander Rio clearly had other ideas.

Kaiden had been offered Rio's job as head of security, but he needed to be on the move, not stuck behind a desk. Still, Rio had never forgiven him for beating him in the exams, marksmanship, and hand-to-hand combat. Secretly, Kaiden believed that Rio saw him as a threat.

"Your boss is waiting for you," Willow said.

TAP security personnel were not part of the military since they belonged to no state and were not part of the International Confederation of States and its associated International Security Agency. But they borrowed military protocols and traditions in an effort to maintain discipline and effectiveness. There was no point in reinventing the wheel, after all.

Kaiden grunted in annoyance. "Yeah," he said as he rose. "See ya."

Willow scowled, and Kaiden felt a pang of guilt. He knew he was being churlish, but he couldn't help it, not after all that had happened. He clambered down the steps and paused to salute his commanding officer. Commander Rio gave him an impatient salute in reply.

"Follow me, Captain," Commander Rio ordered without ceremony. Kaiden fell in behind him, wishing he could sneak off and find his best friend, Quill.

Commander Rio marched down the corridors toward his office. Despite being underground, TAP was brightly lit with white-walled hallways that had a scrubbed-clean feel and smell. Ararat was a huge installation, and Kaiden had never seen all of it. They passed the lower labs and engineering units and took the elevator up to the security wing. Their boots clicked against the tiled floor as they marched to Rio's office.

Rio stalked to his desk and dropped into his chair with an air of fury that set Kaiden's teeth on edge. Rio had no business censoring him while Rio lounged in his nice, air-conditioned office protected by others, like Kaiden, who kept the facility safe from attacks. Kaiden wrinkled his nose at the odd smell of Rio's office. While the TAP hallways were clean and bright, Rio's office was dim and possessed the lingering odor of gun oil mixed with cologne.

"You want to explain what happened up there?" Rio demanded.

Commander Rio pushed a pile of papers aside on his desk and leaned back with his hands behind his head. His skin was charcoal black—much darker than Kaiden's—and he had a way of lifting his upper lip in a sneer. He wore the same security uniform of black tactical pants and a black jacket, but three golden commander stripes adorned his right sleeve. As usual, his uniform was immaculate.

Kaiden snapped to attention in front of Commander Rio's desk, surrounded by holographic images that displayed the feed from several dozen security cameras. He restrained the sarcastic comment that rose to the tip of his tongue. He had relied on the intelligence Rio had given him. Didn't Rio bear as much blame as Kaiden? But Rio was already fuming. It wouldn't do any good to send him over the edge.

"I sent my report, sir," Kaiden said.

Rio sat forward. "I read your report, Captain. Now, tell me what happened."

Kaiden's insides churned as he explained about the bomb and Raven and Willow, while Rio gazed at him with that permanent sneer. Kaiden didn't need Rio to reprimand him. He knew full well that he bore responsibility for the death of his friends. The bitter ache of it hadn't left his chest since he had seen Raven floating amid the expanding bubble of her own blood. Nothing Rio could say to him would make him feel worse than he already did.

"I've ordered a complete investigation," Rio said.

"Yes, sir."

Rio exhaled loudly. "We didn't need this," he said.

"May I see their bodies before they're composted, sir?" Kaiden asked when he had finished recounting the attack.

Rio wrinkled his brow, surprised by the request.

"They were my friends, sir," Kaiden said.

Rio pursed his lips, and Kaiden thought Rio seemed to be considering something.

"You know what your failure has cost TAP?" Rio asked. Rio had always been a hardnose, but Kaiden figured that's why he was the commander. TAP couldn't afford softies. Their work was too secretive and potentially valuable. And Kaiden had just come back with news of the worst setback TAP had experienced in a decade.

Kaiden bowed his head. "Yes, sir."

"Three years' worth of work." Rio clicked his tongue. "I don't know what Noah will decide, but, for now, consider yourself reprimanded until the investigation is complete, and this will go into your permanent file."

Noah was the code name given to the head of The Ark Project. Everyone thought it was a joke, but no one Kaiden knew had ever seen Noah, except maybe Rio. Still, a mere reprimand for a failure of this magnitude seemed overly lenient.

"Yes, sir. Thank you, sir."

"Don't thank me, Captain," Rio snapped. "You're one mission away from probation."

"Mission, sir?" A warm tingle of suspicion rippled through Kaiden's stomach. What mission would Rio have in mind now that the experimental clones were dead?

Rio eyed Kaiden with open dislike. "I'm going to give you another chance to redeem yourself."

Kaiden waited, trying not to fidget. He wasn't sure he was ready for another mission—not after losing so many of his friends.

"I'm sending you on an extraction mission."

"Extraction, sir?" Kaiden was sure he had heard wrong.

"Senator Benton has been making waves lately. We need to help him see the light."

"Sir, my team is strictly security and transport. We don't do offensive operations."

This mission was wrong for Kaiden's team. Sure, they had gone through offensive operations in training, but they specialized in security and transport between Ararat and the lunar seed bank. There was no reason why Rio should want to send them on such a mission—not when he had five experienced offensive operation teams available.

Rio slammed his fist onto his desk, making the pictures and computer tablets jump. "You have no team!" he shouted. "They just died under your watch."

Kaiden struggled to keep his face impassive. "Yes, sir," he said. He hadn't lost his entire team—only those that went on this mission. But there was no point in reminding Rio of that now.

"You do what I tell you to do, Captain," Rio said. "You're an inch away from being disciplined."

Kaiden eyed Rio. He had only been "disciplined" twice since he came to TAP before he figured out how to avoid it. The discipline was a special TAP technology that allowed it to control all of its employees. There was no way to explain what the discipline did to a person, but Kaiden had seen people go crazy. One fourteen-year-old recruit shot himself after being disciplined just so he would never have to experience it again.

"With all due respect, sir," Kaiden said, "I was unaware that TAP was involved in kidnapping political leaders. I thought that's what terrorists did." He knew he shouldn't have said it, but Rio had made him angry.

Rio lunged to his feet.

"You watch your mouth, Captain. Your priority is the protection of TAP. This man is threatening the project. So, you will find him and bring him here. You have one week to reassemble your team. Dismissed."

Kaiden saluted and spun to leave.

"Captain?"

Kaiden turned back.

"Don't waste any more of my men," Rio said.

CHAPTER FIVE
NANO-BOTS

KAIDEN TOUCHED THE button on his wrist terminal as he left Rio's office. Quill's face materialized on the tiny screen. He had short, dark hair and a wide Asian face.

"Whoa, I was expecting you two days ago," Quill said.

"Had some trouble," Kaiden said, holding up his wrist close to his mouth so he could speak in a whisper.

"I heard rumors to that effect," Quill said, "but nobody seems to know what happened."

Quill paused, waiting for Kaiden to explain. When he didn't respond, Quill continued. "Looks like someone gave you a knock on the head. Have you been picking at Birch again?"

"Something like that," Kaiden said.

Quill beamed his big, toothy grin. "I've got the new MG 5 Super-Pack game console fired up and ready to go, but I've been waiting for you."

"I'll be down," Kaiden said.

The idea of spending a few hours relaxing without having to think about his new mission—or the disastrous one he'd just finished—sounded like the best idea he'd had in days. Kaiden skipped the elevator and took the stairs. He needed to burn off some of the anger before trying to relax with Quill. It wasn't just Rio. He was used to Rio's arrogance and animosity. It was his lost crew members and the strange hallucinations or daydreams he was experiencing. His brain had been hijacked and filled with freakish dreams and nightmares. Maybe the injuries he'd sustained in the explosion had done more damage than he thought. His world had flipped upside down, and he was swimming in a fog of memory and emotion that unsettled him.

He could hear Quill's classical music blaring into the hallway when he was still five rooms down. Kaiden smiled to himself. Quill was crazy. That's why Kaiden liked him.

Quill's door swished open after Kaiden knocked.

"Took you long enough," Quill shouted over the music. But he stopped speaking when he saw the expression on Kaiden's face. "What?" he said.

Kaiden stepped into the room and fiddled with his wrist terminal as he gazed around him. Quill's room was like all of the security crew's living quarters. Unlike the cadets who lived together in one large room filled with rows of beds and a common restroom, security officers were given their own private living quarters.

Everything was made of white plastic, but Quill had found ways to make the space his own. The game console and the stereo speakers dominated the front room. A huge picture of a white, sandy beach with a backdrop of palm trees and a clear, blue sky covered one wall, while the other was covered in pictures of the great musical composers.

Quill clicked off Beethoven's Fifth Symphony. The silence rang in Kaiden's ears. His head still throbbed. Quill stuffed his hands into the pockets of his black security pants.

"Well?" he said.

"They're dead," Kaiden said.

"Who?" Quill asked.

"My entire crew."

Quill stared. "All of them?"

Kaiden bowed his head.

"Man, what happened?"

"Raven," Kaiden said, pausing as his throat constricted, and he found the words difficult to say. "She disabled the ship and killed the crew and the clones."

Quill dropped into a chair beside the round table. His wide-eyed gaze took in the bandage on Kaiden's head. "You killed her then?"

"No, Willow did."

"Who's that?"

"A scientist on board. But listen, there's something else." Kaiden hadn't meant to start talking about it right away, but once he began, he couldn't stop.

"The blast knocked me out," he said, "and then Raven's bullet grazed my head and knocked me out again, and I've...look, something isn't right."

"So, spit it out." Quill's brow wrinkled in frustration. He had never been one to mince words.

"I'm seeing things."

"Like?"

Kaiden jumped up, unable to remain still, and began pacing. "I don't know. It's like I'm remembering things that never happened. People I've never known."

Quill opened his eyes wide in that comic way he had that made him look like a pufferfish.

"So, now you're psycho?" he said.

Kaiden kicked Quill's boot.

"I'm serious. Rio's intel was all wrong. Terrorists infiltrated the ship through five levels of security. Then, they murdered my crew and cargo, and now I'm having weird hallucinations. Something is going on here. I mean, it was Raven, Quill. She's been part of our team for two years. Why would she do this?"

Quill eyed him for a moment and seemed to reach a decision. He clicked the game console off and tapped the tabletop to initialize the computer. The holographic screen buzzed to life.

"Sit down," Quill said, kicking a chair toward Kaiden.

Kaiden flopped into the chair beside Quill, who clicked off his wrist terminal and motioned for Kaiden to do the same. Kaiden frowned but followed suit. The wrist terminals held tiny computers that kept the team in contact anywhere they were. They were a special type of nano-technology that could be reshaped into different devices on command, and that could project holographic images. They were secure, but Kaiden knew they could be monitored if someone higher up wanted to listen in.

Quill slipped out a digital wireless jammer, or DWJ, like the ones they used when on operations to jam potentially threatening signals or communications. It was a rectangular black box with two retractable antennae. He tossed a smaller version to Kaiden.

"Keep that on you and use it when you want to be unobserved," he said.

"Why would I want to be unobserved at TAP?" Kaiden asked as he fingered the palm-sized device.

Quill raised his eyebrows as he adjusted the antennae on the larger DWJ. When he clicked it on, it emitted a quiet buzzing sound to disrupt any signal from the WTs that might transmit or the sounds the mic might pick up.

"I haven't shown these to you yet," Quill said, "because I wasn't finished with them, but check this out."

Quill slapped a new wrist terminal on his arm. It formed to his wrist and lit up with a brilliant blue light. A tiny ant-like creature scrambled down the band and onto the table. Something whirred, and another insect about the size of a mosquito rose up to hover in front of Kaiden's nose. Quill grinned.

"Cool, huh?"

"You've been playing with insect-bots again?" This had been Quill's fantasy since Kaiden could remember. His insect-bots had nearly gotten him expelled from cadet school when one fell into the director's soup at lunch. Quill was so good with computers and nano-technology, Kaiden had often wondered why he was in security.

"I'm not playing anymore," Quill said. "These little babies are fully functional, and I can control them with electrical waves from my brain."

"You mean like the one that you exploded on top of Casey's head that left the bald spot?"

Quill grinned as the mosquito-bot zoomed away, and the ant-bot disappeared over the table only to reappear by the door. It squeezed under the crack and disappeared into the hallway. Before Kaiden could nod in amazement, they were both back again facing him.

"Nice," Kaiden said. "Much better than your other ones. What can they do?"

"These are spy-bots. Eventually, I'll have attack-bots too, but, check out what the ant-bot found this morning." Quill swiped his finger across the hologram and opened a file folder that was labeled

The Flood.

"What is it?" Kaiden asked.

Quill glanced at the door as if he expected someone to enter.

"I sent the ant-bot into the main administrative complex," Quill whispered, "and I plugged him into the supercomputer."

"You're crazy," Kaiden said. "You could've been caught."

Quill grinned. "Nobody can detect it. I developed a new cloaking software. It isn't powerful yet, but it can cloak my insect-bots. I'm working on a prototype that can cloak a human body and, after that, a whole airship. I just have to get the chips set in the right places and synced and then ramp up the power supply."

"You mean nobody can see them at all?"

"Nope. Each bot has a chip that allows the software to mirror its surroundings so it can't be seen. The same chip scrambles electrical signals that would allow other software to reveal it."

"That's cool," Kaiden said. Then he gestured to the file. "So, what is it?"

"I don't know. It's encrypted." Quill pushed his black hair from before his eyes.

Kaiden smirked at him. "That's supposed to be your area of expertise, Mr. Cyber Security Specialist."

"No," Quill said, refusing to take the bait. "This is different. It doesn't use any computer language or encryption code I've ever seen."

Kaiden opened his mouth, but Quill rushed ahead with a wave of his hand.

"My ant-bot hacked into the central security system to the highest level, and it found this."

"You're not supposed to do that," Kaiden said. "You're gonna get demoted—or worse."

Quill grinned. "That's what makes it fun. Anyway, I was just testing the system, but I couldn't pass this up."

"Are you suggesting something?"

"The Ark Project and then The Flood?" Quill raised his eyebrows at Kaiden.

"So?" What was he getting at? Did TAP have some plan for raising seawater even higher? All the old coastal plains were already flooded.

Quill rolled his eyes. "You've got to get out of your hyper-security mode more often, Kaiden," Quill said. "The ark? You know what that's about?"

"Some dude built a boat to save humanity," Kaiden said. He bent over to peer through the huge microscope Quill had set on the table. "That's what we're doing with the seed bank and the clones, right? Giving humans another chance."

"Yeah," Quill said. "But that dude was escaping a flood."

"So?" Kaiden glanced up from the microscope.

"So why is this file named *The Flood*?" Quill asked. "And what is it doing saved in the most secure location at TAP? And what's this flood supposed to be?"

Kaiden watched him. Maybe Quill *had* stumbled onto something. But Kaiden couldn't see how this was related to Raven and the terrorists.

"Sounds like it's above our pay grade, Quill," he said. "What I want to know is how Raven passed through our security system. If she did it, others can, too."

"That's my point," Quill said.

"I don't follow."

"Somebody is hiding something," Quill said. "There's more to TAP than we've been led to believe."

The buzzing of the transmitter filled the room. Kaiden blinked and pursed his lips. "What are you saying?"

"I'm saying that maybe there's more to The Ark Project than we've been told. And somebody has discovered what it is and is attacking us from the inside."

"You don't think the Destroying Angels have something to do with it?" Kaiden asked.

Quill rubbed his jaw. "Don't know, but they couldn't have encrypted that file on our central security supercomputer, could they?"

"Willow said she thought there was someone on the inside," Kaiden said.

"That's what I mean," Quill said.

Kaiden picked up a piece of a nano-bot from the table and fiddled with it. "Rio is sending us on a mission to extract a senator," he said.

Quill gawked at him. "We don't do extractions," he said.

"That's what I told him," Kaiden said.

"Something weird is going on here, man," Quill said. He furrowed his eyebrows. "When do we leave?"

"One week."

Quill considered, then reached a hand out to grab Kaiden's wrist. "Don't tell anyone what I just showed you," he whispered, "or we're both dead."

"Now who's being the dramatic psycho?" Kaiden asked.

CHAPTER SIX
THE EXTRACTION

KAIDEN SURVEYED THE plaza through the blue light of the electronic gunsight of his new Model 45 Electromagnetic Assault Rifle. He didn't like what he saw. He lay flat on the top of a square building, concealed by the air conditioning unit. During the night, TAP had inserted his team into the heart of New York City, the greatest megacity in North America. The old city had been rebuilt on a raised platform as the ocean reclaimed the land. Even the large plazas had been lifted up to avoid the advancing waters caused by the melting glaciers. Tens of millions of people milled about the city from which the stinking haze of humanity rose into the air. The day was going to be hot. Kaiden wasn't used to city life, and, once he had seen a city, he had never had the desire to return.

Even if he had liked cities, this was the worst possible place for an extraction. Kaiden peered down on the wide plaza in front of the International Security Agency. The agency's needle-sharp tower cast a long shadow that stretched to where the International Confederation of States building hunched over like a great blob tossed onto the cityscape. Automated aerial-bots and hovercraft zoomed about, somehow avoiding each other—all of them armed with cameras—cameras that would be able to record every move Kaiden and his team made.

A crowd was already gathering around the stage erected at the center of the plaza. Artificial trees and shrubs were scattered about in a vain attempt to make the concrete and metal city feel less fake. Kaiden had to carry out the extraction of a high-profile political figure in the middle of this teeming metropolis. It was insane, but those were his orders.

Kaiden checked his team. He had placed his most experienced team members on the ground. Quill, dressed in blue jeans and a T-shirt, tried to look like a tourist interested in the display in front of the ISA tower. Birch was dressed like a college student with her hair pulled back in a ponytail, and a blue backpack slung over one shoulder. She had a thin face and wiry frame that made her easy to underestimate, but she was sharp as a tack and willing to take risks.

She relaxed on the edge of the stage, flipping through the messages on her wrist terminal. Kaiden could just make out the flickering holographic images. Greyson reclined at the little, spindly table in front of the coffee shop. The blue suit looked odd on him, but only because Kaiden had known him since he was ten and had never seen him in anything other than the black TAP security uniform. The holograph of the news report he pretended to read reflected in his sunglasses.

Kaiden had drawn his three new members from a couple of offensive operations units in an attempt to give his team a fighting chance. Iris, the new sniper, held a commanding position from the top of the Library of Global Studies. She came highly recommended as the most accomplished sniper at TAP with twenty-seven confirmed kills. Her KMH 70 Manslayer Sniper Rifle shot a .408 caliber round and had an effective range of three miles.

Jade and Flint, the other new members of the team, oversaw the cyber interruption equipment from the get-away truck parked discreetly next to the ISA building. Jade ran communications because they didn't need her expertise with explosives on this mission. Flint was a computer geek, like Quill.

Kaiden had worked with all of the new team members before, but this team had never worked together. This only added to his tension. An extraction operation in a public place was not the best way to experiment with a new team. As Kaiden surveyed the site and considered his crew, he tried to ignore the nagging doubt that Rio had sent him here to fail and the fear that there might be another

Raven in the group.

The crowd continued to grow in the plaza as political campaign music blared over the noise of the crowd. Kaiden settled in to wait while officers marked off the helipad and stretched yellow tape to keep the crowd away from the path the senator would walk. The peculiar roar of an airship's engines cut through the air and became louder as it zipped past the ISA tower and halted over the plaza. Its engines rotated, and it descended in a rush of blue flame to settle onto the helipad.

The crowd applauded as Senator Benton emerged from the airship and waved to the crowd. According to the intelligence report Rio had given him, Senator Benton was careful about security, and this was the only time he would be vulnerable. But with this many people in the plaza, there was bound to be collateral damage—with no way to avoid it.

Consequently, Kaiden's team was armed only with tranquilizing darts. These darts delivered a seventy thousand volt charge with a very low amperage, so they were not lethal. They also injected a sedative and paralytic agent to keep the victim immobilized for several hours. Their mission was to capture, not to kill.

Kaiden and Iris rifles both had self-adjusting sites that could be set for non-lethal or lethal status targets. The sites then analyzed the intended target and automatically adjusted the shot to compensate for any operator error. They were sweet rifles. Still, a lot of things could go wrong with an operation like this.

Dressed smartly in a gray suit and red tie, Senator Benton began a boisterous speech about corruption at the highest levels.

"Clones are a curse upon the planet," he bellowed. "Babies are abandoned on doorsteps while we're making fake humans."

"Down with clones," the crowd chanted.

"Positions," Kaiden spoke into the mic. "Prepare to jam communications."

"Down with clones! Down with clones!" The chant echoed around the plaza.

Kaiden's head still ached even after nearly two weeks since Raven's betrayal. He blinked at the pain and suddenly remembered an experience he had long ago. It was foggy and filled with rage.

He was amid a crowd of jostling teenagers pumping his fist into the air.

"Save the children. Kill the clones," he had screamed at the top of his lungs. How could they create clones when the earth's population had already passed twenty billion, and ecosystems were collapsing? People were starving in every megacity on earth. Instead of perfecting food production and combating disease, the government was spending trillions of dollars on a secret clone program that meant they had given up on humanity. It was immoral. It was wrong. "Save the children. Kill the clones," Kaiden screamed again.

"There's one," someone shouted. The mob surged with a roar, and Kaiden was with them. It was time to do something real to stop this evil.

A blonde woman exiting a skyscraper spun around with her eyes wide in terror.

"Get her!"

Kaiden was in the forefront of the mob, the first to grab her. There was no way to tell by sight if a person was a clone, but the crowd was so worked up, no one cared. Kaiden was the first to swing. She was screaming and shrieking, and then the mob overwhelmed them, and Kaiden was trampled until he managed to crawl away. When he came to his feet panting, his body aching from the pummeling he received, he raised his hands and found them covered in blood. Horror filled his chest. What had he done?

"Captain?" Quill's voice blared from his earpiece. "He's moving."

"Jam," Kaiden ordered. "Move in."

Kaiden shivered from the horrible images, clipped into the line hanging over the side of the building, and zipped down into the alleyway. He divided his attention between his team's movements and the necessity of keeping his feet from breaking through the windows. It had been necessary to hide on the rooftop to avoid the security search of the plaza and to oversee his team's movements. But now, he needed to be on the ground helping his team.

He hit the ground, unclipped, and raced into position. Quill approached the senator from the left, Birch from the right, and Greyson from behind. Birch dropped a canister, and blue smoke billowed through the crowd. Someone shouted.

Security emerged from one of the buildings and pelted toward the senator. Kaiden knelt and dropped both of the security officers with tranquilizer darts. They toppled to the ground twitching spasmodically as the tranquilizers did their work. The van rolled forward when Kaiden saw the little boy sitting in the plaza in the path the van would take. The child was scribbling on the stones with chalk, oblivious to his peril. Where had he come from? Where were his parents? Kaiden cursed. Jade wouldn't be able to see him before the truck plowed him over. In a sudden burst of desperation, Kaiden sprinted toward the boy.

"Watch the kid!" He yelled into the mic.

"What?" Quill said.

"Jade, the kid."

The van careened around the corner. Kaiden jumped, grabbed the child, and rolled with him in his arms. The bumper clipped Kaiden's hip and sent him flying. Bullets kicked up fragments of rock all around him.

"We're taking fire," Birch screamed.

"Kaiden! Iris! The sniper!" It was Quill's voice.

Kaiden set the boy in the shelter of a doorway and jumped up to see Quill and Birch, ducking into the crowd toward the van, dragging the staggering senator behind them. Greyson came behind them, his gun drawn. The blue smoke from Birch's smoke grenade wafted over the plaza, providing a bit of cover. Kaiden dove behind a concrete barricade, found the sniper, and shot a dart in his chest. But it was too late. The senator's guards were alerted now and converging. The crowd stampeded for cover, leaving Quill, Greyson, and Birch exposed. Iris began dropping guards with her sniper rifle. Kaiden shot several more guards, but the guards' electromagnetic pistols sliced indiscriminately through the crowd. People shrieked in terror. Quill jerked. He spun and fired, but his feet weren't under him. He stumbled and staggered, desperately trying to reach the van.

Kaiden sprinted for the van, fighting the pain in his hip and shooting every guard he could see through the drifting smoke. Others fell, and he knew Iris was trying to cover them, as well. Quill staggered to his knees, dragging Birch to a stop. She took one look at the senator and released his arm. The senator sagged to the concrete, lifeless and unmoving. This couldn't be happening. Everything was going wrong.

Birched grabbed Quill instead, and they lurched toward the van. Greyson tumbled to the ground, but he rolled and came to his feet, his pistol blazing. The guards dispersed, seeking cover behind trashcans and statues. Several of them grabbed up the senator and dragged him from the plaza. The team launched themselves into the van, and Jade sped off into the streets. Bullets clicked against the sides of the armored vehicle.

"Quill!" Kaiden knelt beside his friend on the floor of the van. The pool of blood was spreading underneath him. Birch ripped two bandages from her bag, threw one to Kaiden, and rolled Quill onto his side. She pressed the bandage to the exit wound while Kaiden pressed another bandage to Quill's chest. Blood soaked the bandage immediately. Birch's gaze found Kaiden's.

"Why isn't the INCR working?" Kaiden said. He grabbed another bandage, desperate to save his friend. This couldn't be happening. Not again.

Birch shook her head. "He's bleeding out too fast," she said. "That bullet must have clipped an artery."

CHAPTER SEVEN
SABOTAGE

QUILL WAS DEAD. It seemed impossible. How could that silly grin and irreverent laughter be erased from the world? Snuffed out in an instant of horror and blood. Kaiden still couldn't believe he'd seen the light fade from Quill's eyes. He couldn't process that he would never stay up all night with Quill, playing video games while Vivaldi, Schubert, and Beethoven blared from Quill's top-of-the-line HHC surround sound speakers.

Kaiden peered out the window in one of the tiny rooms of the T-60 Python gunship sent to extract them from New York. He wanted to be alone. The city spilled out beneath them as the airship banked and turned west. The buildings fell away to be replaced by long strips of green land carefully laid out along the banks of the dwindling rivers. In between the green oases, everything was brown and barren.

He had been told that vast forests once covered the land from the Atlantic to the Mississippi. What might that have looked like? Kaiden grunted. What did it matter if forests once covered the land? Nothing at all mattered anymore since his friend was dead. They hadn't extracted the senator, and every private aerial-bot and hovercraft camera in the plaza probably had footage of the whole thing.

Kaiden toyed with Quill's wrist terminal. He had slipped it off

41

his wrist when it was obvious that he was dead. This whole thing had been wrong from the start. An inexperienced team should never have been sent on such a high profile assignment in such an exposed position. Now Quill was gone forever.

Kaiden tried to breathe normally—to control the choking anguish that burned in his chest and the hot fury boiling just beneath the surface. He couldn't cry. Quill wouldn't want him to. They had rushed Quill away to a hospital unit, but Kaiden knew it was no use.

It was all Kaiden's fault. He should have refused the mission, but he had gone ahead despite his misgivings. He had been trained to trust his instincts, and he had ignored them. First, there was the explosion and the murder of the clones and his crew. Now, his best friend's body was being shipped back to Ararat. He couldn't believe it. He wouldn't.

Kaiden stuffed the wrist terminal into his pocket and clicked on the news feed. He couldn't remember the last time he'd watched the news, but he didn't want to think just now, and he might as well be prepared when he had to face Rio again. Rio would discipline him for sure this time.

Kaiden dropped into a chair as the female broadcaster stepped in front of a huge screen showing the earth with a belt of satellites encircling it. "Now for the news roundup," she began. "The Equitable Trade Association has fined the Greater South America Co-Prosperity Sphere one billion dollars for allegedly selling a stripped-down version of its software to African states for the same price it charges the more developed regions.

"The Chinese Free State has launched an offensive against Indian forces in their decades-long struggle to control the water flowing from their Himalayan stronghold. Water politics continues to promote instability in the International Confederation of States as the United States of North America disputes the United Slavic States for the rights to melt arctic ice for drinking water."

This is why Kaiden didn't watch the news. It was too depressing. He adjusted his seat to relieve the pain in his hip. The music played, and the words "Breaking News" flashed onto the screen.

"We now have more information," the broadcaster continued, "on the terrorist attack at an anti-clone rally in the Plaza of Global Cooperation in New York. It is believed that at least two terrorists were injured in the fighting, but both escaped. Early reports suggest that Senator Christopher Benton was assassinated, and the terrorists attempted to steal his body. Three civilians were mortally wounded, and fourteen remain under medical care."

Aerial images of the plaza with people scrambling in all directions and Birch and Greyson dragging Quill to the van panned across the screen. One of the videos depicted Kaiden scrambling away from a spray of bullets as he ducked behind a concrete barrier with the boy in his arms.

Kaiden sat up, suddenly alert. Those bullets were not coming from the sniper he had shot. The angle was wrong. And Quill had been hit in the chest, not the back. Kaiden tried to remember if any guards had been in front of them, but he was sure they hadn't been. The only sniper he had seen had been in the wrong position to fire those bullets.

"The Destroying Angels deny involvement," the reporter continued. "In response to our request for information, they released the following statement: 'It would be a complete contradiction of our platform to attack an anti-clone demonstration. We support any and all attempts to halt the willful and illegal creation of clones who can only take jobs and food away from our own children.' We will continue to follow this story…"

Kaiden clicked it off and rose.

He tapped his wrist terminal to send on Birch's frequency alone. "Where are Iris, Jade, and Flint?" He whispered into his mic.

Birch's voice came on. "I left them in loading bay cleaning their weapons."

"Where are you?"

"Relaxing."

"Stop relaxing and find Greyson. We need to talk."

"Now?"

"Yes, now."

"What about the others?"

"Just the original members of the team, for now," he said. "Meet me in the weapon room in ten minutes."

Ten minutes later, Birch lounged with her feet propped up on a chair and her arms crossed, the picture of ease. But her gaze followed Kaiden as he entered. Birch was a pretty, slender young woman with light brown hair and big, dark eyes. If you didn't know her, she would be easy to underestimate.

Greyson leaned on the wall by the door with his hands in his pockets. He had not been injured in the fighting as the news reporters thought. Instead, he'd simply tripped over a fallen guard. Greyson kept a little patch of short, black hair on top of his otherwise shaved head. Though he had been top of the class his year, he had been passed over for captain because of an unfortunate passion for alcohol.

Still, he was a genius at grappling and small arms. That's why Kaiden picked him for his team. Still, Kaiden knew Greyson often chafed at having to take orders when he thought he should be the one giving them.

Kaiden gestured for them to turn off their mics and their wrist terminals. Then he pulled out the little DWJ Quill had given him and clicked it on. It didn't matter if TAP knew he was meeting with members of his team. They would expect him to. But he didn't want them to know what he was going to say—not yet, anyway.

"We've got a problem," he said.

"I noticed," Birch replied.

"Quill was murdered," Kaiden said.

"What makes you say that?" Greyson asked. He shifted to stare directly at Kaiden and folded his arms.

"He took that bullet in the chest," Kaiden said.

"So?" Birch said.

"So there were no security personnel to your front. Only one person we know could have fired that shot."

"You're suggesting that Iris killed him?" Greyson said.

Kaiden nodded. "And I took fire from the same direction."

"No," Greyson said.

"No what?"

"You can't shift the focus away from the fact that you botched this job by calling it too late and wasting your time on that kid."

Kaiden bristled. "Be careful, Greyson," he said, "or I'll cite you for insubordination."

Birch shifted nervously.

"Yes, sir," Greyson said, but the muscles in his jaw flexed.

"It was supposed to be a non-lethal extraction," Kaiden said.

"And that included civilians."

"Sacrifices have to be made, sir," Greyson said. He paused, calculating. "But that doesn't explain why you called it too late."

Kaiden ground his teeth. "I didn't call it too late. We had plenty of time. If Iris hadn't wasted time shooting at me and Quill, we would have made it."

Greyson couldn't keep the smirk from his face. "With all due respect, sir, Iris only had tranquilizers like the rest of us."

Kaiden raised his eyebrows. "You don't know that," he said.

"Look," Birch said, interrupting Greyson's reply, "I think the captain is onto something. There's no way Quill could have been hit from the front, but he was."

Greyson snorted. "So, what are you going to do about it? You picked her for the team."

"I'm going to make a full report to Rio." Kaiden raised his eyebrows. "Including your lack of respect for your commanding officer."

"You could get us all disciplined, sir," Greyson said.

Kaiden frowned. He had considered that, and he was trying to work out a way to avoid it. He concluded that honesty was his best option.

"We've lost five members of our club," Birch said. "Why?"

Kaiden shifted. "I think you mean team," he corrected her. Birch had a habit of mixing up her words. It was usually humorous, but not now. He had a good idea why he and Quill had been targeted, but he couldn't tell them—not yet. Raven was a different matter. That had happened before he even knew what Quill was doing.

"I don't know," he said. "Raven was on a suicide mission no matter what happened. She could have just killed the clones and been done with it, but she targeted the entire crew. Iris must be involved with the same group."

"While you work that out, sir," Greyson said, "our faces are going to be plastered over every screen in the world."

CHAPTER EIGHT
THE GENESIS ROOM

"I THOUGHT I MADE myself clear!" Rio shouted.

The images of the aerial-bot cameras from the New York City plaza played across the screens surrounding Rio's desk. Kaiden's own face filled one of them as he ducked behind a concrete barrier with the child in his arms.

"Yes, sir." Kaiden had braced himself for the onslaught. He expected the discipline to flare up at any moment. Still, he had to grit his teeth to keep from shouting back. He balled his fists behind his back.

"And?" Rio demanded.

"We were set up, sir."

"What?" Rio slammed his fist into his desk.

"The extraction point was an impossible situation, sir, and we received friendly fire."

"What friendly fire?" Rio said. "I thought you eliminated a sniper."

"Yes, sir, but the fire came from Iris's position."

"What? You have proof of that?"

"The fire that killed Quill could only come from Iris's position."

"Bull crap," Rio said. "She's the best we have."

"Watch the footage, sir," Kaiden insisted. "Quill was shot in the chest. The sniper I took out was to our right. There is no way—"

"I've heard enough," Rio snapped. He paced behind his desk as he brushed a speck of dust from his immaculate uniform.

"I'm placing you on administrative suspension until I can check into this. You're not off the hook yet. Get out."

Kaiden saluted and left. But he didn't to his room. He was convinced he and Quill had been targeted because of Quill's breach of the security system, which meant that Quill hadn't been as careful as he'd thought. If Iris wasn't the assassin, then Rio must have sent someone else to do it and kill the senator. None of his team on the ground had lethal ammunition. Kaiden didn't know who to trust anymore. Raven had been his friend and comrade for at least seven years, though she'd only been on his team for two. If she could betray him, anyone could.

Kaiden clicked on the DWJ as he walked. It was better that no one knew where he was going. He drew Quill's wrist terminal out of his pocket and used it to enter Quill's room. Now that Quill was gone, the room would be reassigned. That's the way it was. Kaiden was surprised it hadn't been cleaned out already. But he wasn't going to waste this chance. He swallowed the knot that rose in his throat at the sight and smell of Quill's rooms and yanked the pillowcase off the pillow in Quill's bedroom. Then, he dumped all of Quill's bots, computer gadgets, and anything he could find into it.

Using Quill's favorite login, "BEESymp no 3" for Beethoven's best symphony, he opened Quill's computer files. He hurried to download everything in Quill's folders and delete anything that might suggest Quill had been infiltrating the system. Before Kaiden left, he permitted himself one last look around. The rooms felt like Quill. They even smelled like Quill with his wild cologne and the sharp spices he used to flavor his food. Kaiden picked up the picture of him and Quill as cadets. So young. So innocent. So hopeful.

Kaiden blinked against the sting of tears. Quill would never come here again.

"I'm sorry," Kaiden said before he dropped the picture into the pillowcase. "I'll find out who did this, even if it kills me."

Willow slipped into a blue engineering lab jacket and strolled into the vast engineering complex as if she belonged. This was the section of TAP that designed weapons and airships. She passed huge hangars where robots buzzed and whirred as they constructed newer, sleeker hovercraft and big gunships. The sharp smell of hot metal and warm oil stung her nose. Soon she was striding past the armory and the testing range. The rattle and pop of guns reached her ears, muffled by the thick walls.

All around her, blue-clad engineers worked in clusters or rushed between rooms. There was nothing to set this section of TAP apart from other industrial zones in the megacities, save for the fact that most of the engineers were under twenty years of age, like most people at TAP. It was a curious practice that no one outside of TAP would understand, and most inside TAP didn't comprehend. But they all eventually would, to their cost.

Willow took a deep breath to calm the nervous flutter in her stomach as she approached the rendezvous point. Her hand drifted to the pocket where she carried a small knife, just in case. She had never trained in security, but that didn't mean she wouldn't fight like a wild cat to stay alive this time.

The crowd of engineers thinned as she worked her way into the darker corridors where the huge ventilation pipes recycled the air. The corridor narrowed to follow the vents into the deeper shadows, lit only by the pale blue lights set at regular intervals in the ceiling high above. Willow cast about to make sure no one was following or watching her and slipped behind the black pipes. She knew TAP could track her, but she hoped with all the activity in this section, her passage would go unnoticed. If it didn't, she would know soon enough.

Kaiden hadn't come to see her after he started having his spells. It wasn't that they knew each other well, but after experiencing something like that, she felt a bond with him and thought, or hoped, he would feel the same for her.

She slowed as the shadows deepened and slipped her hand into her pocket to grasp the knife. It had a spring-loaded blade that retracted into the handle. Her thumb found the switch. She tensed and stepped around another big pipe.

No one was there. Confused, she checked her WT to make

sure she wasn't early. But she was right on time. She took two steps deeper into the shadow when an iron-like grip seized her wrist, and a hand clamped over her mouth, yanking her close to a body that felt as hard as stone.

"Drop it," a harsh voice whispered in her ear. Whiskers scratched the back of her neck, and she smelled the awful breath of a man who had been drinking. This was a smell she remembered all too well. Her father had been a drinker and a beater.

Rage filled her chest, and she drove the elbow of her free arm back. A grunt came from the man who held her. Then she slammed her foot up and back, driving her heel into his groin. His grip loosed, and she twisted free, jerking the knife from her pocket and pressing the switch. The blade snapped out, and she was ready to fight or die.

But her attacker was on his knees, bent over.

"Crap, lady," he groaned. "You didn't have to do that."

He wore a blue jacket like hers, but she could see the collar of a white t-shirt and the bulge of a pistol stuffed into his pants at the small of his back.

"You touch me again, and I'll slit your throat."

She bent to jerk the pistol free and pointed it at him.

"He told me you were just a lab tech," he said. "I thought you had a gun in your pocket."

The rush of adrenaline made her ears ring, and her knees feel weak. She suddenly wanted to cry. But she held it in.

"What's the message," she said, "that he couldn't send over the WT?"

The man squinted up at her, the pale blue light overhead shining in his eyes. He had a red, scruffy beard and a hard look about him.

"Give me a second," he said. "You might have ruined my chances of ever having a family."

Willow couldn't keep the smile from her lips. "Serves you right for jumping on me like that."

"Well, don't walk around like you plan on killing someone, and you'll make friends a lot easier."

"I didn't know if I could trust you or him."

The man smirked. "Next time, I'm gonna let him run his own errands." He crawled to his feet and extended his hand.

"Name's Hawk," he said.

Willow eyed the hand warily but shook it.

"Now that we have the niceties over," Hawk said, "Can I have my pistol back?"

Willow hesitated and handed it to him. He tucked it into his pants.

"The director sends his greetings," Hawk said, "and says if you're who you say you are, you'll know what the last words are that he said to you."

A horrible wriggly feeling swam around in Willow's stomach. She had thought about those words over and over again. They had invaded her nightmares. She swallowed.

"He said, 'Willow, I am sorry, I tried to save you.'"

Hawk grinned. "Excellent. Now, we're cool."

He slipped a small, black device from his pocket and handed it to her.

"If you need us, you just push this button, and we'll contact you."

"That's it?"

"Yeah."

"Tell him I didn't like what he did on that ship," Willow said. "That was wrong on every level."

Hawk peered at her. "No, I guess you wouldn't," he said. "I'll let him know."

Kaiden bent over the mug of warm ale in the officer's pub. The music and chatter around him provided a dull roar that helped him think and deadened the pain of losing Quill. His thoughts roamed and were filled with memories of his childhood at TAP, where he and Quill had been inseparable. It started that first day of tactics training when Quill followed Kaiden in a flanking movement that secured their objective while everyone else on their team was killed or captured in the mock battle. Then his thoughts wandered into vague, shadowy images of things he had never experienced.

How could he remember things that had never happened? He was less than a year away from a promotion, and his spotless record now held two blemishes that would most likely end his career with TAP. What would he do if they discharged him? He didn't know anything else. He had no family. All he had known was the orphanage where food and water had been scarce, and friends and affection had been non-existent.

But now, there were new dreams and hallucinations, almost like memories—memories of people and places he had never seen, filled with longing and love. Emotions Kaiden had never felt.

The soft glow of lights lit the pub where officers of every kind came to relax after a day's work. Kaiden glanced around at the officers in their various colored coats—white coats for the physicians and geneticists, dark blue for the engineers, red for the computer programmers, green for logistics, light blue for the nursery, and black for security. All of them had a little red ark stitched into the left shoulder.

Warm ale was a rare and expensive treat in which Kaiden rarely indulged. But the unsettling images and dreams haunted him, and the anguish of Quill's death and Kaiden's failure to protect his friends and crew members tormented him.

Kaiden swallowed a mouthful of ale and relished the warmth it spread in his belly. What was he to make of it all? What could the hallucinations mean that crept up on him—flashes of faces and events with no apparent connection—intimate details of a life he had never lived? He remembered playing Beethoven's fifth symphony on a violin—but he had never even seen a real violin, let alone played one. He remembered throwing baseballs with a man in a park—though he'd never even been to a real park. And he remembered singing a lullaby to a baby girl he cradled in his arms. These hallucinations, or whatever they were, came with a dull ache that gripped his heart as if he missed something he loved and valued.

It seemed clear that the bomb blast had rattled his brains. He was having PTSD symptoms of events he had never experienced with people he had never known. He had to accept that conclusion because the other was unacceptable. He could not be losing his mind at only nineteen years of age.

Kaiden had endured the spasmodic flashes of hallucinations and daydreams for two weeks. It was like he was living two lives at once—one in the external world where he could touch, taste, and see—the other in an internal world of emotions filled with pain, doubt, and regret but also of love and belonging. Sometimes he felt that love so powerfully it brought tears to his eyes. Or he struggled against a sense of loss so intense that he would sit and stare at the wall of his living quarters like nothing in the world mattered anymore.

Something had to change, or he *would* go crazy. He couldn't go to the medical ward. They would have him removed from his command. With Quill gone, there wasn't anyone he could talk to about the haunting images that flashed into his mind. Greyson blamed Kaiden for Quill's death, and Birch was too close to the whole mess. Besides, he couldn't let anyone on the team know that his head was messed up. He had to work through this somehow. But who was left? Whom could he trust? Willow? She knew or suspected what was going on inside his head, and apparently, she hadn't told anyone. Maybe she would have some answers, or at least she'd let him talk through his sense of loss.

Kaiden drained the rest of the ale and set out to find her. The smooth, white walls of the corridor reminded him of a hospital, and the woman in the white lab coat. He had gone there to visit her as a child. She had smiled at him, kissed him on the cheek, and given him a lollipop. She smelled of hair gel and sweet perfume. He loved that smell because it was *her* smell. He blinked at the sudden burning in his eyes. These images brought so much pain and longing. Kaiden had never experienced anything like it. Is this what it was like to belong to a family—to be so vulnerable?

Kaiden paused in the hallway near the lab, where Willow worked. He stuffed his hand into his pockets and shuffled his feet, trying not to look so out of place in his black security uniform. Lab techs brushed past him, giving him a quizzical glance that said, "Why are you here?" If he went in there and admitted to Willow that he had PTSD symptoms, she could turn him in, and it would all be over. But he had to have answers. He couldn't live like this.

Willow stepped out of the lab. Her white lab coat flapped out behind her. He experienced a sudden hatred for that coat, but he didn't know why.

"Hey," Kaiden said, trotting to catch up with her.

Willow glanced around but didn't stop walking. Her brown hair fell around her shoulders. In his horror and shock after the first disaster, he hadn't noticed how beautiful she was.

"Are you talking to me?" she said.

Kaiden scowled. "We need to talk."

"Oh, I'm fine. Thank you for asking," Willow mocked. "How are you?"

"What are *you* mad about?" Kaiden demanded.

Willow stopped and glared at Kaiden with her hands on her hips. "Oh, I don't know. Let me think. I saved your miserable life, and you acted like I was the terrorist."

"I lost another member of my team," Kaiden said.

Willow glowered. "Is that all Quill was, to you?" she demanded.

The rebuke hit Kaiden like a slap in the face. He almost spun and left her there, but he needed her.

"He was my friend," Kaiden whispered. "I need to talk."

Willow's glower faded to a sad frown.

"All right." She checked the corridor, considering. "Follow me."

Kaiden clicked on the DWJ as he followed Willow into a small room with no windows just off the lab. No one else was in the room. Computers and monitors littered the countertops, and other equipment Kaiden didn't recognize. Kaiden watched curiously as Willow clicked off the wrist terminal on her arm and motioned for him to do the same. When he had, she touched a few buttons on the countertop, so the hologram screens went blank. Kaiden followed her movements. She shut down everything in the lab that might allow them to be recorded or observed. The DWJ in his pocket would already do that, but there was no point in not letting her take these precautions. One never knew.

"You've been expecting me," Kaiden said.

Willow smiled. "I thought you might come," she said. "Life is easier if you know what to expect."

What was that supposed to mean?

"Well?" Willow said. She raised her eyebrows. She was an attractive girl with little dimples in her cheeks and the freckles on her nose.

"Uh, okay," Kaiden said. "I lied to you in the elevator."

"I figured that out on my own," Willow said.

Kaiden stared at her, thinking she might chastise him, but she just watched him with tight-lipped anticipation.

"And," he continued, "I'm hallucinating about things that never happened, about people I've never met. Weird things—"

"Like Rose?" Willow said.

Kaiden shifted. "Yeah. Like I was playing a violin, and I don't like grapes, and I was—" He almost told her about the rally where he was screaming, *Kill the clones*. But that didn't seem like a good idea, given that the clone program was one of the most important programs TAP oversaw. He didn't know how much he should confide to Willow, but he wanted to trust her with a sudden desperation that surprised him.

Willow tilted her head to one side, pinched her brows together, and set her face in an expression of the utmost pity. "You really don't know, do you?" she said with a little shake of the head.

"Know what?"

Willow threaded her fingers through her hair in an attitude of nervous excitement. Then, she leaned close to him. Kaiden caught a whiff of her sweet vanilla perfume.

"We're clones," she said.

Kaiden gaped and jerked away from her. "What? You're joking."

But she wasn't smiling. She had stopped fidgeting and fixed him with a steely-eyed stare.

Kaiden knew the clones. He had transported them to and from the lunar station for three years now. He'd seen their sad, disinterested eyes and sallow cheeks. He'd seen their bodies, grotesque in death, where Raven had executed them.

"No," he said.

Willow raised her eyebrows at him. "You and I and almost everyone working in TAP are clones."

Kaiden stood up. She was mocking him. This had been a waste of time. He should have known.

"Sorry, I bothered you," he said. Maybe Willow was the one who had lost her mind. Kaiden strode to the door of the lab and then turned back. "How would you know, anyway?" he demanded.

Willow lowered her gaze to stare down at her feet for a moment before raising her head to look Kaiden square in the eyes. Her eyes were a deep rich brown, and her gaze was earnest. "I remember dying," she said.

Kaiden found himself temporarily robbed of his voice. It

couldn't be possible. Was she lying? No one could remember dying. And here she was, wasn't she? Clearly *not* dead.

"You don't have to die to be cloned," he said.

"No," Willow said. She clasped her hands in front of her as if struggling for patience. "But we did. We all died."

Kaiden wanted to leave, to run from this horrible idea. But an undeniable fascination gripped him, and he returned to sit on the stool beside her. "That doesn't make any sense. How come *I* don't remember dying?"

Willow sighed. "First, you need to understand that what we're talking about could get us both killed."

"I'm not stupid," Kaiden said. He knew very well what could happen. Quill had been murdered. He was sure of it.

Willow eyed him like she thought he might be simple before jumping up to pace back and forth.

"The answer is," she said, "you aren't awake yet."

"What's that supposed to mean?" Kaiden demanded. This conversation had been completely derailed. He came looking for help, and all he got was crazy talk.

Willow shot him an annoyed glance but kept pacing. "It means your memories of your real life are still suppressed." She stopped pacing, flopped onto a stool, and dropped her gaze to the tile floor. She clasped her trembling hands in front of her. "I was in a hovercraft accident," she said. "They told my mother I was dead." Willow touched her forehead with her fingers. "My mother kissed me on the forehead, and my mind was ripped from my body, where I existed in utter darkness and silence until I awoke inside a thirteen-year-old body."

Kaiden shifted uncomfortably. "Wait," he said, "how old were you when you died?"

Willow glanced up at him. She bit her lip and blinked back tears. "Nineteen," she said. "The same age I am now."

Kaiden stared incredulously. "I don't believe it."

Anger flashed across Willow's face. She jumped off the stool and grabbed Kaiden's arm, dragging him toward the door. "Come with me," she snapped.

Kaiden yanked his arm free. "What's the matter with you?" he demanded.

Willow ignored him as she strode through the door and into the corridor. Kaiden followed, convinced more than ever that he had made a mistake in trusting her.

She led him deep into the heart of the TAP complex to places Kaiden hadn't been in years—not because he couldn't, but because he had never needed to. His job was transport security. That meant he had the highest-level clearance, but he seldom needed to use it. The dark hallways of the upper levels where the security personnel had their living quarters and training facilities gave way to blue and gray hallways with labs and manufacturing sections.

Willow refused to answer any of his questions until she paused in front of a door, gave Kaiden a meaningful glance, keyed in the entry code, and stepped through. Kaiden strode two steps into the room and stopped.

His gaze roamed the gigantic space. As far as he could see, rows of transparent tanks that glowed green held membrane sacks in which human infants wiggled and kicked. Red, blinking lights overhead cast a ruddy, pulsating glow over the darkened room. Kaiden blinked at the ghostly menace of the lights and shivered.

"It's called the Genesis Room," Willow said. "These are motherless womb chambers called ectogenesis." She paused and turned to watch him. "We all began in a room like this."

Heat spread in Kaiden's chest and rose into his face. He had never felt so violated, so betrayed. Not him, surely. He knew the clones he transported to and from the moon were created and raised at TAP, so he wasn't surprised to find the Genesis Room here. But he had never visited, never seen the cold inhumanity of the motherless womb.

"I...I..." He tried to think of something to say. He wanted to reject the whole idea. He wanted to call her a liar and a lunatic. But the evidence of the hundreds, maybe thousands of wiggling infants that surrounded him could not be wished away.

"I thought the clones were still being studied in a small pilot program," he said. "How can there be so many?"

Willow grimaced at him and gestured for him to walk with her.

"They use an accelerated growth hormone to hasten our arrival at maturity. That way, they can keep pumping us out like manufactured robots. They get clones in half the time it takes a natural child to develop, so they can test their techniques without having to wait ten to twenty years."

Kaiden couldn't tear his gaze away from the babies swimming in the clear fluid. There were blacks, like him, Asians, whites—every variety of human. There must have been thousands of babies in various stages of development, all of them encased in a semi-transparent uterus and fed by tubes that pumped human blood through the membrane. The sight so unnerved Kaiden that he could only gaze wide-eyed at the tanks—row after row of them—awash in eerie green light.

Willow led him through another door and down several corridors that he recognized as they entered the primary ward. He came here when he was ten years old-after being rescued from the overcrowded orphanage where he fought for his food and a place to sleep. How could he have lived so close to the Genesis Room and not even know it was there?

Willow stopped at an observation window, and they gazed out over a crowd of toddlers, all busy with their little hologram screens or sitting on the floor playing with complicated erector sets and diagrams of cells or DNA. They already wore the different colored jackets. Even at this age, TAP had tracked and tested each one. Every child grew up knowing what they would do. A few caregivers dressed in light blue lab coats worked with them. One glanced up and saw them. She raised her hand in a friendly wave.

"Do you remember this?" Kaiden asked because he didn't. He remembered the fleas and the cold, hard floor where he was forced to make his bed out of a bunch of rags. He remembered the beatings and the teacher that smelled of alcohol. If he had been born at TAP, how could he remember the orphanage?

"I do," Willow said. "And I remember my father dropping me off at a real school in Chicago. I remember winning a scholarship to an accelerated high school and getting my doctorate in genetic therapy with a specialty in the field of Cognitive Redesign just after I turned eighteen. And I remember dying with the warmth of my mother's lips still on my forehead and the moisture of her tears on my cheek."

Silence settled between them as Willow stared out over the busy, little children and their caregivers. A great emptiness expanded inside Kaiden. He longed to know who he had been. If what Willow had said was true, he had probably had a family like hers.

"Do you think that's what I'm remembering?" Kaiden asked. "My real life before they cloned me?"

Willow gave him that pitying glance again that confirmed his suspicions.

"But how? They would have to transplant my brain from one body to the next for me to remember things that I experienced in a different clone body. That's how the brain works."

"No. All they have to do is download your memories as binary code," Willow said. "The files can be saved and manipulated and then uploaded into a newly cloned brain that is mature enough to handle it. The problem is that the science of modifying memories or completely erasing them isn't advanced enough to control how much we remember. For example, the manipulation of memories never works on me. I'm always aware, and when they download my memories from one body and upload them again into my new clone, I get everything from the previous clone body plus what I remember from before that."

"That's got to be awful," Kaiden said. "I mean, all I could remember until a few days ago was the brutal life of the orphanage. But now..." He didn't know what to say.

"Seen enough?" Willow asked.

Kaiden stuffed his hands into his pockets.

Willow started back the way they had come.

"Have you ever eaten grapes at TAP?" she asked as they walked.

The question took Kaiden by surprise. "What? No."

"Why don't you like them, then?"

Kaiden pondered, trying to recall that strange memory. "They felt like eyeballs popping in my mouth."

Willow glanced at him and smiled. She shook her head. "Have you ever had an eyeball pop in your mouth?"

Kaiden shrugged. He guessed not, but how could he be sure now?

Minutes later, they stepped back into the little room of the lab where Willow had first taken him. Kaiden plopped down on a stool and popped his knuckles.

"All right," he said. "Let's say I believe you. How does this work?"

"What? TAP?"

Kaiden gestured impatiently with his hands. "Yes, TAP. Everything. How could I not remember who I am?"

Willow didn't smile. Her expression became sad, hopeless. "You've heard of a Synaptic Download?" she asked.

Kaiden rubbed a hand over his course, short-cropped hair. "Yeah, it's theoretical."

Willow shook her head. "No, it isn't."

"That's what you meant when you said they downloaded our memories? You actually believe that our memories were downloaded before we died and uploaded into a new clone of ourselves when the clone was thirteen?"

"Yep. Well, they execute the upload at age thirteen for girls and age fourteen for boys so that we are each near the end of puberty. With the exception of the frontal lobe, the mind's patterns are set by then."

"I don't believe it," Kaiden said. "What happens to our memories of growing up inside TAP, then?" Kaiden asked. "Wouldn't we still have all of those?"

"You do," Willow said. "But most of those memories were overwritten by new ones, so you would think you came here at a younger age."

"Why? It doesn't make any sense. Why not just recruit scientists to work for them?"

Willow took a deep breath and gave Kaiden a sympathetic look. "They do recruit scientists. But you have to understand that we are part of the experiments, Kaiden. We're just rats in a big lab."

"But how?" Kaiden was having trouble grasping all of this. "Memories aren't like computer files. They're stored in brain matter and scattered all over the place. Even I know that."

His world perched on the edge of an abyss. If he accepted what she was saying, then he was nothing—just a cluster of cells and a few computer files being run through a series of tests to satisfy some scientist's curiosity. His identity—his sense of self-worth meant nothing. He had never had a family, just a bunch of other babies reared in test tubes.

Willow picked at a thread on her lab coat. "It's what used to be called whole brain emulation or mind mapping," she said. "Your brain has about 86 billion neurons connected through electrochemical activity. That activity can be recorded, downloaded, saved, manipulated, and even uploaded into another human brain. It's a technique called Cognitive Redesign."

"You mentioned that before," Kaiden said.

Willow averted her gaze. "Yes. It's my area of specialty."

"So you remember growing up in TAP?"

"Yes, because for some reason, the Cognitive Redesign doesn't work on my brain. I remember both the things that really happened *and* the memories they uploaded."

"Could there be others like you?"

Willow smiled. "Most definitely, but usually people only have a few memories that survive from before."

"Which is what is happening to me?" Kaiden asked.

"Yeah. The explosion or the concussion may have triggered it."

It made sense, but something about the way she said this made him wonder if there was something more she wasn't telling him.

"So, what now?" Kaiden asked.

"If you want to know why Quill was killed, and you want to get your memories back, you're going to have to do something more radical."

Kaiden studied her. "You mean like sneaking into TAP's top security files?"

Willow nodded. "But I don't want to die doing it. They have ways of tracking everything that happens inside TAP. Remember, we are part of their experiments. They're collecting data on us."

Kaiden rose. He wasn't going to take this quietly. "Quill can get us in," he said.

Willow stared at him. "I thought you said he died."

The bitter ached filled Kaiden's chest again. "He did. But he can still get us in."

CHAPTER NINE
ALLY

"WHERE HAVE YOU BEEN?" Birch leaned against the wall of the corridor by Kaiden's door with her arms folded. Her short, brown hair fell before her eyes. She had a lithe figure and an open, intelligent face.

"I'm on administrative suspension," Kaiden said. He liked Birch, but right now, he had more important things to do than catch up.

"I noticed," she said. "So, that means you can just ignore your friends?"

"I'm not sure who my friends are." Kaiden hadn't forgotten the discussion in the weapons room on the airship. Birch had sided with him, but Greyson had been surly.

Birch looked as if he had slapped her face. "We have one bad mission, and you decide to freak out on us? Go all haywall."

Kaiden sniffed. "It's haywire, Birch. Not haywall. Besides, it was two bad missions. And Quill was murdered by a member of our team." His voice rose. He had been betrayed, and Quill was dead. He couldn't forget it or forgive.

Birch pushed herself off the wall and stepped toward him. Her face flushed bright red. "You don't know that!" she yelled.

"See what I mean?" Kaiden said as he threw up his hands and pushed past her into his room.

Birch followed him to the door. "Look," she said, "I know how much Quill and the others meant to you, but you can't just push the rest of us away."

Kaiden dropped into a chair at the table where he had left the pillowcase full of Quill's stuff. Birch came in and plopped into the chair opposite him.

"Greyson blames me," Kaiden said.

Birch folded her hands on the table. "He's just sad and frustrated," she said. "They were his friends, too."

"What do you want?" Kaiden said.

"Man," Birch said, "sometimes you are the biggest baby I know. I just wanted to make sure you were all right. I've been worried about you like any good teammate would be." She stood. "But if you're determined to be a pig, then I'll just go find Greyson, and we can argue about how stupid you are." Birch spun to leave.

"Sorry," Kaiden said.

"You should be."

"Things have changed," Kaiden said.

Birch whirled. "Yeah, they have, and we need to move on. We still have work to do."

Birch glanced at the pillowcase and raised her eyebrows.

"Do you normally store your stuff in a pillowcase?"

Kaiden clicked off his wrist terminal and waited for Birch to turn hers off, too.

Then, he extracted the larger DWJ from the pillowcase and set it on the table. He adjusted the antennae and clicked it on. The quiet hum filled the room.

"It's Quill's stuff," he whispered.

"Are you supposed to have it?" Birch scowled.

"No."

"Soooo?" Birch waved her hand, encouraging him to continue.

Kaiden considered. He'd spent two weeks trying to decide who ordered Quill's execution. It could only be Rio or Noah. Rio was the head of all TAP security at Ararat, and he reported directly to Noah, the director of The Ark Project. Either way, Rio must know about it. Maybe Rio had sent Birch to spy on him.

"First," Kaiden said, "I have to know that you're on my side."

"What's that supposed to mean?" Birch's face tightened in anger, and she planted her fists on her hips.

"Give me your word you weren't sent to spy on me and that you won't betray me."

"What? Betray you to whom?"

"Swear it."

Birch threw up her hands and sank into a chair at the table. "All right, I swear it."

Kaiden stared at her. He was taking a risk to trust her, but they were old friends. Birch had been the first to befriend him when he had arrived fresh from the orphanage, frightened and uncertain. At least, that is what he thought. He didn't know what truly happened anymore.

"Do you really want to know?" he asked.

"Are you trying to make me more curious, or what?"

"No," Kaiden said, "but this is what got Quill killed."

Birch sat up straight. "What *are* you talking about?"

Kaiden started pulling things out of the pillowcase. When he had them all lined up in a row, Birch just stared at him.

"Nano-bots?" she said. "You're kidding."

"He used them to hack into the highest classified level on the central computer."

"No." Birch's eyes widened. "What an idiot. He was asking for trouble."

"And I'm going to do it again," Kaiden continued.

For the first time in his life, Kaiden had rendered Birch speechless. A wry smile twisted Kaiden's lips at the thought. "Unless you betray me."

Birch finally found her voice. "You're serious."

"TAP isn't what we were taught it was," he said. "Something else is going on here."

Birch smirked at him. "I could have told you that," she said.

"What?" Kaiden hadn't expected this. As he gazed at the smirk on Birch's face, he realized that he probably didn't know her as well as he thought.

"You know," Birch said, "if you spent more time talking to folks in TAP rather than listening to classical music and playing video games, you might have figured that out for yourself."

"Now, what are *you* talking about?" Kaiden asked.

Birch rolled her eyes and folded her arms. "The Destroying

Angels say we're cloning our own army of super-soldiers. Everyone's been talking about it."

"They're fanatics. And the intel says otherwise."

"And," Birch continued, "we have a Genesis Room with thousands of little babies cloned each year."

"How do you know about that?"

"Because I ask questions." Birch's gaze passed over Quill's equipment.

"I'm in," she said.

"What?"

"Jade will be in, too."

Kaiden realized that he had just lost control of the conversation. "No," he said. "I'm doing this alone."

"No, you're not."

"I don't want anyone else getting hurt. Wait. What did you say?" Kaiden eyed Birch suspiciously.

"You're not alone." She raised her eyebrows dramatically. "Willow?"

"Ah," Kaiden finally understood. "She sent you?"

"No," Birch said. "She just said you were upset."

"How do you know her?" Again, Birch had thrown Kaiden into a tailspin. Were all girls like this? How much more did she know that *he* didn't?

"Do I have to roll my eyes at you again?" Birch said. She snapped her fingers in his face. "Wake up, Kaiden. It's time you popped that little bubble world you live in."

"I haven't been ignoring the real world," Kaiden said. "I just haven't wasted time on information that wasn't relevant to my missions or to keeping my team alive."

"Well, it looks like the big picture just became mission-critical information."

"Yeah," Kaiden said, "and we have some catching up to do." He paused. "Wait, who else have you been talking to besides Willow?" Kaiden was suddenly afraid that Birch had already compromised him.

"I don't know Iris from a giraffe," Birch said. "Greyson needs time, but he'll come around."

"What?" Kaiden asked. Sometimes Birch's verbal gaffes didn't make any sense at all. "What does a giraffe have to do with anything?"

Birch gave him an innocent look. "What are you blabbering about?"

Kaiden sighed but chose to keep going rather than get stalled in an argument with Birch over giraffes. She probably meant she didn't know Iris well.

"Greyson wants to be captain," Kaiden said instead.

Birch nodded. "He *is* two months older than you. But he's loyal."

"Loyal to TAP?" Kaiden asked.

"Loyal to his team," Birch corrected.

"Maybe," Kaiden said. He hadn't forgotten how Greyson criticized him. When he was taken off suspension, Kaiden would have Greyson reassigned to another team. He couldn't have Greyson undermining his authority. It was dangerous. Someone else could get killed.

"Flint is a geek, like Quill," Birch continued, ignoring Kaiden's remark. "He's dang good with computers—the best, even better than Quill. We might need him."

Kaiden considered Birch. *This* was crazy. They could all end up like Quill. But everything he thought he had known about TAP, about himself, had been thrown into question. He felt as if he were staring into a dark room, groping for any spark of light.

The only way to find out what had happened to him and where his memories had gone was to help Willow hack into the system and get the Synaptic Download files. If he could, he was going to find a way to get those memories back—all of them. He couldn't live with this constant confusing flow of contradictory and heartrending memories.

"Okay," he said. "But just you and Jade for now. We'll bring in the others as we need them."

"Best decision you've made in a long time," Birch said.

Kaiden handed Birch two palm-sized DWJs. "Give one to Jade and keep one for yourself. Use it before we gather so we can't all be traced to the same location. If they see us all going to Willow's lab, it will raise suspicions."

CHAPTER TEN
LAB RATS

WILLOW RAISED HER eyebrows as Kaiden led Birch and Jade into the small lab. She had expected Birch, but Kaiden was taking risks with anyone else. She gestured for them all to click off their wrist terminals.

"We already did," Kaiden said, before setting a black box on the counter and handing her a smaller version of it.

"What's this?" she asked.

"A Digital Wireless Jammer," Kaiden said. "Better use it anytime we're going to meet so TAP won't know where we are or who we're meeting."

"Does it really work?"

"It's powerful enough for one person or a small room. The big one boosts the jamming signals quite a bit more."

"Won't this draw attention to us?"

Kaiden raised his eyebrows. "Maybe, but with all the training going on around here, they'll have a hard time knowing if it's for real or just training. And they would still have to find us."

Willow agreed. It was good thinking. Just what she'd expect from Kaiden. But why had he brought Birch and Jade with him?

"New recruits?" she asked. She cocked her head at Kaiden. He shot her a grin, his dark skin tugging at the scar where Raven's bullet had struck him. He may not realize it, but he had a commanding presence about him. That's one of the reasons she had chosen him.

Willow didn't know Jade well. She was one of the few Native Americans working in Ararat, and Willow had heard that Jade had a reputation for being quiet and secretive. Some said she had a grudge against the world. There might be good reasons for it, but grudges had a way of messing things up right when you needed them to run smoothly.

Kaiden raised his hands. "Birch insisted on coming."

"No parties without me," Birch said. She flipped the bangs out of her eyes and winked at Willow.

"And we're going to need help," Kaiden said.

Willow studied Jade. She had light brown skin that was smooth and unblemished. Her high cheekbones gave her an exotic, attractive look. Kaiden's gaze kept sliding to her, and Willow could understand why. Jade was simply beautiful with her slender figure, black hair, and dark eyes.

This was no accident since TAP was selecting for clones with the most appealing features. They were serious about the slogan the best and the brightest, but they also wanted their clones to look good. Jade stared back at Willow.

Kaiden shifted and glanced between the two women. "We invited Jade," he said.

"So, I gathered. Can she be trusted?"

Kaiden glanced at Birch for support.

"I'll vouch for her," Birch said.

Willow raised her eyebrows. "If we're discovered," she said, "we could get killed. They won't bother with discipline. They'll just terminate us. You can't speak of this to anyone—ever."

"We got it," Birch said. "We each have our own tooth to pick with TAP."

Kaiden laughed, and Jade cast her a wry smile. "I think you mean *bone*," she said.

Willow ignored Birch, waiting for Jade to acknowledge that she understood. Jade only nodded to her. Willow considered forcing her to verbalize her acceptance of the terms but decided this wasn't the time for a confrontation. Too much was riding on what Kaiden promised he could do.

Willow tried to smile, though it felt more like a grimace, and faced Kaiden. "So, let's see them."

She waited while Kaiden slapped on the wrist terminal and closed his eyes. The WT fastened itself to his wrist, and a little ant appeared on the band. Its head swiveled back and forth before it leaped off the wrist terminal and onto the counter.

"Cool," Birch said. "How does it work?"

Kaiden pursed his lips. "Quill said it responds to brain waves."

"You don't know how to use it?" Birch scoffed.

"Knock it off," Kaiden said, waving an annoyed hand at her. "How hard can it be?" The ant scampered around in a circle. "I can get the hang of this." The ant scurried off the edge of the counter and fell to the ground.

"You see what I have to deal with?" Birch said.

"Believe me, I know," Willow said with a sardonic smile. Kaiden could be headstrong, but he usually got results.

Kaiden grinned up at her as the ant clambered back up to the top of the counter. "See?" he said. "I just had to get used to it. It's like playing a video game. Did you get the computer set up?" he asked Willow.

"I'm way ahead of you." Willow tapped the countertop, and the holographic image flashed in mid-air. A map of the Ararat compound materialized with a square in the corner showing what the ant-bot could see. It scanned over them, and their images appeared on the screen.

"The main security computer is not connected to this lab's computers," Willow said. "But, you can get in through Rio's computer."

"Excellent," Kaiden said. "Let's make it look like Rio is messing with the files."

"So, how do these nano-bots work?" Jade asked.

"Brain waves," Kaiden said. "I don't know how Quill did it. I think he used the nervous system somehow. But watch."

The ant-bot disappeared under the door, and Willow turned to the screen to monitor its progress.

"Dang, that thing cruises," Birch said. "It can really move."

"Quill knew what he was doing," Kaiden said.

Images of TAP personnel in the corridors flashed past as the ant-bot raced along the corner of the wall. In a few minutes, the ant-bot scampered up to the door to Rio's office, where it stopped.

"What's the matter?" Birch asked.

"He's got a firewall set up around his office," Willow said. "Look, he can't get through it."

"What are you hiding, Rio?" Kaiden said thoughtfully.

"Here," Birch elbowed her way past Willow and keyed in some commands to kill the firewall. The ant-bot started moving again.

"Thanks," Willow said, not trying to hide her annoyance.

This wasn't Willow's first foray into forbidden territory. She had the memories of her other clone lives and the memories of her pre-clone life to go on. Because TAP accelerated the growth of the infants in the Genesis Room, they didn't have to wait for each clone to mature and be terminated before they could start another. Willow had died the first time forty years ago and had lived through four accelerated clone lives. She knew more about TAP than probably any clone alive, though there were still significant holes in her knowledge. Those forty years of planning had taught her that she needed help, so she swallowed her pride and smiled.

Birch grinned and climbed onto her stool, apparently oblivious to the fact that she had just been rude. The ant-bot slipped under the door to Rio's office. It was dark, but the ant-bot was equipped with infrared night cameras that cast the room in an eerie green light. Kaiden directed the ant-bot to the top of the desk and synced it with Rio's computer. It began sending files back with lightning speed. Willow sifted through them, searching for anything that looked classified.

"Quill sure was good," Birch said. "Not even TAP has nano-bots this sophisticated."

"Wait." Kaiden shifted. "Something's wrong." He turned the ant-bot around to scan the room. "Do you hear it?"

"Something is moving in there," Jade said.

Birch gestured to the screen. "Better get him out."

"Not yet," Kaiden said. "Look at the name of the file he's downloading."

Birch leaned in to read the file name. "The Lash. What's that?"

"Sounds painful," Jade said. She stepped up to Kaiden for a better view of the files. Her hair fell onto his shoulder.

Kaiden glanced at her. "Exactly."

"So?" Birch straightened.

"If it's painful, it's probably important," Kaiden said.

"It's getting louder," Willow warned. What or who would be in Rio's office this time of night? "Do you know how to run the cloaking device?" she asked.

"No," Kaiden said.

Then, it appeared. Hooked jaws came over the side of the desk first and then the shiny, black body. Its wings fluttered and clicked as it cleared the ledge and scrambled onto the desktop.

"It's another insect-bot," Willow breathed.

"Get him out," Birch said. "It's a killer-bot."

Kaiden placed a hand on his head as if that would help the ant-bot move faster. The ant-bot spun to scamper across the desk. The beetle's wings whirred as it leaped on top of the ant-bot, caught it in its jaws, and squeezed. The ant-bot crumpled and then exploded with a flash of light and a puff of smoke. The screen blinked out.

"Holy—" Kaiden began.

"Why did it explode?" Birch interrupted.

"Self-destruct mechanism, maybe?" Willow said. She kept her eyes on the screen, watching to see if the file had come through.

"I hope you have more insect-bots to play with," Birch said.

"They were waiting for you," Jade said. She flipped her long, black hair behind her ear.

Willow glanced at her. That much had been obvious. The computer beeped, and she swung back to the screen.

"Can they trace that ant-bot back to us?" Birch asked. She stood and placed her hands on her hips. "I mean, there's gonna be little bits of it scattered all over Rio's desk."

Willow knew Birch was considering whether she should prepare herself for discipline. The file flashed onto the screen.

"We got them," Willow said.

"What?" Kaiden asked.

"What did we go through all of this for?" Willow asked. "The files, of course."

"Well?" Kaiden came off his stool, oblivious to the fact that he was invading her space, and pressed in close. She could smell the sharp scent of his aftershave lotion.

"Give me a sec." Willow scanned the file. Kaiden straightened and faced the others. Willow divided her attention between the conversation behind her and the screen. She tried not to show how excited she was. She had theories about what TAP was doing, but she'd never dared hack into the main computer like this.

"Wait a minute," Kaiden said to Jade and Birch. "You both know about the clones?"

"You're not the only one with weird memories," Birch said.

"What do *you* remember?" Kaiden asked.

Birch grunted and a stool creaked as she sat down. "A teddy bear," she said. "I remember an old teddy bear sitting in a corner and a woman's voice pleading with someone not to take me away."

"Dang," Kaiden said. "Jade?"

She was silent for a long minute. "I just figured it out," she said.

"Do you mind sharing?" Kaiden asked.

"Yes," Jade replied. "It's personal."

"Right, okay," Kaiden said.

Willow chanced a glance at Kaiden. He had been confused by Jade's refusal. But Willow didn't trust Jade. There was something about her that seemed off. She would have to check Jade's background.

Kaiden perched on a stool. "I want to find out what's going on," he said, "and I want to know who I was."

"What if you don't like who you were?" Jade asked.

Willow shot Jade a quick glance. Did Jade know something? But the candid look Jade gave Kaiden didn't seem to hide any ulterior motives. Kaiden had obviously never considered that possibility because he just stared at Jade in silence. Willow *had* considered it. She knew more about Kaiden than he knew about himself, though she hadn't been able to figure out who he had been before TAP, not yet. But she would make that a priority now. She was beginning to think she had been wrong about him. He was more important than she had thought.

"I'll deal with it," Kaiden said.

Willow spun on the stool to face them.

"All right," she said. "Nothing I've read so far looks like top secret stuff, but, with what I already know, we can answer a few questions."

"We're all eyes," Birch said. She settled back on her stool and leaned both elbows on the lab table.

Jade glanced at her with a confused scowl.

"What?" Birch said.

"Don't you mean ears?" Jade asked. "We're all ears?"

Birch waved her away. "It's all the same."

"Um, no. It really isn't," Jade said.

"Forget it," Kaiden interrupted. Once Jade was around Birch long enough, she'd get used to her verbal hiccups.

"It's about Cognitive Redesign," Willow said, "otherwise known as Neuro-Reconditioning. TAP has to harvest memories from real people because complete, realistic memories are difficult or impossible to write effectively. TAP can tweak or add memories to a memory file set but can't create a complete and realistic memory set as of yet."

"Why not?" Kaiden asked. He slipped off the nano-bot wrist terminal and set it on the counter.

"They're too complex," Willow said. "And they're tied into all of the other memories and emotions that form a human personality."

"How would you know if a memory was real or added by the programmer?" Birch asked.

"An added memory would be less rich in detail," Willow said. "I have both kinds of memories, and the ones from my real past are full of sights and emotions, sounds and feelings. The ones of the orphanage are less vibrant, less real."

"You have a memory of an orphanage?" Kaiden asked.

"Many do," Willow said, nodding. "It's a standard memory. Some have memories of hovercraft crashes, airship accidents, political violence, famine, etc."

"In mine," Kaiden said, "we had to fight for our food."

Birch waved an impatient hand at them. "Keep going," she said.

"Well," Willow continued, "the problem with these memory files is that they're tied to the structure of the originator's brain. That's why TAP needs clones of the people from whom they harvested the memories. Otherwise, strange things can happen—like serious brain damage and violent, erratic behavior."

"Hang on," Kaiden said. "TAP has been doing this for, what, twenty years?"

"More like fifty or sixty," Willow said.

"So what?" Jade said. She drew one foot up onto the rung of

the stool.

They all looked at her.

"So, what if TAP took our memories and created better bodies for them?"

Willow stared at her. She had to resist the desire to reach out and slap her. The arrogance of the TAP program and the suffering it caused were intolerable. Especially for someone like Willow, who remembered everything they had done to her.

"Because," Willow said, trying to keep her voice even, "it is an immoral invasion of human dignity and an abuse of science."

"But we've already ruined this planet," Jade scoffed. "Our only hope is to find a new homeland in the stars."

"Why?" Birch said. "So we can invade somebody else's homeland like we invaded yours?"

Jade pinched her lips tight and glared at them.

"Let me tell you something," Willow said. The heat rose in her chest, and she clasped her hands in front of her. "When I died, I experienced indescribable agony. I felt my heart stop beating, my lungs stop breathing, and the whole world became very still. I heard the doctor tell the nurse I was dead. I heard my mother sobbing. I wanted to tell her that I was all right—that I was still there. But I wasn't in my body anymore."

The other three stared at her. But Jade didn't back down.

"I remember," Willow continued, "being downloaded into a computer, having new memories shoved into my mind, and then being uploaded into my child self—not once, but four times. They tried to corrupt my other memories, but it didn't work. I remembered everything. I used to get terrible headaches and flashes of two contradictory memories simultaneously. I thought I was going mad. No one should have to experience that kind of torture. Not once and certainly not over and over again."

Jade shifted on her stool. "I don't remember it," she said as if her lack of memory meant it didn't matter that others had suffered.

Willow came off her stool, hands raised, hot fury burning her face.

"Okay." Birch stepped in between them. "You two aren't going to agree on this."

Willow wanted to push past Birch and start yelling. How could

Jade be so dismissive of another person's suffering?

"Why are you here, then?" Kaiden asked Jade.

Willow backed away from Birch and Jade, surprised that Kaiden had come to her defense. But she didn't sit down. The fury inside her made her legs tremble. She clenched her fists.

Jade bowed her head. "I'm not opposed to cloning, and I think it might have some value," she said. "Why not try it? But I do disagree with the lies, the secrecy, and the murder. I've been on too many missions where we assassinated people whose only crime was disagreeing with cloning. Why are we being terrorists and assassins? What is TAP hiding?"

"Is that enough for you to risk your life?" Kaiden asked. "Because, if it isn't, you need to leave now and never mention this to anyone."

Willow gave Kaiden an approving nod as Jade considered him. Willow half-hoped Jade would get up and leave. She didn't like the way Kaiden looked at Jade, and she didn't like the arrogant disdain that Jade seemed to have for her.

"Is it enough to resist a regime that murders helpless kids and assassinates political opponents?" Jade said. "Yeah. For me, that's enough. I don't have to disagree with cloning, but I can disagree with the methods they use."

"Good," Kaiden said.

"In that case," Willow cut in, still annoyed with Jade, "you should know that we were all carefully selected because we had an aptitude or skill that TAP needed. We weren't rescued from orphanages or airship crashes. We were kidnapped from our families and homes, and our DNA and memories were stolen."

"That doesn't make any sense," Birch said. "Why go through all the trouble of cloning when they could just make us do what they want anyway?"

Willow gave her a sad smile and sat back down on her stool. "Because we are test subjects," she said, "just like those clones up on the moon. TAP is perfecting its techniques and processes."

"How do you know this?" Jade asked.

Willow hesitated. Did she dare tell them? How would they react? She swallowed. "Because I help run some of the tests," she said.

"Whoa," Kaiden said, coming to his feet. "You never told me

this."

"Yes, I did. I told you Cognitive Redesign was my specialty. Why do you think I was sent to monitor the clones you picked up at the lunar base?"

"But I didn't realize you were running the tests on *us*."

Birch glanced at Kaiden in annoyance and waved a hand at him. "Let her explain," she said. "So, what happens when the tests are done? Is that why everyone gets reassigned or promoted on their twentieth birthday?" Birch watched Willow with an air someone who already suspected the answer.

"We die," Willow said.

Birch lunged to her feet. "Just like that?"

"Yep. That's the promotion."

Jade cursed softly, and Kaiden looked like he might be sick. Willow guessed he was thinking of Quill.

"Wait a minute," Kaiden said. "I've been to dozens of promotion parties, and I've read the letters with the new assignments. I even exchanged emails with some of them."

"No, you didn't," Willow said. "The system monitors your messages and uses the information it contains about each clone to fabricate the messages. It's all just an algorithm."

"But why kill us at age twenty?" Kaiden asked. "I mean if they kill us that young, they only get six or seven years of work and testing out of us. Wouldn't it be better to let us live for fifty or sixty years?"

"They're on a different timeline," Willow said. "A study that took fifty or sixty years to complete would have a hard time acquiring financing. The people who pay us want results—now."

"Wait," Birch said. "I still don't have a clear view of the overall system. If we die at twenty, they have to wait thirteen years before they can start again."

Willow sighed. This was proving more difficult to explain than she had expected. "You've got it all wrong," she said. "Look. We were all harvested at different ages. Some folks might have been older or younger than we were. TAP seeks out the most gifted and targets them. If they can be persuaded to join TAP as naturals, they'll be brought in and then cloned when they get older and nearing the end of their productivity. Others, like me, who refused to join, were kidnapped and murdered."

"You don't have to kill someone to clone them," Jade said.

"No," Willow replied, "you don't. But people like me who would resist could be a liability. But to finish answering Birch's questions, as soon as they have you, they begin the cloning process. By the time your clone dies at age twenty, another clone is ready. They perform a Synaptic Download to recover what you learned in the new clone edition for future study, modify the memory files, and re-upload them into the new clone. Always saving a copy."

"But I've been in the nursery," Birch said. "There's no clone of me in there."

"There wouldn't be for precisely that reason. Your clone is being grown and raised at a different TAP center."

"Sounds like a lot of trouble," Jade said. "Wouldn't it be easier just to pay volunteers to collect their DNA and their memories?"

If they only knew, Willow thought. "It's crucial to the TAP program that no one knows what's happening, or the program would be shut down since it's completely illegal. They especially don't want *us* knowing what's happening," she said. "If everyone knew they were just going to be killed, TAP would have a permanent rebellion on their hands. Even clones don't want to die."

"They can just discipline us to control us," Jade said. Her expression became dark. Willow understood. They had all been disciplined at least once.

"How does the discipline work?" Kaiden asked.

"All I know," Willow said, "is that part of our brain has been genetically modified with the genes of an algae that cause it to be reactive to light. Somehow, they expose that part of the brain to light, which causes it to respond in the way it has been conditioned. For us, that means we experience intense pain and fear."

"Yeah. We all know that," Birch said.

"This changes everything," Kaiden said and flopped down onto a stool again.

"Why?" Jade asked. She hadn't shifted from her stool.

"Because I have less than six months before I get *promoted*." He raised his fingers in air quotes.

Birch elbowed Kaiden. "I've got six months longer than you," she said with a wink. "I'll give you a nice promotion party."

"That's right," Willow said. "The test ends at age twenty. Our memories are downloaded again and uploaded into another clone body that has already been prepared."

"So, we never get to die?" Jade asked.

"Oh, we die," Willow said. "And then we die again and again and again until TAP is finished with our DNA or no longer needs our memories to be active in a clone body."

Birch stared at her. "How many times have you died?"

"Four," Willow said. The memories of those experiences were bitter, and she struggled not to think of them.

Kaiden swore under his breath.

"They didn't clone me until they kidnapped me," Willow continued," so they had to wait thirteen years before I could be uploaded into a new clone because they hadn't started the accelerated growth program yet. I've been *promoted* every seven years since then."

Willow could see them all doing the math in their heads. "Forty years," she said to help them. "It's been forty years since I was kidnapped and harvested."

"So your brain is sixty years old?" Birch said.

"Uh, no," Willow said. "It's only nineteen years old, but I have almost sixty years' worth of memories."

"Didn't you ever try to escape?" Birch asked.

"I did. Twice, and I was recaptured each time."

"Wait a minute," Kaiden said. He lunged to his feet. "That means there's another Quill out there?" Hope blossomed on Kaiden's face like a little boy expecting a present.

Willow hated to dash it for him, but she didn't want Kaiden galloping off searching for another Quill clone. It would be a waste of time. *That* Quill wouldn't even know him.

"Probably," Willow said, "but you'll never see him again. TAP is careful about that sort of thing. And, even if you did, he wouldn't have memories of you anyway."

"But you can make one," he said. "If you know how to upload his old files. We just have to find out where his other clone is right now."

"It's not that easy," Willow said.

"Why not?" Kaiden demanded.

Willow studied Kaiden. His desperation to have his friend back was making it so he couldn't think straight.

"I tried to see if they made any new memory files before he died, but I couldn't find anything. He probably died too quickly, which means he wouldn't have any memories of you. Besides, I don't have any of his DNA or the resources to use it if I did."

Kaiden frowned. "But you said you have memories of your other clone lives."

"I do," Willow replied, "because before I die, I secretly perform a synaptic sync, so the new knowledge and experiences I have acquired are preserved. And, as I told you before, my brain doesn't accept the overwritten memories."

"What if they upload an older version of your files," Jade asked.

"That's a possibility," Willow said, "but I update all the files on the central server."

"So, we're nothing but lab rats," Birch said, "being bred in the name of science?" She stalked over and leaned against the door jam.

"That's what Casey called the clones at the lunar station when we picked them up," Kaiden said.

Willow said nothing. If they didn't understand now, they never would. And even if they did understand, they would probably never forgive her for what she planned to do or for what she had already done. But it had to be done. There was no other way. She couldn't fail this time. Something big was coming, and she would not get another chance.

CHAPTER ELEVEN
TATTOO

JADE SLIPPED INTO the Genesis Room. The lights were low, and the motherless wombs glowed an eerie green color. Infants wriggled and kicked in the transparent membrane sacks. Tubes flowing with red liquid that must have been blood stretched to a long row of dialysis machines with blinking red lights.

The tubes carried in nutrients and oxygen and carried away the waste to be removed in the dialysis machines. Row after row of the motherless wombs filled the vast space. There must have been two or three thousand at least, and they were all in different stages of development.

Jade checked the cameras' positions and peeked in to make sure no one was about. Then she strode into the shadows of the line of dialysis machines where the cameras would not be able to see her. It was best that no one knew she came here. It had become a sanctuary for her on restless nights when she couldn't sleep.

She slipped her hand into her pocket and touched the little DWJ that Birch had given her just to make sure it was still there and running. She had clicked it on when she left her room. It was partly their discussion with Willow and Kaiden that troubled her. She desperately wanted to do the right thing, but how did one know what that was? By what criteria did one measure it? Though she knew TAP had bigger plans, she hadn't been surprised to learn that she was a clone. She'd figured that out years ago, which led her to discover the Genesis Room. All of the missions she had undertaken were supposed to be about protecting clones like herself from extermination.

The quiet purr of electric motors covered any noises her boots made on the tiled floor. A caretaker was taking a reading at one of the machines, and Jade flattened herself against the warm dialysis unit until she finished and moved on.

Only two caretakers would be on staff this late at night. It was the best time to come. Jade found him swimming in a motherless womb about halfway down aisle seven. The plaque at the base of the glass bubble had a number and a strange triangular shape. Jade had seen ones like it on the necks of the other female clones in the common showers when she was training. She knew she had one and had heard that all TAP personnel had been tattooed with these triangles, but she didn't know what it meant.

A number. That's all this baby boy was to TAP. But he had nut-brown skin like her own and was developing a nice mop of black hair. It was plain to see that he was a Native American like her. She was sure of it. Cloning itself wasn't the problem for her. It was this—a child cut off from his ancestors and from the land that should have nurtured him—the way she had been cut off from her grandfather and the land her people once occupied.

Scraps of memory and language were all that remained—that and the feel of her grandfather's arms about her. The soft touch of his breath against her ear. "You are the last daughter of our people," he said. "You must survive."

Maybe Willow was right. Maybe this sense of aloneness, this lack of belonging, was the true-crime of TAP. Still, maybe cloning could bring her people back. Maybe it was the only way they could have a future. The baby's hand waved in the water, and a lump rose in her throat. What was his name? Who were his people?

She raised her hand to rest it against the glass. It was warm. A longing to hold the child erupted into her chest, and she jerked her hand away. What was she doing? This didn't help.

Her team had been her family in TAP, but after the last mission where they had been sent to eliminate an entire family, she had requested another transfer to a transport and security team, thinking she could protect better by guarding the clones used for the experiments, rather than murdering innocent people whose only crime was to disagree with cloning or some other TAP program.

Then, she found herself on the first mission sent to kidnap a senator, and she had witnessed Kaiden risking his life to save that child. That's what TAP should be about, protecting and nurturing, not kidnapping. She had finally found a leader she could follow in TAP—someone she could respect.

The quiet slap of running boots on tile drew her attention, and she whirled around, swinging the rifle she always carried to the front. Caretakers didn't run in the Genesis Room.

Jade crouched and shrank into the shadows just as a dark figure raced between the aisles of the motherless wombs. He slid to a stop beside a dialysis chamber and looked around expectantly. Jade slipped between the glass incubators, with their eerie green light, and circled around to get closer. This was an unusual place and time for a meeting—and certainly not a romantic one.

She peered around a dialysis machine, careful not to let the red blinking lights illuminate her form. A man, older than the average TAP employee, maybe in his late twenties, wore the engineers' blue coat. A woman stepped from the shadows.

"I told you not to come here unless it was urgent," she said.

"Kaiden knows about The Flood." His voice was still breathless from his run.

"Shut up. I told you never to talk about that."

The woman looked around and dragged the man closer to the dialysis machine. Jade tried to get a view of her face, but she couldn't.

"He'll have to be neutralized," she said.

Jade's pulse quickened. Someone was spying on Kaiden and was conspiring to kill him. She raised her rifle to nestle it against her shoulder. She couldn't let them leave here if they intended to murder Kaiden. It was her job to protect him. She sighted on the man through the scope.

"I'll contact the asset," the man said.

Jade squeezed the trigger once and swung to squeeze it a second time. Two shots rang out in rapid succession. Two bodies fell. She straightened and strode out from her hiding place to peer down at their still-quivering forms. The male was a young communications officer, but the woman was an older black woman—much older than most people who worked at TAP. The woman wasn't dead yet, but Jade didn't have the stomach to shoot her again. She would die soon enough. Jade never liked the sight of dead bodies or the act of killing. It always seemed like a failure. Her job was to protect, but to protect, sometimes you had to kill. It was one of the awful realities of life.

"I'm sorry," she said and strode from the Genesis Room, being careful to walk in the dead zones where the cameras would not pick up her movement. Kaiden needed to know he was compromised.

"Kaiden. Get down here!" Willow's voice burst from Kaiden's wrist terminal.

He jerked upright in bed. "What?"

"Get down here, now."

Kaiden glanced at the clock. It was barely four in the morning. He'd only been in bed a few hours.

"Why? What's going on?"

"Just come now!"

Kaiden slipped the DWJ into the pocket of his pajamas and clicked it on as he headed out the door in his bare feet. He found Willow sitting at her desk with a holographic image shimmering before her. The bright lab lights shone in her hair. The little brown freckles on her nose were striking against her pale white skin

"What?" Kaiden said.

Willow glanced at him and then took a double-take.

"You came in your pajamas?"

He glanced down at his T-shirt and baggy blue and white striped pajamas. "You said now," he said. "So, I came now. What did you want me to do, put on my formal uniform?"

Willow wrinkled her nose. "Clothes would have been nice."

"Just tell me what you got me up for," Kaiden said. He was in no mood for games.

"Quill left you a message."

Kaiden blinked at her, trying to decide if he had heard her

correctly. How could Quill leave him a message?

"Look." Willow pointed to the screen, and Kaiden read the bold, blue lines.

"Hey, Kaiden. I think they're onto me. Watch your back. I wouldn't trust anybody on the team. Rio's behind it somehow. I found some top secret shipments going out that I think are tied to that Flood file. If you can track them, you might be able to figure this thing out. That encryption code is some ancient language. I slept through most of history class, but I've seen it somewhere before. Anyway, if you're reading this, I guess I'm gone. Thanks for everything, Dude. Good luck."

Kaiden blinked at the sudden sting in his eyes and the warmth in his chest. Quill had known he would be targeted. He had expected to die. Why hadn't Quill said something?

"How come you got this and I didn't?" Kaiden said.

"I found it in the trash files," she said. "Somebody in communications must have seen it and tried to delete it."

Kaiden bowed his head so Willow wouldn't see his unshed tears.

She placed a cool hand on his. "I'm sorry," she said. Kaiden let her hand linger. It was comforting as he wrestled with his emotions, too overwhelmed to speak.

"Well?" Willow soothed. "Do you know what he's talking about?"

Kaiden swallowed. "Quill broke into the central security system and found a folder called *The Flood*. He thinks...thought...it was a play on the old story about Noah."

"Obviously." Willow withdrew her hand. "The Ark?" She raised her eyebrows.

"I get that," Kaiden said. "It's The Flood that Quill was worried about. The file was encrypted with some ancient language, and Quill thought The Flood is supposed to do what it did in the days of Noah."

"Like destroy humankind?" Willow prompted.

"That's the idea."

"And it didn't occur to you to tell me this before?"

Kaiden bristled. "No more than it occurred to you to tell me you were running tests on all of us before they kill us."

Willow grimaced at him. "Okay, genius. What's your next move?"

Kaiden dropped into a chair. "I don't have a next move." He paused as the idea came to him. "But I want to know what happened to Quill's body. Has it been composted yet? I wish we could have funerals with…" He paused, trying to remember the word.

"Caskets?" Willow said.

Kaiden nodded as he remembered the red rose and the little girl in the casket. He realized that he had a memory of a funeral, though he didn't understand it. It had been painful, but it had also been necessary, somehow. Something about being able to place the rose on the lid and say goodbye filled him with a strange longing that hurt and made him feel better at the same time. He wanted to be able to have that feeling about Quill—not this empty sadness.

Willow's expression softened. "We're just lab rats, Kaiden. When are you going to understand that?"

"So, where's his body?"

"I don't know," Willow said.

"Find out."

Willow clicked her tongue. "You could say, *please.*"

"Please," Kaiden said. How could he explain why this was important to him when he didn't understand it himself?

Willow gave him an exasperated glare. "This is going to take a while."

"I can't sleep now anyway. Not since you dragged me out of bed."

"Deal with it," Willow said, but she turned to the computer.

Half an hour later, Willow kicked Kaiden's foot. His head rested on his arms, and he was drooling on the table.

"I found it," she said.

When Kaiden lifted his head to blink at her, the drool dribbled off his chin.

"That's attractive." Willow grimaced.

Kaiden swiped at it with the back of his hand.

"Where is he?" Kaiden said.

"It's his number."

Maybe Kaiden was just sleepy, but Willow's answer didn't make any sense. "Number? Like our ID number?" Kaiden glanced at the black tattoo on his right arm.

"Kind of. It's your clone number. That's how TAP keeps track of us."

"What's this?" Kaiden pointed to a symbol next to Quill's number that was composed of several little triangles with thin lines coming off one end.

"I think...wait a minute," Willow said. She spun in the chair to stare at Kaiden. "Turn around."

"Uh, why?"

"Just do it."

Kaiden rolled his eyes and spun his back to her. Willow was demanding and headstrong. Kaiden couldn't figure her out, so he humored her.

She grabbed the back of his collar and pulled it down.

"What the...?" Kaiden jumped as her icy fingers touched his back. "Your hands are cold."

"Hold still," she said. Her cool fingers brushed his skin. He shivered, but not from the cold this time. "I thought so," Willow said.

"Care to share?" Kaiden asked.

"You have a similar mark on your spine right above the shoulder blades."

"Oh, that," Kaiden said. He shrugged the shirt back up and faced Willow. "All the security personnel have one." Kaiden had seen it often enough in the showers while he was in cadet school.

"I think all the *clones* have one," Willow corrected him.

"Really?" Kaiden snickered. "You want me to check to see if you have one?"

Willow smirked at him. "I don't think so. I've already seen it in the mirror."

"Just an idea," Kaiden said. "Any time you want to know what it looks like, all you have to do is ask." In the dimmed light of the lab, her face had a soft glow to it. He wanted to touch her cheek, but he didn't know how she might react.

Willow wrinkled her nose like she had just encountered a bad smell. "Can we stay on subject?"

"Sure," Kaiden said. He dragged a chair over to sit next to her. "Why do we all have a number and a bunch of long triangles tattooed on us?"

"Search me," Willow said as she shifted so she could see the holograph screen. "I haven't figured that out yet."

"All right," Kaiden said, "so, where's Quill's body?"

"Why?"

"We just went through this. I need to say goodbye."

Willow took her time answering. When she faced him, her brow pinched together and a frown formed. "You're too late," she whispered.

Kaiden waited for her to continue, but she just slouched without looking at him.

"He was put into recomposition last night," she said.

Kaiden's stomach somersaulted. "And the rest of my crew?"

He had learned of recomposition in school as a child. Burials and cremation all used too much energy, contributed to pollution and global warming, and had been abandoned years ago. Too valuable to be wasted, all dead bodies were placed in special recomposition units, which used natural bacteria to decompose them into the soil. In a few weeks, there would be nothing left of Quill.

"Why don't they let us see our friends' before composting them?" Kaiden said. "Why can't we say goodbye?"

Willow shook her head and laid a hand on Kaiden's knee.

"I'm sorry," she said. "We're just clones to them."

Kaiden bowed his head. TAP wasn't playing around. In six months, he would be composted, and his remains would be used to grow plants in some isolated farm community, just like Quill, and nobody would know or care.

Willow leaned in and hugged him. "I'm so sorry," she said. Kaiden stiffened in surprise and then let her hold him. She smelled of vanilla, and her embrace was warm. He couldn't remember a time when anyone had hugged him.

Jade tapped quietly on Kaiden's door as she tried to calm her ragged breathing. The hallway was empty, and the lights were dimmed for the night. She had raced from the Genesis Room, desperate to warn Kaiden that he was in more danger than he knew. Nothing stirred inside the room. She knocked louder. Silence.

She leaned with her back to the wall to catch her breath and then clicked on the WT and set it to contact only Kaiden before raising it close to her mouth.

"Kaiden," she whispered. "Wake up."

Something shuffled down the hallway, and she stiffened. Easing her rifle around to the front, she prepared to fight. Had they followed her? Had she not avoided the cameras in her haste to reach Kaiden?

The shuffling paused and then came on.

"I've been awake," Kaiden's voice came over her WT, making her jump. "You women won't leave me alone."

Now, his voice came from both the WT and the direction of the shuffled footsteps. Jade straightened as Kaiden came around the bend and into the glow of the dimmed lights. She lowered her rifle as relief flooded into her chest. He was alive.

"Do you usually wander around in your pajamas?" she asked.

"Only when women call me from bed," he said.

"What woman?" Jade asked, suddenly suspicious. She had just shot a woman. He couldn't mean the same one. Could he?

"Willow found something about Quill, so I went to find out what it was." He paused by the door and swiped his ID in front of the Access Control, and it swished open. He glanced at her and waved her in.

Jade experienced a sudden and unexpected pang of jealousy. What was wrong with her? She was a soldier, not some lovesick school girl.

"Do you usually wander around the base dressed in full battle gear?" Kaiden asked.

She stepped inside and brushed the hair from her face. "Sometimes," she said.

"Did you turn on the DWJ before you came?" Kaiden said. "I don't want any accusations floating around."

Jade nodded. What would he say when she told him what she had done? "I just shot two people," she blurted.

Kaiden froze and turned slowly to face her.

"Why?" he said.

"They were spying on you. They said you knew about The Flood and that you needed to be *neutralized*."

Kaiden dropped into a chair by the table and ran his hands over his head.

"Where was this?" he said.

Jade shuffled her feet and studied her boots. She didn't want to tell him, but how could she avoid it? "The Genesis Room," she mumbled.

She glanced up in time to see the scowl on Kaiden's face.

"What were you doing up there this time of night?"

Jade shook her head. "It doesn't matter. I left their bodies on the floor and came to tell you."

Kaiden rose and checked his WT. "They'll be found at the next change in staff in one hour."

He stripped off his shirt and pajama bottoms without any warning and reached for the uniform he had draped over a chair. Muscles rippled under his dark skin, and Jade felt the heat rising in her cheeks. Did he have any idea how attractive he was?

"You could have warned me," she said as she turned away.

"Sorry," Kaiden said, "but we've got to move. Fast."

Jade glanced over her shoulder to see him buckle his belt and slide on his boots. He touched his WT as he bent to tie them. "Flint," he said, "I need you." There was no answer.

"Get up, you old mophead," he said louder.

"What's got your knickers in a twist?" Flint's voice came over the WT, sounding sleepy and annoyed.

"We've got a situation, and you're the only one who can handle it."

"Of course. Do you have any idea what time it is?"

"Meet me by the nursery in five minutes and bring your most sophisticated computer."

Kaiden snatched up his rifle and grabbed Jade's arm. "Let's go."

CHAPTER TWELVE
COLLEAGUES IN CRIME

JADE LED THE way through the darkened, silent corridors. Once or twice, they had to pause to avoid a security patrol. Kaiden had Quill's DWJ switched on so he couldn't be tracked, but they had to be careful of the cameras. Jade seemed to know how to avoid them, so he let her choose the path. Conflicting emotions boiled in his chest. How could anyone know that he knew about The Flood? Was it Quill's deleted message? And if they were ready to kill him for it, why was he still alive? If those bodies were found before he could hide them, his career and his attempt to discover why Quill had been murdered would be over.

He glanced at Jade. She was another mystery. She crept along silently, carefully, checking her back trail, and monitoring the location of the cameras. Jade was good at this. Why had she been so willing to kill to protect him when they barely knew each other? When they arrived at the blue nursery door, they found Flint crouching in the shadows, waiting for them. He spun as they approached.

"What's this all about?" he snapped. His thick, black hair was a mess, and he'd missed a button on his shirt.

"Relax, cowboy," Kaiden said. He gestured to the door to the Genesis Room. "Can you do something about all the cameras in there?"

Flint narrowed his eyes. "Why?" he said.

"We have a mess to clean up before it's too late."

Flint glanced and Jade. "I have a feeling I don't want to know what it is." He pulled out his computer and switched it on. Leaning his back against the wall, he slid to the floor, cradling the computer on his knees. The blue light from the screen lit his face, which tightened in concentration. Kaiden had to force himself to not fidget while he waited.

"There," Flint said and rose to his feet. "I've got them all diverted, but you can't leave it for long, or someone will notice."

"Right," Kaiden said and strode to the door. He peered through a tiny observation window. The sight of the motherless wombs with the babies wriggling inside made his stomach clench tight. It was so inhumane, so crass and calculating. He still hadn't reconciled himself to the fact that he began his life in a room like this. How could human beings be reduced to mere experiments in a petri dish?

Flint joined him. "Kind of makes you feel sick, doesn't it?"

Jade elbowed past them and keyed in the access code. "This way," she said and pushed through the door.

They ghosted from shadow to shadow along the long line of whirring machines under the red lights from the blinking instruments until they reached the first body on the floor. It was a young man Kaiden recognized but couldn't place his name. A pool of blood had spread under him. Another puddle lay beside him, but it had been disturbed. A trail of blood led off into the rows of motherless wombs with their eerie green lights.

Flint swore. "I can't believe you got me involved in this."

"There was a lady," Jade said. "I was sure she was going to die."

"INCR can work quickly, especially if you missed the heart," Kaiden said. "Any ideas where we can dispose of the body?" He didn't like the subterfuge or the fact that another clone had to die, but Jade had done what she thought best. He picked people for his team who could think on their feet. He wasn't going to second guess her now.

"There's a new section under construction at the back of the hall," Jade said.

"Flint, help me lift him. Jade, see if you can find something to clean this up."

Kaiden bent and grabbed under the young man's arms while

Flint hefted the legs. Together, they carried the body through several rows of chambers to a dark area where some new dialysis machines were being built. They clambered up onto one and wedged the body inside so it couldn't be seen from the floor. Kaiden found an old rag one of the workers must have left behind and used it to clean up the blood trail they had left behind. By the time they returned to where Jade was mopping up the blood, she was almost finished. She swiped the mop over the last bit of blood and plopped it back into the mop bucket. Then she nodded to him and hurried away to dispose of the evidence.

"Care to tell me why I just committed several crimes?" Flint asked while they waited for her to return.

"Later," Kaiden said. He checked his watch. "We've only got five minutes before the shift changes."

The sound of footsteps echoed in the immense hall. Kaiden swung around to find a security patrol advancing toward them.

"Down," he whispered, and he and Flint crept into the shadow of a dialysis unit. Jade's figure reentered the hall from the cleaning room. Kaiden clicked is WT to warn her, but it was too late. She closed the door with a soft click. The security guard paused and faced the sound.

Jade froze in place. Where were Kaiden and Flint? The green lights of the motherless wombs lit the chamber. The sound of boots on tile echoed faintly. Then she saw him. A black-clad security guard was working his way through the rows of incubators coming toward her. Had he seen her, or was he simply following the sound of the closing door?

"Get out of there," Kaiden's voice whispered over the WT.

Jade snapped her rifle up and then lowered it. She wasn't going to kill an innocent guard if she didn't have to. She crouched and jogged to the nearest motherless womb before the guard came through the row. Throwing her back against a tank just as he stepped out and scanned the area, Jade peered through the translucent liquid with its tiny infant waving its hands. The guard's image was distorted, but she could see his head shift from side to side. *Just keep going*, she thought.

He checked the closet where she had washed the bloody water down the drain and rinsed out the mop and bucket. Finding nothing, he came out and strode toward her again.

What was with this guy? Did he have a tracking device on her or a death wish? Jade slipped from hiding and scampered behind a looming dialysis machine and waited breathless while the thud of the boots faded into the distance. She let out a long sigh and stepped out from hiding to find Kaiden and Flint racing toward her.

"That was awkward," Flint said. "But I still want to know what's going on."

"We'll fill you in on the way back," Kaiden said, "but you aren't going to like it."

"You've got to be kidding," Birch said as Kaiden and Jade filled in her and Willow on the night's adventures. Flint had to report to early duty and couldn't join them, but Kaiden and Jade had explained everything to him already. Kaiden wanted them all to understand the seriousness of their situation before he laid out his plans.

"We've got a real problem now," Willow said. "Whoever the woman was, she has probably already reported what happened."

"Which is why," Kaiden said, "we're going to have to work fast and plan on escaping if things go bad."

"I'll work on that," Birch said.

"I may have another way if Birch's idea doesn't pan out," Willow said.

"Good," Kaiden said. "I'll want the details later, but for now, here's what I want you to do."

He had lain awake long after returning to his quarters, figuring out how best to organize his team.

"Jade," he said. "On your off-time—"

"Uh," Birch interrupted. "We aren't on suspension yet, in case you didn't notice. We can't sit around drinking and playing video games all day, like some people."

Kaiden smirked at her but continued. "Jade, I want you to check every hangar and search the cargo of every ship that comes or goes. Quill said there were strange shipments tied to this Flood thing. We need to find out what's on board."

"I'll get Colt to help me," Jade said.

"Who's Colt?" he asked.

"You've met him," Birch said. "He's the crazy one."

"Right," Kaiden said. "I'm not sure we should bring anyone else in."

"He can be trusted," Birch said.

"TAP already knows I'm up to something," Kaiden said. "The more people we bring in, the more opportunities for accidents."

"Stop sweating," Jade said. "I got this."

Jade pushed her hair behind her ear in a way that sent a thrill up Kaiden's spine. He didn't know Jade well, but she had been brave and self-assured the night before, proving that he had made the right choice in selecting her for his new team. He found that he liked to look at her. She had a wild exotic look that stirred him. He cast a guilty glance at Willow. He had started to feel really connected to her, and it didn't seem right that he should be attracted to anyone else. *What a night*, he thought.

Kaiden turned to the other two. "Birch," he said, "I need you to figure out where these stupid triangles we have tattooed on our backs came from, and, if you can play around with Quill's cloaking device, we need to figure out how it works and if we can improve it."

"Quill was a genius," she said. "Improving on his design is going to be tough. Maybe Flint will have some ideas."

"See what you can do," Kaiden said.

Flint had protested all the way back to their rooms after disposing of the body. He had pointed out that it wouldn't stay hidden for long, and Kaiden was under no delusions that they would be able to remain at TAP much longer. Flint had agreed to secrecy and promised to help him. So Kaiden was fine with Birch working with him.

"Willow, we need to know why these triangles are associated with our ID numbers, and we need more intel on the clone program. You're our point man on the clones."

Willow raised her eyebrows. "Man?"

Birch snickered.

"It's just an expression," Kaiden said.

"What are *you* going to do?" Jade asked.

"I am going to play video games." He winked at her.

Birch clicked her tongue and smirked at him. "You gave us all the dangerous work so you can play video games?"

"I never said the game wasn't dangerous," Kaiden said. "I'm going to find out what TAP is hiding from us. I'm hacking into TAP's security system."

Willow waited until the others left before swiping to the holographic photo of a boy in blue jeans with soft brown hair. It had taken her years to recover this photo, and it meant more to her than anything she owned. Her memories of that last day with her brother were confused. Things had happened so fast. She had been giving a presentation on her research that did not go well. The scientists wanted to exploit her discoveries in unethical ways. Then, the glass walls had shattered, the guard was lying in a pool of blood, and her brother was dragging her from the room.

The high-speed chase in the hovercraft had ended with her dangling from an open door as her brother stared at her with wide, frightened eyes, blood dripping from the wound on his head. Everything after that was black until she awoke in the antiseptic operating room.

She shivered at the memory and swiped away from the picture. There was no time to get sentimental now that things were moving so quickly. Years ago, she had figured out how to isolate two memories, and she had tried to find a way to send them to him. She wanted him to know that she was still alive and thinking of him. But she had never managed to figure out how to send them in a format he would be able to read. She still had the files and carried them with her everywhere she went, just in case.

Willow sighed and opened the file named The Flood. She swiped through the pages of thin, triangular-shaped arrows. Somewhere in the deep recesses of memory, she recognized them.

But she couldn't focus. She, too, was still struggling with what happened on the lunar transport. The image of the clones with their brains blown out and the security crew floating in grotesque circles, their blood trailing around them like it was trying to form a cocoon, still haunted her. Even though she had known something like it would happen, the shock of death still troubled her. She took the first opportunity to snatch a gun from what she thought was Burl's dead body, followed Raven, and shot her before she could kill Kaiden—shot her while Delano's body twisted in death beside her.

Willow swallowed the knot in her throat. She had to kill Raven. Kaiden couldn't die. He was too important. She needed a good security officer, but deep down, she knew it was more than that. Kaiden had come to mean something to her. The thought of him dying sent a wild shiver through her. Whatever happened, she would make sure he survived.

Kaiden clicked on a Mozart concerto and dumped all of Quill's computer stuff onto his table. He hooked up Quill's new game console and rerouted the system through Quill's portable computer. He hacked into the security layout through a series of TAP servers to make it difficult for anyone to locate his position, and then wrote some simple software to keep it all working. He even created a tiny mouse avatar to show him where he was in the schematic. When he was satisfied that everything was in place, he began to play.

This game wasn't the complicated virtual reality games he and Quill used to play. It was more like a spy game in which Kaiden had to navigate his way through the security layout to the TAP compound, searching for anything suspicious while remaining hidden from detection. He counted on his sophisticated hack to mask his movements through the security files and layout.

The schematic was a complex set of blue lines, like an architect's drawing, with labels and notes on the appropriate security protocol. They were layered by level and stacked on top of each other. When he finished one, he moved on to the next level.

Of all the assignments he had made, this was the most dangerous.

He was the most likely to attract attention, and it would be impossible to explain why he had hacked into the system—especially after what had happened to Quill. But Kaiden needed to do this. He needed to know why Quill had been silenced.

Kaiden guided his avatar through the system, searching for any locked doors, any hidden spaces, any sections that couldn't be explained. If TAP was running secret programs, they had to be housed somewhere, and they had to leave some sign or clue to their existence in the system. The trouble was finding those places in the vast underground complex.

TAP had seven levels with nine sections per level. Since he didn't have any idea where to start, Kaiden began at the uppermost and worked his way down. He wandered virtually through the dining and shopping areas, the gymnasium and training rooms, and into the living spaces. TAP was a world all its own. It even had hydroponic gardens and farm space where genetically modified chickens and pigs were raised in tiny cages.

When Kaiden's avatar reached the lab area on the fourth level, he found several rooms with heightened security, as shown by the flashing red light he had programmed the system to make when it encountered heavily secured areas. He noted the location in his search log for further exploration and continued. Hours passed as he worked methodically through the complex. Every time his avatar encountered a red light, he noted the location. By the time he reached the last level, he had half a dozen places listed. But the last level had a surprise—something different from all the other levels. Directly in the center, he encountered a vast area where there was a blank space in the schematic. It was simply empty. The security schematic had no information about what this enormous space contained.

"What have we here?" Kaiden said as he sat up straighter. He worked his avatar around the blank area, seeking an entrance. No red lights flashed. He double-checked his security layout. Nothing was there. But the space was occupied by something—something invisible to him.

"Why would TAP have such a huge blank space in the center of its operation?"

Kaiden made note of the location and decided to finish his exploration of the last level when a metallic voice burst from the computer speakers. "Hello, Kaiden." The word Atra- Hasis flashed in the center of the blank space.

Kaiden jumped. "Holy crap," he gasped.

He rushed to click out of the program and shut down the computer. His mind raced. What had just happened? How had he been detected? How could the system possibly know that it was him and not Quill, since he was on Quill's computer? Mozart blared in the background as Kaiden leaned back and passed a hand over his head, trying to decide what he should do. That's when the pain hit him.

It felt like a knife slicing through his brain. He groaned, slid to the floor, and curled up into a ball as the lightning flashes of agony rebounded inside his skull—gigantic spiders chewed on his body, their fangs stabbing into him with the rhythm of the flashing pain. Then he was trapped in the space elevator in free fall as it plummeted to Earth. He flailed about, searching for something to grab onto— anything to relieve the horrible swooping sensation in his stomach. The pain and the terror competed for his attention as the discipline went on and on. He wanted to die, anything to escape the torment.

Then, a thin brown hand rested on his brow. The woman bent close and kissed his cheek. "The fever will be over soon," she said. Her voice was soft and tender, filled with compassion and love. He smelled the hair gel and sweet perfume. He gazed up at her through the fog of fever and tears. He loved her. She was his mother.

It ended as suddenly as it had begun. Kaiden sprawled on the floor, panting. Tears slipped from his eyes. His body trembled, and his limbs jerked as he struggled to regain control. He hadn't been disciplined since his first year at TAP, and he'd almost forgotten the horror of being tortured from inside his own brain. But he had never experienced the soothing presence of the woman—his mother— before. The afterglow of the torture lingered alongside the longing for that tender touch, for that sense of being loved and wanted.

Kaiden struggled against the tears. He had to force his mind to focus. TAP was onto him, now. How long would it take before they moved from discipline to simple execution—like they had done to Quill? ·

Kaiden clicked his wrist terminal on. "Willow," he gasped. His voice cracked, so he tried again. No one answered. "Birch." Silence.

"Jade." Kaiden was surprised at how weak his voice sounded.

"I gotcha," Jade's voice came out of his wrist terminal. Kaiden sighed in relief.

"Listen," he said. "We need to meet. Can you contact the others? They don't respond to me."

Jade didn't reply.

"Jade?" Silence.

Terror constricted Kaiden's throat. TAP was coming for him. They would be intercepting his transmissions. Now, he had endangered his friends.

A knock sounded on Kaiden's door.

CHAPTER THIRTEEN
CAUGHT IN THE SNARE

KAIDEN LUNGED TO his feet. They had come for him already. He scooped up Quill's equipment and shoved it under the bed. He knew it was futile to try and hide what he had been doing, but what else could he do? The knock sounded louder, more insistent. Muffled voices came through the door. Kaiden prepared himself. His hand fell to his sidearm. He would not die like Quill—not without a fight. He touched the button to open the door. Jade hovered in the doorway, giving him a peculiar expression. Her hair fell over her shoulders. She looked good in the black security uniform.

"Expecting someone else?" Jade asked. Birch and Willow poked their heads over Jade's shoulders.

"You look sick," Birch said.

"Get in here," Kaiden said. He grabbed Jade and dragged her into the room. The others followed.

Jade slapped his hand away from her arm. "Don't yank me around," she demanded.

"He's a bit jumpy," Willow said this as if Kaiden wasn't standing in the room.

"He's not usually like this," Birch said. "Cool as a meese in a lake."

Kaiden had no idea what Birch had just said, and he could tell by the baffled expression on Willow's face that she didn't either.

"You mean moose," Jade said.

"That's what I said," Birch replied. "But, I get the feeling Kaiden doesn't really trust us to cover his back."

Kaiden gestured for them all to click off their wrist terminals and fidgeted with his sidearm while he waited for them.

"Are your DWJs on?"

They nodded.

"Why didn't you two answer when I called?" Kaiden demanded. "I thought something had happened."

The three women dropped into chairs. Jade picked up one of Quill's nano-bots that Kaiden had missed and examined it.

"We were busy following your orders," Birch said. "Now, what's got your pistol all in a twist?"

"That doesn't even make sense," Kaiden said. He scowled at them. "Look. I got caught."

Jade dropped the nano-bot, and they all stared at him, openmouthed. Now, he had their full attention.

"I hacked in through a complicated series of servers, and the system still knew I was there and who I was."

"How do you know it knew who you were?" Birch asked.

"Because, it said, 'Hello Kaiden.'"

"The computer spoke to you?" Willow said.

"Yes. Then, I was disciplined."

The girls paled, and Willow raised a hand to her mouth. Jade scowled.

"We've got to find a way to turn off that switch," Birch said.

"Are you all right?" Willow asked.

"Yeah, now listen." Kaiden didn't want their sympathy. "I found a big empty space in the center of level nine. The place was called Atra-Hasis."

"I thought you said it was empty," Jade said.

"The name appeared just as the voice spoke."

"What kind of name is that?" Birch said. "Sounds like a sneeze."

"Maybe," Willow said, "Atra-Hasis is the name of the person who spoke to you."

"What do you mean?" Kaiden asked.

"I don't know, but it's a possibility. The point is," Willow continued, "we've been compromised again. We need to figure out a way to escape in case one of us is caught."

"I already took care of that," Birch said.

"Good," Kaiden said.

Birch batted her lashes at him. "I've got your back, Captain," she said.

Kaiden shook his head at her. Birch was impossible. "Right," he said. "So, what did you all find out?"

"I've got people watching all the hangars," Jade said. "And Colt is searching for records."

"He won't find any," Willow said.

Jade picked up the nano-bot again.

Birch held up her hand with a devious grin. "Watch this," she said. She wiggled her eyebrows at Kaiden, and her hand disappeared.

"Whoa," Kaiden said.

"Not too bad, huh?" Birch said. "Quill made one little error in his cloaking software that was messing him up. Flint says we can make this go bigger. It's all about controlling the light waves to mask your presence and having the nano-chips in the right places in your clothing. I've been inserting the nano-chips into our clothing, so eventually, the software will be able to mask an entire group if we don't get too far apart."

"That's cool," Kaiden said.

"It's dang cool," Birch said. "And I have Flint playing with Quill's nano-bots. He thinks he can improve those, too. But it's gonna take time."

"Don't know how much of that we're gonna have," Kaiden said.

Jade's wrist terminal buzzed. She glanced around at them and clicked it on. "Yeah," she said.

"Colt here." The voice whispered. "We've got an unauthorized flight leaving bay twenty-two right now."

"What do you mean unauthorized?" Jade asked.

"The airship filed no flight plan," Colt said. "It has no markings, and it does not appear on the register."

"What's it carrying?"

"My source told me it's carrying genetic material for South America. Wait. I thought I saw..."

The voice fell silent.

"He cut out," Birch said.

"Colt," Jade said into her wrist terminal. "Colt."

When Colt didn't answer, Jade sprang to her feet. "Dang it," she said. "That son of a moth-eaten blanket better not have been discovered. I told him to keep his head down." She strode to the door and disappeared into the hallway.

Kaiden chuckled at her weird way of cursing. "Do we have some special operation in South America?" he asked.

"Seriously?" Birch said. "We collect DNA from every ecosystem on the planet. Of course, we have operations in South America."

"I understand that," Kaiden replied.

"But why are *we* sending genetic material there?" Willow said. "It usually comes to us for processing before being sent to the seed bank."

"That's the question," Kaiden said. He stood. "I think we should follow Jade."

As the door swished open, Kaiden found himself facing Rio with an armed escort. He froze. His hand drifted toward his weapon.

Rio smirked. "Don't give me an excuse."

Kaiden snapped to attention and saluted, trying to act like he normally would, though his insides were writhing. Why would Rio appear at this moment?

"Sir?" Kaiden questioned.

He eyed Rio and the guards warily. His mind raced as he estimated how quickly he would have to move to eliminate them all before they could neutralize him. His odds weren't good.

Rio peered over Kaiden's shoulders to Willow and Birch. "Ah," he said. "Two ladies at once. You're finally learning from Greyson."

"Can I help you, sir?" Kaiden demanded again.

Rio winked at him. "*I* don't want anything, lover boy," he said. "But, Noah wants to speak with you."

Noah? Kaiden's throat tightened, and his heartbeat pounded in his ears. He was going to end up like Quill.

"Should we disarm him?" one of the men asked.

Rio appraised Kaiden. "I don't think so," he said. "He's not a prisoner—yet. But give him time. He's working really hard at becoming one." Rio clicked his tongue in disapproval. "Two failed missions, several dead officers, and years of TAP work wasted? Now, hanky-panky on his off hours?"

Not a prisoner yet? Then what did Noah want? Hadn't he been discovered hacking into TAP security files? Had the body in the Genesis Room already been found?

"And to think everyone thought you should be the commanding officer," Rio said. "You're pathetic." He gestured with his chin toward Kaiden, and the guards stepped forward and each grabbed Kaiden by an arm before marching him away.

Chapter Fourteen
Noah Sees

"YOU MAY LEAVE HIM."

The deep bass voice sent a shiver up Kaiden's spine, but there was something wrong with it. It didn't sound natural. Kaiden knew the rumors about Noah, the head of TAP. He was said to personally execute any traitors found in TAP, and he liked to use a sword. Kaiden didn't know how true this was—especially since Quill had been quietly shot. But still, the chances of leaving this interview alive were not in his favor. Sweat trickled down his back.

The guards shoved Kaiden through the door, and he stumbled in, blinking at the glare of a bright light as he examined the circular room. Chairs and computer consoles sat in orderly rows with blue holographic monitors hovering above them, filling the room. Kaiden felt like a fly that had been drawn to the center of a spider's web. This must be the hub of Noah's intelligence-gathering operation. From here, Noah could monitor everything that happened at TAP. The door swished closed behind him, and he searched the room for Noah, but no one was there.

This seemed odd. Surely someone had to monitor all of those computers. What good would an intelligence-gathering center be without people to gather the intelligence?

The big screen flickered to life in front of him, and Kaiden found himself staring at an old man with white hair and a long beard seated in a high-backed chair. He wore a black jacket, like the security personnel, with a large, red ark stitched at his left shoulder. The old man didn't smile or blink. He simply stared.

"Why did you hack into our security system?" Noah demanded. His voice, deep and menacing, echoed off the walls.

Kaiden stiffened. He had half-hoped this meeting would be about his last two missions as Rio seemed to think. But this was far worse.

"How—"

"Do not presume," Noah interrupted, "that you can do anything like that inside my complex without my knowledge."

Kaiden's palms began to sweat. How much did Noah know? Was he only talking about his latest attempt or also about Quill or the raid on Rio's computer, or the body hidden in the Genesis Room? And if Noah knew about Quill and had had him executed, why was Kaiden still alive?

"Yes, sir," Kaiden said in a weak attempt to buy some time to think of a plan.

"I'm waiting," Noah said.

"Curiosity, sir," Kaiden said.

Noah wasn't convinced. "Your curiosity has now become dangerous."

Kaiden shifted his feet. "Yes, sir."

"You understand that I cannot allow you to continue?"

"Yes, sir." Kaiden shifted his leg and felt the holster strapped there. He let his hand rest on his thigh as he noted the location of the cameras in the room and the two other doors. If he had to, he would shoot his way out.

Noah glowered down at him with an expression that Kaiden didn't understand. Was Noah angry? Concerned? Worried? The silence stretched on. Kaiden squirmed. Sweat beaded on his brow as he glanced around the room again at all the flashing lights and flickering screens. Noah *was* the great spider sitting at the center of thousands of threads listening to every tremor, sending his minions to silence opposition. Perhaps they even rewrote memories so he could reconstruct the world to his own liking.

Kaiden realized that this old man had robbed him of his past, ripped his mind from his body, and forced him into a life he had not chosen. The heat rose in his chest. He clenched his jaw. His fingers itched to hold his sidearm.

"I know, sir!" he shouted with belligerent recklessness. "I know what you've done to us!"

The expression on Noah's face hardened. "And what have I done?"

"You've made us all freaks," Kaiden shouted.

To Kaiden's surprise, Noah grinned. "Now, I understand," he said. "It took you longer to figure it out this time."

Kaiden started as the bottom fell out of his stomach. *This time?* What was Noah talking about? "What?" he murmured.

Noah grunted in satisfaction. "You're three years late," Noah said. "We *are* making progress."

Kaiden could only gape. Had he been engineered to be uncritically loyal to TAP? He still hadn't internalized what Willow had been trying to tell him. He was just another experiment. Nothing more. Noah had been genetically engineering him to make it so that he never doubted TAP, never questioned. And this time, the experiment had almost worked. If it hadn't been for the explosion on the lunar transport, he might never have figured it out.

Noah jerked his head around to stare at something Kaiden couldn't see or hear. Noah barked an order. The screen flickered, and something or someone else flashed behind Noah's image for just an instant. Then, Noah turned back to Kaiden.

"We will not meet again," Noah said. "You have one hour to turn over all of Quill's files, nano-bots, and software to Rio and to submit yourself for reconditioning. If you fail to comply, you will be terminated."

The screen flashed, and Kaiden found himself staring at a flickering blue screen.

"Wait!" Kaiden called. "What's reconditioning?"

The door swished open behind him. Iris and Greyson entered.

Kaiden stiffened. "What are you two doing here?" His hand drifted to his sidearm. Greyson and Iris both wore the ear receivers they usually wore when on missions and had their weapons with the safeties off. They were ready for combat.

Greyson raised a finger to his lips. "Our orders are to escort you back to your room." He gestured with his head toward the door.

Kaiden hesitated. Where were the guards that brought him here?

"Did you do it?" Kaiden demanded of Iris. "Did you kill Quill?"

Iris's black hair was cut short, almost shaved. The tattoo of the sniper rifle showed underneath her short shirtsleeve, deep blue against her light brown skin. Her nostrils flared, and she strode up to him, standing nose to nose. "Believe me," she said, "if I had shot at you, you would be dead. I never miss. Ever."

"Then who did it?"

"I didn't have any live ammo," Iris growled.

Greyson grabbed Kaiden by the arm and dragged him through the door. "Look," he said in a low whisper when they were outside in the hallway, and the door closed behind them, "we're taking a big risk coming to get you."

"I thought you had orders," Kaiden said.

"We do," Greyson said. "When we heard they'd arrested you, we volunteered to escort you."

"Why?"

Greyson glanced at Iris. "You're our team leader," he said as if that was explanation enough. "Now, come on before Rio gets suspicious."

They marched down the busy corridors for a good fifteen minutes before Greyson yanked him to a sudden stop and placed a hand on his ear.

"Yes, sir," Greyson said. "A body, sir? Where? Right. We're on our way."

"Sorry, Captain," he said to Kaiden. "A body seems to have appeared where it doesn't belong. We'll circle back to your room if we can. If not, Willow will know where to find us. Good luck." And he and Iris sprinted down the corridor.

Kaiden stared after them, trying to figure out what had just happened. Iris denied killing Quill, but he still had a gut feeling she had been involved. And Greyson was being unusually polite. Why would Willow know where to find them? A few people edged past him, glancing at him curiously. It wasn't every day you saw a security officer standing alone, staring down a hallway. Still, he hesitated.

Should he follow Greyson and Iris to verify that the body of the man Jade had killed had already been found? No, Noah had given him one hour. If he was going to save himself and his friends, he needed to act now. Kaiden clicked on his wrist terminal as he broke into a jog.

"Willow?" he said. "Birch? Jade?"

"Where have you been?" Birch's voice crackled from his wrist terminal.

"I'll explain later."

"There is no later," Birch said. "Did Greyson and Iris find you?"

"Yeah."

"He's gone." It was Jade's voice.

"Who?"

"Colt. He's gone."

"Meet me in my room," Kaiden said. "Use the DWJ." He wasn't even sure the things worked anymore after what Noah said, but maybe the old man was exaggerating.

He sprinted through the corridors, surprised to find security personnel out in force. He knew most of them, but he couldn't understand why a single body would generate this kind of response.

When he burst through the door of his room, he found Willow there. She glanced at him and stuffed the last of Quill's equipment into a backpack. She wore a black security uniform that fit her like a glove, and her hair was pulled back in a ponytail. Kaiden slid to a stop and stared at her. Without her lab coat, she was really beautiful.

"What are you doing?" Kaiden demanded.

"It's time to go," Willow said.

"Noah knows everything," Kaiden said. "He's probably listening to us right now."

"So, it's time to go," Willow repeated.

She was right. "We'll try Birch's escape plan," he said.

Willow handed him the backpack. "I worked out a backup plan if that doesn't work." She gestured to the short, automatic security rifle Model 35. This one didn't have the features of the 45, but it was a fast shooting, accurate, and dependable rifle. Kaiden had trained with it, and, until the 45 came out, it had been his rifle of choice. A pile of loaded clips rested on the table.

"Do we really want to try to fight our way out of here?" Kaiden asked.

"I'm not going to fight," Willow said. She wrinkled her nose playfully. "You are. Now, suit up." She checked her wrist terminal.

"They'll be here in a couple of minutes."

"Are you prepared to kill our own people?" Kaiden asked as he eyed the loaded clips. He had never liked cloning much, but he had felt pity for the clones and didn't want to kill them, especially now that he understood what had happened to them—now that he was one of them.

"You think they'll hesitate to kill us?" Willow asked.

Kaiden frowned. After what Noah just told him, he was certain they wouldn't.

"Anyway," Willow said, "those are all loaded with tranquilizers. Hopefully, they'll get us out."

Kaiden hesitated. Things were moving so fast. He had never known anything but TAP. Even if they could somehow escape the compound, how were they going to survive? Where would they go? They needed time to prepare, to organize. He hadn't had time to review Birch's escape idea. You just didn't go into a major operation like this without contingency plans. He knew enough about the world outside of TAP to understand that food and water were precious commodities and in very short supply. He also knew that the cities were filled with violent, desperate people.

"This is crazy," he said.

Willow smirked. "You have less than an hour before you're dead," she said, "because unless I've guessed wrong, you had no intention of giving up Quill's files and betraying all of us to Noah."

Kaiden gaped. "How did you hear that?"

"I keep telling you, I'm not just a lab tech," Willow said.

She was right. He had been prepared to fight. In fact, he had already decided to fight even though he knew it was hopeless. But if they left TAP, how would he ever recover his lost memories? How would he ever find out who he really was? He couldn't turn over Quill's files, or Noah would know that he had involved his friends in his crimes. Kaiden cursed. His friends would have to come before his memories. He had lost too many friends already.

The door swished open, and Kaiden spun, drawing his pistol. Jade and Birch rushed through the door, eyes wide and expectant. Kaiden noted the automatic Model 45 rifles in their hands and the fully-packed rucksacks on their backs. They also wore their black security uniforms. Jade's black hair was pulled up in a ponytail to keep it out of the way.

"Well?" Birch said. "Grab your battle rattle, and let's go."

Willow glanced at Jade as if she expected her to correct Birch, and she gave Kaiden a confused expression when Jade didn't speak. "Am I supposed to know what that means?"

"It just means your combat gear," Kaiden said.

"Right," Willow said.

"You know we're about to be disciplined?" Kaiden said. "All of us."

Birch grinned. "Flint is running interference on the discipline switch for now," she said. "Should give us some time."

Flint was quickly earning Kaiden's admiration. Maybe he was as good at this stuff as Quill, after all.

"Where is Flint?" Kaiden asked as he swung the pack on his back and reached for the rifle.

"He's coming a different way," Willow said.

"Let's go," Birch said and dashed off.

"I guess we follow," Jade said.

Willow and Jade raced after Birch, and Kaiden scrambled to catch up with them. As they pelted down the white-walled corridors, something kept nagging at the back of Kaiden's brain. He was missing something. Something wasn't right.

Why would Noah bother calling him to warn him when he had simply ordered Quill to be murdered and made Colt disappear? Why not just kill Kaiden? And why the elaborate scheme to get Quill killed in full view of the public? Why not simply have him imprisoned and executed? And why had Noah left Quill's stuff for Kaiden to find?

"Where are we going?" Willow asked as they ran.

"Hang on," Birch said.

Kaiden dragged himself from his musings and realized that Birch was leading them toward one of the lower airship bays. They avoided the elevators and pounded down several flights of stairs.

"It'll be on lockdown," Kaiden called.

"I got us covered," Birch shouted.

They burst through the doorway and skidded onto the hangar level, where the hallways were wider. Now, they could run side by side. They raced around the last corner to find the wide bay doors closed and the red security lights flashing off the bright white doors.

"We can go down and come around through the loading bays," Kaiden said.

"No time," Willow said.

Birch never paused. She strode up to the keypad and clicked in the numbers. She stepped back, expectantly. Nothing happened. Birch keyed the numbers in again. Nothing.

"I thought you had the codes," Jade said.

"I have the override codes," Birch said. "These should work."

"Let's blow it," Jade said.

Birch glanced at Kaiden. "Do it," he said. "We don't have time to play around."

Jade unslung her pack, set the tiny explosives, and rushed to join the others who sought cover around the corner and flattened themselves to the ground. The explosion rocked the corridor as the shockwave swept over them. Debris flew past them, and billowing smoke choked the air. Kaiden lunged into the smoldering rent in the door. He knelt on the platform that overlooked the airship bay. A guard rail obscured his view, but the stairs dropped off to his right. The zip and whine of bullets buzzed over his head and slapped into the jagged remains of the entryway.

"Down," Kaiden yelled as he dropped to his belly. Security weren't shooting tranquilizers. They were shooting to kill. Noah had known everything. How did they think they could escape so easily? Still, maybe they could fight their way to an airship.

Kaiden peered over the rail to find the airship bay empty. His stomach tightened. If Birch had expected an airship, she had been sadly mistaken. A line of security personnel formed a giant semicircle around the door. That could only mean that they had been expected, and TAP was prepared for them.

"They're going to trap us!" Kaiden yelled. "Out. Out!"

Kaiden sprayed the line of security with a burst of fire and leaped back through the hole. Jade knelt beside the rent, using the twisted metal as protection as she covered his escape. Then, she tossed another explosive into the hole as they sprinted back the way they had come. Kaiden knew she was blowing the stairs so the security couldn't follow.

"Time for your backup plan," Kaiden yelled to Willow, trying to still the growing panic.

"Follow me," Willow called.

"Where?" Jade asked.

"Watch out," Birch shouted as a line of security personnel burst into the corridor in front of them. Kaiden recognized many of them. As he squeezed the trigger in short bursts and watched them fall with blue tranquilizer darts protruding from their twitching bodies, he was grateful that Willow had grabbed the non-lethal ammo. He didn't know if he could have killed the people with whom he had grown up and trained. Not when this mess was his fault.

"This way," Willow called.

Bullets punched into the walls and whined and buzzed around their heads. Birch rolled a concussion grenade toward the TAP security as Kaiden's little team sprinted after Willow down a side corridor. The explosion rocked the corridor, but some security had already sped past the grenade and were firing at them.

A bullet slammed into Kaiden's backpack. He stumbled but kept running. He paused at a corner and released a burst of darts into the oncoming security. Several dropped. The rest scattered. Kaiden spun and sprinted down the corridor.

Willow led them lower and lower, down to levels that Kaiden never visited except in his virtual exploration of TAP a few hours before. Willow drew up short before an elevator with blinking red lights. They gathered around her, panting. Kaiden scanned each of them quickly to make sure no one was wounded.

"I'm not sure I want to jump into an elevator with TAP hunting me," Birch said. "There's no guarantee the door will open again. We could get stuck in there like fish in a fish tank."

They all gazed at Birch.

"You have the weirdest way of expressing yourself," Willow said.

"What?" Birch said. "The fish can't get out, can they?"

The elevator door slid open, and Kaiden spun to face it. Greyson and Iris filled the doorway.

CHAPTER FIFTEEN
DESCENT

"WHAT THE..." Kaiden jerked his rifle up, but Willow grabbed the barrel and cast him a confused expression.

"Hang on," she said. She glanced at Greyson. "Are you ready?"

Greyson scowled at Kaiden's rifle. "Didn't we just save your bacon?" he said.

Iris clicked her tongue. "I told you I didn't do anything."

"Not now," Willow said. "We don't have time."

Kaiden didn't miss the petulant glare Iris shot at him or the way her finger kept moving toward the trigger of her KMH 70 Manslayer Sniper Rifle. When loaded with a .408 mm x 60 mm exploding round, that gun would leave a hole the size of a grapefruit in a person. The new accelerated power gave it much higher velocity and an effective range of three miles. The big gun wouldn't be of much use in a running battle, but Iris never fought without it. Her eyes narrowed as she noticed Kaiden's scrutiny of her weapon.

Kaiden grabbed Willow's arm. "What makes you think this is a good idea?"

"They're part of your team," she snapped and yanked her arm out of his grasp. She scowled in confusion. Then she drew Kaiden aside so the others couldn't hear.

"I thought you trusted them."

"I did," Kaiden said, "but I think they might be responsible for

Quill's death."

Willow blanched and cast Greyson and Iris a furtive glance. "You never said. How was I supposed to know?" Willow raised a hand to touch his cheek. Her fingers were cool. "Let's just get out of here, and then we can discuss it," she whispered.

"We really don't have time for this," Birch said, raising one eyebrow at the sight of Willow's hand on Kaiden's cheek.

Willow spun away from him. "Take off your wrist terminals," she ordered.

"Why?" Jade asked. Her chin came up, and her eyes narrowed. She raised her rifle without taking her gaze off Greyson and Iris.

"Because they'll use them to track us, even with the DWJ," Willow said, "and we need to do something about that." Willow pulled out several new wrist terminals from her pack. "These are set to a different frequency. They won't be perfect, but at least they'll make it more difficult for TAP to track us."

Birch tugged a little drone out of her pocket and attached their discarded wrist terminals to it. She sent it flying down a different corridor.

"That should give them something to chase for a while."

When they finished, Iris tossed a bag full of climbing harnesses to Jade and held up a thick blue line that dropped through the floor of the elevator. Six other lines dangled beside it.

"Hook up," Iris said.

"Where are you taking us?" Jade asked.

Iris pointed to Willow. "Ask her. We're just following instructions."

"I have another way out," Willow said. "It's our only chance."

They all buckled into their harnesses, but Kaiden kept an eye on Greyson and Iris. He couldn't figure them out, and he couldn't escape the lingering doubt that Iris had been the sniper who killed Quill. If she had, then why would she be helping him now?

The touch of Willow's cool fingers against his cheek and the quiet hug she had given him earlier had stirred him more than he cared to admit. Still, he couldn't escape the nagging feeling that there was something she wasn't telling him.

Kaiden almost decided to leave them all and go his own way, but he couldn't abandon Birch and Jade. And he hadn't had time to formulate any other plan. He had thought he might have a couple of days at least, but things had taken a sudden turn for the worse, and the best they could do was improvise until he did have time to get reorganized. They all crowded into the elevator, being careful not to step through the hole in the floor, and the door swished closed.

"Why are we repelling down an elevator shaft," Jade asked, "when we could simply push the button?"

Greyson grinned. "The buttons don't work, sweetheart," he said.

Jade pointed her rifle at him. Her eyes narrowed. "You call me that again, and I *will* shoot you."

Greyson held up his hands, but the grin never left his face.

"Go," Birch said.

Greyson winked at Jade and dropped through the hole. Iris followed.

Someone pounded against the door.

"They've found us," Birch said.

"They'll blow it," Jade said.

Willow dropped through the hole. Jade followed. Then Birch. A terrible screeching sound shook the elevator as Kaiden jumped into the black hole. The rope buzzed through the belay device as he fell. Slits of light blinked past, marking each floor. Kaiden counted fifteen before the roar and flash of light filled the shaft. His line went slack, and he plunged into the darkness.

Kaiden's mind ripped open as the TAP discipline lashed into him. He screamed in agony. Terror boiled in his chest and squeezed his stomach tight. Nausea swept over him. He was curled up inside the box, suffocating in the complete darkness. Spiders tore at his flesh. He was going to die. Even through the horror and agony of the discipline, he knew he was falling. If the discipline didn't kill him, the fall most certainly would.

Then, the sound of his mother's voice echoed in his mind. "I love you, darling," she said. Her arms encircled him. Her soft lips touched his cheek. He was safe.

Kaiden didn't fall far before he slammed into the ground. The pain jarred him out of the fog of the discipline. Someone was screaming. Hands grabbed at him, tugging at his clothing.

"Move," Birch's voice penetrated the pain and the fear.

Kaiden tried to scramble to his feet. Someone was dragging

him. Debris crashed around him. Pain lanced through his arm as he slammed into a wall. The discipline ended, and he reeled in confusion, reaching for the wall to support him. Birch gripped his arm and dragged him to a sitting position.

"Kaiden!" Birch yelled again. "What's the matter with you?"

Kaiden coughed. "Discipline," he mumbled.

Birch clicked her tongue in irritation. "So much for Flint jamming their ability to administer discipline," she said to the others.

Bits of the elevator still rained down around them. The acrid smell of high explosives, hot metal, and burning oil filled the air. Kaiden coughed again and scrambled to his feet. Jade dragged him toward the door, stumbling over the wreckage. They burst into a corridor to find the others waiting for them. Their discarded harnesses lay in a pile.

"Are you hurt?" Willow asked. Her face tightened in concern.

Kaiden shook his head and glanced at his arm. Blood was starting to soak the sleeve. Something poked out of the ragged tear. "I'm fine," he said. "Let's go."

"Don't be stupid," Birch said. She pulled a bandage from her bag, sliced his sleeve away with her knife, and gazed at the wound.

"That's a nice piece of metal you've collected," she said.

Jade bent to inspect it. Then, she yanked it out.

"Holy..." Kaiden yelled.

"Nothing serious," Jade said. "You've got INCR like the rest of us."

Kaiden glared at her. Jade smiled prettily as Birch applied an antibacterial salve and a bandage.

"Now, let's act like we're trying to escape," Birch said as she shouldered her pack. "Unless you want to hang around and see if you can collect any more metal souvenirs from TAP."

"Weren't any of you disciplined?" Kaiden asked.

They all stared at him.

"Guess you're just special," Greyson said. "Maybe Noah really cares about your future."

"Or maybe," Jade said, "Noah knows you're the leader, and he's trying to scare you."

Kaiden grunted and snatched at the flashlight Willow handed him. They all knew Kaiden wasn't calling the shots on this mission.

This was all Willow's plan. Maybe she had been manipulating them from the start. The smile that had twitched at the side of Willow's mouth when Birch had teased him faded to a deep frown as if she knew what Kaiden was thinking.

"Come on," Kaiden said.

Willow rested a hand on his arm. "Trust me," she whispered. And she winked at him before she led them into the darkness.

Kaiden scowled after her. He couldn't escape the feeling that he was going to regret this, but he waited for the others to fall in line before he followed.

His mind still felt cloudy from the discipline, and his head ached. But he couldn't forget the powerful emotions that surged through him as his mother embraced him. Somehow, the memory of her presence had pushed the fear and the pain away. And it seemed that the discipline triggered these memories of the woman he now knew was his mother. But, if she was his mother, why did he love her and hate her at the same time?

Kaiden flexed his arm. The wound throbbed, but it hadn't been serious. The INCR would soon repair it, even though it had failed to save Quill. He glanced back at the tangled remains of the elevator. The beam of his flashlight cut through the settling smoke and dust. Noah had been serious. Kaiden was now an outlaw, and the best-funded, most secretive organization in the world would be chasing him no matter where he went. All he had done was postpone the inevitable. TAP would find him in the end.

Greyson and Jade had taken up positions at the back of the line. Kaiden slung the rifle over his shoulder and plodded along behind them. What could he do but try to survive as long as possible?

The walls of the corridor were round, smooth, and gray. Its ceiling rose twenty feet over their heads. A musty dampness coated the inside of Kaiden's mouth.

He noted with some amusement that Greyson kept glancing at Jade. Greyson had long prided himself on his abilities with the ladies in TAP. It was true that his close-cut black hair, dark eyes, and narrow face had turned many a young lady's head, but Kaiden thought maybe he had picked the wrong lady this time.

"So, where's your family from?" Greyson asked.

"TAP," Jade said in a flat disinterested voice.

"That's not what I meant."

"I know what you meant. Now, leave me alone."

"You always this friendly?"

Jade ignored him.

Kaiden liked Jade's spunkiness, and it did him good to see Greyson get a bit of her temper. He deserved it.

"I thought Indians were supposed to be these spiritually sensitive people who respected everyone," Greyson said.

Jade jerked the butt of her rifle sideways. It slammed into Greyson's ribs. He doubled over, and she swept his feet out from under him, so he fell flat on his back. She leveled her rifle at his nose.

"I told you to leave me alone," she said. "When I want to hear you talk, I'll ask you. Until then, keep your fool mouth shut."

Greyson slapped the rifle barrel away from his face and crawled to his feet. "Grow up," he growled as he stomped off after the others.

Jade let Greyson get ahead.

"Thanks," Kaiden said to Jade as he fell in beside her.

Jade glanced over at him.

"I've been wanting to do that for a while," he said.

Jade grinned. "My pleasure."

"By the way," Kaiden continued, "I never thanked you for trying to protect me last night."

"It's my job," Jade said.

"Not like that," Kaiden said. "You risked your career and your life for me. I won't forget it."

"Looks like I just lost my career, anyway."

"Yeah, sorry about that."

"Don't be."

Kaiden glanced at her. "I'm still not clear why you decided to join us."

Jade looked over at him. Tears glistened in her eyes.

"Because I'm alone," she said. "I don't want to be alone anymore."

This statement surprised Kaiden. Jade seemed so tough and professional. But maybe that was just a façade to hide her real feelings. Still, he wanted to comfort her—but how? He didn't want to make the situation more awkward or get a rifle butt shoved into his ribs.

"We may not be much," he said, "but we're a team."

Jade reached over and grabbed his hand. She squeezed it. Her grip was firm, and her hand smooth. "Thank you," she said.

A little shiver ran through Kaiden, and he squeezed her hand back before letting go.

The corridor narrowed and pressed in around them, forcing them to walk single file. They stopped talking because the others were closer now, but their arms brushed, and each time they did, Kaiden experienced the desire to feel her hand in his again. It was a strange feeling. He had never felt drawn to any woman before—and now there were two.

Greyson, who was the tallest, had to hunch over as the concrete tunnel narrowed and gave way to solid rock. It smelled of earth and age, probably because the moist air didn't circulate much down here. The team traveled in silence for some time until a blue light flashed ahead. Willow answered with her flashlight, and the light flashed again.

"It's safe," she said.

"Who's waiting for us?" Kaiden asked.

Willow hesitated. She glanced down and pursed her lips. "You'll see."

As they approached the blue light, a tall man with a rifle over his shoulder stepped out of the shadows into the beams of their flashlights. He wore jeans and a T-shirt stretched tight over his muscles, and he had a scruffy red beard.

Willow shook the man's hand. "This is Hawk," she said. "He'll lead us out of here."

"And who are you?" Greyson demanded.

"Your guide."

"Evading the question?" Greyson said.

"He belongs to the Destroying Angels," Willow said.

Five rifles snapped up to point at him.

Hawk raised his hands in surrender and glanced at Willow. "I told you," he said. "You should have warned them."

"Relax," Willow said. "All of you."

"What are you doing, Willow?" Kaiden demanded. What made her think this was a good idea?

"I'm saving our lives," Willow snapped.

"Funny way of doing it," Greyson said. "Turning us over to TAP's worst enemies."

"I'm not turning anyone over to anyone," Willow said. "And in case you didn't notice them shooting at us with live rounds and the explosion at the elevator, TAP is actively trying to kill us. *We* are now TAP's enemies."

"She has a point," Birch said, lowering her rifle.

"Besides," Willow added, "they can get us out of here."

"And then what?" Kaiden asked.

Willow looked away. "I don't know," she said. "First things first."

"You never said anything about joining a terrorist group," Greyson said. "If I'd known that's all you had planned, I would have stayed behind."

"No one's stopping you," Willow said with an angry gesture back down the tunnel. "No one knows you came with us."

"They do now," Greyson said. He raised his hand to show her the new wrist terminal.

"All right," Birch said. "Greyson, if you want to go back and face the clowns, go for it. Otherwise, let's get going. We're wasting time."

"I think you mean *face the music*," Jade corrected her.

Birch's lips shrank into a pout. "It's all the same."

Kaiden glanced around at them, refusing to be distracted by Birch's linguistic mess-ups. Had Willow really betrayed them? He didn't want to believe it. What were the chances the terrorists would let any of them live? He tried to come up with an alternative to the options before him but failed. His chances couldn't be any worse with the terrorists than with Noah. At least, he knew for certain Noah meant to kill him.

"Let's go then," Kaiden said.

"Right," Hawk said. "Follow me."

His headlamp flashed against the stone walls that glistened with moisture as he spun to face the darkness.

CHAPTER SIXTEEN
INTO THE DARK

WILLOW CAST A GLANCE at Kaiden, though she hoped he wouldn't see it in the darkness of the tunnel. Then she spun to follow Hawk. She had known they wouldn't like her escape plan. That's why she hadn't told them and why she had let Birch try her plan first. If it had worked, none of this would have been necessary. But after spending forty years at TAP with the accumulated memories that she was not supposed to have, Willow had known that Noah would be tracking them. And she knew it wasn't just the wrist terminals. That's why she had led them deep underground. Down here, with miles of rock around them, TAP wouldn't be able to track them. TAP security might come down the elevator shaft and follow them, but they would be long gone by then if her plan worked.

Willow had also been able to overhear Noah's interview with Kaiden. Something about it bothered her. Why Kaiden? What was so special about him? Quill had simply been executed. Colt had disappeared. But Kaiden had been given several chances, and he was still alive. There were only two possible explanations. He was a plant Noah was using to uncover conspiracies inside TAP, or Noah had something more personal planned for him. Maybe Kaiden had some special genetic modification that Noah was testing. That would explain why Kaiden had been so slow to question what was going on at TAP and why he had such a visceral reaction to the fragmented memories of his pre-clone life.

Willow had been watching Kaiden for a long time. She had selected him first because out of all the clones she had met at TAP, he was the only one she recognized from her pre-clone days. She had met him once while interning in a science lab, but the details were still fuzzy. He had been cloned at least as many times as she had, but he was apparently more important. She had a growing suspicion why, but she needed to do a bit more digging. She needed to have time to examine the files she had downloaded before they left.

The tunnel narrowed, and the ceiling dropped so low that Willow had to crouch.

"We seem to be running out of space," Greyson called from behind her.

"Just a bit farther," Hawk said.

He stopped and shined his light into a jagged crack in the side of the tunnel.

"You're kidding," Birch said.

"Nope," Hawk replied. "You'll have to remove your packs."

"And what's on the other side?" Greyson asked.

"You'll see." Hawk shoved his pack ahead of him and disappeared through the crack.

Willow glanced back at the beams of light that marked the location of her companions. She couldn't see their faces, but she could feel their gazes. They were angry with her. Maybe they should be.

Willow slipped off her pack and squeezed into the crack behind Hawk. The space was tight for thirty yards, and then it widened into a narrow chamber barely high enough for her to stand up straight, but she couldn't turn around. She had to force herself to think about something other than the confining space.

Panic tightened her throat. The narrow gap made her sweat and breathe harder. She struggled to keep from scrambling over Hawk. She now understood the images of dark confined spaces that TAP used to punish her when she was disciplined. She tried to control her breathing as she squeezed through several narrow slits, shoving her pack in front of her with more desperation than she cared to admit.

When she finally entered a long chamber with a sandy floor, she breathed a sigh of relief and shined her light on the walls. The pitted basalt rock glistened with moisture. It must have been a lava tube of some kind. The drops of moisture refracted the light of the flashlights, making the walls shimmer like sheets of silver inset with diamonds. It was an astonishingly beautiful sight in an otherwise dark and ordinary cavern. Water dripped somewhere. The echo magnified until it sounded like a rain shower. The air smelled fresher.

Hawk slipped his backpack on and waited for the rest of them to join him. Willow hadn't known him long, only a few days, but he was a brave man to sneak into TAP just to give her a message, and now he had risked his life to save them from certain death.

"Thanks," she said to him.

He smiled. "Anything for an old sparring partner."

"Sorry about that," she said.

"I feel like a cockroach," Birch said as she squeezed into the cavern. "Couldn't you find a better tunnel?"

"Sorry," Hawk said. "That's the best we could do." He pointed his flashlight to the end of the tunnel, where a dim light could be seen. "We're almost there. One more narrow crawl space, and we'll be out."

"Out where?" Greyson asked with a glare of distrust.

Willow glanced at him. She had brought Greyson and Iris in because they were already a part of Kaiden's team, and she thought he trusted them. Birch had told her that they were all loyal to the team—that team loyalty was the most important thing for any security group. Since they hadn't been actively involved in Kaiden's other plotting, she thought they would be a good choice to prepare the ropes and harnesses at the elevator shaft. If Birch's escape route worked, they could just return to their jobs without too much trouble. There was no evidence to connect them to Kaiden's activities.

"I'm not supposed to tell you where the entrance is," Hawk said, "but our people will be there to get us out."

Greyson released the clip from his rifle, tucked it into a pocket, pulled out another clip, and clicked it into place. Iris followed his example.

"What are you doing?" Birch demanded.

Willow gave Kaiden a nervous glance.

"I'm not walking out into a crowd of terrorists without some protection," Greyson said. "I'll go first." He glanced at Iris.

"That's enough," Kaiden said. "Greyson, you agreed to come. If you don't like it, head back."

"I didn't say I was going back," Greyson said. "I said I'm not going out there unprepared."

"We can't afford to have you do something stupid," Kaiden said.

Greyson smirked. "I'm not the one you have to worry about."

"Look," Kaiden said, "once we're out, you can take off if you want, but I won't let you risk our lives by being an idiot."

Greyson sneered at Kaiden. "Man, you're just hell-bent on believing we betrayed you even after we rescued you from Rio and helped you escape. What more do you want from us?"

"Proof of your innocence," Kaiden said. He stepped toward Greyson, the muscles in his jaw working. He held out his hand. "Give me the clip with the live rounds."

"We just betrayed TAP for you," Greyson said. "I don't have to follow your orders anymore."

Kaiden snapped his sidearm from its sheath and leveled it at Greyson's head. Greyson blinked in surprise and started to raise his own rifle only to find Jade and Birch aiming their guns at him, as well."

"Hand it over," Kaiden said. "Or you won't walk out of here."

Greyson cursed and let the clip drop to the sand.

"Unchamber that round," Kaiden said.

Greyson rammed the slide back, and the shell jumped out to fall with a quiet thump in the sand.

"You too, Iris," Kaiden said.

She clicked her tongue in annoyance and followed Greyson's example.

"You're a fool," Greyson said.

Kaiden pointed a finger at Greyson. "Once we're out of here, I want you two gone." He holstered his pistol.

"Gladly," Greyson snarled. "I thought maybe something was going to change around here, but I see it's just the same old nonsense."

"You can reload the tranquilizer rounds, just in case," Kaiden said. They both did. "But don't fire unless I give the order."

Willow guessed that Kaiden didn't want to leave them both unable to defend themselves when they were approaching a potentially hostile situation.

"Keep a gun on each of them," Kaiden whispered to Jade and Birch. Then he gestured to Hawk. "Now Hawk, lead the way."

Hawk cast Greyson a wary glance and waved a hand at them to follow. The beams from their lights flashed against the damp walls as the others fell in behind him. Greyson edged in behind Hawk with Birch right behind him. Kaiden and Willow followed her with Iris behind them. Jade took up the rear.

"What's he playing at?" Willow whispered to Kaiden.

"You invited him," Kaiden snapped.

Willow shined her light on his face and found him scowling at Greyson's back.

"How was I supposed to know you didn't trust him?"

Hawk paused as they approached a large, V-shaped crack through which a fresh breeze blew. The warm, clear air tasted good after the stale damp of the tunnels. Pale daylight penetrated the darkness, illuminating Hawk's thin face as he turned to look back at them. Greyson lunged toward Hawk. Their flashlights glinted off of steel, and Greyson plunged a knife up under Hawk's ribs. Hawk fell sideways. Iris raced to Greyson's side and spun with her rifle up. Kaiden grabbed Willow and dragged her down as Jade and Birch dove onto the sand. Greyson tossed a blinking grenade into the narrow gap that led to the exit.

"Stay down," Iris shouted. "And no one else will get hurt."

Two shots rang out from behind Willow and Kaiden. Willow flinched, but Kaiden snapped his rifle up, aiming at Greyson. Iris jerked with the impact of the bullet and sank to her knees with a grunt. The heavy sniper rifle slipped from her grasp. Greyson crumpled sideways, going limp as a rag. Then the stone cavern erupted with a flash of light. A shock wave from the detonation washed over them. The cavern shuddered, and the ceiling collapsed with a roar.

CHAPTER SEVENTEEN
TRAPPED

WILLOW LAY ON her stomach, with her hands clenched over her head as the debris rained down around her. The ringing in her ears was so loud it seemed as if her head were underwater. Her lungs contracted, trying to find some air in the thick cloud of dust that settled around them. Grit coated the inside of her mouth and ground between her teeth. How long could she stay conscious without clear air to breathe? Something pressed against her legs, and her head ached.

Her flashlight lay beside her. Its beam pushed against the haze that surrounded them. Something shifted beside her. Kaiden laid a hand on her back. In the light of her flashlight, she could see his lips move, but she couldn't hear anything over the ringing in her ears. Kaiden picked up her flashlight and swept it around them.

They were lying in a tunnel of debris that was propped up by great slabs of stone. By some miracle, the slabs had fallen to either side of them. Kaiden crawled to his knees and then swiveled the light behind them. Willow tried to rise, but her feet wouldn't budge. She squirmed around until she could peer over her shoulder. Her stomach clenched, and she struggled to remain conscious as a swooping nausea made it feel like the cavern was rolling onto its side. A slab of basalt lay across her legs from the knees down, pressing them into the sandy floor of the cavern. Why didn't she feel any pain?

Kaiden shook his head at her and motioned for her to stay still. She blinked, trying to control the panic. She couldn't die down here. Not now. Not when she was so close. Forty years of laying the groundwork, watching, waiting, preparing. If she died without having her brain downloaded in preparation for a new synaptic upload, the knowledge of the last six years she had acquired since her last upload into this clone body would be lost. Her new clone, if they had even made one, would be blind to what she had so recently discovered. She thrashed against the weight on her knees.

Kaiden laid a hand on her shoulder. She peered up at him through the haze. His lips were moving again. He gestured more urgently for her to remain still. She swallowed the panic and tried to breathe in the thick air. Kaiden crawled away, and Willow stared into the darkness. She pressed on her ears, trying to get the ringing to stop.

Kaiden returned with Birch, who, like Kaiden, was covered in dirt. Birch said something and fished around in her pack until she drew out two little black earpieces and pushed them into Willow's ears. Then, she clicked on a receiver. The ringing diminished but didn't go away.

"Can you hear me?" Birch whispered. Her voice sounded far away.

Willow nodded. "Yes," she murmured.

Birch smiled in relief and exchanged a glance with Kaiden.

"I'm going to find Jade," Kaiden said. "Then, we'll get you out."

"What about the others?" Willow asked.

"I can't find Greyson or Hawk," Kaiden said. "Iris is alive. For now. She's mumbling something about Noah and promises." Kaiden laid a hand on Willow's arm, and an expression of concern passed over his face. "I'll be back," he said. "Sit tight."

Then, he was gone.

Jade covered her head with her arms and curled into a ball as the ceiling collapsed with a roar. The earth shook, and bits of stone pummeled her. The air became so thick with dust, she couldn't breathe. And yet, her only thought was for Kaiden and the others.

As soon as the rumbling quieted, she scrambled to her knees and drew her jacket up to cover her mouth and nose, hoping it would filter out the dust. She tasted the earthy grit as she flashed her light in the direction she had last seen Kaiden. She blinked in the shrouded haze.

The beam fell on a great stone slab that had been driven into the earth. The only thing that saved her was that the slab above her had fallen at an angle instead of straight down. This left her trapped in a little triangle just high enough for her to stand and long enough for her to lie flat. Her ears still rang from the blast.

Greyson and Iris had betrayed them. Kaiden had been right to suspect them. And she had been right in putting a bullet into each of them. Twice now, she had killed to save Kaiden's life. He was likely trapped under the rubble.

Tightness gripped her throat, but she fought it down. She wouldn't despair. Her grandfather told her that she must survive, and she would. She hadn't told Kaiden she ran out of tranquilizing rounds back at the landing bay and had loaded exploding rounds before they reached the elevator, but it was a good thing she had.

Swinging her rifle onto her back where the sling held it, she scrambled through a narrow opening between the great slab and a pile of rubble. Kaiden had to be alive. He just had to be. Her grandfather had been ripped away from her, leaving her alone. Now, she had allowed herself to feel close to Kaiden, and he might have been taken from her, as well. Maybe she was supposed to be alone.

She reached the top and shined her light up into the black crevice that expanded above her. They had to get out of there before any more rocks fell. The place had been unstable, and the rockfall probably wasn't over yet.

A beam of light flashed through the haze, and she almost cried out. Scrambling down the other side and over several more large boulders, she worked her way toward the bouncing beam of light. A dark figure stumbled behind the light.

"Jade," Kaiden called. His voice was muffled in the dirt-filled air. "Can you hear me?"

Warmth burst into her chest. Kaiden had come for her. "Over

here," she called and clawed up another pile of rubble. Kaiden slid down a stone slab. He grabbed her shoulders.

"Are you all right?"

"I'm fine. How are the others?"

"Willow's trapped, but Birch is with her."

Jade peered up into his face, gray from the dust that clung to his sweat, and shuffled her feet. An awkward silence fell between them as pressure expanded in her chest. He had come for her. He had been concerned about her. She couldn't remember the last time anyone cared whether she lived or died. She grabbed him in a hug.

"I was afraid you were dead," she said into his shoulder.

His arms encircled her. "I got you," he said.

Willow rubbed at the sting in her eyes. She raised her head to blink at Birch. "Are you all right?"

"Just a few bruises and having a hard time hearing," Birch said, "but I'll be all right. Those little nano dudes they injected into our blood are already repairing the damage."

"Why did he do that?" Willow said.

Birch bowed her head. "Greyson? I don't know. I never thought he would try to kill us."

"Maybe he was doing more than that," Willow said. "Maybe he was making sure this entrance was closed for good."

"You think Noah put him up to it?" Birch said.

"Who else? Noah sees more than we know. I bet he knew the terrorists had a secret way in, and he used us to find it and seal it." It did Willow good to think about something other than her legs that lay trapped beneath what could be thousands of pounds of stone.

"Maybe," Birch said. "That might also explain why no one was chasing us. They expect us to come back to them."

"I doubt that he expected the whole ceiling of the tunnel to collapse," Willow said.

A circle of light bobbed on the slab of basalt, and Kaiden and Jade scrambled down to kneel beside them.

Jade was covered in dirt like the rest of them but otherwise looked unruffled. She always had that infuriatingly calm expression on her face no matter what happened.

"That's all of us," Kaiden said. "Now, let's get you out."

The three of them crawled behind her and began working around her legs.

"The slab isn't resting directly on her leg," Jade said. "It's propped up here and here." Willow couldn't see what she pointed at.

"It's a good thing," Kaiden said, "or her legs would be crushed."

"I'd prefer it if you didn't talk like I wasn't here," Willow said. The thought of losing her legs sent a wild shiver through her. No INCR would heal that. She would be crippled.

"Sorry," Kaiden said. "The floor is sand, so we can try to dig you out."

Willow listened past the ringing in her ear and waited. They jostled her legs, and she still felt no pain, but there was pressure and a tingling sensation as if her legs had fallen asleep. Something grated, and the rock shifted.

"Watch out!" Jade yelled.

Willow covered her head as debris rained down on her.

"It's all right," Birch said. "Just a bit of shifting."

After clawing at the sand and scooping it away with his arms, Kaiden said, "Try to move your legs."

Willow pulled, and her leg budged a bit. Pain lanced up her thigh, and she bit off a cry. At least, the pain meant she wouldn't be paralyzed.

"Now, try a bit more," Birch said.

Willow kept tugging, and her legs came out an inch at a time as the others scooped and scraped the sand away. Finally, she dragged herself free and rolled to her back, panting and covered in a cold sweat. When she tried to sit up, Birch laid a hand on her arm.

"Not yet," Birch said. "Let me look at it."

Willow's toes tingled and stung like someone had shoved needles under her toenail. Her right leg ached, but otherwise, she felt okay—especially considering what *could* have happened.

"You're lucky," Birch said. "That stone could have cut your legs off."

"Yes, thank you, Birch," Kaiden said with a note of irritation in his voice. Maybe he didn't want Birch to frighten her. She was already frightened, so it didn't matter.

Birch smirked at him. "Looks okay," she said. "Just some scrapes. Can you wiggle your toes?"

Willow did and felt them move inside her boots. "Yes."

"Are you in a lot of pain?"

"No, just some aching and tingling."

"Give it a try."

Willow sat up and flexed her legs. The relief flooded into her chest as they responded to her commands. She blinked back the tears. "All good," she said.

Kaiden took a deep breath. The expression of relief on his face made Willow blink more rapidly. Maybe he could care for her, despite everything.

Willow glanced at Jade. "Did you shoot them?"

"No one else was handling the situation," Jade said, "so I did."

"Well, thanks," Willow said, though the word burned in her throat. She didn't like to admit Jade had done something right, but if Jade hadn't shot Greyson and Iris, they might all be dead. "I thought they could be trusted."

Kaiden narrowed his eyes. "There seems to be a lot of deceit going on around here these days."

"I'm sorry I didn't tell you about the terrorists," Willow said. "There wasn't time. Things were moving too fast."

"We appreciate your friendly apologies," Jade said, "but what now? Unless you fancy sitting here until we either suffocate or die of thirst, we ought to see about getting out of here."

Birch was already digging in her pack. "Now, we'll see if Quill's nano-bots can actually do something useful."

She clipped on the wrist terminal, and two mosquito-sized drones rose into the air.

"I'm getting the hang of this," Birch said as the mosquitoes disappeared in opposite directions. Birch slipped the screen from her backpack and clicked it on. Two images appeared side by side. The green light lit her dust-covered face, casting it in a sickly pallor.

"Wow," Birch said. "That bomb really messed up this tunnel." She gazed at the screen in disbelief.

The ceiling had collapsed along most of the tunnel, but some slabs propped up enough of the ceiling that the nano-bot was able to work its way to the back of the corridor and the crack they had crawled through. It zipped into the crevice.

"Looks like the way back is more or less clear," Kaiden said.

"Do we really want to do that?" Jade asked.

Kaiden wiped at the dirt in his eyes but didn't answer.

The other drone worked its way over the pile of rubble and then slipped into a tiny crevice. It passed out of the cave into a wide-open area bursting with sunlight. An old T-50 Cobra Gunship waited with its engines running in a valley of jumbled boulders. A crowd had gathered to peer into the rubble. Most of them wore simple jeans and T-shirts, and they were all armed to the teeth. Willow recognized one of them. A young man of Indian descent with thick, black hair framing an open face, now pinched with concern, peered up into the crevice from which a dust cloud was still rising.

"Flint?" Kaiden exclaimed. "What's he doing here?"

"I sent him," Willow said.

Kaiden's brow furrowed, and he glared at her. "What else have you done that is almost going to get us killed?"

Willow opened her mouth to protest, but Birch cut her off.

"Look," she said.

A group of men wearing jeans and T-shirts like some kind of uniform hurried forward, struggling under the weight of a huge laser drill. "They're going to dig us out."

"Are these terrorists your friends?" Kaiden accused. All the tenderness and concern he had shown earlier were gone. His face was tight with anger.

"I never said they were my friends," Willow said. "But they're necessary if we want to get out of here alive."

"That's proving to be quite the challenge," Kaiden said.

Birch tapped the screen.

"Hey, Flint," she said. Flint jerked and glanced around. So did the others.

"I got eyes on you," Birch said. "You mind giving us a hand? We've got a tiny little problem in here."

Flint grinned. His hair fell into his eyes as his gaze focused on the nano-bot hovering before his face.

"We'll have you out in a jiffy," he said.

CHAPTER EIGHTEEN
TO BE HUMAN

KAIDEN SLUMPED WITH his face pressed against the observation window as the old T-50 Cobra gunship hurtled over the broken, barren landscape. It was a wider and faster gunship than the T-60, but it had fewer armaments. The jagged mountainside raced by, littered with the skeletons of long-dead trees. Nothing green grew there now—just like most of the western half of the continent.

They were flying low, very low. Kaiden knew the terrorists were trying to avoid TAP radar, but he didn't think they could do it. TAP had the most up-to-date technology, most of it designed by their own engineers and scientists, who were supposed to be the best in the world.

Kaiden let his head fall back against the headrest and tried to ignore the newsfeed that babbled in the background. How long would it be before TAP airships attacked them? He kept his rifle across his lap, which was still loaded with tranquilizer rounds. He had been prepared to resist should the terrorists try to disarm them, but no one had said anything. They had rushed to carry Iris away and to extract Hawk's mangled body from the rubble. No one had been able to find anything of Greyson beyond the barrel of his rifle that lay crushed beneath a slab of basalt the size of an airship. It was too big to try moving.

Kaiden shifted his arm and tried to ignore the ache where the piece of metal had ripped his flesh. His throat was still raw from breathing in the dust from the cavern, and his mouth tasted of mold and earth. He glanced around at Birch, Jade, and Willow, who were all covered in the same gray dust.

Willow was curled up on the bench beside him, apparently asleep. Her brown hair draped over her neck. The white skin was so pale and smooth. Scratches on her face were transforming into thin, pink lines as the INCR did its work. Kaiden experienced a sudden surge of warmth for Willow. Even though he knew she had not trusted him enough to tell him about the terrorists, he had to admit he would have been dead already if she hadn't been thinking ahead. For a lab tech, she had handled herself pretty well. He told his team to show initiative, and she had done that, though in the future he would need to make sure she remembered to include him decisions as important as joining forces with terrorists.

Birch fidgeted with her rifle in pensive silence. Jade kept her head bowed but cast him a furtive glance now and again. She seemed to be embarrassed about her show of affection in the cave, but Kaiden hadn't thought it wrong. It had surprised him to find that Jade was vulnerable because she broadcast such a sense of calm self-control. Yet, her hug had been fierce, almost desperate. The memory of it warmed his chest and confused him at the same time. Could he feel affection for two women simultaneously? Should he? He had no experience in such things. It wasn't a part of TAP training protocol. Maybe it was just these confusing bursts of memory that seemed to be wrenching him in two different directions.

It hadn't taken the laser drill long to penetrate the rubble. Kaiden had carried Iris through and handed her to two men who rushed away with her. She had a hole in her chest that was bubbling blood. Kaiden didn't know if the INCR could save her. It hadn't saved Quill from a similar wound. But he needed her to explain why she and Greyson had betrayed them. And why she had kept mumbling something about Noah and promises.

"Okay," Birch said. "I'm going to say what you're all thinking. Greyson and Iris tried to kill us."

Jade raised her eyebrows in agreement, but Kaiden shook his head.

"I don't think that was the idea," he said. When Birch smirked at him, he continued. "They could have just tranquilized us and killed us with ease." He glanced at Jade. Her lips lifted in a smile. She had been the only one of them to have lethal rounds and had shot Iris and Greyson.

"I didn't trust them from the beginning," she said.

"Me neither," Kaiden agreed. "But they thought we all had non-lethal rounds. Iris has the best kill record at TAP, and Greyson was an excellent shot. Together, they could have tranquilized us all in a second if they took us by surprise."

"They blew the exit to close it for the terrorists," Jade said.

"That's what Willow thought," Birch said.

Kaiden glanced at Willow. Curled up like she was, with the dirt clinging to her face and hair, she seemed so vulnerable. He wanted to reach out and brush the hair from her cheek.

But if what she said about her memories was true, she knew far more than she had told them. She had five lifetimes of untampered memories of being inside TAP. He wanted to trust her because she had saved his life, not once but twice, and he knew he no longer had much choice. But she had delivered them into the hands of a bunch of religious fanatics—terrorists who believed that the existence of clones was a sin against God. He couldn't see how this was going to turn out well.

"But who ordered them to do it?" Kaiden asked. "Was it Rio or Noah?" He needed to know who had corrupted members of his crew and how.

The music of the news stream played, and the words *Breaking News* flashed across the screen. Kaiden glanced up at it, half-expecting a news report on their escape from TAP.

"The Destroying Angels strike again," the newscaster said. Kaiden exchanged glances with Jade and Birch as the image on the screen panned over the smoking remains of a mansion. Emergency hover-vehicles floated in the air with their red and blue lights flashing while fire drones poured fountains of water and foam onto the building. The camera zoomed in to show two charred bodies being laid on stretchers.

"Moments after the drone strike," the announcer said, "the Destroying Angels posted the following message on their website. 'You are God's temple, and God's Spirit dwells in you,'" it read. "'If anyone destroys God's temple, God will destroy him. For God's temple is holy, and you are that temple. The holy Sons of God have stretched forth their hands to cleanse the earth of two perversions of God's temple. Justice rained down from the sky on those who would take God's power unto themselves. We have punished Senator Benton Newborn and his wife for using their political connections and vast wealth to create clones of their bodies. Praise be to God.'"

Willow sat up and rubbed at her eyes, smearing the dirt around her face.

"And these are the people you brought us to?" Kaiden asked without any preamble.

Willow glanced up at the screen where the terrorist's message still played as the newscaster described the destruction in detail.

"They want all clones dead," Kaiden said. "You get that, right?"

"The International Confederation of States," the newscaster continued, "denies the existence of any government-funded cloning program and insists that cloning human bodies remains illegal under international law."

"Since when has that stopped anybody?" Jade said.

"It's more complicated than it appears," Willow said.

"Of course it is," Kaiden said. "But I think you owe us an explanation."

Willow scowled. "I was going to tell you, but everything just happened so fast. I was afraid if I told you once everything was in motion, you wouldn't go, and we would have all been trapped." She paused and licked her lips. "There's something else I need to tell you before—"

The door swished open. Kaiden snapped up his rifle, but it was only Flint.

Flint beamed at the sight of them, and he pushed a shock of black hair from his dark face. Sometimes Flint reminded Kaiden so much of Quill. They both loved computers, though Kaiden didn't much like Flint's taste in music.

"Not a bad ship for a bunch of terrorists, eh?" Flint said. Wild punk music played from his wrist terminal. Kaiden would have preferred classical, but if it helped Flint focus, he wouldn't say anything.

"Where have you been?" Kaiden said.

Flint grinned and turned off the music. "I've been playing with terrorist technology," he said. He glanced at Birch and winked before he clicked something on his wrist terminal and scanned the corners of the room. Then he bent forward to whisper to them. "I managed to download most of their onboard database while I was uploading Quill's cloaking software."

"You gave them the software?" Kaiden demanded. "What if we need to hide from them?"

Flint didn't stop smiling. "Shh," he said. "I just disabled the mics and cameras they have in this room, but they could be listening at the door." He glanced at it. "Don't worry about the software. I didn't give them the latest version, and I installed a bug so I can disable it anytime I want."

Kaiden shook his head. "You've got guts," he said.

Flint grinned again. "Better turn things back on before they get suspicious."

"So, how did you hook up with the terrorists?" Kaiden asked. Willow had never explained.

Flint glanced at Willow. "I took a hovercraft to the coordinates Willow gave me, and this old guy in a T-shirt was waiting for me."

"That was risky," Kaiden said to Willow. "They could have just shot him."

"They wouldn't," Willow said, "because my—"

The door opened before she could finish, and Flint jumped as he clicked his wrist terminal again and spun.

Kaiden snapped his rifle up again and found himself staring at a tall, muscular man with white hair in his late-fifties. He wore blue jeans and a white T-shirt just like Hawk had worn. The man's gaze swept over them before it came to rest on Willow. She backed up half a step as the man stepped into the room.

"Hello, Willow," he said.

Kaiden glanced at her. Willow paled and pinched her lips tight. Her eyes were wide with fear.

"Who are you?" Kaiden demanded as he came to his feet.

The man never took his gaze from Willow's face. Kaiden tried to read what was going through the man's mind, but he couldn't.

"It's good to see you," the man said.

Willow swallowed. "Hello, Oakley," she said in a soft voice.

Tears shimmered in her eyes.

Kaiden stared in confusion. How could a clone, who had been locked up in TAP for forty years, know a terrorist? That thought gave him pause. How had she been able to communicate with them from inside TAP? Willow hadn't been lying about one thing at least—she was more than a lab tech.

"How long has it been?" Oakley asked. "Nearly forty years?" His gaze swept over her. "And you don't look a day older."

"I'm sorry," Willow said. "It wasn't what I wanted."

Oakley took two great strides toward Willow, and before Kaiden could so much as point his rifle, Oakley enfolded Willow in an embrace. Willow stiffened for a moment and then melted into his arms and cried.

Kaiden glanced around at the others to find the same shock and incomprehension he felt written on their faces.

Birch shrugged helplessly. "Old boyfriend?" she mouthed.

The awkward silence stretched out for several minutes until Willow started sniffling. She pulled away and gave them a guilty smile. She wiped at the tears, leaving muddy smudges on her cheeks.

Then, she gestured toward Oakley, who stood with an arm around her waist. Kaiden experienced a sudden pang of jealousy, which surprised him.

"This is what I was going to tell you," Willow said. "Oakley is my little brother."

Kaiden gazed up at the tall man.

"Little?" Birch said.

"Younger," Willow corrected.

"And he's a terrorist?" Kaiden said.

Willow glanced up at Oakley. "He's their leader. That's what I was trying to tell you."

The statement hit Kaiden like a punch in the stomach. He dropped into the chair. Now, he understood why Willow had wanted to join the terrorists and why she hadn't told him. She was gambling with their lives so she could reconnect with the life that had been stolen from her.

"You're joking," Flint said.

"All right," Birch said, "let's hear it." She flopped into the chair, folding her legs under her. Jade and Flint sat down, as well.

"There's not much to tell," Willow said. She glanced up at Oakley. "Our father got himself killed in a coup in Africa. Our mother raised us." Her lips trembled, and Oakley squeezed her against him. "The last time I saw Oakley, we were being chased by a hovercraft that crashed into us. I fell, and I never saw Oakley again." She bit her lip. "I was dead. Harvested by TAP."

"They tried to tell us that the hovercraft was just malfunctioning," Oakley said, "but I knew better. I was there."

"What are you saying?" Jade asked.

"She was targeted for harvesting," Oakley said. "I figured it out and tried to get her out of there. But I failed."

They stared at him in silence, waiting for him to explain.

Willow picked up the story when Oakley remained silent, the muscles working in his jaw.

"TAP has been harvesting the most gifted children for decades," she said.

"Harvesting?" Birch asked.

"That's what the leadership calls it," Oakley said. "They harvest your DNA and your memories before they clone you."

Flint scowled at them. "You mean they killed us so they could clone us?"

Willow and Oakley both nodded.

"That doesn't make any sense," Flint said. "There's no need to kill someone to take their DNA."

"So what?" Jade cut in.

Willow glared at her. She didn't like Jade. That was plain enough.

"So," Willow said with measured calm, "they murdered us to steal our genetic and psychological identities so they could use us as lab rats in their search for the perfect clone."

"I get that," Jade said. "I don't like their methods either, but cloning may be the only way to save humanity from this mess we live in."

"I'm with Jade on this one," Flint said. "Look at what natural humans have done to the planet and to each other. I've been in the megacities. Those natural humans are more like animals than humans."

"Exactly," Willow said. "So why not take all the money TAP wastes on clones and put it to better use?" Her face flushed pink.

Instead of wasting money on all this research, why not try to clean up the planet and make it livable and equitable for the humans who inhabit it? Why not pay for birth control and medical facilities? Why not set up micro-ecosystems on earth where they could rejuvenate our world and feed our people instead of running to the stars where we know humans can't live?"

"I don't think we know that," Jade said. "And you still haven't answered my question. If we can help humanity by making genetically modified humans who will take better care of the earth and be able to thrive in space, don't we have a moral obligation to do it? Isn't the sacrifice of a few kids worth it?"

Oakley scowled, and the muscles in his jaw twitched.

"Sacrifice?" Willow snapped. She stepped toward Jade, but Jade wasn't intimidated. "Let's talk about the costs. Robbing people of their right to die with dignity. Trapping them in a perpetual existence as lab rats. Murdering promising children simply to rip their minds from them and then clone them—without permission—only to use them as a slave labor force and an armed militia to attack natural-born humans. Murdering a sentient human being that feels the drive to survive and that is conscious of being murdered just so they can run experiments on them."

Willow wiped savagely at the tears spilling down her face, smearing mud everywhere. She glared at Jade. "Only a vicious amoral being could sanction such a program."

"She has a point," Flint said.

"Look," Jade said, "I'm not saying it's morally unambiguous, or even right, but we're talking about the survival of our species here. Is it better to treat a handful of people as you describe, which I admit is horrible, or force billions of humans to a slow death on a dying planet? If science has found a way to save humanity when religion and politics haven't, why not take it?"

"Because," Birch said, "it'll probably fail. Cloning makes identical copies of the DNA, which destroys genetic diversity. If something happened and only clones were left, we might not have the diversity necessary to permit long-term survival. Cloning could doom humanity if it became too widespread."

Jade considered. "That's a better argument than the one the terrorists use. But even that doesn't work. Look at us. It's clear TAP has been harvesting clones from every ethnic group."

Oakley shifted. "To those who believe in a god, cloning is sacrilegious."

"That's a lame argument," Flint said. "It might work on your ignorant recruits, but it won't work on us. Besides, Buddhists aren't opposed to cloning. Neither are most Hindus. It's only some monotheistic religions that oppose it."

Oakley scowled at Flint. "You scoff at religion, but a person's religious beliefs aren't any less significant than your scientific ones. Cloning meddles with the balance of nature. It assumes that humans know everything there is to know about the generation of life. It's a perversion of the natural world."

"I'm not scoffing at religion," Flint said. "But that doesn't make any sense, either. Clones aren't any more a perversion than a twin is. Twins are clones of each other."

Willow gave Oakley a nervous glance as if she was anxious not to offend him. "Um," she began, "Flint is right. Cloning is a form of asexual reproduction that is quite common in nature. Some fish, lizards, such as the Kimono Dragon, insects, like bees and aphids, and some frogs engage in parthenogenesis. Some call it *virgin birth*. But all it means is that the female egg develops into a fully formed individual without fertilization. The offspring is effectively a genetic clone."

"You see?" Flint said.

Oakley didn't respond immediately. A war seemed to be raging within him. Kaiden decided then and there that he didn't like Oakley. He seemed duplicitous, scheming. He wasn't putting up a good defense of his position.

"Even if God chose to allow some creatures to reproduce asexually," Oakley said, "he clearly never intended that for humans. As all of you should be keenly aware, artificial cloning of social animals, like humans, can only cause intense personal suffering and emotional and psychological dislocation." Oakley gazed directly at Willow. "We were created, or evolved, if you like, to be born into families. We need to be tied to other human beings who share our genetic heritage."

"He does have a point," Birch said. "I mean, I'm all right, but the rest of you are really messed up."

Flint chuckled, and Kaiden smiled despite himself. "What about orphans and adopted kids?" he said. "Are you saying they can't have fulfilling lives unless they're with their biological kin?"

"And what about marriage?" Flint said. "Married couples aren't genetically related, and they can live happily together."

Jade shifted in her seat. "I would think," she said, "that after all of these years, you would have better arguments. Your entire position is hypocritical. Here you are accusing TAP of playing God by deciding who lives and who dies when you're doing the same thing." She pointed to the screen where the newsfeed continued to play. "Murdering clones, or people you suspect as being clones, isn't any better. What do your recruits do when they figure out you're a hypocrite?"

"We vet them carefully," Oakley said. "You may not like our religious arguments, but you can't deny that stopping an evil like TAP is a good thing. Spending billions of dollars to replace humanity with experimental clones is short-sighted and dangerous, especially when they may not be able to survive. Shouldn't we save the genetic heritage evolution has left us?"

"Sure," Jade said. "I agree with you on both points, but it isn't like TAP is trying to replace natural humans. It's just trying to make humans who are better adapted to living on other planets."

"That's the official line," Oakley said. He reclined on one of the round, padded chairs. "We think they're planning to replace natural humans with a genetically modified population they can control."

"That's a wild conspiracy theory," Jade said. "And we are proof that TAP can't control its clones."

"You want to talk about the discipline?" Oakley asked.

"How do you know about that?" Flint demanded.

Oakley traced the length of his rifle with a finger. "We know a lot more than you might think, and I suspect a lot more than you know yourselves."

"For worrying so much about money being ill-spent," Jade said, "you seem to be pretty well-funded."

"We have to fight an organization like TAP," Oakley said. "Besides, there are people who value human life and who are willing to pay to protect it."

"What do they get for their investment?" Flint said.

Oakley shifted.

"I see," Birch said. "He's selling the technology he steals from TAP."

"So much for the moral high ground," Flint said.

Oakley cracked his knuckles. "Sometimes you have to fight fire with fire."

"All right," Kaiden said. "We're not going to agree on this. To me, it's about my right to choose who and what I am. That right was stolen from me. I don't really care about the scientific or religious arguments. I care about not knowing who I am. I care about the family I can barely remember."

"If TAP hadn't uploaded your memories," Jade said, "but had simply cloned you and let you grow up a different person entirely, would you have a problem with it?"

Kaiden considered. That thought had never occurred to him. He shook his head. "With cloning itself? No. But with creating a secret army populated by clones of people who had no choice in the matter and then sabotaging their identities by stealing their memories? Yes."

"That's what Willow and I have been trying to say," Oakley said.

"Well," Birch said, "as interesting as this little discussion has been, we still don't have any idea what we're going to do next."

"TAP will be tracking us," Jade said.

"Nah," Flint said. "I disabled the discipline switch and tracking chip, and we have new WTs, so they can't use those."

Kaiden appraised Flint. "I was disciplined back in the elevator shaft," he said, "after you say you disabled it."

But Flint was already shaking his head. "I was just running interference then," he said. "But I got a better read on it from Oakley, and I think I have it disabled for now."

That would explain why Kaiden hadn't had any more disciplinary episodes. Flint was more talented than Kaiden had thought.

"But that doesn't explain why I was disciplined, and none of the rest of you were."

Willow clicked her tongue in annoyance. "You did just defy a direct order from Noah and then helped us escape."

"I'll make you a deal," Oakley said. "I'll help you remove your switches and the controls in return for your assistance."

Kaiden glanced at Oakley while the others considered his words in silence. Was the man boasting? Could he really do something like that?

"You know how to do that?" Jade asked.

Oakley raised an eyebrow. "We haven't done it yet, but we think we know how."

"Wait a minute," Flint said. "How have you been infiltrating TAP?"

"Raven," Kaiden said.

Oakley gazed at him without expression.

"You sent Raven," Kaiden said.

Oakley cast him a wicked grin. "We captured her while she was on a secret assignment, one not even you knew about," he said. "We gave her a few new memories along with a mission to kill the clones."

"She tried to kill us!" Kaiden shouted, lunging to his feet. "She slaughtered half my team."

"I'm sorry about your friends," Oakley said, "but we couldn't leave anyone alive to give us away. Not if we could help it." He glanced at Willow. "I didn't know Willow would be on that mission."

"Okay, man," Birch said. "Your whole position is screwed up. You don't mind slaughtering clones who had no choice in the matter, but you would make an exception for the clone of your sister?"

"Even terrorists have feelings," Oakley said.

Kaiden blew out his air in disgust. Oakley's position was more than hypocritical. It was self-serving in the worst possible way. Kaiden didn't want to have anything to do with these terrorists, but if he was going to survive, he would need to have the discipline switch and tracking controls removed, and if they could write new memories, maybe they could help him recover his.

"What do you want in return?" Kaiden asked.

"Kaiden," Jade warned.

He raised his hand. "Just a minute. I want to hear what he has to say."

Oakley smiled at Kaiden, making the age lines crinkle at the side of his eyes and mouth. "I want to infiltrate TAP and bring it down."
"I want to destroy their operation."

"That's a tall order," Birch said. "TAP is huge. There's no way a terrorist organization is going to do it. You would need a massive army with an armada of airships that could assault every TAP installation simultaneously."

"No," Oakley smirked, "all I need to do is kill Noah and corrupt or delete their databases. The whole system will come crashing down."

"Impossible," Flint said.

Oakley considered them. "Not if I have your help."

CHAPTER NINETEEN
THE IRIS WILTS

KAIDEN LET THE DARKNESS wrap itself around him while one of Mozart's string quartets filled the room with music. He settled into a corner with his back against the cool wall of his room in the terrorists' base. The base was an old hospital in some abandoned city in the heart of the Rocky Mountains. Hospital rooms had been haphazardly repurposed as sleeping quarters. The room had a single bed, a round side table with two chairs, a sink, and a bathroom with a shower off to one side. A single window overlooked an empty parking lot where camouflaged shelters had been erected to hide the terrorist airships. Kaiden had drawn the curtain so he could be alone in the dark.

The journey to the base had occupied much of the day. The airship flew at low altitudes and made several detours to ensure they weren't being tracked. Kaiden didn't know where he was, and, right now, he didn't care. Iris was still in critical condition, and Kaiden couldn't shake the feeling that there was more going on with her and Greyson than met the eye.

Greyson and Iris had received orders to check on a body and then had appeared at the elevator. Why weren't they still dealing with the body found in the Genesis Room? Greyson had said, "Yes, sir." So Rio must have called them away and given them new orders. Maybe it was simple team loyalty, but Greyson had been chafing for months under Kaiden's leadership. It was unlikely he would have agreed to help Kaiden unless he stood to gain something by it. Iris hadn't awakened yet, and until she did, he wouldn't be able to get any answers.

This and his uncertainty about Oakley and Willow and the nature of their rekindled relationship had kept him from giving Oakley a straight answer about the removal of the discipline switch and tracking device. Oakley and Willow had not told them everything. He suppressed the sudden surge of rage and a sense of betrayal. What was Willow playing at? Not only had Greyson betrayed him, but Willow had manipulated him and his team into coming to her brother—the terrorist leader. There were too many agendas even among his own group for him to have any confidence that they would all play the parts they had agreed to play. Every time he let himself relax, something went wrong.

Still, what choice did he have? There was nowhere he could hide from TAP with the tracking controls and the discipline switch embedded in his body. The image of his mother's face flashed through his mind. A deep longing, like he had experienced in his dreams, filled him. It was maddening to have these feelings and this knowledge without being able to put it all into context—to fill in the holes. What had happened to her? Where was his father? Had he loved his father? Had his mother and father loved him? What would they think of what he had done, of what he had become? Unless he could recover the lost fragments of his pre-clone identity, it would torture him for the rest of his life.

A knock sounded on his door.

"Come," he said.

He straightened and laid a hand on his pistol. But when the door opened, Jade stood there with the light from the corridor framing her slender figure against the darkness of his room. Jade had bathed, and her still-damp, black hair clung to her neck. She brushed it away and smiled at him as she stepped through the door. She had changed out of her soiled uniform into a T-shirt and jeans. Kaiden cringed at the thought of her being dressed like a terrorist.

"Do you usually sit around in the dark, listening to classical music?" Jade asked.

"Only when it's necessary," Kaiden said.

The door closed, and Jade flipped on the light. Kaiden blinked up at her until his eyes adjusted.

"I thought you might like some company," she said.

Kaiden gestured for her to sit down. She leaned against the wall and slid down beside him. "You know what those chairs are for, don't you?" she said.

Kaiden sniffed. "They aren't as comfortable."

Jade pulled her knees up and hugged them. "Your room looks about like mine."

"Yeah," Kaiden sighed. "What do you think we should do?"

"Do we have a choice?"

Kaiden considered her. She had never said exactly why she joined them except that she didn't want to be alone, and she had argued forcefully in favor of cloning.

"Beyond self-preservation, why are you so willing to accept clones?"

Jade smiled, and two dimples formed just beneath her high cheekbones. "You've been dying to ask me that, haven't you?"

"Just trying to understand."

Jade's smile faded. "I keep having these dreams. My grandfather comes to me and tells me that my people have finally lost all of our homelands. Our once beautiful mountains have become wastelands. Now, we must seek a new home in the stars. We must travel up the way our ancestors did into a new land."

"Then why join us?"

Jade sniffed. "I've been sent on many so-called 'extractions' of political figures. But they weren't extractions. They were political assassinations. Why are we acting like terrorists and lying about what we're doing? Why not tell people the truth that we can clone humans better adapted to survival in space? We've ruined this planet, and I don't know if it can be saved. We might have to find another one. I don't like lies or the murder of innocent children to do it. I have long had a feeling that TAP is up to something bigger, more frightening."

"You argued pretty forcefully in favor of cloning with Oakley."

Jade blew out her breath. "He's a hypocrite, and he knows it. Murdering suspected clones to stop TAP from harvesting? He's no better than they are. He just likes to hide behind his religious platitudes."

"So religion is irrelevant?"

"I didn't say that," Jade said. "Religion is important to me and to a lot of people, but it shouldn't be used to persuade people to engage in acts of evil. It should be about nurturing and brotherhood. It should help us learn to live together peacefully."

Kaiden considered Jade with renewed respect. She thought deeply about things, and she had a profoundly moral stance. He liked that. He found that he felt comfortable talking to her, more comfortable even than Birch or Willow.

"So, should we help the terrorists destroy TAP?" Kaiden asked.

Jade bowed her head. "I don't know. It seems like such a waste, but if they really intend to murder billions of innocent people, we might have to."

"If we don't," Kaiden said, "then TAP will eventually kill us—again."

"What if the terrorists decide to kill us all anyway?" Jade asked.

"That's a risk," Kaiden agreed. "But if we don't help them, we're still going to die. Either they'll overwhelm us, or TAP will find us."

"We might be able to survive."

"How?"

Jade stared at the wall and shook her head. "I don't know." Then she turned to look at him. "I think we need each other."

"She's dead," Willow said without any preamble.

Kaiden glanced up at her. Like the rest of the team, she had changed into jeans and a T-shirt. They drew less attention that way, though he had noted the sullen glares and hostile whispering among the terrorists. He and Jade had just sat down to breakfast at a table in the cafeteria of the old hospital.

The small room with a low ceiling was filled with round tables and a self-serve line. Low-hanging lights lit the area with a dull, yellow glow. The fluorescent light fixtures looked like they were leftovers from the last century. They sat alone, but dozens of terrorists filled the chairs at the other tables, casting them sideways glances and whispering in close huddles.

Kaiden bowed his head. He wasn't surprised that Iris was dead. The INCR hadn't been able to save Quill or Burl. Why should it save Iris?

"No great loss," Jade said. She shoved a spoonful of artificial eggs into her mouth and grimaced.

"Maybe not," Willow said. "But now, we'll never know what she and Greyson were up to."

"You think she would have told us?" Kaiden asked.

"I don't know," Willow said, "but you mentioned that she was mumbling the name Noah. The order must have come from the top. Maybe Noah realized we had a way out, and he wanted it sealed. After they blew it up, Greyson and Iris were going to arrest us and take us back."

"Like that would have worked," Jade mumbled from around a mouth full of scrambled eggs. "These eggs taste terrible."

Birch joined them and sat beside Jade. Her light brown hair was pulled back in a ponytail. "Did any of you have hot water in your rooms?" she asked. "And they could use some sanitation-bots." When no one spoke, she glanced around at them. "What?" she said.

"Iris didn't make it," Kaiden said.

Birch considered. "Good rider," she said. "She was always thorny."

Kaiden raised his eyebrows at her odd wording.

Jade shook her head. "You mean good riddance," she said. "And I believe the other word you wanted was prickly."

Birch grunted over her mouthful of toast and shrugged away Jade's corrections.

Kaiden wondered if the speech center of Birch's brain had been damaged when they uploaded her memories. Willow smiled at him, but he didn't smile back. He still hadn't unraveled his confused feelings about her. He was drawn to her in a way he had never been drawn to another woman, except maybe Jade, and yet he was afraid to trust her fully.

"Anyway," Willow said, "we still have to decide if we're going to accept Oakley's offer."

"Do we have a choice?" Jade said. She glanced at Kaiden.

Kaiden stuffed something that resembled a sausage into his mouth to avoid answering the question. The sausage had a sharp, unpleasant flavor. He wondered what was in it.

"I don't think we do," Birch said.

Kaiden swallowed and nodded. "I'm getting the switch removed first."

The others stopped eating.

"I'm not letting any of you do it, until I make sure it's safe," Kaiden said. "I got us into this mess. If anyone is going to die with the experimental operation, it's going to me."

"Kaiden," Willow began to protest, but a large man with short-cropped hair strode past their table and bumped Kaiden's arm.

When Kaiden glanced up at him, he found the man scowling down at him. Kaiden tried to ignore him, but soon several men and women in white T-shirts had gathered. Kaiden rose to face the man. Jade and Birch followed his example.

Kaiden studied his opponent. He didn't need any trouble at the moment, not with a room full of clone-hating terrorists.

The man glanced down at Kaiden's forearm, and Kaiden realized that the TAP tattoo had attracted their attention. The man sneered.

"You don't belong here, freak."

Kaiden said nothing, but he noted the way the rest of the group spread out, preparing for a fight. He thought of drawing his sidearm but decided that killing terrorists in their own base wouldn't be a good idea.

He glanced at Jade and Birch. They were ready. The burly man reached out to shove Kaiden, but Kaiden intercepted the man's fingers, bent them back and down, and held him there. The man tried to twist away from the pain, but Kaiden swung his leg over the man's head, kicked him in the face with his heel, and sat on his arm. The man cried out as he slammed into the chair with a clatter and then onto the floor.

Jade and Birch jumped to cover him with kitchen knives in hand as the others surged forward. The crowd paused.

"That's enough," a voice rang out in the cafeteria. Oakley strode up to them.

"Let him up," he said to Kaiden.

Kaiden considered breaking the man's arm but decided against it. He rose and stepped out of the man's reach.

"Get up, Klinton," Oakley ordered.

The man rose to his feet with a surly expression. Blood dripped from his nose. He glared at Kaiden.

"Get out of here," Oakley said.

"They're clones," Klinton grumbled. He pointed to the tattoo on Kaiden's arm.

"That's none of your concern," Oakley said. "Get out before I change my mind."

Klinton grunted and pushed his way through the crowd. Oakley waited until the crowd dispersed.

"I'll ask you not to rough up my fighters," Oakley said to Kaiden.

"Then you had better keep a tighter leash on them," Kaiden said.

Oakley scowled. "Do you have an answer for me?" he said.

"Yes," Kaiden said. "I'll go first."

CHAPTER TWENTY
TRIGGERS AND SWITCHES

"YOU NEED TO understand the risks," Oakley said.

Kaiden stretched himself out on the cold, aluminum table in the medical lab. The walls were bright white. The hum of medical equipment filled the air, which smelled of plastic and antiseptic. Willow hovered over him protectively, while Oakley loomed behind her. A physician and several white-gowned assistants busied themselves by hooking Kaiden up to monitors and strapping him to the table. The rest of his team had gathered on the other side of the observation window to watch the procedure. Kaiden noticed that Jade and Birch both carried their rifles as if they expected trouble. A surgical-bot hummed overhead.

"The nano-imager," Oakley explained, "shows several chips attached to the tattoo on your arm." Oakley pointed to a screen where the tiny structures below Kaiden's skin could be seen. "We've seen this in all the clones we've examined, and we think it's the trigger to the discipline episodes. If we can cut it out, we should be able to stop them."

"Risks?" Kaiden asked.

Oakley raised a bushy eyebrow. "Coma, paralysis, death."

"Very nice," Kaiden said.

Willow patted his arm. "Don't worry. I've got you." She smiled at him.

Kaiden grabbed her hand and drew her close. "If anything happens to me," he whispered, "don't trust Oakley, and, please, save my team."

Willow's brow wrinkled, and she glanced at Oakley. She squeezed Kaiden's hand. "I will."

Kaiden released her and turned to Oakley. "You've given me your oath that all you want is to kill Noah and destroy the TAP operating software."

"You have my word."

"You promise that you won't go in there and start killing every clone you see?"

"My word."

Kaiden locked his gaze with Oakley's as the surgical-bot maneuvered and descended toward Kaiden's arm. He knew he was taking a risk, but he couldn't allow TAP to keep this nano-leash on him, or he would never be able to discover who he was. He would never be free. But he wasn't going to trust Oakley—ever.

"Hold still," the physician said. Kaiden felt the stab of pain as he injected Kaiden with a local anesthetic at the site of the tattoo. "That should dull most of the pain," the physician said and nodded to his assistant.

The surgical-bot hummed as a blue light throbbed inside it. The blue laser flashed. It felt like ice and fire stabbing into Kaiden's arm. He tried not to flinch.

"The switch is located in the dermis," the doctor said, "so we're going to cut just beneath it and remove the dermis intact."

"Do it," Kaiden said.

"Here goes," Willow said.

The robot hummed again and then sizzled in a flash of blinding blue light. Pain surged up Kaiden's arm through the back of his neck and exploded into his brain. Terror constricted his throat. He couldn't breathe. He couldn't move as the discipline pierced his brain.

A monster spider landed on his chest and sank its fangs into his throat. The brightly lit surgical room blinked and plunged into darkness. Kaiden floated in a weightless nothingness. He opened his eyes, and everything was blue and wet. He tried to breathe but fluid-filled his lungs. He coughed and flailed about. His head emerged into a brilliant yellow light. Someone squealed with laughter, and he spun around, treading water to find a beautiful black girl clapping her hands. A large black man picked her up. "Catch," he said. And he launched her toward Kaiden. The girl squealed in delight as she flew through the air and plunged into the water, and Kaiden submerged to catch her and drag her to the surface. The girl clung to his neck, coughed, and then giggled.

"Do it again," she said. "Again."

Kaiden groaned. The vivid memory, with its powerful emotions, faded. His head ached. A finger caressed his cheek, and he blinked at the light. He was still in the operating room with its white walls and antiseptic smell.

"That didn't work," Willow said as she peered down at him. "Apparently, the switch can protect itself."

"What happened?"

"Well," she said, "the trigger has an old cloaking software that interrupted the nano-imager the first time we used it. Flint disabled it, and we found that the tattoos on your arm and on your neck are connected under the skin by nano-hairs that tie into your central nervous system and your brain. The tattoos on your neck are connected to nano-chips that attach to your spinal cord with nano-wires, and a thicker cord penetrates the left side of your brain, which must be where the discipline switch is. We were lucky to save you."

She laid a hand on his arm. Her hand was cool and smooth. He read the concern and tenderness in her gaze. It touched him. She had been worried about him.

"So, the tattoos have a kill switch?" Kaiden asked.

"Looks like it."

"So, what now?"

"I've been thinking about that while you slept," Willow said. "We could try to temporarily disable the two switches with a focused electromagnetic pulse. Then, if we set up two surgical-bots to remove both switches simultaneously, it could work."

"Let's do it," Kaiden said. He closed his eyes and massaged his temples. His head felt like it would explode.

"This could kill you," Willow said.

"Do it anyway," Kaiden murmured without opening his eyes. When she didn't say anything, he glanced at her.

Willow leaned back in her chair and gaped at him. "Do you have a death wish?"

"I want my freedom," Kaiden said. "Then, I want to get my

memories back from TAP."

Willow shifted and glanced at the door.

"What?" Kaiden asked.

Willow avoided his gaze. "I actually have them," she said.

"What?" Kaiden tried to sit up, but a wave of nausea and stabbing pain in his head made him lie back down.

Willow placed a cool hand on his bare chest and smiled. "I found and pulled your memories from TAP's files just before we left." "I didn't think we would be able to go back, and you were so driven to get your memories, I…"

Kaiden grabbed her hand. "Do you know how to upload them?" The excitement of knowing that he might be able to untangle this confusion of fragmented memories surged through him.

Willow shrugged, but left her hand in his. "I designed the procedure," she said, "but what do you think this is going to get you?"

"My memories. My identity." Kaiden couldn't see why this was so hard for her to understand.

Willow withdrew her hand. "That body is dead, Kaiden. The body those memories belonged to doesn't exist anymore."

Kaiden grabbed his aching head with his hands. "I want to know who I am," he moaned.

"Who you are?" Willow lunged to her feet. The sound of the chair scooting backward echoed off the sterile white walls. "You're a clone," she insisted. "You're a clone who works for TAP, which has been using you as a scientific experiment. That's who you are."

Kaiden jerked his hands away from his face. "No," he said. "I was born with a family. I had a mother. I had a father. I had a sister. I want to know who they are."

Willow threw up her hands. "They're dead, too!" she yelled.

Kaiden glared at her. "*You* remember," he accused.

"Yes, I do," Willow said. "And I wish I didn't."

Kaiden snorted. "Easy to say when you don't have to wonder who and what you were."

Willow shook her head. "You don't have any idea what it's like."

"I could say the same thing to you," Kaiden said.

Willow paced. "It doesn't matter anyway," she said, "because we don't have the equipment here. We would have to get back into TAP and…"

"No, you don't." Oakley's voice came from the doorway.

Kaiden jerked his head around as Willow spun.

Oakley leaned against the doorway with his arms folded. "We have the technology here," he said. "It's an older version of what TAP uses now, but it works."

"How do you know it works?" Kaiden asked, suddenly suspicious.

Oakley stepped toward them. "Because we've used it before."

"On Raven?" Kaiden wanted to throw something at him.

"Yes." Oakley stopped by Willow's side.

"Why doesn't that surprise me?" Kaiden said.

Oakley stuffed his hands in the pockets of his jeans. "I'll let you use it *if* you survive Willow's little experiment with the switches."

Kaiden studied him. Oakley was up to something. He wouldn't offer to let them restore his memories unless he expected to gain something from it. But Kaiden was feeling reckless. "All right," he said. "Let's give it a whirl."

"Ready?" Willow asked.

"Yep," Kaiden said.

Willow studied him. He lay on his stomach with his shirt off. Black straps bound him securely to the operating table. His dark brown skin was taut and smooth. She had always liked the look of him. He was lean and well-muscled, with a few dark scars crossing his back. The blue wedged-shaped tattoos at the base of his neck showed where the nano-hairs reached out to encircle his spine and pierce his brain. The wires were attached to the tattoo in a way that meant they would have to cut the skin away to remove the wires.

A nervous flutter rippled through her stomach. If anything went wrong, Kaiden could die, and his death would be her fault. She had started him down this path. She was trusting Oakley and his surgical-bots with Kaiden's life. She licked her lips with a dry tongue. She would never forgive herself if he died.

The medical equipment hovered over him with its blinking

lights. They had to test the electromagnetic pulse before they could try to operate, but she was far from confident that it would work. She suppressed her doubts and touched the pad. The focused electromagnetic pulse discharged into Kaiden's arm and neck. He jerked, cried out, and thrashed on the table for a moment with an expression of the utmost horror on his face. Then, he lay still—utterly still.

His heart rhythm ceased, and the monitor flat-lined with a steady tone. Willow and the other medical staff swooped down on him with drugs and monitors. They rolled him onto his back. No heartbeat. No brain activity. No breathing. He was dead.

"No," Willow whispered.

"Oxygen!" the head doctor called. An assistant injected the oxygenated microparticle solution directly into the IV in Kaiden's arm.

"Defibrillator," the doctor called.

As the staff rushed to comply, Willow grabbed Kaiden's hand.

"He's been injected with INCR," she said.

"That should help," the doctor said. "Stand clear."

Willow dropped Kaiden's hand, and the doctor pressed the button. Kaiden jerked as the electricity entered his body from the defibrillator machine. He sucked in a deep breath and opened his eyes. He scowled and blinked at the pain in his head.

"Dang," he said. "That hurt."

Willow squeezed his hand, hoping he didn't see the terror in her expression or the unshed tears that burned her eyes. She had almost lost him.

"Did it work?" he asked.

Willow pursed her lips. "We managed to disable the discipline temporarily, but when it shuts down, it kills you," she said.

Kaiden blinked. "But you brought me back? How long was I out?"

"Only a few seconds."

"Let's get them out then."

"I don't think we should risk it," Willow said. "We have it disabled for now."

Kaiden snorted. "Until TAP figures out we're doing it and finds a way around it. No, I want this thing out of my head."

"We might not be able to revive you again." Willow's face darkened, and she studied him with an intensity that surprised him.

Kaiden gave her a wry smile. "I'm just a clone," he said. "You said so yourself. I've already died several times."

"That's not funny," Willow said. She stepped away from him. It was her fault he was acting this way. She was the one who had convinced him being cloned against their will was wrong. She had been the one to show him the casual, brutal way TAP treated them.

"Just do it," Kaiden said. "We have to experiment on someone."

Willow took a deep breath to steady her nerves. She glanced at the doctor.

"What do you think?" she asked.

The doctor rubbed his chin. "It might work, but—"

"Just do it," Kaiden said again.

The doctor shrugged, but Willow noticed the curious excitement he couldn't hide. He probably didn't care whether Kaiden lived or died. He just wanted to see if they could do it. Willow wondered for a moment if the physician was under orders from Oakley to figure this out so he could capture clones and send them back to infiltrate TAP. Or worse, to kill Kaiden and make it look like an accident.

"This time," the doctor said, "we're going to sedate you."

Willow hovered nearby as the team prepared Kaiden for the surgery. What if they had missed something? What if another defensive system existed? Kaiden glanced over at her and smiled before he closed his eyes. How could he trust her after everything she'd done? If he knew the secrets she was keeping from him, he would never forgive her. She longed to tell him, but it was too dangerous. She couldn't risk losing him. Besides, she wasn't certain yet. There was so much she still didn't know.

The doctor positioned the surgical-bots and stepped back from the table.

"We're only going to have about thirty seconds, I think," Willow said.

The doctor checked Kaiden's vital signs. "He's good," he said.

"One," Willow counted, "two, three." She touched the screen. Kaiden jerked on the table and thrashed against the constraints. An arm slipped free of the straps and knocked one of the surgical-bots aside. An aide scurried to reposition it. Kaiden fell limp.

"Now!" Willow shouted.

The bots whirred into motion. The blue lasers sliced into Kaiden's dark skin. Acrid smoke rose from the burning flesh. The synchronized bots ripped the flesh free, dragging the nano-wires with them at the same instant. Kaiden jerked again.

"Oxygen," the doctor called. "Defibrillator."

Kaiden's body remained limp.

"More oxygen."

Willow glanced at the monitor. No pulse. No breathing. No brain activity. Only the steady heartrending tone from the machines indicating a life had been snuffed out. She backed away in horror. She had killed Kaiden.

CHAPTER TWENTY-ONE
RESTORATION

KAIDEN'S MOTHER GLARED *at him. Her straight, black hair framed her smooth, chocolate-colored face and stood out against her white lab coat. Her lips were unnaturally red—the color of blood.*

"Where have you been?" she demanded.

Kaiden rolled his eyes and smirked.

"Since when do you care?" He wanted to hurt her. "The only thing you love anymore is your new, classified operation."

"That's not true, and you know it," she said. "If you don't shape up, they're going to throw you out of the academy."

"I don't care about the academy!" Kaiden yelled. "I want my sister back." He knew what he said wasn't entirely true. He did care about the academy. He had always wanted to be a scientist, but after Rose's death, he couldn't concentrate. It all seemed so useless when everyone you loved could disappear in one heartbeat, and all the science in the world couldn't stop it. And his mother had failed him. She had let his sister die.

"You actually went to an anti-clone rally?" she demanded.

"All that money we waste on cloning could have been used to save Rose," Kaiden snapped. "But you wouldn't care about that."

His mother pinched her lips tight, and this time he saw the mist of tears in her eyes. He sneered in satisfaction. He had finally managed to make her feel something of what she had done.

She gripped the edge of the desk. "I'm withdrawing you from the academy

161

myself," she said.

"Fine."

"You can waste your life chasing conspiracy theories," his mother said, "and blaming me for things I couldn't control. But it's your life to waste."

The memory faded, and Kaiden blinked at the blare of bright lights. A metallic taste filled his mouth, and the room smelled of sanitized metal and plastic. The lingering aroma of burnt flesh made him wrinkle his nose.

"Feeling better?" Oakley's deep voice filled the room.

Kaiden rolled his head to the side to find Oakley lounging in a chair, studying him. His white hair fell into his eyes. Willow lingered behind him as if unwilling to approach Kaiden.

"A bit," Kaiden said.

"You're lucky to be alive," Oakley said.

"Yeah, thanks."

"Don't thank me. Thank Willow. She wouldn't let them give up."

Kaiden looked past Oakley to Willow. She gave him a weary smile and folded her arms.

"I know who you are," Oakley said.

"What?"

"I know who you are," he repeated. "They haven't erased *my* memories."

Kaiden knit his brows together. Why was Oakley telling him this?

"Well, that gives you the advantage," he said.

Oakley smirked. "I thought you would be interested."

"I would be if I thought you would tell me the truth."

"Suit yourself," Oakley said. "But if you restore your memories, you might not like what you find."

"So, you can manipulate memories just like TAP?" Kaiden asked.

"Not as well, but we can do it."

"Sounds hypocritical to me," Kaiden said. "If you hate TAP so much, why do what they do?"

"Sometimes you have to fight fire with fire," Oakley said. "Sometimes, you have to embrace evil to destroy it."

Kaiden sneered at him. "What's that supposed to mean? Sounds like a lame excuse to be just as evil as TAP."

Oakley raised his bushy, white eyebrows. Kaiden knew what it meant. It meant that the terrorists had been stealing clones and messing with their memories. They had done this to Raven and turned her into a sleeping cell, just waiting for the opportunity to strike.

"How many others do you have inside TAP?" Kaiden asked.

"A few."

The door burst open, and Flint, Jade, and Birch rushed in.

"What's he doing here?" Jade snapped. She still had her rifle, and she raised it toward Oakley.

"Relax." Oakley waved a hand at them. "If I wanted to hurt him, you couldn't stop me."

"Wanna bet?" Jade said.

Flint rushed past her. "Hey, man," he said to Kaiden with a grin.

"You look wretched," Birch said.

Jade slipped by Oakley with a glare and came around the other side of the bed. "How are you?"

Willow stayed back as the others approached.

"Well, that was easy," Kaiden said. "Who's next?"

They all glanced at each other.

"You do realize," Flint said, "that you died, like three times?"

"I'll be next," Willow said.

Kaiden glanced at her. She still had a guilty expression on her face.

"I should have gone first, anyway," she said.

"Actually," Kaiden said, "before you do it, can we recover my memories?"

He didn't want to say it, but if Willow didn't survive the operation, he wouldn't be able to recover his memories. He wasn't about to let Oakley do it.

Willow scowled. "That's all you want me for?"

Jade glared at her. "You're the only one who knows how to do it."

"All right," Willow said. "But I already warned you. You may not like what you remember."

"Oh, he won't," Oakley said and gave Kaiden a big grin of satisfaction.

Willow peeked over a counter full of computers and medical equipment to where Kaiden lay with his head inside the scanner. She had already sedated him so he wouldn't be awake to feel the memories upload.

She knew from experience how awful it could be. The others hadn't arrived yet. She was alone with Kaiden in the room. Willow touched the holographic screen and then checked the monitors. Kaiden's brain activity was normal. She could do it now before anyone knew.

Kaiden had made her promise not to let Oakley or any of the terrorist staff work on him. But she wasn't naïve enough to believe that Oakley's staff couldn't manipulate the equipment without her knowledge. They might even try to make Kaiden a weapon like they had Raven. And she wouldn't let them do it.

She had had time to examine the files she downloaded before they escaped TAP and discussed the matter with Oakley. He had been cagey about exactly what he knew, but Willow now understood why Kaiden was so important.

When Kaiden found out what Willow knew, he might want to restore his memories to what they were now. He might not want to remember. She didn't know if these older memories would completely overwrite the others or not. It was best to be prepared just in case.

Willow touched the screen again, and the scanner hummed. The upload initiated, and Kaiden's memories were copied to the hard drive of her mobile computer. The procedure only took about five minutes, and it had barely completed when the door opened, and Birch came in.

Willow touched the screen, and it blinked out. She didn't want anyone knowing she had made a copy of the Kaiden they all knew. They wouldn't understand why she might want to overwrite the memories he was about to receive.

"Is he ready?" Birch asked.

Willow glanced at Kaiden. He was fully sedated.

"Yeah," Willow said. "Just waiting for everyone to arrive."

"What's wrong?" Birch asked. "You've been moping around since you took out Kaiden's switches."

Willow scowled. "We could permanently damage his brain or even kill him."

"He knows that."

"What if the memories change him?" Willow asked.

Birch grimaced. "How would they change him?"

"What if he becomes a really different person?"

"He's a clone," Birch said. "How different can he be?"

"Very," Willow said. "No two clones are alike. "They have differences in attitude and temperament, likes and dislikes. They don't always look exactly alike, either."

Birch chuckled. "It's not going to change how he looks."

"No, but it will probably change how he sees us."

"He's dead-set on getting his memories back," Birch said. "I don't get it. But that's a risk we have to take."

The others arrived, and Willow turned away from Birch. None of them understood what it was like to have the memories of multiple lives inside your head. Sure, they each had a few things they remembered, but not the entire experience. Each time she had been uploaded into a new body, she had wanted to die. Only the hope that she might be able to strike back at TAP and make the horror stop for good had given her the courage to survive.

Jade and Flint dropped into chairs beside her. Flint fiddled with the computers, setting up the firewalls that they hoped would keep the terrorists from corrupting Kaiden's memories.

When Flint nodded to her, Willow reached to initiate the download. Jade grabbed her hand.

"If anything goes wrong," Jade said. "I'm holding you responsible."

Willow jerked her hand away. "Blame Kaiden," she said. "He's the jerk who made me do this." She initiated the download.

"Will it hurt?" Birch asked as Kaiden twitched on the table. Birch lifted Kaiden's hand into hers.

"Not at first," Willow said. "His brain is about the same age it was when he was first downloaded, so it might not be as painful for him."

The scanner continued to hum as the files downloaded. Kaiden groaned. He shuddered.

"Doesn't look pleasant," Flint said.

"Almost done," Willow said.

The scanner clicked and fell silent.

Willow glanced at the others. "I don't know what's going to happen when I reset him."

"Can you reverse it?" Flint asked.

Willow hesitated, then nodded. "But if he resists, it could be difficult."

Birch dropped Kaiden's hand and backed up.

"Here goes," Willow said. The scanner withdrew from Kaiden's head.

His eyes snapped open. His head swiveled from side to side as he took in his surroundings. He raised a hand to his head and grimaced. "My head." He struggled to a sitting position and swung his legs over the side of the table.

"You should rest," Willow said.

"Where am I?" he demanded. He studied Birch and then Jade and then Flint. When his gaze fell on Willow, his brow furrowed.

"I know you," he said. He leaped to his feet and strode to her. Willow rose and backed away. Terror gripped her throat and twisted her insides. She had been afraid of this.

"You were there. In her office."

Willow shook her head. "Don't," she pleaded.

Kaiden glanced around again. "Is this her lab? Do you work for her? What have you done to me?" His eyes widened. "You're one of them. You're a clone!"

He lunged over the table. His hands closed on Willow's throat.

"Filthy clone!" he growled through clenched teeth.

Willow struggled and kicked, but Kaiden was incredibly strong. Sweat beaded on his brow. His face twisted in rage and hatred. Willow's lungs spasmed. The pressure in her head became unbearable.

Willow could hear the scrambling and shouting all around her, but her mind could focus only on Kaiden's terrible visage. He meant to kill her. Despair swelled inside her to compete with the pressure in her lungs and the desperation to breathe.

"Let her go!" Flint shouted and grabbed Kaiden. Jade tried to pry his hands loose. Birch loomed behind him with a syringe, which she plunged into Kaiden's neck. He jerked and swatted at her. Willow sucked in air as Kaiden released his hold. Her chest throbbed. Kaiden reached for her again. But Flint tackled him and grappled with him for a few seconds before his eyes rolled up into his head so that only the whites were showing, and he became limp.

Birch lifted Willow to a sitting position.

"Are you okay?" Birch asked.

Willow nodded, but she couldn't speak. She needed to wait for the INCR to repair the damage to her larynx. Tears dripped from her cheeks as she glanced over at Kaiden's prostrate form. This is what she had feared. She had seen him once long ago while she was interning at a genetic research lab. That and his reputation as one of TAP's best captains had initially drawn her to him.

Only recently had she started to unravel how connected they really were, how opposed he had been to cloning. But his attack had come as a surprise. There was no way she could have known how radically opposed he was—so much so that he would murder a clone with his own hands.

"Now what?" Flint said. "We can't have Kaiden running around trying to strangle us all because we're clones."

Willow knew what she had to do, but she didn't know how much it would help. It was like the old memories she had uploaded overwhelmed the Kaiden she knew and replaced him with the clone-hating radical he had been when he died. Maybe if she replaced the memories she had downloaded moments ago, he would be able to find his way back to them. Maybe he would become the Kaiden she had learned to love.

"Get him back on the table," she croaked. The effort to speak made her throat burn.

Jade glanced at her. "Why?"

"I'm going to restore his memories of us."

"You can do that?"

Willow gazed at them, stone-faced. "I think so."

"But that will just confuse him even more," Birch said.

Willow folded her arms. "Maybe, but it might also stop him from trying to kill us all."

She didn't really know what it would do. The memories might compete for the same synapses in the brain and leave him paralyzed or psychologically damaged. But to have a Kaiden who hated clones without the understanding of what had happened to him was unacceptable. He would be worse than dead. He would be dangerous. Willow suppressed a twinge of guilt. But he was the stubborn idiot who wanted this. He would have to deal with the consequences.

CHAPTER TWENTY-TWO
THE AGONY OF MEMORY

KAIDEN GROANED. The rush of memories overwhelmed him—swamped him in a chaos of emotions and circumstances, of people and events. And with the rush came the terrible bone-rending pain that exploded from every fiber of his being. He curled up and wept.

He wept for his little sister, who had died of a wasting disease that his mother couldn't heal. He wept for the absentee father who sacrificed his children and his marriage for his political career. He wept for the mother he had wanted so desperately to love. The loss and disappointment consumed him. But that wasn't the worst of it.

He had become the thing he loathed. At age sixteen, he had joined the terrorists to rid the world of the plague of fake humans that were sucking resources from real research and real programs that would help humans deal with the world they had wasted. Kaiden helped to plan and carry out the murder of clones. The memory of the young, blonde woman he and the mob had caught scampering away from TAP now haunted him. He had helped them kill her.

Kaiden cradled his head in his hands, wishing the memory would go away. He tried to rationalize what he had done, but he couldn't. The woman may not even have been a clone. But what if she were? Would that justify what he had done? She didn't have any more control over being a clone than he did.

If cloning had been any good, his mother would have used it to save little Rose. But she hadn't because she couldn't. Or she hadn't tried hard enough. The world's foremost genetic researcher should have been able to do so much more. He hated her for it, and now he hated himself because he was one of them—a clone, not once, but several times.

And he had spent the last forty years helping TAP perfect its clones. How could he live with himself? How could he endure the pain, the humiliation, the betrayal? Willow and Oakley had both been right. It would have been better not to remember. It would have been better just to die.

Images flashed before his mind in vivid color, full of raw emotions. They seemed so old and familiar, and yet, so new and strange. The feel of the violin vibrating as he drew the bow over the strings. The liquid pop of the grape as it burst in his mouth. The sharp aroma of raw onions that burned his eyes. The terror of the furry spider that crawled up his arm. The soft touch of Rose's kiss on his cheek. The agony of his mother's betrayal when Rose died.

The bright lights glared down at him from the laboratory ceiling as his wasted body devoured itself. He hadn't known then, and he didn't know now what had killed him. His mother, with her bright red lipstick, gazed down at him with a determined, defiant expression on her face. He had died and left his decaying body behind. Why wasn't he dead? Why did the anguish continue? Why was it so cold and so silent?

Raven had killed his crew. Willow had betrayed them to the terrorists. Or had she brought him home? Was this where he belonged? In the belly of the terrorists' lair, chanting slogans of hatred about clones, working to destroy every clone that polluted the world?

"Kaiden?"

The voice pierced the chaos.

"Kaiden?"

He knew that voice. It was soft and inviting.

"Kaiden?"

He opened his eyes. The room was shadowed. Silky black hair spilled over his cheek. The smell of fresh sage filled his nostrils. Someone stroked his hand.

"Hey," Jade said.

"It's cuneiform," Kaiden said. He didn't know why he said this, but it was among the clutter of memories he hadn't yet processed, and it seemed important. Cuneiform was an ancient form of writing that hadn't been used for thousands of years—not since ancient Mesopotamia. Why would TAP be using it for the tattoos on the clones?

Jade smiled, and the dimples formed beneath her cheekbones.

"You've been unconscious for two days, and that's all you can say?" she said.

"I was one of them," Kaiden said. "I was a terrorist."

"I figured as much when you tried to strangle Willow."

Kaiden struggled to sit up. His head reeled, but he forced himself to remain upright. "Did I hurt—"

"No. She's fine. The INCR fixed her up good as new."

He had gone to his mother's lab just before Rose died, and Willow was there in a white lab coat. At the time, he hadn't known about the clones.

"This changes everything," he said.

Jade studied him. "What? Now you have to kill us all yourself?"

Kaiden stared at her. Is that what he wanted? No. But death might be a peaceful escape from the horror that presently consumed him.

"No," he said, "but I'm...I'm a fake human."

Jade smirked at him. "That's the dumbest thing I've ever heard you say. You've known you were a clone for weeks now."

"I know," Kaiden said. "I'm just so confused. It's like there are two of me vying for control of my mind." Then he raised his hands to stare at them. "This body didn't even have a mother or father," he said. "It was hatched in a big glass bubble, like bacteria in a petri dish."

"And that makes you fake?"

"Doesn't it?"

"Is the bacteria in the petri dish fake?"

When Kaiden didn't answer, Jade lifted his hand again and held it in her lap.

"Look," she began, "your DNA is the product of all the ancestors who went before you. TAP may have tinkered with some of it, but they can't create it. And all those memories bouncing around in your head right now belonged to a living, breathing human, no matter how he was created."

The words sounded good. Kaiden wanted to believe them. It was as if he had two personalities, two identities warring with each other. He rubbed his face with his hands, trying to push back the growing ache.

Jade draped an arm around his shoulders and pulled him close.

"What am I?" Kaiden mumbled.

"A human being created by alternate means," Jade said.

Kaiden lifted his head and gave her a weak smile. "Alternate means?"

Jade raised her eyebrows. "How else would you describe it?"

Kaiden shook his head. "Are we really humans?"

"What difference does it make?" Jade said. "Is a human who has had an organ transplant less human? We belong to the sentient world the same as all other living things. We have value because we exist."

Kaiden smiled despite the agony in his soul. "You have a way with words."

"If it helps," Jade said, "you can think of it as a type of reincarnation. Ancient religions often believed that people returned to earth after death in the form of another creature. Instead of coming back as a pig or a cockroach, you came back as an upgraded version of yourself."

"That's a pleasant thought," Kaiden said sarcastically.

Jade leaned in. Her breath was warm on his face. She smelled of sweet sage. "I'm glad you're back," she said. "You scared me."

Kaiden blinked at her. She was so alluring. Her lips were parted and moist, and she looked him in the eye. The unspoken question passed between them. Would he kiss her? The warmth rising in his chest confused him. What was this feeling? What did he do with it? He swallowed, and their lips touched. Her lips were soft and warm. A tingle of excitement rushed through his gut, and he kissed her back. It was a gentle, lingering kiss that sent a fire coursing through his belly.

She pulled away and smiled at him. "See," she said, "you are human, after all."

THE AGONY OF MEMORY

Two days later, Kaiden fidgeted at the observation window to the surgery with his hands clasped behind his back as each of his companions underwent the operation to remove the switches. It disturbed him to see them writhe on the table. They might be sedated, but the switch's defense mechanism tore through the body, nonetheless. His jaw clenched and unclenched at the enormous arrogance of TAP and its complete disregard for the dignity of the children it swept into its clutches.

He raised a hand to push against the sudden stabbing pain that flared at his temple. He closed his eyes, trying to wait it out. When he opened them again, he saw his reflection in the window, and he realized that he didn't know where he was. Fear gripped his stomach. Was this his mother's lab? Who was the beautiful woman that lay on her stomach with the surgical-bots hovering overhead? What were they doing to her? He blinked at another flash of pain, and he was back at the window, watching the surgical-bots remove the switches from Jade's neck and arm.

Kaiden ground his teeth in frustration. He had expected a sudden understanding of who and what he had been with the return of his memories, but all he got was a confusing rush of contradictory emotions and memories that battled for his attention. He had hoped for some miraculous clarity. But it hadn't worked. The memories returned slowly like the flowing of hot lava, bringing moments of understanding followed by confusion, anger, and pain.

And always, the self-loathing remained. He was a freak, a monster, a scientific experiment with no purpose other than to be poked and prodded in the name of science. TAP had done this to him—left him in mental anguish and robbed him of his family. He had been violated in the worst possible way. He had been stripped of his body, his mind preserved as a computer file against his will, and then forced into a cloned body with no real connection to anyone or anything other than the evil institution that created him. But he had known this for weeks. Why did it bother him so much now? What could he do about it?

Willow was the last to lay down on the table despite her earlier declaration to be the first. The doctor had insisted that he needed her help, so now she was the last to have the devices removed. She turned her head so that she could see him as she lay on her stomach. Their gazes met. Kaiden looked on in growing confusion. Willow had been quiet and standoffish since she had restored his memories. He tried to apologize for attacking her, but she brushed him off. Either she was afraid of him, or she was afraid of his memories.

The muscles in his jaw worked in frustration. Willow's expression of sorrow and helpless grief infuriated him. But he didn't know why he was so angry. He didn't know why he had so violently attacked her—other than that he opposed cloning as a teenager and actively sought to stop it.

Willow's eyelids fluttered closed. Her body jerked. The monitors went blank. Kaiden's heart beat faster as it always did at this stage. The surgical-bots did their work and held up two pieces of pale flesh with dripping nano-wires dangling beneath. The doctor and his assistants began working to revive her. Kaiden watched them inject the oxygenated solution and attach the defibrillator. Willow's body jerked again. Kaiden glanced at the monitors. They remained blank. Kaiden scowled as the warmth rose in his chest. Willow was not responding. The others had already responded by now. Something was wrong.

The surgical-bot dropped the switches on a stainless steel tray, and Kaiden glanced at the black cuneiform tattoo on the piece of pink flesh. He didn't know why he knew it was cuneiform, and he didn't know why he could read it, but it said, "The Breath of Life."

Why did this make his blood run cold? His stomach clenched tight. *Come on*, he thought. *Come on, Willow.*

The nurse prepared to inject her with another syringe of oxygenated microparticles. He remembered that Willow had told him that the oxygen system had stopped working after the explosion on the lunar transport ship after the bomb blast. And yet, she had continued to function with no apparent problems. He had never pressed her to explain why, but it suddenly became very important.

"No," Kaiden screamed. "He slammed his fist against the window and then rushed for the door and threw it open. "No more oxygen!" he yelled.

The doctor spun to face him, and the nurse paused.

"Get him out of here," the doctor said.

"No, listen." He had to convince them. "You're killing her!"

"Get him out!" the doctor yelled.

Oakley grabbed Kaiden from behind.

"She's been modified to live in low oxygen environments!" Kaiden yelled.

The doctor gazed at him. "Are you sure?"

"Yes."

"That would explain why her O2 saturation was so low," the doctor said and waved away the nurse with the syringe.

"If she dies because of you," Oakley whispered in his ear. "I'll make you pay."

Kaiden shook him loose. "We lost oxygen on the shuttle after the explosion," he said, "and she suffered no side effects while she had to put me on oxygen."

Oakley stepped back to study Kaiden with interest. "They can be that specific?"

Kaiden pointed at the piece of flesh attached to the switches. "It's cuneiform," he said.

"What's cuneiform?" Oakley asked.

"It's the writing of the ancient Sumerians, and it's being used to note specific genetic modifications on each clone."

Oakley stared at him. "Who are the Sumerians?"

"The people of Mesopotamia. The ones who supposedly built the ark."

"Right." Oakley eyed him suspiciously. "And you can read it?"

Kaiden shook his head. "Not really. I just understood...I mean..." He tried to think why he had understood it. "My dad was an archaeologist who studied ancient Mesopotamia before he got involved in politics. He taught me some cuneiform when I was a kid. It was a game we played."

Willow lurched on the table and sucked in a great gulp of air. Her eyelids fluttered, and she lay still. Kaiden glanced at the monitors. Her heart rate came up and leveled off. Her oxygen saturation was in the twenties—so low she should have been dead. But she seemed to be breathing fine. The doctor glanced at Kaiden and nodded.

Kaiden let out a long breath. He had almost lost her. Somehow, that knowledge had focused his mind like nothing else since she restored his memories. He didn't want to lose her. She was his friend. He had lost too many already.

"I'm sorry," Kaiden said.

Willow blinked up at him from the table where she was recovering from the surgery. Confusion clouded her face before a weak smile played across her lips.

"I know," she whispered.

He took her hand. "I wasn't myself, I…" How could he explain the horrible conflict of emotions bursting within him? The sense of being two people at the same time—one who hated everything about clones, who thought they should die, and one who kept repeating in his mind, "I am a clone. My friends are all clones. We are good people."

Willow squeezed his hand. "I warned you that you might not like it. Remembering isn't always a good thing. Sometimes it's easier to forget."

"Maybe," Kaiden said. "But I have to know why I remember you—why I attacked you. Can you tell me?"

A frown tugged at the corners of Willow's mouth. "I was an intern at a lab where you used to come to visit someone," she said. "I saw you there once, but I don't think we ever talked."

"You mean we knew each other before TAP harvested us?" That would explain the one memory he had of her.

Willow nodded. "A bit."

"I only have a vague memory of seeing you that one time, and every time I think of it, I'm filled with this rage. Why?"

"Oakley told me that you were a protester like him," Willow said. "Maybe that's why you were there."

"Your lab was working on cloning?"

"No, I only worked on Cognitive Redesign, but by then, TAP was already experimenting with it because they stole my research and used it to perfect their system. Then, when my memory files were uploaded thirteen years later, I found the program fully developed and advanced beyond what I had discovered."

Kaiden bowed his head in shame. "I really am sorry."

Willow raised her hand to stroke his cheek. "I know you would never hurt me on purpose. And I'm sorry for not telling you about Oakley. I was just so afraid that if you knew, I would lose you, and we would all be killed and composted, and TAP would just go on doing what they're doing."

"Is there anything else you haven't told me?" he said.

Willow lowered her hand and shifted. An evasive look slipped across her face, and she averted her gaze. Then she pinched her lips tight and faced him.

"I don't think we can trust Oakley," she said. "He's different from when he was a boy. And I think he's hiding something about Iris and about this mission into TAP."

"All right," he said. "I'll make contingency plans."

Willow lifted his hand and drew it to her lips and kissed it. "Thank you," she said. "For not hating me."

Kaiden didn't say anything. He couldn't tell her that even now, he was struggling with the terrible hatred. It was irrational and frightening, like he was two people in the same body.

CHAPTER TWENTY-THREE
THE LOST KISS

TWO DAYS LATER, Willow peered down at Iris's corpse, trying to understand why she had died. She yanked the T-shirt over her nose to cloak the stench of Iris's decomposing body. Iris's wound had been serious, but with immediate medical attention and the INCR, she should have recovered. Oakley said they had done everything they could for her, but something wasn't right.

Oakley and Kaiden had called a meeting to plan their next move. But Willow needed some answers before she could agree to any further action—especially since she now thought she understood why Noah hadn't killed Kaiden. While she was recovering, she spent some time working through Quill's files and doing research of her own. She had long suspected something like this, and Kaiden was not going to like what she found.

She glanced around to make sure she was alone before clicking on her computer. She hacked into the medical computer and started searching. Iris's vital signs had been dangerously low, then they had stabilized, and several hours later, she was dead. Willow kept searching, but there was nothing else. She chewed on the edge of her lip and scowled. If Flint had deactivated the switches, then TAP couldn't have killed her. Since the INCR had been working and she had stabilized, there was no reason she should have died. That would leave only one other option. Oakley had ordered her execution. But why? What did Iris have to hide?

Willow paused. Had Oakley captured Iris or Greyson—or both—before all this happened? Had they been working for Oakley all along, like Raven? What else was Oakley hiding from her?

She slipped out the door into the hallway. She encountered a few terrorists who glared at her, but by now, everyone knew she was Oakley's sister, so they left her alone. This suited her fine. Right now, she needed to be alone. When she came around the corner near her room, she found Kaiden waiting for her. She stopped. He leaned against the wall, his arms folded, and he didn't smile.

"Hey," Willow said.

"Now, who's ignoring people?" Kaiden asked as he pushed himself off the wall.

Willow stepped up to him. "I'm not ignoring anyone," she said. "I've been busy."

Kaiden glanced at the computer in her hands. "Where've you been? I've been looking for you for hours."

Willow pulled the computer closer. She couldn't tell him that she had been digging into his past and trying to figure out who he actually was and why Iris had betrayed them. He already had a hard time trusting her now that she had restored his memories. Should she tell him that she suspected that her brother had made sure that Iris never woke up?

"Trying to find out everything I can about Noah and these terrorists," she said.

"That's what I want to talk to you about." Kaiden poked a thumb toward the door to her room.

Willow let him in and sat at the tiny plastic table that would only seat two people. Willow watched him, afraid he was going to question her about Iris. She didn't want to go there. Not yet. She needed more time to figure out what Oakley might be planning.

"Do you remember your other cloned lives?" Kaiden asked.

"Yes," Willow said.

"How come I don't remember any of my cloned lives?" He poked a finger at his head. "Shouldn't I have them running around in here somewhere?"

Willow tapped her computer with a slender finger. "I didn't have time to find them. Besides, I thought you only wanted your original memories."

"Yeah," Kaiden said. "I suppose so." Then he narrowed his eyes at her. "I think you're right about Oakley," he said. "I don't trust him."

"You shouldn't," Willow said. "I already told you that."

Kaiden picked at a spot on the table. "You have any idea what he might be doing?"

Willow shook her head. "I don't. I barely know him anymore." She hadn't been able to admit this to herself, and she'd never said it out loud. But the more she interacted with Oakley, the more he reminded her of their father.

Oakley seemed secretly pleased at the power he had over the terrorists. It was just the kind of thing their father would have enjoyed. Power was the only thing he admired and respected. Even his pursuit of wealth had been aimed at exercising power over others. That's what made her uneasy around Oakley. She had never trusted power, especially when it was exercised by those who craved it.

Kaiden stared at her. "Did he plant any weird stuff in my head?"

Now Willow understood. Kaiden was worried that Oakley would do to him what he had done to Raven. Kaiden would rather die than betray his friends. That was another one of the reasons why she'd picked him to help her in the first place.

"I personally oversaw the uploads," Willow said. "I took the files from my computer that has never left my possession since we got here."

"Are you sure?" Kaiden's lips pinched tight, and he stared at her as if trying to bore a hole through her.

"I'm positive," Willow said.

"If I turn into a Raven," Kaiden said, "I want you to promise to shoot me quickly."

Willow frowned. Raven was the only person she had killed in any of her lives. She didn't think she could shoot Kaiden. She got up and poured two cups of water.

"You won't become a twisted fanatic," she said as she sat back down and slid one over to Kaiden. "All those memories making you so miserable are your own."

"How can you know that?" Kaiden said. "What if I'm being manipulated again? What if I never had a real family?"

Willow reached over and took his hand. She squeezed reassuringly. "You'll just have to trust me."

Kaiden sipped at the water, but he studied her from over the rim of the cup. "You promise you're not secretly in league with Oakley to do something horrible?"

"Why would you think that of me?" Willow demanded. "I already told you I don't trust him either, but I did what had to be done. If I hadn't contacted him, we would all be dead by now. And we need his help to get back into TAP." She waved a hand. "After that, we can go our own ways."

"Okay," he said. "But if you find out what Oakley is up to, I want you to tell me immediately."

Willow nodded her agreement. "Tomorrow, he's going to try to get us to play his game," she said. "And we're not going to play along."

Jade haunted the corridor outside Kaiden's room. They had barely spoken in the days after she kissed him. They had all been recovering from the surgery, and Kaiden's new memories troubled him far more than she might have expected. The self-loathing was apparent, and it disturbed her. What did he think of her if he thought clones were freaks?

Kaiden finally arrived, looking careworn and exhausted. He smiled when he saw her. At least he wasn't angry about the kiss.

"How are you?" he asked.

She shrugged non-committally. "I'm all right. Feels strange to know the leash TAP has had on me all my life is gone."

He opened the door and gestured for her to enter. She did, and he followed her in. She stuffed her hands into the pockets of her jeans and glanced at the floor. How did she say what she wanted to say without sounding like a jealous schoolgirl?

"Do you think you can trust Willow and Oakley?" she asked.

Kaiden nodded as if he had had similar thoughts. "I think Willow's okay, but Oakley I definitely do not trust."

"He's going to try something," Jade said. "We can't let him inside

TAP."

"I know."

"I think you need to be careful with Willow, too."

"Do you know something?"

"No," she shook her head. "But something's off with her."

Kaiden studied Jade, and she guessed he was trying to decide if this was simple jealousy on her part.

"She knows too much and not enough at the same time," Jade said.

"What's that supposed to mean?"

"If she has forty years of knowledge about TAP, shouldn't she have known about the tattoos and tracking devices?"

"She didn't work in that department."

"Maybe," Jade said. "Anyway, I just think you should be on your guard."

"Okay," he said.

Jade stared at him, shuffled her feet, and then turned toward the door. Kaiden grabbed her hand and pulled her back.

"You don't have to go," he said.

Jade turned to him. Did he really want her to stay? "Have you decided if you're human yet?"

Kaiden sank into a chair. "Depends on how you define humanity."

"That's a question that's been debated for thousands of years," Jade said as she sank into the chair opposite him. "The problem is we keep insisting there is something special about us that makes us unique—more important—than other species."

"We are the most powerful species."

"In some ways," Jade said. "But all species are equally important to a thriving ecosystem. It's our success that has created massive imbalances and placed the earth in jeopardy."

"Sure," Kaiden said. "I know all that."

"Some philosophers say we're unique because we're self-aware," Jade continued. "Isn't that what René Descartes meant when he said, *Cogito, ergo sum*? 'I think. Therefore I am.'"

"I didn't know you knew Latin," Kaiden said.

"Neither did I," Jade said. "I'm starting to think I worked in the humanities before I was cloned—though why TAP would need me,

I don't know. I'm not really useful. I think I was selected just to add genetic diversity."

"No," Kaiden said. "You were selected because you were the best and the brightest."

"Anyway," Jade pressed on despite the warmth rising in her chest. Kaiden thought she belonged—that she had value. "Maybe humanity should really be defined by our values or emotions and our relationships more than by mere biology."

"So, you really don't think it matters if we were born naturally into a family like Oakley said?"

"That might be the ideal," Jade said, "but it doesn't account for the scope and variation of human experience. I think it's about being connected to each other, to our ancestors, to our friends. If we don't have a biological family, we can still create fictive ties of kinship and be happy."

"That makes a lot of sense," Kaiden said. "But I have this horrible gnawing hatred of clones."

Jade flinched. "Even me?" The thought of him despising her for something over which she had no control pained her.

"No," Kaiden said and took her hand. "I know I'm being stupid. It isn't about you. It's about me. These competing memories and the knowledge of what TAP did to me have so warped my self-identity that I don't know who I am anymore."

Jade rose and knelt before him. She took his face in her hands. "You are a man," she said. "A good man." She raised her face to his hoping he would kiss her again. Wanting him to accept her. To choose her.

Kaiden leaned forward and then paused. He drew back. "Thank you," he said. "That means a lot to me."

The pain of rejection stabbed into her chest, and a knot formed in her throat. She let her hands fall from his face and rose to her feet.

"Well," she said, "Think about it. The sooner you wrestle through these feelings, the better off we all will be."

Then she strode through the door before he could see her cry.

Kaiden watched her go, sick at heart. He'd never intended to hurt her. But that look on her face was so full of pain and sorrow. He rose, thinking he should go after her. But what could he say? He did like her—a lot. In fact, he felt more relaxed with her than he did with anyone else. But right now, his mind was in turmoil. He hadn't even decided on his own identity. How could he form an attachment now when they needed to stay focused on their mission?

Besides, he couldn't use her like that. She didn't deserve it. If he kissed her again, she would think he was getting serious about her. The truth was he was afraid of her and Willow—at least in that way. They stirred feelings and ideas in him he'd never experienced, and deep down, he knew he should only be attracted to one of them. He would have to sort this out after they destroyed TAP and defeated Noah. Maybe by then, he would have worked through the confusing feelings the jumble of memories caused. Maybe things would be clearer.

Jade retreated to her bedroom and crouched in the corner without the lights—alone in the comforting embrace of the darkness. She was always alone. Perhaps that was her destiny. She wiped at the bitter tears and tried not to think of the expression on Kaiden's face as he pulled away from her. She thought he was interested in her. He had kissed her back when she kissed him, and she was sure he enjoyed it. She also noticed the way he looked at her. There was a longing there, a desire to be close to her. She was sure of it.

People had told her frequently that she was beautiful, but maybe that wasn't enough for him. Maybe he needed something else. Maybe he wanted a scientist, not someone who spouted off information about culture and philosophy.

The silence weighed down upon her like a suffocating shroud. What options were left to her? She couldn't request a transfer this time.

"Grandfather," she whispered, "what should I do?"

The memory of her grandfather's grizzled hair that he wore in two braids came back to her. These were the memories she cherished amid the jumble of confusion TAP had given her. He handed her a burning sage bundle, and she drank in the sacred smoke. It was so rich and cleansing, a rare gift in a desiccating world.

His hands had been rough and wrinkled from years of grinding labor in the factories of Denver, and his voice had a low, comforting ring to it.

"You must survive," he had told her.

His words filled her with a bitter sadness followed by a sudden determination. She would survive, and she would make sure that Kaiden survived no matter the risk. Willow might be his first choice, but Jade would be his guardian. She would find meaning and belonging in protecting the one man who had earned her respect and love.

"I am strong," she said. "I will survive."

"We can't just stroll into TAP and expect a warm welcome," Birch said. She clicked her pistol's safety on and off absentmindedly.

Kaiden had gathered Birch, Jade, Flint, and Willow together in a circular room that acted as a briefing center for the terrorists. Oakley leaned against the wall in a posture of casual disdain. Like the rest of the compound, the room was in ill-repair. The furniture was worn and tattered. Kaiden found himself thinking about the news report of the last attack by the Sons of God and the charred bodies on the stretchers.

"Obviously," Kaiden said.

He glared at Birch. For some reason, everything anyone said set his teeth on edge. He wanted to lash out, to get even. Now that Iris was dead, he would never know why she and Greyson had attacked his team. And if Iris hadn't killed Quill, who did? In a moment of clarity, Kaiden understood.

The sniper had tried to kill him, as well. The only reason he was alive was because he had jumped to save the little boy. But if Noah had meant to kill him, why hadn't he just finished the job later? Kaiden shook his head and clenched his jaw. Everything always came back to Noah.

"Don't be such a pea-brain," Birch snapped. "Somebody had to say it."

"I can get you in," Oakley said.

Kaiden didn't like the smug expression on Oakley's face.

"Then, what do you need us for?"

"Because getting in into TAP isn't the hard part," Oakley continued. "Destroying their entire computer network and erasing their files is more complicated. You all know the system, and you have the necessary clearances or hacking capabilities to get me into the computer network."

"They'll have revoked our clearances by now," Kaiden said.

"But you understand the system better than anyone." He gestured to Flint. "You designed half of it."

"Maybe," Flint said. "But finding and killing Noah seems like the real challenge to me. He's not stupid, and he'll be expecting something."

"We need a distraction," Kaiden said.

Jade scowled, and Kaiden tried not to think of the way she had kissed him. It always left him with a confusing rush of excitement and guilt. And he couldn't forget the pain in her eyes when he had refused to kiss her a second time last night.

"Distractions usually end up with dead bodies," Jade said. "I'm against killing clones if we can help it."

"Sacrifices have to be made," Oakley said.

Willow spun to face him. "That's exactly the kind of thing TAP would say," she said. "Jade's right. We need something else."

Kaiden studied Willow. He hadn't been satisfied with their conversation the day before. She hadn't come looking for him after she recovered two days ago, though after the way he attacked her, maybe she had a good reason. Now, Willow glared at Oakley as if she suspected something.

Flint smiled. "What if we could play with memories?"

At first, Kaiden thought Flint was poking fun at him. The angry reply died on his lips when he saw that Flint was serious. Still, Kaiden didn't like the idea of toying with people's memories—not after what he'd experienced—what he was now experiencing.

"I took a peek at that chip they stuck in my neck," Flint said. "Guess what I found?"

"What? A happy birthday message?" Birch mocked. "Spit it out."

Flint kept grinning. "I found that the chip contained a standard memory file."

"Which means?" Jade asked.

"It means," Flint said, "that I should be able to hack the standard memory files of all the clones and insert our own memory files and then trigger a reset that would upload those memories."

"Hang on," Birch said. "If they could reset our memories at any time, why didn't they just do that to all of us?"

"It's called reconditioning," Kaiden said, finally understanding what Noah had been talking about when he demanded that Kaiden submit himself for reconditioning. "But then, why would they need to murder Quill?"

Flint shook his head. "I don't know. Maybe it wasn't intended as a reset. It was located with the discipline files. I'm not sure they understood the possibilities."

"You can't just reset the memories of thousands of people at once," Willow said.

Flint grinned again. "I can."

"How?" Jade demanded.

"Wireless," Flint said. "Once I'm inside TAP, I can hack the central communication system and use it to broadcast a wireless signal to the chips. That's how the discipline works, isn't it? We'll just hijack the system."

"You think it'll work?" Kaiden asked.

"If we have a memory to upload, I bet I can do it."

"But you're not certain," Willow said.

Flint pursed his lips. "Nothing is ever certain, is it?"

"We don't know how to write memories," Jade said.

"We do," Oakley said. "Well, simple ones anyway."

"What kind of memory are you thinking of?" Kaiden asked.

Flint waved a hand in front of him. "I don't know. How about something like, 'We really like these ex-TAP infiltrators, so we shouldn't kill them'?"

"I'll vote for that one," Birch said. "But that's not going to help us find Noah."

"No," Willow said. "It needs to be more powerful. We need to give them a real memory that will convince them that TAP needs to be stopped."

"What do you propose?" Oakley said.

"Take one of mine," said Willow.

After a moment of stunned silence, Birch spoke up. "And how do you propose that we do that? Your mind's not a computer. You can't just pick a single memory file, or TAP would have been more effective at erasing our previous memories and writing new ones."

"I have one I isolated and downloaded years ago," Willow said.

"How?" Flint asked.

Willow dismissed him with a wave of the hand. "I've had forty years to figure it out," she snapped.

"What is it?" Jade asked.

Willow bowed her head. "It's one of me dying and being uploaded into a child's brain."

"Dang," Flint said. "And you have that as a simple file?"

Willow nodded.

"Why?" Birch asked.

Willow glanced at Oakley. "I wanted to send it to my mother and to my brother, so they would know what happened to me."

Oakley stared at her. Kaiden noted the war of emotions that played across Oakley's face.

Willow continued in a quiet voice. "But I could never figure out how to send it in a format they could read."

"That's sad," Flint said. "And really cool, too, in a weird way, like..." He paused and glanced around at them. "Okay. I'm just going to shut up now."

"Good idea," Birch said.

"Anyway," Willow said, "I can provide the file. The question is, what do we do if it works?"

"I kill Noah," Kaiden said.

It seemed clear to him now. Noah had been the one who had stolen his rotting body and his DNA. He had been the one who had robbed him of his identity and transformed him into a genetic freak. Jade had tried to convince him otherwise, but he just couldn't feel it. Not for himself.

Willow gazed at him with wide eyes. "Are you serious?"

"He did this to me," Kaiden said. "And I'm going to get even."

"I don't think you should," Willow said.

Kaiden scowled. "Why?"

Willow fidgeted. "I don't think you'll want to live with that on your conscience."

"I have to," Kaiden insisted.

Willow bowed her head. "Maybe you do," she mumbled.

"I want my people there to make sure you don't mess this up," Oakley said.

"No," Kaiden, Jade, and Willow said at the same time.

Oakley shook his head. "That's the deal. I helped you, now you help me."

"We *are* helping you, in case you didn't notice," Birch said.

"But no terrorists go inside TAP," Kaiden said.

"Then, I guess we're done here," Oakley said as he stood. "I'll drop you off in Chicago, and you can see how long you make it on your own." He strode toward the door.

Kaiden exchanged glances with the others.

"Sit down," Kaiden said. He had no patience for displays of bravado.

Oakley spun to face him. His silver eyes flashed annoyance, but Kaiden waved it away.

"You can't expect us to let the Sons of God into TAP," Kaiden said. "How do we know you won't start slaughtering every clone you see?" Even though Kaiden questioned his own humanity, he wasn't about to get involved in killing clones—people like him, people he knew. Not if he could help it.

"I haven't killed *you* yet, have I?" Oakley said.

"You need us," Jade said, "for now."

"I already told you that I want Noah dead and the TAP system so corrupted it can never restart," Oakley said. "If you'll give me that, I'll let the clones live."

Kaiden exchanged glances with his team. But he didn't trust Oakley.

"Why?" Jade asked.

"What?"

"Why will you let the clones live?" Jade studied him as if she could read his expression.

Oakley considered her. "Because without TAP, clones aren't

dangerous."

"How do you figure that?" Birch said.

Oakley smirked. "Because there will be no one to control them. And the resources wasted on their development can be redirected to real human beings."

Willow snapped her head around to stare at Oakley. Tears brimmed in her eyes, and Kaiden experienced the sudden urge to punch Oakley in the face. Oakley had just admitted that the sister he pretended to love wasn't a real human.

His continued hypocrisy forced Kaiden to confront his own. He saw himself as a freak, but not Willow or the others. To hear Oakley deny their humanity rankled in his stomach. It was one thing for Kaiden to question his own identity, but what right did Oakley have to judge them for what someone else did to them without their consent?

"Okay," Kaiden said, in an attempt to redirect Willow's attention away from her calloused brother. "But, you can only have five men accompany us. And they have to have express orders not to kill any clones unless attacked. If they do, then we will shoot them on the spot."

"Agreed." Oakley sat down, and Kaiden eyed him with suspicion. That had been too easy.

"Now, to the details," Oakley said, rubbing his hands together.

CHAPTER TWENTY-FOUR
INVASION OF ARARAT

KAIDEN CROUCHED IN the shadows of a dilapidated brick building in the stifling heat, waiting for Oakley to give the signal that the way was clear for them to board the airship. Jade, Willow, Flint, and Birch huddled next to him. It had been two weeks since they had escaped TAP, and now, they were going back in. They were insane. This could never work.

The dull roar of the megacity surrounded them like the incessant whine of an insect. Apartment towers bulging with humanity hovered over them, their windows glowing in the gathering darkness. Hovercrafts hissed and whirred as they zipped overhead. The stink of human waste clung to the still air.

Sweat trickled down Kaiden's back and beaded on his forehead. He hadn't often been in the cities, and now, he remembered why he avoided them. The menace of the city loomed over him as if eagerly waiting for the moment when it could fall and crush the life out of him. It sucked at his soul. Something about the mass of concrete and steel and the oily, empty streets made him feel less human than he already did.

Among Kaiden's restored memories were the ones of his youth in New York. He struggled to remember that it was forty years ago, but so much had changed. The earth's climate had been mostly stable then. Cities still had parks. The ocean levels had risen but hadn't yet devoured the coastlines. People had walked and driven their own hovercrafts. Now, this street, with its lonely emptiness, filled him with despair. Maybe TAP was right. Maybe humans needed clones to save them.

A shuffling sound drew Kaiden's attention. A small child wandered onto the street. She stooped here and there to investigate some bit of trash lying in the road. She was barefoot, and her clothes hung in tatters about her thin, little body. Kaiden followed her progress with growing disgust and pity. This is why he had opposed cloning from the start. This child could have been his sister, Rose. All the resources wasted on cloning could have been spent to give the numerous helpless children, like this one, a warm meal and a place to sleep.

Contradictory emotions and beliefs competed inside him. Part of him hated TAP and wanted it destroyed. The other part saw the decadence and savagery of these natural humans caught in a global crisis of their own making and saw no way to save them from themselves without engineering a new, improved species to guide them. Kaiden cursed softly. TAP had even robbed him of his own peace of mind.

A low growl sounded from somewhere. A mangy dog bounded in front of the child, who screamed and tried to run, but the dog was on top of her in two bounds. Kaiden wheeled to shoot the dog, but he was too late. Jade and Birch both fired at the same time. The explosion echoed off the brick walls. The dog yelped and stumbled away from the girl who had buried her face in her hands. The dog tried to hobble away, but Jade's next bullet dropped it. It fell without a sound. The smell of gunpowder temporarily masked the stench of the city.

Willow rushed to the child's side and lifted her into her lap. The girl slid her hands from her face and stared up at Willow. The child's face was stained with layers of grime. Her cheeks were gaunt. The way her gaze searched Willow's face made Kaiden cringe in pitying revulsion. The child seemed more animal than human. This was the way Kaiden had always seen the clones he transported to and from the lunar field station. Now, it was a natural child.

"It's okay," Willow said. "You're safe."

The girl wriggled free of Willow's grasp, jumped to her feet in the ruined street, and whirled to face Willow.

"There is no safe," the girl said. She bent and picked up a wrapper. She glanced at the dog as if considering how she might eat it and then started toward it.

"Wait," Willow said. She pulled out one of the packets of food rations the team carried with them and handed it to the girl. The girl studied the packet, grabbed it, and scampered away.

"What the…" Birch stared after the girl, horrified.

The girl hadn't gone far when another child twice her size jumped from behind an old, rusted hovercraft and snatched the packet from her.

"Hey!" Willow called and sprinted after him. The boy shrieked and dropped the packet. The girl seized it again and scurried away.

"That's so sad," Jade said as Willow jogged back to them. "I don't know how to save naturally born humans, but maybe clones can help stop this savagery."

"I don't know if clones would be any better," Birch said. "If we made clones go hungry and forced them to live in their stinking refuse, they'd behave like animals, too."

Willow spun on Jade with a snarl. "We need to care for our own," she snapped, "and to stop wasting money creating people like us."

"Drop it," Kaiden ordered. He couldn't have his team arguing hours before a dangerous operation. Especially not Jade and Willow.

Willow glared at him.

"There's nothing we can do about it now," Kaiden said.

Oakley returned, but Willow kept scowling. Maybe she was remembering what Oakley had said about her. Maybe she was starting to feel the same conflicting emotions churning around inside Kaiden's own chest.

"It's now or never," Oakley said. "The airship is ready. Once you have the system down," he gestured to Flint, "and you do the reset," he glanced at Willow, "if we get separated, my team will meet you at the command center. Then, we take TAP down for good."

Oakley's eyes shone with excitement, just like a little boy on Christmas morning, waiting to open his packages. Kaiden was surprised by the idea. They didn't celebrate Christmas in TAP. He hadn't seen a present since he was fifteen. But, he didn't have time to reminisce even if the memories were still so new.

Kaiden nodded. "Only five, like we agreed," he said.

Oakley flashed him an annoyed glance. "Of course," he said. "Now, let's go while we can. They might change the clearance codes before we get in."

Willow grabbed Kaiden's hand and dragged him to the back of the cargo bay where they could sit beside each other. Oakley had arranged to smuggle them in on an old TAP supply ship the terrorists had captured, and the group separated to conceal themselves in the hold among the boxes in case anything went wrong when they landed.

Kaiden caught the warning glance Jade cast him as Willow dragged him away. He shrugged to let her know this wasn't his idea. He had read the expression on her face and couldn't help but feel guilty. She had wanted him to kiss her, and he had wanted to, but it didn't feel right. It felt like he would be using her, and he respected her too much to do that.

Willow pulled him down between two rows of shelves.

"This could be an ambush," she said.

"Oakley?" Kaiden asked.

Willow glanced at him. "No, I was thinking of Noah. I'm not convinced the cloaking software is going to work. He's going to expect us to come back, especially since he knows that the terrorists helped us escape. He'll be ready."

Kaiden considered her. Something about the way she talked about Noah seemed familiar. "Probably," he said. "Do you have something in mind?"

The ship rocked as it lifted off the pad, and Kaiden had to steady himself.

"I need you to trust me," Willow said.

"I have been," he said.

Kaiden studied her more carefully. Willow was a complicated woman. Every time he thought he understood what motivated her, she would do or say something that made him think he had imagined everything he knew about her. And yet, she had saved his life several times now when she could have let him die. They had formed a bond ever since the explosion on the lunar mission. She was smart and capable, always able to be flexible in the face of catastrophe. She was a survivor.

"What are you getting at?" Kaiden asked.

"You just need to be ready," Willow said. "We don't know everything about Noah or TAP."

"What's that supposed to mean?" Kaiden thought it probably meant he didn't know as much about TAP as she did, which was true. But it annoyed him that she just wouldn't come out and say what she had to say.

Willow avoided Kaiden's gaze. "I can't say because I'm not sure, and if I'm wrong..." she trailed off. "If I'm wrong, it could hurt you."

"What if you're right, and you don't tell me?"

She gazed at him now with pleading eyes. "You may not like what we find." She swung her rifle around from behind her and laid it across her lap.

"You're being cryptic on purpose," he said. "Not telling me something I need to know is the same as lying."

She grabbed his hand. "Don't go to kill Noah," she said. "Send someone else."

"Why?"

Tears brimmed in Willow's eyes. "Don't make me say it," she said. "I could be wrong. I hope I'm wrong."

"No," Kaiden said.

Her eyes widened, and a single tear slipped from her eye.

"I won't send anyone else. It has to be me," he said.

"Why?"

"Because I'm the leader and because Noah has stolen everything from me, even my own identity and sense of self-worth."

Willow stared at him, working her jaw. "All right," she said, "if you must, but where are you going to look for him?"

"The central command center, like Oakley said."

"He won't be there," she said. "It's too obvious, and you said yourself that he was only on a screen."

"Then, where?"

Willow didn't answer immediately because one of Oakley's men clomped down the aisle in front of them.

She leaned close to whisper to Kaiden. Her hair brushed his cheek. "You should look in the section where Noah caught you snooping around," Willow said. Her lips had a gentle curve to them, and they were moist and alluring in the pale light that filtered through the cargo bay. He felt suddenly guilty. How could he be drawn to two women at the same time? Was he no better than Greyson and his womanizing?

"What?" He dragged his gaze away from Willow's lips. His mind had wandered.

"The section called Atra-Hasis," she said.

Kaiden cocked his head in suspicion. "Why?"

"Because." Willow said this like it should be the most obvious thing in the world. "Noah stopped you from snooping around there, didn't he? He let you wander all over until you got too close."

"What makes you think he'll be there?" Kaiden lifted a small box from off the shelf next to him and examined it. He needed to refocus his mind.

"Because Atra-Hasis is the name of the Noah character in the old Sumerian story of the Flood. It predates the biblical story."

"I know," Kaiden said. He hadn't sat around doing nothing while they waited at the terrorist base. He'd done his research. "TAP is following the original flood story, not the biblical one."

"That's right," Willow said.

"But how does it matter?"

"The Flood," Willow said. "In both stories, the gods sent The Flood to destroy humankind."

"So?" He placed the box back on the shelf.

"The Flood file Quill found was all in cuneiform," she said. "I think it's a blueprint for what TAP plans to do with the clones."

"You don't think it's about building a clone army?"

Willow smirked. "Not a chance," she said with a shake of her head. Her ponytail bobbed around her face and brushed Kaiden's cheek again. "In the original story, one of the gods warned Atra-Hasis that another god was going to send a flood to destroy humanity. I think Noah plans exactly that—something that will sweep over humanity like a flood, and the clones are going to be the only ones who will survive somehow."

Kaiden grimaced at her. "You really think TAP would waste its time playing with fairy tales? Maybe humans are the flood, and TAP wants to fix them by introducing clones to improve the species." Kaiden hadn't forgotten the child wandering the streets in search of food.

Willow was shaking her head before he finished speaking.

"No," she said. "It's more sinister. I think The Ark Project has more than one agenda."

The airship shuddered and decreased its speed as it dropped in altitude.

"Looks like the show is about to begin," Kaiden said.

Willow grabbed his hand. Her teeth bit her bottom lip, and her eyes were over-bright. "No matter what happens," she whispered, "remember that I…" She paused and swallowed. "Remember that I'll always care for you and that this was your idea to go after Noah, not mine."

Before Kaiden could respond, Willow leaned over and kissed him on the cheek. Then, she rose abruptly and left. Kaiden gazed after her, utterly confused at the warm feeling that surged into his chest.

The airship settled onto the pad inside in the hangar at Ararat. Personnel went about their work of repairing, loading, and fueling the two dozen airships already docked in the hangar. A double set of iron stairs ran up to the next floor above wide bay doors that allowed materials and equipment to be delivered to the various departments. The team waited until the activity in the hangar quieted, and then they slipped out.

Willow shouldered her rifle and fell into step behind one of Oakley's men. Flint and Birch led the way as they strode from the rear hangar where the captured TAP supply airship landed. Flint monitored the cloaking software that concealed them all from view, and Birch kept an eye on the tablet she carried with the images sent from the new nano-bots she and Flint had built on a nano-fabricating machine the terrorists had.

The nano-bots buzzed along in front of them and behind them to help them avoid any unwanted surprises. Kaiden glanced back at Willow, and she tried to smile at him, but she had seen the way he looked at her when she kissed him on the cheek.

He didn't trust her. She wished she could tell him all that she knew or suspected, but she couldn't risk it. Not now. After nearly forty years of planning, she was on the cusp of shutting down TAP and stopping its brutal "harvesting" of brilliant, young children. Kaiden wouldn't believe her if she did tell him what she thought. She almost didn't believe it herself.

She tried to convince herself that this wasn't about revenge, but deep down, she knew that it was. Willow had expected to feel elated and triumphant, but, as she crept down the corridor concealed by Quill's improved cloaking software, a strange sense of detachment overcame her, like she was moving in someone else's body.

She worried about what Oakley had planned. His initial affection toward her had cooled, and she was convinced that Iris had not died of her wounds. If Oakley had, indeed, killed Iris to keep her from telling Kaiden what she knew, then Oakley had another agenda entirely. What if Oakley wanted access to TAP technology so he could clone his own army? It might be a contradiction of his own beliefs, but as Oakley was fond of saying, "sacrifices had to be made," and "you have to fight fire with fire." Oakley was hiding things from her—just as she was hiding things from him.

She touched the pocket where she kept the file Flint was going to upload into the clone chips—the file she had so desperately wanted to send to Oakley and her mother, so they would know she was alive. She hadn't let anyone else see it or handle it. Only she knew what it contained.

Willow had been so absorbed in her own musings that she didn't notice how empty the corridors were. She glanced at her wrist terminal. This time of day, TAP should be busy. The labs would still be running. Where was security?

She elbowed her way up to Kaiden's side.

"Something's wrong," she whispered.

Kaiden nodded without looking at her. "The corridors are deserted. They're expecting us."

"What are we going to do?"

"What we came to do."

"But—"

"We won't get another chance," Kaiden interrupted.

"We're here," Flint whispered.

The team came up short in front of Rio's office. Flint bent over his computer in silence for several seconds. His black hair fell into his face.

"This guy's nifty to have around when you need to get past a locked door," Birch said.

As the door swished open, the alarms screeched to life. Red security lights flashed.

"That's not good," Jade said.

"Move!" Kaiden yelled.

The team rushed into Rio's office. Flint and Willow dashed to the computers and set to work. Birch sent the nano-bots down the corridor to warn them of anyone approaching while Kaiden, Jade, and Oakley, and the four men he brought with him took up positions by the door.

"I get the feeling they expected us to come here," Jade shouted over the screaming alarms.

Blue holographic screens buzzed to life all around them, showing video feed from all over TAP. Red security lights were flashing, and TAP personnel spilled into the corridors.

"It's gonna get ice cold in here real fast," Birch said.

"I think you mean it's gonna get hot in here real fast," Jade said.

"Let's go for uncomfortable," Kaiden said.

"Ah-ha!" Flint exclaimed. "Dang. That was easy. I thought they'd...Wait a minute."

"I think I like it better when you keep your thoughts to yourself," Birch said. "You're making me nervous."

"Hurry up," Oakley demanded from the doorway where he waited with his four men.

Willow tried to ignore them as she concentrated on hacking into the main laboratory computer and from there into the memory server. She initiated the download of all the memories of the crew just in case, and then she uploaded the two she had selected from her own memories. She let the download work in the background while she keyed into where Flint was struggling with the complicated firewall TAP used on their wireless system. She uploaded her file to his computer.

Flint glanced at her. "I'm in."

"You keep saying that," Jade said.

"Well, this time, I'm in. Here goes."

Willow stepped back from her computer to peer over Flint's shoulder.

"It helps that I wrote some of this software," Flint said.

"What?" Willow said. "You remember writing it?"

"Didn't I tell you?" Flint said. "I remember dying, too."

Willow stared at him. All these years, she thought she was the only one with complete memories. But how could she have been so naïve? That meant there must be others. What would it do to them to upload her memory into their brains? Would it even work?

"Do you remember everything?"

"Almost," Flint said, "but there are blind spots where they damaged some of the parts they tried to overwrite. I can't remember my mother or childhood, for instance."

"Guys?" Birch said with a note of warning as the holographic images showed the halls filling with TAP personnel. A squad raced toward Rio's office.

Flint winked at Willow. "I wrote it, so I could get in." His finger paused over the enter key. He glanced at Willow for confirmation. Willow's stomach churned. This was it.

"Do it," she whispered.

Flint clicked the key. The slap of running feet sounded in the corridor.

"Here they come," Birch shouted.

Willow glanced up at the screens where TAP personnel in every color jacket scampered here and there, following their security protocols. She knew the labs would soon be locked down. Security personnel in their black outfits sprinted down the corridors, securing the vital areas. She caught sight of Rio heading their way, leading a group of armed security.

Then, people began collapsing. Willow winced as their bodies jerked and writhed on the floor, and she was glad they had removed the switches from their bodies. Otherwise, all of them would be experiencing the same horror. Some curled up into balls. Others rolled and thrashed. She wished Flint had found a way to upload the memory without triggering the discipline. It was horrible to watch, especially when she knew how terrible it really was.

"Better get started," Jade said to Kaiden. "We'll be right behind you once genius here is done with the computers."

Oakley and his men stepped to follow Kaiden when Birch leveled her rifle at them. "Not you," she said. "You're not invited to this party."

"We had a deal," Oakley said.

"A deal with the devil never stands," Birch said. "Isn't that your philosophy? Now, drop your guns. We're not having you running amuck shooting clones for fun."

When they hesitated, Jade stepped up to them. "I'm against killing clones," she said. "But terrorists are at the top of my shoot-on-sight list. So, unless you want to be filled with lead, you should do as she says."

"You'll regret this," Oakley said and gestured for the men to drop their guns.

"Letting you live?" Jade said. "I already do."

As Birch and Jade secured the five terrorist prisoners and deposited them in a side room for safekeeping, Kaiden glanced back at Willow as if to say, "I'm trusting you," and raced off at a sprint. She followed his progress on the cameras as he leaped over and around the sprawled bodies. Maybe she should have resisted and forced Kaiden to send someone else. But he never would have relented. He wouldn't have believed her.

"Where's he going?" Birch asked. "That's not the way to—"

"There are terrorists in the building," Flint said. "Lots of them."

Willow spun to face the screen. Sure enough. Dozens of T-shirt clad terrorists were swarming in from the landing bay.

"They waited until we neutralized everyone," Jade said, "and then just flew right in the open doors."

"Oakley planned this," Willow said.

She raced for the door to the room where they had secured Oakley and his men. There was a flash and a bang. The door was ripped off its hinges and flew at her. She ducked, but the door still caught her a glancing blow on the shoulder. She tumbled to the floor and crouched until the rush of debris ended. Then, she bounded to her feet. The room was empty. Oakley was gone.

The screens went blank, and the lights blinked out. Willow gasped and bolted for the door. She had to warn Kaiden that Oakley was loose, and his thugs had infiltrated TAP. They had been duped. She had underestimated Oakley.

"Kaiden," she yelled into her WT.

Silence.

"Kaiden," she tried again, but he didn't answer.

CHAPTER TWENTY-FIVE
BROTHER AGAINST BROTHER

THE LIGHTS FLICKERED out as Kaiden arrived at the stairwell. He skidded to a stop until the emergency lights flashed on. A blackout hadn't been part of their plan. The little globes cast an eerie, blue light over the whimpering bodies of the clones who had had their memories reset. Some were crawling to their hands and knees. Some vomited in the corners. Some didn't stir at all.

Kaiden kicked through the door to the stairwell and bounded down the stairs two at a time. He had no idea what the reset would do to the other clones, and he needed to reach the lowest level before anyone discovered what he was doing. He knew the cameras would probably warn Noah he was coming—especially without Quill's cloaking software. Birch and Flint were the only ones who knew how to operate it. But he couldn't do anything about that at the moment.

He flew down the stairs past four levels when he heard a door bang open below him. He paused on the landing to catch his breath and to see who was in the stairwell below. Boots thumped on the stairs. They were climbing.

He peeked over the railing and saw a close-shaved black head that could only be Rio's. Kaiden cursed. "Not now," he whispered. But he didn't have a choice. He had to reach level nine, and Rio was in the way. He shouldered his rifle and aimed. The red button of light in the scope settled on Rio's head.

One squeeze of the trigger, and Rio would never order him around again. Kaiden would never have to endure his sneers. He started to squeeze the trigger and then stopped. He couldn't do it. Not like this. Rio had been his commanding officer just doing his job.

Kaiden flipped the rifle over his back to let it hang by its sling and waited until Rio was just beneath him. Then, he leaped over the rail, grabbing it with both hands as he pivoted and swung feet first at Rio's body.

Rio spun to meet him, but Kaiden's feet slammed into his chest, sending him sprawling against the wall and then tumbling down the stairs. Rio's rifle bounced between the handrails and crashed to the stairs below.

Kaiden bounded down the stairs and was on top of Rio as Rio's hand found his sidearm. Kaiden caught the arm with both hands and rammed his knee into Rio's face. Rio jerked and sent Kaiden flying over his head. Kaiden kept a hold of the pistol and dragged it, along with Rio, as he spun through the air and slammed onto the stairs. But he didn't have control of the pistol. It discharged with a loud crack that made his ears ring. The bullet grazed his shoulder. His elbow banged against a stair, making his left arm go numb.

Kaiden rolled to his feet just as Rio leaped forward and smashed a big fist into his face. Kaiden stumbled and reached out for the wall.

"Traitor," Rio snarled and swung again, but Kaiden ducked and punched Rio in the groin. Rio cursed and doubled over as Kaiden brought the butt of the pistol crashing down on the back of Rio's head where the spine connected to the skull. Rio grunted and fell.

Rio groaned. Kaiden knew he wasn't dead, but he didn't have time to wait and see. He jumped over Rio, snatched up his own rifle, and sprang down the stairs.

When he reached the ninth level down, he slowed to a walk, trying to catch his breath. His head ached, and his shoulder burned. His elbow was beginning to swell. He could feel it tugging against his shirtsleeve. The blood from the small bullet wound had soaked into his clothes, but he could already feel it closing. The INCR was working.

Kaiden needed to calm down. He took a few steadying breaths as he strode down the corridor. He knew the door was on this level about halfway down the hall, but the door might be hidden.

A massive explosion rocked the compound. The safety lights flickered. Something had gone wrong.

Willow sprinted down the corridor now lit by the little blue safety lights protruding from the ceiling. She had to catch up with Kaiden. She couldn't let him do this alone.

She tried her WT again, but Kaiden didn't respond.

Clones were starting to come around from the effects of the discipline. Some were standing, gazing around in confusion. Willow slowed as more and more of them staggered to their feet. A few glanced at her and then started down the hallway. Others scowled as she jogged past. Realizing that she was drawing attention to herself, Willow slowed to a walk. She tried to control her breathing and the desperate fear that choked her. What if Kaiden couldn't do it and everything failed? And what was Oakley planning? The electricity wasn't supposed to go out. He had set something in motion that taking him prisoner wouldn't stop.

A male clone in a white lab coat glared at Willow as she passed. What had her memory done? She had sent them two memories. One of her waking up inside the head of a thirteen-year-old child with all the pain and agony of that experience. She had also sent the memory when she had first understood that she had been cloned. But memories were tricky things. She knew that trying to upload a full memory scan into a brain that was not structured like the original brain could result in paralysis and death. She had no idea what two short memories would do in a completely different brain, or if they would even take hold.

Willow approached the body of a clone in a red jacket that was not stirring. She paused and knelt beside the young woman. The woman wasn't breathing. Willow swallowed. The reset must have killed her. She would never know if it was the discipline or the memories that had done it. Maybe she didn't want to know. Willow rose and continued.

Most of the clones were awake now. Some were still vomiting.

Others were staring around at each other, dazed and disoriented. Some of the security personnel picked up their rifles and glared around at the other clones. Willow knew she needed to hurry to catch up with Kaiden, but she had to know what was going on in the minds of these clones. What had her memories done to them?

She stopped a clone in a blue engineering jacket who had a surly expression on his face.

"What's happening?" she asked.

He glanced at her lab coat and glared at her. "Did you do this to me?"

"What?" Willow said. She tried to control the trembling in her voice. She hadn't been trained in security. If this man decided to take out his frustration on her, she didn't stand a chance.

"Are we all clones?" he asked her. Others stopped to listen. Some drew near.

Willow glanced around at them and steeled herself for their reaction.

"Yes," she said. "We're all clones."

"Not me," someone shouted.

Willow spun to find a female security officer striding toward them through the growing crowd of people.

"We're all clones," someone echoed Willow.

"It's a lie," the security officer yelled. "Someone's hacked the system, and you're all confused. You just need to stay calm."

A massive detonation rumbled through the compound, knocking Willow to her knees. The lights flickered. Someone screamed.

"It's the terrorists," the security officer called. "Stay calm."

"You're the terrorist," someone shouted.

Others took up the cry, and the security officer backed away.

"Remain calm," she said. She lowered her rifle. "Let's everyone just relax."

Then, they were on her. She fired, and three clones fell before she collapsed under their combined assault.

"No!" Willow screamed as she scrambled back to her feet. It wasn't supposed to be like this. They weren't supposed to attack each other. Clearly, the memories didn't upload the same way in all of the clones, and some of them took the memories badly. It had made them hysterical and vicious. What had she done? How could she stop this?

She tried to drag the attackers away from the officer, but she got punched in the face for her efforts and was shoved away. She tasted the blood in her mouth. The despair and desperation drove her down the corridor. She had to get to Kaiden. She had to find a way to end this madness.

Kaiden paused by the narrow outlines of the door. The lines were barely visible in the pale blue glow of the emergency lights. There was a keypad, and he didn't have Flint or Willow to hack the system for him. He pulled out the stackable explosive charges Jade had given him, set them stacked three deep, and dashed back down the hallway.

The door blasted inward with a roar and shower of metal and smoke. Kaiden rushed into the smoke and leaped through the door. He paused to take his bearings and froze.

There she was, picking herself up from the ground amid the wreckage of the door. A battery of computer monitors flickered above her. Some showed the pandemonium raging in the corridors of TAP. Clones were attacking clones. Terrorists in T-shirts were spreading down the corridors, shooting as they advanced.

The room's quiet elegance contrasted with the chaos and horror displayed on the flashing screens. It appeared to be a sitting room or living room. Plush furniture, now covered in a fine layer of dust from the blasted doorway, and paintings of floods and a huge tree had been artfully placed. A table with a plate of sandwiches on top stood off to the side.

The woman righted herself and studied him as he entered as if the blast had meant nothing to her. Behind her, two more women peered at him from computer monitors for an instant before the monitors went blank. Kaiden's mind reeled. How could this be?

The woman had dark skin, straight black hair, and bright red lipstick.

"Mother?" he gasped.

The woman smiled. The sight of that beautiful smile he had so longed to see sent wild shivers coursing through him. A lump rose in his throat, and his eyes stung. He stepped toward her. All the longing and heartache that had been stirring inside him since the blast on the lunar transport boiled to the surface. Here she was. The mother he loved. The mother he hated. The mother he had lost.

"Hello, son," she said.

CHAPTER TWENTY-SIX
FOR GOD SO LOVED THE WORLD

WILLOW ROUNDED THE corner near the stairwell and skidded to a stop. She needed to catch her breath and figure out where she was. What was the fastest way to reach Kaiden? The emergency lights illuminated the hallways in a pale blue glow where a gigantic hole had been ripped in the corridor. She gazed up at the dangling wires and the jagged rent with sky-blue paint that curled and cracked on the bent metal. The explosion had torn through several floors and collapsed a huge portion of the Genesis Room. The chatter of machine-gun fire echoed through the hallways. Clear liquid spreading over the floor and dripping through the rent brought her heart into her mouth.

"No," she whispered. "He wouldn't."

She stepped up to the hole and peered through. The Genesis Room had been destroyed. The glass artificial wombs had been shattered, and the corpses of innocent babies lay strewn over what remained of the floor. No motherless wombs remained intact. They were dead—all of them. Bile rose in Willow's throat. The horror gripped her stomach. She struggled to keep from throwing up.

How could they do this? How could anyone do this? Oakley had known all along they would never let him and his terrorists roam free in Ararat and had planned for his rescue. He let them overwhelm the security system from within while his men waited outside to rush in once the base was defenseless.

The rattle of gunfire galvanized her into action. She wiped savagely at the tears that dripped down her cheeks and sprang down the corridor to the last door, yanked it open, and sprinted through the lab. She rushed down the next corridor as the gunfire grew louder.

"Please, no," Willow whispered.

She panted as she slid to a stop in front of the glass window overlooking the nursery where she had stood with Kaiden a few weeks before. Oakley and a group of terrorists were systematically working their way from room to room, leaving a trail of bodies behind them and pools of blood that spread out on the white tile floor. He must have raced directly here after escaping from Rio's office.

Willow pounded on the glass. "No!" she shouted. "You promised." One of the terrorists loosed a burst of gunfire at her. She ducked as the bullets smashed through the window, showering her with glass.

When she looked up again, Oakley was striding for the door to the stairway that led up to the observation window and waving the terrorists on. Willow rushed to meet him. She had never felt so betrayed in all her life—not even when she discovered what TAP had done to her. No crime TAP had committed could justify what he was doing to innocent children. What had happened to the sensitive boy she remembered who had liked love songs and toy trucks? The boy who had cried after biting a playmate in the nursery because he felt bad for hurting him?

Oakley stepped through the door and waited for her to approach. The rifle dangled from a strap around his neck. He rested one hand on it as if he wanted to be sure it was there. Willow raced up to him and slapped him across the face as hard as she could.

"What are you doing?" she screamed. "Stop it! Stop it now!"

Oakley grabbed her fists and held her.

"I saw you fall from the hovercraft," he said. His voice was calm.

Willow gaped at him. "So, that justifies killing innocent children?"

"They aren't children," Oakley said. "They're freaks."

"You promised!" Willow said. She jerked her hands away from Oakley's grasp.

Oakley sneered. "A promise to a monster doesn't have to be honored."

Willow gaped at him. She wanted to slap him across the face again. "We aren't the enemy," Willow said. "It's not our fault they did this to us."

"It's a perversion," Oakley said. His lips lifted in a sneer.

"Would you kill a deformed natural human child?" Willow demanded.

"It's not the same thing." Oakley wiped a drop of blood from his eyebrow.

"We are just as innocent as natural children," Willow insisted.

Oakley shook his head. "You have no idea what they have planned, do you?"

Willow threw up her hands in frustration. "I've heard of The Flood if that's what you mean."

"Then, you understand why you all have to die?" Oakley said.

Willow backed away from him. Oakley had become just like their father—driven by hatred and the lust for power. Their father had gone to Africa to engineer coups so he could rise to power on a fountain of blood. He had never cared who he killed or how many. Now, here was Oakley, his white T-shirt spattered with the blood of innocent children, sneering at her the way her father used to do.

"I'm your sister," Willow said.

Oakley laughed bitterly. "My sister is dead," he said. "You're a freak. A dangerous lab experiment."

The tears welled up to blur Willow's vision. Her heart ached for the life that TAP had stolen from her. It ached for the little boy who had become so vicious and filled with rage. It ached for the children Oakley had murdered, for his betrayal. It ached for what she had sent Kaiden to do. Willow swallowed the lump in her throat.

"Why?" she said. "Why do you hate us so much? You don't really believe all the lies you tell."

"Look at you," Oakley said. He gestured to her with his rifle. "You're sixty years old, and you still think you're nineteen. You clones all think you can cheat death and live like gods."

"You're crazy!" Willow yelled. Her hands balled into fists. "We. Didn't. Choose. This!" She enunciated every word.

Then, in a sudden moment of clarity, she understood. "Ah," she said as she backed away from him. "You're jealous. Is that why you killed Iris? Did she know what you had planned?"

Oakley sneered. "Iris knew who tried to kill Kaiden. I couldn't let her tell him."

"It was you?" Willow said in disbelief. "You were working for Noah?"

"Only when it suited my purpose," he said. "How do you think I had such good access to the base and to TAP equipment?"

Confusion boiled in Willow's chest. Why would Noah work against himself? Then it dawned on her. Noah needed the Sons of God to precipitate a crisis. A crisis he could use to justify unleashing The Flood, whatever that was.

"You're a filthy hypocrite," Willow shouted, "just like our father."

Oakley's face twisted in a snarl as he snapped his rifle up. Willow's blood ran cold. He was going to kill her. She didn't want to die. Not like this. Not now. Kaiden still needed her.

"You want to be immortal," she said. "You don't want to destroy TAP's files and technology. You want to take them for yourself. You want to make a clone of yourself."

Oakley smiled a cold, bitter smile that sent shivers through Willow's body. He held up a computer chip. "I have everything I need here," he said. "TAP did all the work for me. Now, I'm going to watch you die a second time."

A shot exploded in the corridor behind her. Willow flinched, but Oakley jerked, and his eyes opened wide. A red stain spread on his chest. Another shot rang out as Willow lunged to the side. Oakley stumbled into the wall of the corridor, spitting blood. Another shot barked. Oakley slid to his knees and collapsed to the floor. He stared up at her as the blood pumped from the holes in his chest.

Willow jerked her head around, trying to decide which way to run when Jade and Birch stepped out into the corridor. A little curl of smoke trailed from Jade's rifle. Willow glanced at Oakley's body.

A red pool expanded grotesquely on the floor as he twitched and reached a hand toward Willow. She blinked at the tears that slipped down her cheeks. Her little brother was dying, the one who had risked his life to save her from being harvested forty years ago, but she had to let him die.

She stepped away from him and peered up at Jade and Birch.

"Thanks," she whispered.

But Jade was staring at the ruined door of the Genesis Room. She raced to it and let out a cry of dismay. Birch joined her.

"No," Jade sobbed. "They murdered the babies. Why did they kill the babies?"

Birch draped an arm around her shoulder.

"He's dead," Jade sobbed.

"Who?" Birch asked.

Jade didn't answer. She jerked her head around to glare at Willow. "Where's Kaiden?" she demanded. Tears still streamed down her face.

Birch stepped over and kicked Oakley onto his back. The surprise had frozen onto his face—his blood-soaked T-shirt now bright red contrasting against the white tile floor.

"Where is he?" Jade demanded again.

Birch offered Willow a hand. "Come on."

Willow wiped at the tears. "Level nine. That's where Noah will be."

Jade whirled and sprinted down the hallway. Birch followed. Willow hesitated as she stole one last glance at the brother she had loved. The brother who had murdered innocent children and who had intended to murder her in cold blood. Maybe he was right. Maybe he was no longer her brother. Maybe clones had no family. She bent and snatched the computer chip from Oakley's lifeless hand before racing after Jade and Birch.

Jade raced down the corridor as the tears streamed down her face. Even she had never suspected that Oakley would murder helpless babies. The little Indian boy would be lying on the floor in a puddle of embryonic fluid like the rest of them—cut off from life before he even had a chance to taste the air, to feel the warmth of another human body, or the touch of a loving hand. A burning ached filled her chest. Stopping TAP was supposed to protect him and all those like him. But they had let the wolf in, and he had slaughtered the lambs.

What if Kaiden had also died without her being there to protect him? Then where would she go? What would she do?

"I am strong," she mumbled and renewed her speed. She had to reach him in time.

"I don't understand," Kaiden mumbled as he searched the room through the smoky haze for the old man he had seen on the video. Noah was supposed to be here. He had a job to do. There was no time.

But there was only the woman. His mother. He wanted to rush into her arms, to have her kiss him and hold him the way she used to do when he was small. But the sad look on her face and his own confusion at finding her here stopped him.

"No, you don't understand," his mother said. "You never would. That's why I had to put you in security. I couldn't have you in the science lab where you'd be exposed to sensitive information."

The harsh tone in her voice startled Kaiden. She wasn't pleased to see him. Somewhere in his fragmented imagination, he had assumed she would embrace him and weep on his neck, telling him how much she had missed him, how much she loved him. And why wasn't she surprised that he hadn't aged at all since she last saw him? She just stood there in her white lab coat, glaring at him. Her lips, painted red as blood, lifted in a sneer.

"What are you talking about?" Kaiden demanded. He was torn between his desire to be with his mother, the woman who had occupied his dreams for weeks, and his need to find Noah. He had so little time. He had to find Noah. The others were counting on him.

His mother considered him as her sneer shifted to a bitter smile. "Will you believe what I say?" she asked. "Or do you still hate me?"

"I..." Kaiden didn't know how he felt. He loved her, and yet, he hated her. But how could he feel that way about the same woman?

"I am Noah," she said. "I am the leader of TAP."

Kaiden stared. "I thought...You can't be." Kaiden had seen Noah. He was a wrinkly old man. He remembered the odd quality of the voice and the flickering screen.

"Sit down and let me explain," she said.

Kaiden shifted and glanced around but did not sit. Willow had warned him of a trap. She had told him he wouldn't like what he found, tried to convince him to let someone else do this. Willow had known.

His mother strolled to the red velvet couch and settled into it.

"I was appointed head of The Ark Project just before Rose died," she began. "Your father oversaw the International Department of Environmental Cooperation that had been tasked with collecting the genome of every species of every ecosystem in the world. He employed thousands of scientists and originally developed The Ark Project as a top-secret, international effort to transfer earth's genomes to a massive data bank on the lunar surface where it could be later transferred to other habitable planets when we discovered them."

His mother motioned for him to sit again, but Kaiden ignored her. He raised his rifle and then lowered it again. He had come to kill Noah only to find that Noah was his own mother—the person he had longed to see. He tried to swallow the horrible lump in his throat, and he blinked at the stinging in his eyes. This couldn't be happening.

"The Ecosystems Recovery Institute," his mother continued, "began designing planetariums on the moon to reconstruct lost or dying ecosystems. Meanwhile, I continued my clandestine work on human cloning for the International Security Agency. My colleagues had been developing the ability to download the human mind as a binary code that could be stored and uploaded into another human brain. We had a brilliant young technician in Cognitive Redesign, Willow, who developed the software for us."

A knot coiled in Kaiden's gut. Willow had created the software TAP used to harvest their memories? The one TAP had used on her? She had told him as much, but to hear it from his mother's lips sent a cold horror coursing through him.

His mother stared off at a picture on the wall. "I was too late to save Rose, but I could save you." She paused. "I knew you would hate me. You already blamed me for not saving Rose."

"Why didn't you save her?" Kaiden demanded, feeling the old

rage surge up inside him.

"You don't think I tried?" his mother yelled, lunging to her feet. "I tried everything. There was no cure!"

"You let me die, too!" Kaiden shouted.

"No, I saved you. I resurrected you."

"For what?"

His mother stopped and bowed her head. "I couldn't use medical science to save my children," she said, "so I used the science of cloning. Before you died, I downloaded your memories, and I harvested your DNA and cloned you. I tried to upload your memories into an eight-year-old cloned body. But it failed, and the brain died. When I was finally successful, I kept you away from the labs because I feared what you would do. But I had to keep you close."

"Why didn't you just let me die?" Kaiden said. "Now, I have to live knowing I'm a freak, all while I remember the family I should have had. The family you stole from me."

His mother snorted. "I gave you immortality."

"Wait," Kaiden said. "You tried to kill me that day in New York. The day you killed Quill."

His mother considered him. "You left me no choice," she said. "You and Quill were meddling in things that did not concern you."

"But, why didn't you kill me after you caught me searching the security system? You let me go."

His mother bowed her head. "I was weak. After I discovered that you remembered me, I couldn't bring myself to do it. It was too much like killing my own child."

Now, Kaiden stared. "I am your child!" he shouted again.

His mother gave him a sad smile. "Yes," she said. "I made you immortal, or rather, I extended your mortality. I keep you on a schedule, so when you have to be composted, I have a new son to replace you. You will go on living as long as I do."

Kaiden stared in horror. What did she mean? "Schedule?" he said, but she ignored him.

"And then," she continued, "I found plenty of people who were willing to pay big money for immortality. And, while I had them hooked up to my machine, I inserted new memories of loyalty to me and a secret belief that cloning was good. I used these people to gain access to political power at the highest levels, and then, I developed The Flood to save humanity."

"Your clone army?" Kaiden said, though he was pretty sure The Flood was something else.

His mother laughed. "What do I need a clone army for? I'm creating a new species to replace the one that is so intent upon self-destruction."

"Species?"

"I have designed clones to be more altruistic than natural humans," she said. "More intelligent, less belligerent, less greedy. I also designed clones that could live in low oxygen, high radiation, and low gravity environments, just in case. I have prepared humanity to start anew and to colonize the stars. Because of me, humanity will survive."

"Start anew?" Kaiden could hardly speak. The idea that his mother intended to wipe out every living natural human—even that little child he had seen in the city—repulsed him.

"That's your Flood?" he asked. "You're going to kill them all?"

His mother smirked. "Don't paint me as the villain," she said. "I've spent my life trying to save humanity, and what have you done? Before I gave you a second chance, you moped around and protested against the only future humanity had. I'm going to save them the way I saved you."

A second, though smaller, detonation stuttered through the compound. Kaiden glanced toward the door. What was going on out there? A female voice came from the computer. "Sync complete," it said.

Kaiden snapped his head around to stare at the computers. "What are you doing?" Kaiden demanded. She had distracted him to give herself time to complete a computer sync of some kind.

"I'm ensuring that my son doesn't doom humanity to extinction," she said.

Kaiden knew what he had to do. She hadn't left him any choice. He raised his rifle. Tears spilled down his cheeks. His heart pounded against his rib cage. She had made him a monster, stolen his identity, corrupted his mind, kidnapped and murdered innocent children. And now, she was going to slaughter billions of innocent people.

"Please," he said, "you can't do this."

She watched him. His own mother. He had longed to see her, to have her wrap her arms around him, and make all the pain and hatred go away. Kaiden swallowed. He couldn't do it.

"You can't kill your own mother," she said.

"Please, don't make me," he said. "Please stop."

He experienced a sudden clarity. Maybe without intending to, his mother had created him to stop her. That was why he was still alive. He steeled himself.

"I'm going to ensure that my mother doesn't become the greatest mass murderer in history," he said.

"I love you, Mom," he whispered as he squeezed the trigger.

Gunshots rang in the corridor outside.

A second blast rolled through the compound, making the stairs shiver under Willow's feet.

"What did your reset do?" Birch yelled as Willow caught up to her and Jade. They slowed to descend the stairs, bounding down them as fast as they could. Fighting had erupted everywhere. Clones were killing clones in a horrible blood bath.

"Looks like you screwed up," Jade said.

"Shut up," Willow choked. "I didn't do this."

"I can't figure out why Kaiden trusts you," Jade said. "Seems to me that you're behind all of it."

Willow resisted the urge to kick Jade in the back as they descended the stairs. But Jade was right. Kaiden shouldn't trust her. She was using him the same way Oakley had used her. But she wouldn't betray Kaiden—not really. Everything she was doing was for the good of humanity—for Kaiden's own good.

"Hello," Birch said as she paused in bounding down the stairs. Commander Rio had crawled to his hands and knees. He blinked up at them. Blood dripped from a cut on the back of his head.

"Have you seen Kaiden?" Birch snapped.

Rio reached for a knife at his hip, and Birch slammed the butt of her rifle into Rio's head. He slumped to the ground.

"I've wanted to do that for years," Birch said as she leaped over him and continued down the stairs.

Birch paused at the door to the Level Nine corridor, panting as she waited for the other two to catch up. She signaled for Jade to cover her and edged the door open. Beyond, Willow could make out a piece of equipment that might have been a floor cleaner. Birch jumped through the door and dropped behind it. Gunshots rang out, and Jade knelt, slipping her gun through the crack in the door. Her rifle jerked and spent shells jumped to burn against Willow's face. She leaped back as the slap of bullets echoed in the stairwell. They were trapped.

Kaiden's rifle bucked, and his mother jerked with the impact of two explosives rounds. She fell back on the couch as a red stain blossomed on her chest and spread to her white lab coat. The gun slipped from Kaiden's grasp, and he leaped to his mother's side. He wrapped his arms around her and drew her close. She still smelled of hair gel and perfume the way he remembered. She blinked at him and raised a hand to his cheek. More gunshots echoed in the corridor, but he ignored them.

"I'm sorry, Mom," he said as a sob escaped his throat. He buried his face in her neck. How could he have done it? His own mother? The horror burned his chest. He was a monster. Only a monster could so callously murder his own mother.

The pulse in her soft brown neck continued to beat for a few moments before it ceased, and she lay limp in his arms. Kaiden started, half-expecting the INCR to kick in and save her. But, just like Quill, Burl, and Iris, the nano-organisms hadn't had time to do their work.

Through the blur of tears, he saw the blue-black cuneiform tattoo on the back of her neck. It took him a moment to realize what he was seeing. The blue wedged-shaped tattoo read, *For God So Loved the World*. He jerked away from her body and came to his feet.

He stared at the computer. What had she done? Why hadn't it occurred to him that she had not aged at all? Kaiden fell to his knees, burying his head in his hands. It had all been for nothing. He had murdered his mother for nothing. He sank to the floor, vaguely aware of the sound of gunfire and booted feet pounding in the hallway. Then, someone smelling of sweet sage was lifting him into an embrace. He clung to her in desperate agony.

CHAPTER TWENTY-SEVEN
CARBON COPY

"WHO'S THIS?" Birch asked as Jade lifted Kaiden into a hug. The sound of running feet made Birch swing back to the doorway. She fired off three bursts, and the hallway went quiet. The smell of gunpowder drifted in the air.

Willow stared down at Kaiden's mother's body. A cold horror swept through her. Kaiden should have listened to her. When she began planning to attack TAP all those years ago, she had no idea who Kaiden really was, just that he was important to TAP for some reason. And she had remembered seeing him at the lab where she designed the synaptic transfer system.

She had only discovered clues to Kaiden's true identity a few hours before they left the terrorists' stronghold. Still, she had hoped she was wrong. If she had known, maybe she wouldn't have selected him to help her destroy TAP. But now, she understood why Kaiden had been so violent when she had restored his memories. His own mother had cloned him when she knew how much he opposed the idea. His sense of betrayal must have been overpowering.

The feeling of triumph she had expected when Noah was finally destroyed didn't come. Only sadness. Kaiden had been forced to kill his own mother. Willow should have insisted that it be someone else. She shouldn't have let him come. But he wouldn't have believed her. He would have thought she was trying to hide things from him again.

"I recognize her," Jade said as she peered over Kaiden's shoulder. "She was the one I shot in the Genesis Room."

"So she was ordering Kaiden's death?" Birch said.

"She's Noah," Willow said.

Birch glanced back from where she guarded the entrance. She smirked at her. "Um, maybe in your lab, male and female names don't matter, but Noah is definitely a male name, and I think it has been ever since that dude in the big boat saved all those animals and insects."

"She's Kaiden's mother," Willow said.

Birch gaped. "No." She glanced over to where Kaiden was pulling away from Jade's embrace.

Willow strode to the computer console. "Better keep an eye on the corridor," she said to Birch. Then she clicked on the computer. The words "Sync Complete" flashed on the screen.

"Hallway's still clear," Birch said, "but you better hurry."

"What was she syncing?" Willow asked.

Kaiden stepped over to study the screen with her. His eyes were red and puffy.

"I don't know," Kaiden said. The defeated, gruffness of his voice made her cringe. Would he ever be able to recover from this?

"She's deleting files," Willow said as her fingers clicked the keys. "We have to stop this."

Willow heard shuffling behind her but ignored it as she hurried to cancel the delete command. Noah had been trying to hide something. Willow managed to interrupt the delete command and discovered that it was a folder entitled The Flood. She clicked on it. These files weren't in cuneiform, but they were also corrupted. The image of a huge tree with great spreading branches filled the screen. In the center, the words Tree of Life flashed.

"She likes to mix her cultural references," Jade said.

"What?" Willow asked as she stared at the tree.

"Cuneiform from Mesopotamia, The Ark from Israel, and now, the Tree of Life from Mexico—at least this one looks like the one from Mexico."

"What's it supposed to mean?" Birch asked.

"I think for the Aztecs," Jade said, "the tree represented the world. But for some eastern religions, it represented immortality. In the west, the Tree of Life has its roots in hell and is able to destroy the earth."

"How do you know that?" Kaiden asked.

Jade shrugged. "I don't know. Maybe it's leftover from whatever I did before they harvested me."

"Whatever it means, I think we should go," Birch said. "Oh, hello."

Willow didn't turn to see who Birch was talking to. But Kaiden and Jade spun away. She heard the snap of rifles being raised. She was already downloading the file, transferring everything she could grab to Flint's computer that was still hooked into the system back in Rio's office.

Once the download was running, she turned to find Jade, Birch, and Kaiden all facing a narrow stairwell to an upper level of the room with their rifles up. Rio stood on the bottom step with his handgun leveled at Kaiden's chest. Blood dribbled from the wounds on his head. His nostrils flared, and his lip curled in a sneer. He must have known a back way into Noah's chambers. That was unexpected.

"Careful," Birch said, settling her rifle against her shoulder.

"What have you done?" Rio demanded as his gaze took in Noah's body draped over the sofa. Streaks of blood stained his face, which was wet with sweat. He was panting hard.

"We're stopping you all from murdering billions of innocent people," Kaiden said.

A third blast somewhere above rattled the dishes on the table.

Rio glanced at the ceiling. "You let the terrorists in here?"

"Only a few, and they're secure," Kaiden said.

"They're killing us all," Rio said.

Kaiden glanced at the others in confusion. "What's he talking about?"

"Oakley lied to us all," Willow said. "He had ships waiting outside to come in when we uploaded the memories."

Kaiden cursed as a fourth explosion shook them, toppling pictures from the walls.

"Okay," Birch said. "We can stand here pointing guns at each other all day, or we can get the heck out of here and maybe save a few of our friends."

Kaiden lowered his gun. "It's your call Rio," he said.

Rio strode the three steps between them and tried to slam the butt of his pistol into Kaiden's temple. But Kaiden caught his arm and drove his elbow into Rio's face. Rio twisted, catching Kaiden's leg, sweeping it out from under him. Kaiden slammed onto the floor.

"Hey," Birch yelled. "Drop your pistol, or I'll fill you full of lead."

Rio paused and glowered at her. Jade fired a round past his ear. He ducked and raised his pistol. Jade's second bullet slammed into his shoulder. Rio stumbled back, clutching at the sudden burst of red on his black uniform.

"You people play around too much," Jade said.

"Don't kill him," Kaiden shouted. "We may need him to get out of here."

Birch sniffed and stepped up to Rio. She leveled her gun at him. "Unless you want to die," Birch said, "I suggest you drop your gun."

Rio cursed, letting the pistol slip from his fingers, and then he spat on the ground beside Kaiden, who had crawled to his hands and knees.

"Someday," Rio said, "I'm going to get my hands on all of you and beat some sense into your thick heads."

"That's nice," Jade said. "Now, move."

"What about my shoulder?" he said.

Jade cast him a disdainful glance. "That's not my problem, and I don't really care if you bleed to death."

"Nice of you to drop by," Flint said as they raced into Rio's office twenty minutes later.

"Come on," Kaiden said, anxious to get out of there.

"What are you doing?" Rio demanded.

Flint held up his hand. "It's almost finished." Then he took a second glance at Rio, taking in his bloody shoulder and the muzzle of Jade's rifle fixed on his back. "Tried to arrest them, didn't you?"

Kaiden glanced to the door. "Come on, Flint. We've got to go." He had to get them out before they became trapped.

"I expected more of you," Rio said.

"If you want to get into a discussion about job performance," Flint said, "you won't come out on top."

"We need to go," Kaiden said.

As much as he might like to hear Flint give Rio a dressing down, he saw the corpses scattered throughout the corridors. He smelled the death that lingered in every hallway. He had to stop this.

"Just a minute," Flint said. "Almost there." A ping sounded. "Got it."

The holographic screens flashed on, and they gazed at the pandemonium in the corridors. TAP had become a war zone.

"Where are our people?" Rio said.

"I'm looking for them," Flint said. "Those that are alive are congregating in the hangar on the third level."

"That would explain why we didn't run into any terrorists on the lower levels," Jade said.

"They must be herding them there," Birch said.

"We have to do something," Rio said.

"Wait a minute," Flint said.

"I'm gonna beat you silly if you don't stop saying that," Rio snapped.

"You touch anybody," Jade said, "and my next bullet will punch a hole in that wooden lump that you call a brain."

"Besides," Flint said, "we don't want to race in there just to have our fellow clones kill us, now, do we? Give me a minute to get the message ready."

"What message?" Willow asked.

"You'll see. Now, be quiet and let me work." Flint keyed something into the computer.

A fifth detonation growled through the corridor, causing the holographic screens to blink and flicker.

"Sounds like Oakley's ordered them to blow up the compound," Birch said.

"He already blew up the Genesis Room," Willow said, "with the first bomb."

Kaiden spun to face her as dread filled his chest. Birch and Jade didn't look at Willow. They had already known. But Jade's face paled, and her eyes glistened with unshed tears.

"And the nursery?" Kaiden asked.

"He killed them all," Willow said, tears streaming down her face.

A pit expanded in Kaiden's stomach. All those innocent children. Even if they were clones, they didn't deserve to die like that.

"Now, who's the monster?" Jade asked. Her face was grim, and Kaiden knew she had visited the Genesis Room just to see the babies.

Rio's gaze swiveled between them. "You led a man in here so he could murder the babies?"

"No!" they all yelled at the same time.

"He promised us there would be no killing," Kaiden said. "We only brought in five, and they were neutralized."

"You believed a terrorist whose only goal in life is to kill clones?"

"It's a bit more complicated than that," Willow said.

"It was a risk," Kaiden said, "but we made contingency plans. We can still stop this."

"I have a nice surprise for them," Flint said. "Internal Nano-Cellular Repair is going to come in handy today." The computer pinged again. "There." Flint snatched up his rifle, grabbed his portable computer, and headed for the door.

The intercom crackled to life as they made their way down the hallway. Dead clones lay everywhere. Here and there, the body of a terrorist in his distinctive blue jeans and white T-shirt mingled with the rest. The smell of viscera, gunpowder, burnt plastic, and hot metal filled the corridors, making it unpleasant to breathe.

"Attention TAP personnel," the intercom said. "We have been invaded by the Sons of God terrorist organization."

"That's a hopeful message," Birch said.

"Just listen," Flint said.

"Evacuation airships are preparing in the hangar on Level Three," the voice continued. "Arm yourselves, if possible, and destroy any terrorist you see. Do not turn your weapons on each other. Commander Rio will be directing the evacuation with the TAP leadership team from the hangar on Level Three. All security personnel are to protect TAP workers and lead them to the hangar."

"That's a nice touch," Birch said.

Rio grunted. "You fools have wasted decades of research and development. If we get out of here alive, I'm going to see that all of you are disciplined to within an inch of your lives."

"Good luck," Jade said.

Rio scowled at her.

"You didn't think we'd find a way to remove those stupid switches?" Birch said. "You can't control us any longer."

"I'll find a way," Rio said.

The message repeated. It echoed in the deserted corridors.

"That didn't seem like much of a surprise," Birch said. "I thought you had something big up your sleeve."

"It's coming," Flint said. "It's gonna be painful, but we'll all recover quickly enough."

"I'm gonna thump on you," Rio said, "if you don't start talking straight."

A white gas drifted down over them from the air ventilation system.

Flint grinned. "You might want to cover your mouth and nose," he said. "That way, you won't get such a high dose."

Shouting and screaming echoed down the corridor. Kaiden pulled his shirt up over his mouth and nose. "Flint, you're crazy," he said from behind his shirt.

"It won't kill anyone," Flint said.

The burning began at the back of Kaiden's throat, and soon his airway felt like it was on fire. Tears dripped from his eyes.

"But I'm gonna kill you," Birch choked at Flint.

"Keep moving," Flint said.

They stumbled along, hampered by the growing crowd of wheezing, coughing TAP personnel. They shoved their way into the stairway and elbowed past staggering clones until they reached the third level. The sounds of scattered gunfire still erupted here and there. They came across a squad of terrorists bent over, gagging and vomiting. Two of them sprawled unconscious near the wall.

"Disarm them," Kaiden ordered.

Birch and the others confiscated their guns and then bunched them in a group. A TAP woman in a nursery jacket snatched up one of the guns beside Kaiden with a horrible shriek and started shooting into the group of terrorists. Red stains blossomed on their white shirts, and several of them fell before Rio wrestled the gun from her hands. Her face was distorted in rage and streaked with tears.

"They murdered our babies!" she sobbed.

"We know," Rio said, "but we need them to talk." He glanced at his pistol and then at Kaiden as if he considered using it on him.

Jade grunted and gestured with her rifle for him to set it down. He smirked and handed the gun to a man in a security uniform that had just made his way out of the stairwell.

"Guard them," Kaiden said.

"You're all going to die anyway," one of the terrorists croaked. "This place is going to burn and roast you all." He spat on the floor.

Kaiden suppressed the sudden burst of guilt. He had been one of the terrorists in his first life. He considered kicking the man in the teeth but decided against it and joined the rest of the group as they muscled their way down the crowded corridor toward the hangar.

"What was Oakley planning?" Kaiden asked Willow.

She glanced at him in annoyance. "I don't have any idea," she said. "He told me what he told you. But I don't think he meant to destroy Ararat. He wanted to clone himself."

Kaiden stared at her. "Are you serious?"

She nodded. "He told me before Birch and Jade shot him."

Kaiden sniffed in disgust. "Even I didn't think he was that much of a hypocrite."

Gunfire sounded in the corridor behind them. Kaiden jerked around.

"They executed the terrorists," Willow gasped in disbelief.

"Doesn't look like clones are any better than naturals," Birch said.

"They just witnessed babies and children being murdered," Jade replied. "Any human would react the same way."

"We tried to be humane," Rio said. "I guess they listened to Flint's little message."

They found the level three hangar filled with people—desperate and panicking. Most seemed to have recovered quickly from the effects of the gas because of the INCR, and several groups of terrorists lay dead or tied up in little bunches. Bodies were strewn everywhere. Several airships had already taken off. Flint's surprise was unorthodox, but he had effectively neutralized the terrorists.

"Where are you going to send them?" Kaiden asked. His throat still burned, but the sensation was fading.

"The nearest TAP facility is in northern Mexico," Rio said.

"Is that a good idea?" Jade asked.

"You have a better option?"

Jade shook her head.

"I'm not going there," Kaiden said.

"Suit yourself," Rio said. "But you're not taking one of the large gunships. I need those."

"That one will do," Birch said, pointing to a small F-205 Vulture transport.

"Get out of here," Rio said. "You've done enough damage for one day." He raised a hand to squeeze his injured shoulder. "Next time I see you, you're dead."

Kaiden hesitated and then sprinted toward the F-205 transport, the others following close behind. He clambered into the cockpit with Birch, who was running through the pre-flight checklist.

"Better get this thing into the air," he said. Jade and Willow crouched behind them as Birch fired up the engines.

"Look!" Willow shouted and pointed out the window of the airship. "It's Noah."

Kaiden glanced up. A tall, beautiful black woman dressed in a white lab coat strolled calmly toward another F-205 transport. A black child in a pink dress held her hand. The woman paused at the door to the airship and looked over her shoulder at Kaiden.

"Rose?" Kaiden whispered. It wasn't possible. His mother was leading Rose by the hand.

Chapter Twenty-Eight
Pursuit

KAIDEN LEANED FORWARD with his head in his hands, listening to the quiet thrum of the engines as the airship hurtled through the night. He left Birch to pilot the craft while he tried to get control of himself. His head ached, and his elbow still throbbed. The INCR nano-particles would soon take the pain away.

He still couldn't believe what had occurred—his mother was Noah, he had pulled the trigger, Oakley had murdered the children. It all happened like a dream or a bad nightmare. The shock of it left him feeling numb, unable to cry anymore. How could he have stopped this?

The sight of his mother falling onto the couch with his bullets in her chest haunted him. How had it come to this? He'd become the monster he feared. So many died—for nothing. TAP hadn't been destroyed. He hadn't stopped his mother, and little Rose was alive— or at least a clone of her was. She was almost the same age she had been when she died. What did his mother do? Keep recycling Rose's clones to keep her perpetually ten or eleven the way she did his?

Kaiden groaned as the realization hit him. Nineteen. He had died at the age of nineteen. His mother only kept her clones alive through the age of nineteen. When they turned twenty, she killed them. It was sick, deranged. His mother had loved him, after all, but in a selfish, perverse way. She had tried to resurrect the children she had loved to freeze them in time. Freeze their relationships in time.

Worst of all was the earth-shattering understanding that if multiple clones of his mother existed, then there was certainly another fully-formed clone of himself out there, living out an independent existence. This idea had never been a subject of contemplation for him because he had no reason to believe it possible. But if there was another clone of him out there with the same mental structures and memories, what did that mean for his own identity? Was he just a carbon copy with no independent self?

The numb shock slowly gave way to burning rage. She had betrayed him. His own mother had cloned him despite his own feelings. How could a mother be so selfish?

"You all right?" Willow sat beside him on the padded bench in the tiny common room at the center of the airship.

Kaiden lifted his head and nodded.

"Head hurting again?"

"A bit," Kaiden said.

"I'm sorry."

Kaiden turned to her. "You knew, didn't you?"

She looked away. "I guessed just before we left. But I wasn't sure. I thought it might be your father."

"And you let me go there to kill my own mother anyway?" Kaiden yelled. The rage, frustration, and horror had built up so much he had to let it out. "After you knew how much I wanted my family?"

"I'm sorry," Willow said. "It was your idea to go after her. I did try to convince you to send someone else. Besides, I could have been wrong—then what would you have thought? Maybe you had to see for yourself. You never would have believed me otherwise, and if I killed her, or Jade or Birch had, you would just blame us."

"She was my mother," Kaiden shouted.

Willow lunged to her feet. Her face burned bright red as the anger flashed in her eyes. "You're not the only one who's suffering! My brother tried to kill me after he butchered those innocent children." A sob escaped her throat. "I had to watch him die. And I never lost my memories of him. I've been longing to be with him for forty years. You've missed your precious mother for only a few weeks."

Her outburst so startled Kaiden that he sat back against the wall of the airship and stared at her. She was right. She had tried to warn him, to convince him not to go himself.

"So, I don't want to hear any more crap about how much you've suffered," Willow finished. "We're all suffering." She loomed over him in a blood-spattered lab coat with her fists clenched, daring him to contradict her.

Kaiden bowed his head. He had directed his frustration at her, but he was really angry with himself.

"You know," Birch said as she stepped into the room. "You two have it all wrong."

Willow whirled to face her.

"How's that?" Kaiden asked.

"First of all," Birch dropped onto the cushioned seat and yanked Willow down beside her, "if your mother cloned herself, you aren't technically related. Her clone didn't give birth to you. Your own DNA did."

Kaiden scowled. He didn't like what Birch was saying. "Like that hardly matters," he mumbled.

"And you," Birch said to Willow, "you're what, four generations removed from Oakley. He hasn't been your brother for forty years."

"We still share DNA," Willow said.

Birch scoffed. "Those memories you two go on about are connected to bodies that no longer exist," she said, "to lives that were snuffed out years ago. You're both products of a test tube, and until you accept that fact, you're going to run around like pigs with their heads cut off, trying to find some identity that doesn't exist."

"It's chickens," Jade said from the doorway in a flat voice. "Not pigs."

"It still works," Birch said with a wave of her hand.

"No, it doesn't," Jade said. "Chickens flop around after their heads are cut off. Pigs don't, at least not as much."

"How would you know?" Birch said.

"I just do," Jade said.

Kaiden smiled to himself. Birch was crazy. He glanced at Willow. "Sorry," he said.

"I'm sorry too," Willow said, "for keeping information from you."

"It's about time you admitted it," Kaiden said.

Willow gave him a sad smile. "Do you want me to reset your memories back to the Kaiden who I first met on the lunar transport?" she asked. "That way, you can forget that you ever knew…well, you can forget what happened."

Kaiden considered. Willow was serious. Her jaw was set, her expression grim. What did she mean? Before or after the attack on the lunar transport? After the way he'd acted with his restored memories, he couldn't blame her for wanting to go back before their relationship had become so complicated. But he shook his head. "These memories are who I am."

"I think we're making headway," Birch said.

"But this means," Jade said, "that what Willow said about how TAP has us on a schedule to be replaced every six or seven years is wrong."

Kaiden glanced up at her. "How do you figure?"

"If multiple clones of your mother are walking around all about the same age, then she must have dozens of them in production at any one time, which means she could have dozens of us in production."

"Maybe not dozens," Willow said, "but certainly several copies."

"You mean, I'm not myself?" Birch asked.

"What?" Jade said.

"There is no self if I have five copies of me running around. There's a…" she struggled to find the word, "…a plurality. I'm freaking out about this."

"There's only one you," Jade said with a smile. "Believe me."

Kaiden understood exactly what Birch meant. It was a shock to the foundation of individual consciousness. If there were multiple copies of a single individual coexisting, then what did self even mean?

"Identity is a complex thing," Jade said. "We all construct our sense of self from our personal experiences and our beliefs about the past and about morality. No two people—even clones—will have the same sense of self. It's impossible."

Despair clutched at Kaiden's chest. Maybe it would have been better to let TAP kill him. At least then he would be free of this pain.

"My mother is still going to release The Flood," he said, "and there won't be any natural humans left if we don't do something."

"Then, we just have to stop her," Birch said.

"We have to figure out what that tree means," Jade said.

They all turned their attention to where Jade leaned against the doorway with her arms folded.

"Why?" Willow said.

"Because I just got an image from Colt."

"What?" Kaiden couldn't believe it. Colt had been killed, like Quill. He'd disappeared weeks ago before they escaped TAP the first time.

Jade walked over to them and showed the tiny image of the tree that glowed brightly on her wrist terminal. It looked just like the one they had seen on Noah's files.

"How did you get this?" Birch asked.

"I just received it."

Birch grabbed her arm to get a better look at the WT. "Did you reply?"

"Yes, but he hasn't responded," Jade said.

"Look in the background." Willow pointed to the small screen.

They all bent low over Jade's wrist terminal to peer at the tiny image.

"Is that a shelf?" Kaiden asked.

"Looks like it," Willow said. "He's on an airship. He must have stowed away."

"He's insane," Birch said.

"He's a genius," Kaiden said. "Why didn't we recruit this guy for our team earlier?"

Kaiden realized that he had left Birch piloting the ship after they had taken off from TAP. "Wait. Who's flying the ship?"

"Flint," Birch said.

"Has he qualified to fly an F-205?" Kaiden asked.

"We haven't crashed yet, have we?" Birch said.

"That doesn't make me feel better." Kaiden rose and started toward the cockpit.

The speaker above their heads crackled. "I heard that." Flint's voice boomed overhead.

They all laughed.

"Well," Birch said, "where to now, fearless leader?" She wiggled her eyebrows at him.

Kaiden shook his head. "I don't know. Flint's flying the ship."

"Ever been to Florida?" Flint asked.

"Isn't most of it under water? Why would we want to go there?"

"Because that's where the ship Noah took is headed," Flint said. He paused. "Umm, we have company."

Willow lunged to her feet. "Is it TAP?"

"Looks like a TAP airship," Flint said.

Kaiden rose. "How well can you fly?"

"Hang on," Flint said.

The airship dropped into a dive.

CHAPTER TWENTY-NINE
MESSAGE FROM THE ENEMY

KAIDEN CAUGHT THE arm on the bench he'd been sitting on as the bottom of the airship fell out from underneath them. Fortunately, the bench and table were bolted to the floor. Willow grabbed his leg, but the others careened into the wall.

"You're going to kill us!" Birch yelled.

"I'm going to be sick," Willow said.

"Just a bit of fun," Flint said over the intercom. "You might want to buckle up. This could get interesting."

The airship leveled off, and they all scrambled for a seat. Kaiden raced toward the cockpit. If they were going to have to fight, Flint would need all the help he could get. But when he stumbled into the cockpit, he found Flint listening to punk rock music and smiling.

"Buckle up. They're gaining again." Flint called up an image of the airship, chasing them on a monitor as Kaiden dropped into the seat.

"How many hours have you logged in an F-205," Kaiden asked.

Flint grinned. "Enough."

Kaiden raised his eyebrows at him.

"It's all math and engineering, my friend," Flint said.

Kaiden monitored the radar and the radio. "Do we have any guns or missiles on this thing?" he asked as he reached for the radio switch.

"Nah," Flint said. "This one's too small. But, give me a sec, and I'll have the cloaking software ready to go. I'm hacking into the smart chips already installed in the skin of the ship."

"Someone's transmitting on another frequency," Kaiden said as a red light flashed on the communications console. He flipped the switch to hear what was being said.

"Dude," a voice crackled over the speaker. "Stop trying to get away from me. I'm running out of fuel."

"Who's that?" Flint asked.

Kaiden shook his head. It wasn't an official TAP communication. He had heard the male voice somewhere before.

"Come on," the man said. "Just answer the stupid signal."

Flynn rolled to the left and dived. Kaiden's stomach did a somersault.

"Who's flying that tin can?" the man said.

Kaiden tried to swallow the sudden rush of nausea. He was used to flying, but not like this. "Maybe we should find out who it is before you make us all throw up."

Flint didn't answer, so Kaiden spoke into the microphone. "Identify yourself," he said.

"Dang. It's Colt, man. Set that stupid thing down before I crash."

Flint grinned. "I thought I recognized your dulcet tones."

Kaiden scowled at him. He knew Flint hadn't recognized Colt's voice any more than he had. Colt had been the one Jade sent to spy on the unregistered TAP shipments. They all thought he had been caught and killed.

"How did you find us?" Kaiden demanded.

"Dude, I am running out of fuel. I can answer your questions later. Just put that stupid thing down somewhere."

Flint winked at Kaiden. "Your call, boss man."

Kaiden smirked at him. "Set it down. Let's see what this lunatic has found."

Jade grabbed Colt into a fierce hug before pushing him away and punching him in the arm.

"Ouch," Colt said. "What's your problem?"

"I thought I told you to keep your head down," Jade demanded.

Colt lounged in the doorway to the cockpit of the F-250, where they had all gathered after Flint lifted it off the ground and set it to autopilot. They abandoned the airship Colt had been flying because they didn't have any fuel to spare. Colt massaged his shoulder and scowled at Jade.

He was a short, stocky Japanese kid fresh out of cadet school. Kaiden guessed he couldn't raise a beard if he'd wanted to. Colt wore the same black security uniform they all had, but he was covered in dirt and some type of phosphorous material that made him glow.

"Easy girl," Colt said to Jade. "How did I know you guys were gonna blow TAP to pieces?"

"We didn't do it," Birch said.

"That's not the word on the street," Colt replied. "I was heading toward TAP when I received Rio's bulletin sent over all secure TAP channels that you are to be arrested on sight. Seems he's got a full-scale rebellion on his hands."

Colt glanced at them. When none of them said anything, he gestured to them. "Care to explain?"

Jade gave a quick summary without most of the details. But it was enough to cause Colt to stumble to a chair and collapse into it.

"You people are crazy," he said.

"Don't look at me," Flint said. "I got all my peas in my pod." He gestured to Kaiden, pointed a finger at his own ear, and made circular motions. "That one, I'm not so sure about."

"Well," Colt said, "while you guys were ruining the lives of thousands of unlucky clones, I found out a few things you might want to know before you go blundering into another fight with Noah."

Kaiden flinched at the name and averted his gaze. The pain he had been trying to suppress rose up in his chest.

Jade shoved her wrist terminal in front of Colt's face. "What is this?"

Colt pulled a face. "That's not my problem, sis. You all are the geniuses around here. I just gather intel."

Kaiden thought Jade might knock Colt's block off for mouthing off to her, but she gave him an indulgent glare and said, "Spit it out, moron."

Colt grinned. "I saw my chance to hop on that secret transport, so I took it—all the way to Mexico City, where I jumped ship, stole that hunk of metal, and tried to get back to you. But you all left me hangin' out to dry."

"You disappeared," Jade said.

"Like that's an excuse," Colt said. "I was maintaining radio silence, and Flint's little cloaking device and disrupter in my WT helped me avoid TAP's tracking software."

"Disrupter?" Kaiden.

"It's a prototype," Flint said. "It's like the one I used on the nano-imager to find your tracking device."

"Right," Kaiden said. "We're going to have to get that tracking chip out of Colt."

"I might have another way," Flint said.

"Get on with it," Birch insisted. "I hate it when people stop a story right in the middle."

"All right, all right," Colt said. "Keep your skirt on."

Birch sighed in disgust and cocked her head toward Kaiden while pointing at Colt. "This is why we didn't recruit him from the start."

Kaiden smiled. He liked Colt. He reminded him of Quill.

"As I was saying before, these beautiful ladies so rudely interrupted me," Colt continued, "that transport wasn't carrying any DNA that I could find. All they had were piles of crates with that tree symbol all over them. And they were headed toward Bogotá and then on to Rio de Janeiro."

"So, what's in the boxes?" Willow asked.

Colt shrugged. "When I tried to take a peek, things got real scary, real fast. Alarms went off, and I had to hide in some nasty places until they landed in Mexico City." He glanced down at his dirty clothes. "Did you know TAP personnel never clean that little tool locker in the engine room?"

Jade gave a dramatic sigh. "So, you don't know what was in the boxes?"

"Did I say that?"

"I'm gonna kill him," Birch said.

"I said it got scary," Colt said. "I tried to snag one, but I didn't have time. I snapped this, though." He clicked his wrist terminal, and a fuzzy image appeared.

"Tubes?" Jade said.

"Are those metal cylinders?" Willow asked.

"I just got a glimpse," Colt said. "But the crates are filled with these tiny, little vials. They looked like colored glass to me."

"How tiny?" Flint said.

"Geez, I don't know. Teeny tiny." He held up his forefinger and thumb about an eighth of an inch apart.

Jade dropped into a chair. "That's it? That's all you got?"

For the first time, Colt frowned. "Hey, sis. That's not cool. I just about got killed finding out what's on that ship for you."

Kaiden was distracted by the buzzing of his wrist terminal. He glanced at it. These were the terminals Willow had given them. But they were all here, and none of theirs were transmitting, nor were they buzzing.

Willow's brow creased. "Who's that?" she asked, apparently thinking the same thing.

"Someone is sending me a message," Kaiden said. He hesitated. No one should have been able to hack Willow's terminals. Flint had checked them himself. He glanced at Flint, who raised his eyebrows.

"This one's not on me, man," Flint said.

"Wait," Kaiden said. He scowled at Colt. "How did you send that image to Jade? We switched wrist terminals."

Jade tossed her hair behind her back. "I sent a message to him after we got out of the tunnels. I was still trying to find him."

Kaiden glanced down at his wrist terminal and clicked it on. A short message scrolled across the screen. "Well done, son," it read. "Watch your back. They're coming for you."

CHAPTER THIRTY
MISCONCEPTIONS

THE F-205 TRANSPORT settled onto a little rise covered with the charred skeletons of trees. Below them, the mouth of a cave yawned wide. Cement steps with metal handrails descended into the darkness. Flint cut the engines, and their dying whine shook the airship as it powered down.

Kaiden peered out the window at the black mouth of the cave and the dark rock walls. The slanting shadows of evening stretched over the burned-out landscape.

"I came here with my parents when I was nine or ten," Willow said. She stood with one hand on the window. "It's called Mammoth Cave, one of the largest cave systems in North America. Unless someone else has taken up residence, we should be able to stay here for a bit while we decide what to do."

"Someone like whom?" Colt asked.

"Terrorists?" Birch said.

"No heat signatures register on the monitors," Flint said.

"Like anything could live in this wasteland," Birch said.

"Actually," Jade said, "this whole area used to be a lush forest."

Kaiden glanced at her. He hadn't had time to talk to her alone since they went into TAP. He wished he knew what to say to her. The pain on her face still bothered him. What was wrong with him? Why couldn't he just have a normal relationship? The thought almost made him laugh. What was normal, anyway? It troubled him to see that she was still hurt and that he was the cause.

"Yeah, I see the burned stumps," Colt said.

"The fires started a few years after I visited here," Willow said. "They burned for months. That's when people abandoned the area."

"I'm gonna have a look around," Flint said.

"If we had time," Willow said, "we could go down into the caves. They're really interesting."

Flint climbed out of the pilot's seat, snagged a rifle, and headed for the exit.

"Think I'll tag along," Colt said. "Can't let the old man have all the fun."

"That one's got serious issues," Birch said as Colt followed Flint.

"We're going to need help," Willow said. "We should try to establish contact with the clones we can trust."

"Why?" Birch asked.

"Because." Willow stared out the window. "We need an army if we're going to go after Noah again."

"A clone army?" Kaiden said. He didn't try to keep the irony out of his voice.

Willow stared at him. "If that's what it takes."

"I don't like the idea of us using clones to kill clones," Jade said as she passed an oily rag over her rifle.

"You have a better idea?" Willow snapped.

Jade paused and glared at Willow.

"We don't have a choice," Kaiden interrupted the debate before it could get started. "If Noah went to the base in Florida, we're going to need help to get to her."

"Anyone been to the base in Florida?" Birch asked.

Jade nodded and continued wiping her rifle. "Once, after we assassinated a police chief who was rounding up clones."

"You assassinated one?" Willow glared at her.

"That's what TAP ordered us to do," Jade said. "Don't tell me you've suddenly developed a conscience."

Willow glared and rose to her feet. "Any recommendations on who we should contact?"

"Our message will have to be encrypted." Kaiden turned his

WT around his wrist thoughtfully. "And only for those we know we can trust."

"Dale and Twig in engineering can be trusted," Birch volunteered. "I know for a fact they've been wanting to escape TAP for a while."

"Twig?" Jade said with a wry smile. "Somebody took this fad of using earth names a bit too far on that one."

"I know a couple of people in the lab," Willow said.

"There's Fawn, from the nursery," Jade said, "if she's still alive."

"All right." Kaiden leaned back against the seat and clasped his hands behind his head. "Check with Colt and Flint and then send it. But make sure it's encrypted and tell them to only bring in people they have absolute confidence in. We don't need any sleeping cells sneaking in."

"And you have to set a deadline," Jade said. "We might be betrayed or tracked. We can't sit around here for long."

"I'll get on it," Willow said and strode from the room.

Birch's gaze followed Willow. "What's got her ponytail all in a bun?"

"That doesn't make any sense." Kaiden shook his head. "Did you think that through before you said it?"

Birch gave him a wide-eyed, innocent look and said, "What? She's been grumpy ever since we shot her brother."

Kaiden sniffed and raised his hands in helplessness. He looked to Jade for help, but she refused with a noncommittal shake of the head. "Don't ask me. I try to keep her straight."

"You can't see why watching her brother get killed would upset her?" Kaiden asked.

"He was going to kill her," Birch insisted. She glanced at Jade, who nodded her agreement.

"Anyway," Birch continued, "you want to explain how you're getting messages from your dear, dead mother?"

Kaiden scowled as he leaned forward to stare at the floor. "How would I know that?"

"Who's coming after you?" Birch persisted.

Kaiden had considered that very question, and there was only one conclusion.

"It's one of her clones, obviously. She's trying to scare me."

"Well done, son?" Birch quoted the message. "Perhaps your clone mothers are schizophrenic. How many personalities can a clone have?"

"One for each clone," Jade said. "Clones can't be schizophrenic."

Birch dropped the clip from her rifle and refilled it. "Why not."

Jade laughed and tossed her the rag she'd been using to wipe down her own weapon. "Because they're individuals," she said. "Schizophrenia happens inside one person's mind."

Kaiden rose. "I think we have to assume that they're all dangerous."

He grabbed a rifle and a flashlight and climbed down the ladder. He wanted to take a look around so he understood the landscape in case they had to stand and fight or needed to make a rapid exit. A blast of hot, dry air hit him, abrading his face with tiny grains of sand. Kaiden squinted and bent into the wind. His flashlight beam cut through the gathering darkness.

He slid and scrambled down the hillside to the cavern entrance, trying not to think about everything that had happened. His movements kicked up a fine ash powder that coated his mouth and made him cough.

How many clones of his mother existed? How many Roses, and maybe Kaidens? Should he try to save them? How could he not? Would killing all the Noahs put an end to the mad plan to murder billions of natural-born humans? He didn't know if he could pull the trigger again—even though he knew they were clones this time. Kaiden snorted. He had murdered his own mother in cold blood, and he was planning to do it again.

The valley stretched out before him, long and narrow with tumbled boulders and blackened corpses of trees that stabbed skyward like needles. It was a forlorn place. He found a boulder near the wall and plopped down onto it, laying his head back against the rock. Sweat dribbled down his face. He would have to go in soon. It was too hot to stay there, even in the gathering darkness.

Kaiden glanced at his wrist terminal. What if his mother would respond to him? What if she would answer his questions? He knew it was a risk. She could just be sending him messages in an attempt to try to locate him. But if she had hacked the WTs, she probably already knew where they were. He clicked it on and punched out a quick reply, "How many are you?" He sent it and waited.

To his surprise, the response came back almost instantly. "We are three—one for each of the three sons of Noah. Only three at a time possess all the memories. To stop The Flood, you must kill us all."

Kaiden's gut tightened. The message continued.

"I am watched. I will help you if I can. The others have sent soldiers to kill you. I love you, son. You have the strength to do what must be done, unlike the ones who came before."

"What's that supposed to mean?" he typed in. "How many times have I been cloned?" He wished he had thought to ask Willow to download the memories from his other lives. Maybe he could have learned something useful.

"Many," she typed back.

The sound of boots crunching on gravel startled him. He clicked off the wrist terminal and snapped up his rifle.

Willow paused in the beam of his flashlight. "It's just me."

Kaiden lowered the gun, trying to blink the hot emotion from his eyes. His mother had said she loved him. Even though he knew she was just a clone like he was, reading those words on the screen gripped his heart with a terrible longing he couldn't describe.

It was like having a split personality where the two sides warred for his emotional allegiance. He could love and value the lives of his clone friends while hating his own clone existence. He could respect his clone friends while seeing all clones as a type of corrupted humanity. It was maddening. He blinked at the sting of tears, grateful that the darkness hid them from Willow.

She sat beside him. "Thinking of her?" she asked. "I'm sorry it happened that way."

"Yeah, well," Kaiden said, "I have to go on killing her until they're all dead, don't I?"

Willow laid a cool hand on his. "I know it's hard. I keep thinking of Oakley as a little boy playing with a tiny hovercraft. I can't understand how he became such a monster."

Kaiden glanced at her. "People who kill their family members are monsters, aren't they?"

"Hang on," Willow said, "that's not what I meant."

Kaiden stood, but Willow grabbed his hand and pulled him

back down.

"You have every right to be angry with me," she said. "But you must understand I'm just doing the best I can. I've made mistakes, but I wasn't trying to hurt you." Her voice caught. "I was trying to help you. To keep you safe."

Kaiden sighed. How could he get her to understand when he didn't really understand himself? Everything that had gone wrong with his life began when he let Willow onto his ship at the lunar base. And now he had these horrible, explosive feelings toward her he didn't understand.

Maybe none of it was her fault, but after Oakley and his mother, how could he be sure? "You allied us with terrorists who slaughtered innocent children," he said, "and worse, you kept information from me that could have jeopardized the life of everyone on our team."

"What could I have done to stop you?" Willow said. She grabbed his arm, but he yanked it away. "Stop blaming everybody else and accept some responsibility yourself."

Kaiden grunted, but she was right.

"Please, Kaiden." Tears blossomed in her eyes. "I know I've made mistakes, and I'm sorry. But I warned you, and you wouldn't listen. Besides, if Jade or anybody else had killed her, you would have attacked them."

He shook his head.

Willow grabbed his arm. "Don't deny it," she said. "You've been so caught up in finding your family that if anyone else had done it, you would have killed them on sight. I should have tried harder to stop you, but you have to admit I'm right."

Shame and rage burned in Kaiden's chest. He wanted to grab her and shake her. How could she be so rational about it? Couldn't she see how much it hurt him? If he was going to be honest, this wasn't about her at all. This was about him.

Kaiden bowed his head. "I've become the monster I hated in more ways than one, and the only way to save humanity is to become even more horrible and kill my mother over and over again."

Willow pulled him into an embrace, pressing her body close to his. "I'm so sorry. I would take the pain away if I could, but I can't do this alone. I need you."

Kaiden stiffened, wanting to continue fuming. At least the anger helped to quell his despair and self-disgust. But she was so earnest, and he had made his fair share of mistakes. He wrapped his arms around her and pulled her to him, desperate to find some sense of balance, some way to escape the emptiness and self-reproach.

"I'm so sorry," Willow whispered into his ear. "I would never hurt you intentionally."

She drew away, leaving wet tears to cool on his neck. Her eyes glistened. She had that same look Jade had had, and it scared him. What should he do? He didn't want to hurt her the way he had Jade. She raised her hands to his face and leaned in. Inviting. Pleading. At the last minute, he shied away.

"I'm sorry," he said.

Willow drew back and stared at him. Her bottom lip trembled.

"I don't think you're a monster," she whispered. Then, she stood and stepped toward the airship on the rise above them.

"Wait," Kaiden said. He wasn't sure what to say. Willow wanted him to know that she cared for him, despite everything that had happened between them. And he cared for her, even though his feelings were so conflicted where she was concerned. Maybe it was that conflict that drew him to her in some weird, psychotic way he didn't understand.

Willow paused and looked back. An awkward silence lengthened between them as he searched for the right words. The blue lights of the airship shone eerily in the darkness.

"When you're finished here," she said, "I have something important to show you."

When he only nodded, still uncertain what to do or say, she turned and disappeared into the darkness.

Kaiden lingered. How should he feel? First Jade, and now Willow. He had been so absorbed with his struggle with his memories and their plans to destroy TAP that he hadn't had time to really consider what he would do after it was all over.

Jade remained in the shadow cast by the engine of the F-205 transport. Bitterness clawed its way up her throat. She had been on her way to speak with Kaiden, to explain that she had never meant to make him uncomfortable. But Willow was already there. Kaiden drew her into a close embrace and held her for a long moment.

Her first inclination was to stride out there and tell him he couldn't trust her. That Willow was using him. But if Kaiden had chosen Willow, what would that accomplish? She had suspected there was something between them. She just arrived too late. Willow already found a way into his heart.

Kaiden stared after Willow, and Jade whirled away, not wanting to be seen. There was no point in trying to force herself into his affections. She would not belittle herself by begging. If Kaiden didn't come to her of his own will, she would let him go. It was better to be alone than to grovel.

Willow watched with a sense of satisfaction as the airships carrying clone refugees began arriving the next day. Kaiden and Flint made one of the big T-60 Python gunships their new command center. She listened as Kaiden and Flint debated what to do.

"We can't stay here," Flint said as he scurried around, deleting the TAP tracking software on the ships, uploading Quill's cloaking software, and waiting while it synced with the ship's smart chips.

"They might have tracked them to us already."

"We have to wait at least another hour," Kaiden said. "If we move now, they won't be able to find us."

"If we hang around here, TAP will," Flint said.

"I know," Kaiden said. "I've already sent some of the security personnel down to set up a laser cannon battery in case we're surprised, and I have a T-60 in the air to give us cover and a T-40 Stinger circling. We should have warning and be in a position to fight if we have to."

"And when they come?" Flint asked.

"You'll take this T-60, and I'll get the other one. The four gunships will cover the transports. I've already talked to the pilots. They know what to do."

"Let's hope they're still in disarray at Ararat," Flint said.

Trying to piece together what was happening at Ararat, Kaiden and Birch set about interviewing the new arrivals while sorting them into groups by their expertise and skill sets.

Willow and Jade treated those who were injured and tried to organize the sleeping arrangements. Colt wandered about getting in the way.

"If you're just going to stand there," Jade said to Colt, "hand me that bandage."

Willow smiled to herself as she bandaged a young man who had worked in engineering. She didn't like Jade much because she knew she had her eye on Kaiden, and Kaiden acted differently around Jade than he did Birch, but Willow had to admit that it was entertaining watching Jade go after Colt. They were like brother and sister.

She had also looked into Jade's background and found nothing but an impeccable record. Jade had moved around between teams because she requested transfers, but she had always been highly recommended. In some ways, Jade's obvious competence irritated her the most.

One of the few children to survive the slaughter at Ararat sat on a table with wide eyes, following Jade's every move. She was an adorable African child with curly hair. A bullet had grazed her arm, but she was otherwise unhurt.

Willow's stomach tightened at the thought of Oakley and what he had done. He had dared call clones monsters. This poor child had seen horrors no human being should ever have to witness, let alone a child. How could anyone think she was a monster?

Colt winked at the little girl and tossed a bandage to Jade. "She's always grumpy," he said. "But anybody with beautiful, black hair like hers can get away with it."

Jade glared at him. "Colt is one of those people who never manage to grow up."

"Why did they hurt us?" the girl whispered. Her face contorted in pain as Jade treated her wound.

A knot twisted Willow's stomach. This was her fault. She should never have trusted Oakley. She had been blinded by her desperation to reconnect with her family, to recover something of the love and life that had been stolen from her. And she had been determined to make TAP suffer. But she never expected innocent children to get caught in the crossfire. Tears burned her eyes. What could she have done differently?

Willow felt the color drain from her face as Jade eyed her. None of them had training for caring for the young. But Colt never missed a beat. He knelt in front of the child and grasped her hand in his.

"Some people think clones are dangerous, and they're afraid of us."

"But I'm too small to hurt anyone."

Colt patted her hand. "That's why we brought you here. To keep you safe." He glanced up at Jade. "Come on. Now that she's done poking at you, I can show you something really cool."

He lifted the child from the table and carried her from the room in his arms, holding her close and whispering in her ear.

Jade shook her head. "Even an idiot like Colt can be human."

Willow felt the irony of Jade's words along with the bitter guilt that she hadn't been able to comfort the girl—a girl whose life had been ruined because of her. This was the question all of the clones were now asking. Were they fully human?

Perhaps it was nonsense, but it was a real worry for people whose identities had been stripped from them in one quick stroke. A broken identity had to be reconstructed somehow, and that would mean a lot of self-questioning.

She wanted to say something to Jade to break the wall that had grown between them, but she couldn't find the words. Kaiden was interested in Jade, and he had refused Willow's offered kiss the night before. She couldn't help but feel the prickle of jealousy whenever Jade was around. Kaiden apparently liked women who carried guns and blew things up. Maybe she didn't have the right to be jealous, but she was.

Jade broke the silence. "Don't hurt him," she said.

At first, Willow thought she was still speaking of Colt, but the sad resignation in her gaze and her slouching shoulders convinced her she was speaking of Kaiden.

"I have no intention of hurting him," Willow said.

"But you mean to keep using him, don't you?" Jade said.

Willow frowned. "I'm not—" she began, but Jade cut her off.

"Don't bother denying it. I'm not blind." Then she shifted and looked away. "He prefers you, but he deserves to be able to trust the woman he loves."

Willow shifted uncomfortably. The rebuke stung, and she opened her mouth to shout an angry retort. Then closed it. What could she say? She was pretty sure Kaiden didn't love her, at least not the way Jade intended. He wouldn't even kiss her. But why would Jade think Kaiden preferred her?

He had come to Willow before retiring last night, and she had told him she suspected that his mother had been syncing memory files before he killed her, but he had remained distant all day. She wondered what she might have done differently. She had exposed her true feelings and thought Kaiden had too until she looked into his face and saw the turmoil there. He didn't know what he wanted, and she would just have to give him time.

Jade left to care for another injured clone, leaving Willow to wrestle with her conflicting emotions. What if Jade was right? How would she get Kaiden to understand all that she had done?

It took them much longer than expected to get organized so that they knew what skills each clone had to offer and which airship they were assigned to. Flint had several DWJs in every ship in the hope that they would jam any tracking signals the clones might be giving off. So far, there was no indication that TAP had found them.

Their little army had grown considerably. Willow gathered all the older clones into the loading bay of the T-60 gunship, which served as their command center. The space was small but large enough to fit the clones who had come to them.

Narrow window slits lined the sides of the loading bay, and Flint set up a series of computers from which he could monitor all the complicated security hardware and software he'd spent hours installing on the dozen ships that had joined them.

Over one hundred clones had gathered, ranging in age from nine or ten to nineteen. They brought stories of a civil war erupting in the corridors of Ararat and of Rio and the security forces resorting to mass discipline to put it down. Those who could escaped. They carried word that news of Ararat's turmoil had spread to other TAP installations, and the insurgency was expanding.

This surprised Willow. Once again, she had allowed her naiveté to convince her that she was the only one to remember her previous lives in any detail, but it was becoming obvious that TAP misjudged the success of their programs. The discipline had effectively terrified any who retained memories to keep their mouths shut. Now, they felt liberated.

Flint elbowed Willow. "From the look of it," he whispered, "we've started a flood of our own."

Willow had to agree. But would this flood be big enough to stop the one threatening humanity?

"Can I have everyone's attention, please?" Kaiden shouted over the murmur of voices. He carried his rifle on a strap over his shoulder.

The crowd quieted.

"We need to know," Kaiden began, "if anyone here knows about a top-secret TAP program code-named The Flood." People gazed at each other, but no one spoke. Then, a single hand emerged from the back of the crowd.

"Yes?" Kaiden said.

All heads turned.

A tall, thin man with a narrow face and high forehead rose. When he spoke, his voice was unusually high-pitched and nasally.

"I believe we are The Flood," he said. "Why else would they be creating us in such numbers?"

"How many clones do you think there are?" Kaiden asked. Willow had tried to find this out but hadn't been able to discover any statistics.

"I don't think. I know," the man said. This statement caused a murmur to sweep through the crowd.

"Okay," Kaiden said, with a note of annoyance in his voice. "How many do you know exist?"

"Eight million clones have been produced by TAP in the last four decades. Another four million are now, or will soon be, in production. TAP is seeking ten million viable clones by the end of the year."

"And how do you know this?" Kaiden asked.

"Because it was my job to know."

"Spit it out," Kaiden snapped. "We don't have time for bull crap."

The young man looked insulted, but he answered. "I worked in the Data and Statistics department."

"Then, why do they kill us when we turn twenty?" someone called out.

The young man grimaced. "That wasn't part of my department, but I have no evidence that we are killed."

Kaiden stepped forward. Willow tried to wave him down, but he ignored her.

"I have seen clones executed by TAP," he said. "We have the files to prove it."

"What has any of this got to do with The Flood?" someone shouted.

"I believe," the young man continued, "that we were created to replace humanity. Ten million is the projected number of humans the earth can support while its ecosystems recover. Why else create ten million clones from every ethnic group?"

A murmur swept through the crowd.

"What's your name?" Jade asked.

"Glenn," he said.

"May we consult you if we have any other questions?" Willow asked.

Glenn nodded.

"Anyone else?" Kaiden asked. The muscles in his jaw worked.

No one responded, so Kaiden gestured for Willow to continue. Willow called up the image of the tree they found in Noah's files and projected the holographic image in front of her. "Has anyone seen this anywhere?"

Several hands shot up.

Willow pointed to them one by one. A white woman with short, blonde hair and a gray jacket spoke. "I've seen that image on a computer in the nano-machine lab."

Willow glanced at Flint, who raised his eyebrows dramatically. If nano-technology was being used, that would explain the tiny glass vials Colt had seen. They could be some kind of nano-bot.

"Do you know what work they were doing?" Willow asked.

"No. I wasn't part of that project."

A black man with light brown skin stood next. "We loaded boxes with that symbol for shipment to other TAP bases."

"Do you remember which ones?" Kaiden asked.

"It was all hush-hush," the young man said, "so I don't know much. But I know some were sent to China, India, California, and Russia. I think we just sent a load to South America somewhere."

Willow glanced at Kaiden, who studied the speaker intently. The way his brow pinched and the way his mouth was set let her know he was thinking of Colt's discovery.

"Any place else?" Kaiden said.

The young man shook his head. "That's all I know."

Willow pointed to a brown-skinned man who wore a white lab coat and had a long blue tattoo on the side of his face.

"There was a lab program with that tree symbol," he said. "And no, I didn't work on it. I had a friend who did, but the terrorists killed her." He didn't try to keep the anger out of his voice.

Willow's stomach tightened. Oakley's betrayal had damaged so many lives.

"Anyone else?" she asked.

"Isn't that the Tree of Life?" someone asked. Willow searched until she found a stocky white girl who couldn't be more than twelve or thirteen. She was too young to have gone through the memory transfer yet.

"Yes, it is."

"Why would the Tree of Life be associated with a flood? The Tree of Life was meant to protect and nurture, not kill."

"The best and the brightest." Flint murmured. "TAP wasn't kidding."

"That's what we're trying to work out," Willow said. "Though in western symbolism, it could be used as a symbol of destruction with its roots fixed in Hell."

"So, why should we care?" A tall boy who looked Middle Eastern who couldn't be more than sixteen pushed his way toward the front.

Willow glanced at Kaiden, trying to decide how much she should tell them. But Kaiden didn't wait for her to respond.

"Because," Kaiden said, "we believe Noah plans to destroy all natural human life on earth."

"Including clones?" the boy demanded.

"I don't think so," Kaiden said, "just the naturals."

"Then why should we care?"

Cries of anger followed his words so loudly that Willow couldn't calm them.

"Quiet!" Kaiden yelled.

The crowd calmed, and Kaiden spoke over the remaining voices.

"Whether you know it or not, you all have relatives out there who will also be killed. Billions of innocent people will be slaughtered for the crime of being born naturally into a world they did not create nor destroy."

"That doesn't explain why I should care," the belligerent boy persisted. "So long as I live, what do I care what happens to anyone else?"

Kaiden glanced at Willow. "So much for the more altruistic species she was trying to create." Then he turned back to the boy. "You're free to leave," he said. "Those who remain will be dedicated to stopping TAP from destroying humanity. If anyone wants to leave, now is the time. We won't stop you. But, if you rejoin TAP, we will be forced to do what we must to stop Noah."

"Is that a threat?" the boy asked.

Kaiden strode toward him. "I don't make threats," he said, poking him in the chest. "I make promises. If you betray us, I will hunt you down, and I will kill you."

"Looks like I came to the wrong place," the boy said. He faced the crowd. "I thought we were going to save TAP, not destroy it. I'm not risking my life to save some natural-born who thinks I'm a monster."

A rumble of assent followed his words.

Alarms sounded harsh and blaring in the enclosed space. Willow whirled to find Flint frantically clicking away at the computer.

"Incoming!" he called. "Five airships."

Kaiden, Jade, and Birch joined him.

"More refugees?" Birch asked.

"They're not transmitting the code we sent," Flint said. "I'm initiating the cloaking software."

"Everyone to your assigned ships!" Kaiden bellowed.

Willow glanced out the window. Colt was walking hand in hand with the little girl from the infirmary. They came up the last of the stairs from the caves when he glanced up at the sky, scooped up the girl, and raced up the hill toward the gunship. She clung to his neck. Willow's heart skipped a beat as Colt stumbled and fell.

"Come on," she whispered.

Colt righted himself, took two strides, and exploded in a flash of light, followed by a deafening boom. The shock wave rocked the ship.

CHAPTER THIRTY-ONE
RIO'S REVENGE

"NO!" JADE SCREAMED as Colt evaporated in a flash and cloud of dust and smoke.

People rushed for their assigned ships. Kaiden spun away from the computer with a curse and began shouting orders.

Willow could only stare. Why would TAP attack Colt and the little girl?

"Birch," Kaiden shouted. "Get this thing up in the air."

Birch sprinted toward the cockpit.

"I'll get the other T-60 up," Kaiden said and raced out the landing bay. He raised his WT to his mouth. "Fire up that laser cannon," he shouted, "when a rocket launches, lock onto the source and fire. Where are the T-60 and T-40 we had in the air?"

As if in answer, an explosion burst over them, raining debris onto the ships below. The bay doors closed as the T-60 rose into the air.

"Get that cloaking software up!" Jade yelled. "I'll man the guns."

She bolted from the loading bay, leaving Willow and Flint behind. Not for the first time, Willow bitterly regretted not having any security or flight training. She felt useless, helpless—just like that little girl in Colt's arms. A bitter ache filled her chest. No child, clone or otherwise, should die like that. Despite her best efforts, it seemed that everywhere she went, some child suffered.

She stepped to the window slit in the side of the gunship to see if Kaiden had made it to the T-60. Several airships shimmered and disappeared as the cloaking software went live. The C-121 transport beside them burst into a ball of flame. She shielded her eyes from the blast as debris pinged against the ship.

Birch swung the T-60 around, and Willow found Kaiden. A jolt of terror clenched her stomach tight. He hadn't made it to the gunship. He was picking himself up from the blast, and the T-60 he had been racing toward sagged to one side with an engine in flames. He glanced up at them and then raced toward the laser cannon battery he had ordered to be set up the day before.

Two more ships exploded as the rest managed to get off the ground. The cloaking software connected with the smart chips engaged, and the rest of the ships shimmered and disappeared. The T-60 she was in rotated to face the direction from which the missile had come.

"What's Kaiden doing?" Willow gasped. "He can't even see them."

"Lock us onto them," Kaiden's voice crackled over Flint's receiver.

"That's what he's doing," Flint said. He touched a few buttons. "You've got the first one," he said into the mic. "I'm going after the big T-60. Jade, follow that signal."

"How can you see them if they're cloaked?" Willow asked.

"Because I wrote the dang software so I could."

The laser cannon fired, and the tranquil blue sky erupted into an inferno of fire and debris. Willow watched the pieces of smoking metal and still churning engine of the TAP gunship fall in slow motion from the airship she hadn't been able to see. It was an odd experience, seeing a fireball boil through the clear blue sky when nothing was supposed to be there. Their gunship shook, and another explosion sounded high above them.

"Nice shot, Jade," Flint yelled. "Birch, let's go after the other T-60."

As the ship passed above the smoke billowing in and around the cavern, a line of black-clad TAP security personnel advanced on foot toward the rise that overlooked the cave. Willow's blood ran cold. Kaiden and his little band were alone and trapped.

Jade locked onto the signal Flint sent her and squeezed the trigger. The T-60 shuddered with a burst of fire as the gunship banked and swung away. Tears blurred her vision. Colt had been her only real friend at TAP before she met Kaiden and Birch. She had asked for his help because he was good at covert operations, and she knew she could trust him. Now, he had died just because he was kind to a little child. She couldn't believe he was gone.

Flint sent her another signal, and she locked on. The gunship banked, and she squeezed the trigger. The gunship shuddered, and she followed the trail of the missiles as they streaked through the sky to explode into a ship she couldn't see. Maybe she couldn't save Colt, but she could still punish them for killing him, and she could keep Kaiden alive. The gunship banked again, and her window tilted toward the ground. The sight that met her gaze sent a jolt of terror through her. Kaiden was on the ground at the laser cannon battery, looking up at her. Why wasn't he on a ship?

Kaiden watched the debris of the ship settle to the earth with a grim sense of satisfaction. This wasn't the ideal situation for a commander in battle, but what choice did he have?"

"Give me another one," he said into his communicator.

"You've got bigger problems," Flint said. "They're on foot on your right flank."

Kaiden snapped his head around. A line of TAP security personnel advanced over the rise on the other side of the gully.

"Fall back to the boulders," Kaiden ordered. He grabbed the laser cannon and half-dragged, half-carried it downhill toward the cave where a pile of boulders offered protection. He and his men had almost reached them when bullets fell among his team. The bullets kicked up the dirt and whined past his ears to slap into the boulders and the stone walls. These were exploding rounds intended to kill clones. Three of his team fell before the rest dove behind the rocks.

Kaiden scrambled to get the cannon set up while the rest of his little group returned fire. He set the cannon on the tripod, aimed, and fired. The laser cannon tore a hole in the line of TAP soldiers, and they sought cover among the boulders and burned stumps of trees. Kaiden set the laser for rapid pulse firing, and soon TAP soldiers were aflame and screaming as the laser ignited their clothing and roasted their flesh. He swept the laser along the length of the advancing soldiers. Some of the charred stumps ignited, as well, burning like candles. Acrid smoke smelling of burnt flesh and charred wood filled the gully.

The scene sent the shame and horror burning up his neck and into his face. Those men and women were just following orders. A few weeks ago, he would have been among them. Clearly, Rio was serious about following through with his threat to hunt them down and kill them.

Two more of his team fell.

"Get down," Kaiden ordered. "Stop the bleeding. Let the INCR do their work."

Several explosions echoed through the canyon, and Kaiden hoped Flint and the gunship were taking out the TAP ships. But, if TAP had landed the soldiers, they had more than five ships, and at least one of those must have been a transport to carry that many men.

Heavy machine-gun fire rolled across the dirt, kicking up great bursts of dust and rock splinters. Kaiden whirled the cannon, aimed it toward the little spurts of flame and smoke that showed him where the cloaked ship was and raised the cannon to its highest setting. He couldn't believe that TAP had already developed cloaking software without them knowing. It clearly hadn't worked as well as they thought because Flint had seen through their cover and was able to target them.

Kaiden fired. An explosion burst in the clear blue sky. The image of a ship with a ragged hole in it flickered and materialized as the cloaking software failed. Kaiden hit it again, and it careened toward the floor of the gully. An earsplitting crash ripped through the air, followed by the grinding screech of metal on stone.

Kaiden tried to fire again, but nothing happened. He glanced at the battery indicator on the cannon. It was drained. He tried again just in case, struggling to still the growing panic, but the cannon was no longer effective. Kicking it aside, he flipped his rifle around from his back and took careful aim. That's when Kaiden saw him.

Just behind the ragged line of soldiers, Rio stood with his head bare, staring at Kaiden's position. He wasn't firing. Just watching.

"Son of a test tube," Kaiden cursed.

He leveled his rifle. He should have killed Rio earlier when he had the chance. Just as he squeezed the trigger, Rio dropped to his belly and rolled behind a boulder.

"Filth," Kaiden said. Then, he sucked in a deep breath to relax and let his training take over. He couldn't afford to let his emotions get away from him. Not now. But he would save the last bullet for Rio.

"Flint, where are you?" Kaiden shouted. He should have stayed on the T-60 with them instead of trying to get the other one in the air. He was blind down here. No answer came.

"Aim carefully," Kaiden called to the half dozen men and women he still had with him. "Conserve your ammo."

"There's too many," a young woman called to him.

"Maybe," Kaiden said. "Make every shot count. You know they aren't going to let any of us leave this valley alive if they can help it."

The firing from Kaiden's team slowed, but the incoming rounds continued to screech and slap against the boulders. Two of his men were hit in the face with flying debris from the rocks. The heat was unbearable. He could feel his hands and face baking in the direct sunlight. Sweat rolled down his face. He had to get his people out of here. They wouldn't last long in this heat without water.

The roar of a gunship engine burst over them. Kaiden glanced up, but he could see nothing of the cloaked ship.

"Down!" he yelled. "Everybody down."

The huge guns on the gunship rattled, and a rocket launched. Kaiden prepared for the end, but it didn't come. Men yelled. An explosion echoed off the valley walls. Kaiden peeked over the boulder. TAP soldiers lay scattered over the ground, writhing in their final death struggles. Others were sprinting back over the small rise. He waited as the airship pursued the retreating soldiers with the staccato beat of its big guns. His team cheered.

As the noise of the pursuit drew away, Kaiden stepped out from behind the boulder. His rifle was up, and he was prepared. But nothing stirred amid the smoke and debris of battle, save the TAP soldiers still dying in the dirt. His first instinct was to go to help them. He stepped toward them before he stopped. They had come to kill him and his friends. They had attacked them without any warning. One of them might still be hiding, waiting to pick them off. They had the INCR, too, and some of them might be coming around already.

The sound of another airship made them dive behind the boulders again. But it set down and flickered into view. It was their T-60. Birch smiled down at him from the pilot's window. The door dropped down. "Let's go," Birch's voice crackled from his communicator.

"Go!" Kaiden waved the others toward the ship. "I'll cover you." The last four of his team sprinted up the rise to the gunship carrying two of the injured who were still alive and clambered aboard. A few others who had been stranded on the ground in the attack joined them. As the last one disappeared inside, Kaiden rose up, stole one last glance at his dead companions, and rushed toward the ship. A single gunshot cracked. Kaiden felt the bite of the bullet as it passed through his thigh.

He stumbled and rolled. He came up with his rifle to his shoulder, saw the movement behind a boulder, and squeezed off two rounds. Dust kicked up, and the slap of a bullet against flesh sounded. Kaiden scrambled to his feet and tried to limp toward the airship. Jade leaped from the gunship and pelted toward him. The team members laid down a covering fire all around the cavern as Jade dragged him aboard the airship.

It lifted from the ground, and Kaiden saw, through the still-open door, Rio stand up from behind the rock, a rifle dangling loosely in his hand.

CHAPTER THIRTY-TWO
LONG LIVE THE CLONES

"WHERE ARE THE other ships?" Kaiden asked as Willow cut through his pant leg to expose the wound in his thigh. He stretched his leg on the table in the T-60's medical ward. So many had died. Hollow fury boiled in his gut. It was so senseless. He was trying to save lives, and so far, he had been forced to do little more than kill.

"They ran," Willow said. "Flint says he knows where a couple are hiding, but TAP took out nine of our ships. Everyone on board those ships was killed."

"So much for our army," Kaiden said. The bitterness of it galled him. They had come to him seeking safety.

"We're just going to have to do this alone," Jade said.

"I suppose it was always going to be that way," Kaiden said.

He didn't want to think of all the bodies he left behind in the gully and on the rocky hillsides. It was becoming more difficult to see himself as a freak when the other clones were all so human. So alive. He was just one of them. How had his brain become so warped? Still, he had killed them. Colt, the little girl, his men. They were all dead. He glanced at Jade as the bitter sorrow expanded inside him.

"I'm sorry about Colt," he said. "He was a good man."

Jade worked her jaw and blinked rapidly. "I can't believe he died that way," she said. "I'll miss him."

They brooded in silence for a long time as the airship hurtled through the skies.

"Flint says Noah is still in Florida," Jade said. "I don't know how he knows, but…" She shrugged.

"I need to tell you all something," Kaiden said. He hesitated. Would they think he had betrayed them? "Noah contacted me again."

"What?" Jade said.

"She said there are three Noah clones," Kaiden explained, "and they each possess all of Noah's memories. That must have been what was happening when I killed my mother. I saw two other images of her on the screen. I didn't know what to make of it at the time, but Willow says they were syncing their memories."

This is what Willow had explained to him the night before.

"Ouch!" Kaiden clenched his teeth as Willow used a syringe to squirt antiseptic into the bullet hole. Fortunately, Rio had been using steel-jacketed rounds that allowed the bullet to pass clean through the flesh of his thigh without causing serious damage.

Jade sniffed as he winced. "Time to toughen up."

"Thanks," Kaiden said.

"Anyway," Willow continued. "Noah is following the old flood stories. There were only three sons of Noah that represent the three branches of humanity as early people saw it."

"That's what she told me," Kaiden said.

"Did she say anything about the tree?" Jade asked.

Kaiden shook his head.

"That's the other thing I wanted to tell you," Willow said. She finished wrapping the bandage and pulled the cut pant leg over the wrapping. "I've been researching the Tree of Life and trying to read through the garbled files we took from Noah's computer. Did you notice that the tree in both pictures is deciduous? It's not an evergreen."

"So?" Kaiden said.

"So," Jade interjected, "in the ancient world, the deciduous Tree of Life represented renewal and regeneration. In Egypt, it was the mother goddess that sheltered and protected, and it represented the beginning and ending of cycles of renewal."

"That's right," Willow said.

Kaiden waited for them to explain. This was all very interesting, but he didn't see the point.

"So, The Flood is about renewing humanity, and the tree is their symbol," Jade said.

"What about the little black tubes?" Kaiden asked.

Willow dried her hands. "Maybe you should ask your mother."

Flint and Birch came in. Birch punched Kaiden in the shoulder and scowled at him.

"What did you think you were doing?" she demanded.

Kaiden grimaced. "In case you didn't notice, the T-60 I was going to fly had its engine explode. There weren't any ships left on the ground, so I did the only thing I could."

"Forget it," Flint said. "We're on our way to Florida. We only have a few hours to plan."

"Who's got the ship?" Kaiden asked.

"Blaze is at the controls."

"Blaze, who?"

"He's a flyer," Flint said. "We have five others still with us."

"How are they? Any injured?"

"They'll live," Birch said. "With those five, plus us, that gives us ten battled-hardened veterans to storm TAP."

Flint dropped a tiny device in Kaiden's lap. "That's how I've been tracking Noah. It's connected to the software on the ship she took to escape Ararat. I can't guarantee she hasn't taken another ship, but that's the best we're going to get."

"Speaking of Noah," Willow said, "Kaiden was just going to try to contact her again."

Birch scowled. "Care to fill us in?"

Willow quickly summarized their conversation.

"But do we trust what she says?" Flint asked. "I mean, this *is* Noah."

"No, we don't," Willow said. "But she might give us clues that will help."

"Do it," Jade said. "I want to make them pay for killing Colt and that little girl."

Kaiden glanced at her. He had never seen Jade cry, but the tears hovered in her eyes. She blinked rapidly. He clicked on his wrist terminal and typed a quick message.

"Mother, we need your help."

Almost instantly, a reply came. "You must act quickly."

"Why?"

"My sisters want to begin The Flood. I can't stall them much longer."

"What is The Flood?"

"Trees of Life have been planted across the earth in a vast network. They bear the black fruit that will destroy humanity."

"You mean there are actual trees?" Birch asked.

"The black fruit must be the tiny glass tubes," Jade said.

Kaiden typed in another message.

"What is the fruit?"

"A nano-virus created to destroy humanity."

"And the clones?"

"They are genetically modified to survive the virus."

"How do we stop it?"

"You must kill us. If no Noah clones possess the codes, The Flood cannot be activated."

"How do we find you?"

"My sisters will come when I call."

"Why would you help us?"

"We're not all the same. Not even clones are perfect replicas." There was a pause. "I love my children," the message said. "I don't want their mother to be a mass murder. Nor will I consent to this mad plan to murder billions of innocent people."

"Is she schizophrenic?" Birch asked.

"We already went over this," Jade said. "They're three different people. That's not schizophrenia."

"Ask her how we make sure another Noah clone doesn't reappear," Willow said.

Kaiden keyed in the message.

"I will destroy the files before you arrive. Once you kill us all, Noah will cease to exist."

Kaiden's stomach tightened. That meant his mother would cease to exist. How could she ask him to do this?

"But what about the replacement clones?" Jade asked.

Kaiden keyed in the question.

"I have already seen to that," Noah answered.

"What about Rose?" Kaiden asked.

There was a long pause.

"There are three. I have terminated the other clones in production of that model. You will need to care for these three once we are gone."

"Dang," Birch said, "she is cold."

Coordinates flashed onto the holographic screen. "Come find us. We will be waiting, but beware. I cannot know what the others have planned. They will stop at nothing. Now, I must go. I may have jeopardized everything already."

"Holy jumping toadstools!" Flint said. "She's insane."

"Definitely a split personality," Birch said.

Jade clicked her tongue.

Kaiden scowled. How could the clones have such different personalities? So far, he had met the loving mother and the scientist. What was the other personality like?

"It's a trap," Birch said. "It has to be."

"Probably," Kaiden said. "But do you have any better ideas?"

The pounding of running boots brought them all to their feet. Blaze thrust his head into the doorway, panting like he'd sprinted a mile. His eyes widened at the sight of four guns leveled at his chest. He raised his hands.

"You need to see the newsfeed," Blaze said.

"I thought you were flying the ship," Birch said.

"It's on autopilot. You really need to see this."

Flint fiddled with his computer, and soon a holographic image of the newsfeed filled the center of the room.

A tall man wearing a TAP security uniform straddled the body of a man in a blue suit. He was waving his gun over his head and screaming. "Long live the clones."

While that image played in the upper right-hand screen, a camera panned across a city where the people were rioting. Dead bodies littered the street. Some dangled from lampposts, rotating in slow pirouettes. Mobs swept through the streets, attacking people apparently at random, screaming, "Down with clones."

The news lines across the bottom said, "Breaking News: A self-proclaimed clone has assassinated the chief minister of the International League of Unified Nations. People are rioting in every major megacity in North America. Thousands of people are being slaughtered on suspicion of being clones. The Sons of God are leading the rioting in several cities."

The group stared in stunned silence as the newsfeed repeated itself.

"This must have been part of Oakley's plan," Kaiden said.

Willow gave him a pained look and nodded. "He used us to destabilize TAP and sent that clone to assassinate the chief minister. Now, the only way TAP can survive is to initiate The Flood."

"I can't believe this," Kaiden said.

"It's worse," Willow said.

"How can it be worse?" Birch asked.

Willow let out a long sigh. "He told me that he had been secretly working with Noah to destabilize everything." She glanced at Kaiden. "His men killed Quill and tried to kill you. It wasn't Iris."

"I should have known," Kaiden said.

Birch shifted. "Why would Noah do that?"

"Because," Jade said, "it would give her cover and an excuse for what she was really planning."

"Nice," Birch said.

"Are we going to save them," Jade asked, "just to have them kill us for it?"

Kaiden buried his head in his hands. What a mess. Natural humans had become so depraved. But he also knew he could have been in that mob. He probably *would* have been in that mob. And what about the clone murdering the chief minister? Clones weren't any better. They were all just humans. His agonizing over whether he was human or not seemed so silly now. Then, he thought of Rose. He had to save Rose from being murdered for being a clone. The rest could go to Hades for all he cared.

A memory came to him in a flash. *He was lying on a couch with a blanket draped over him and a hot pack nestled against his neck. He swallowed, igniting the horrible burning in his throat. He moaned, and his mother glanced up from where she worked at her desk.*

"It's going to hurt for a while," she said. "But those tonsils had to come out."

Old books were piled so high on the desk, he could only see her head. Her lips were bright red, and her stiff black hair had been straightened. Nobody used books anymore, and he couldn't figure out why she wanted them.

Maps and pictures of boats and trees spilled over the edge of her desk.

Behind her, a massive screen flashed images of floods. Brown waters raged through city streets, rolling cars over, collapsing buildings, and carrying houses away.

She noted the direction of his gaze, glanced at the screen, and smiled at him, showing white teeth against her black skin.

"Inspiration," she said.

Kaiden wanted to ask her what it was an inspiration for, but his throat hurt so badly, he didn't want to talk. On the wall above his head was a huge painting of a flood. Naked people clung to a rocky crag and a fallen tree, while others were swept away in the blue torrent. Rain fell from a ragged sky in great, black sheets, and a red sun dropped behind the horizon. A funny-shaped boat bobbed on the waters of a huge sea illuminated by a ray of light, secure in an otherwise drowning world. The caption below the painting read, "Francis Darby, The Deluge, circa 1840."

Kaiden wasn't old enough to know what a deluge was, but the painting and the photos of floods cycling across the screen behind his mother left him with a penetrating sense of despair.

Chapter Thirty-Three
The Deluge

FORREST GREEN CROUCHED over the holographic feed from his wrist terminal as his band of refugees huddled around him. The images tied his stomach into a knot and brought tears to his eyes. The earth groaned and coughed. It heaved and rolled. The slow roar of a shock wave rumbled up the valley toward them, and they grabbed each other for stability. It was here—the earthquake he had predicted finally hit.

In the holograph, the skyscrapers of Los Angeles, San Francisco, and Sacramento swayed, caught in a hypnotic dance before they buckled and fell into each other like drunken partners stumbling across a dance floor. Aerial drones buzzed about, broadcasting the devastation to the whole world. California was finally ripping itself apart.

A gasp from Forrest's wife dragged his gaze away from the horrible scenes. She covered her mouth with her hand, and her face was pale as plaster. She balanced their four-year-old boy, Cedar, on her hip, tears trickling down her cheeks.

This is what he had feared. As a seismographer, he had warned this day was coming—the big one—the earthquake that would topple California's megacities to the ground. No one had prepared for it, despite his warnings. When the government dismissed his final plea, he packed up his family and with a few friends, headed for

Denver. Their airship had mechanical problems and dropped them in the barren foothills of the Sierra Madre.

So now, they followed the tiny sliver of green that clung to the stream that had once been a great river. They had enough supplies to last a few months. If the water held, they might be able to reach Denver or, if necessary, make a home far from the chaos and death of the cities—far from the sunken symbols of human arrogance now crumbling into a pile of useless rubble.

"Let's keep going," Forrest said.

There was no point sitting around blubbering about the devastation. The sun beat down on them with unrelenting fury. Skeletons of dead trees and brush littered the landscape. Forrest struggled to keep his despair at bay. So much had been lost. What real chance did they have at surviving? After several hours more clambering up the rocky river bed, he called his little band to a halt to rest while he and several men scouted the trail ahead.

They hadn't gone far when they came across a great oak tree that soared sixty feet into the air. It was a strange thing to see a real tree, especially out here all alone. Its leaves seemed unnaturally bright in the barren wasteland, but he led the men to it, anxious for a respite from the torturing heat. They scrambled up the broken hillside and collapsed in the shade.

Forrest gulped down the warm water from his canteen and peered up at the towering branches overhead. The trunk was at least three-men wide, and branches as wide as a man's torso forked off in perfect symmetry. Clusters of black acorns filled the tree. Limbs bent under their weight. He peered at the bark, which had a waxy appearance to it—too regular to be natural. What kind of tree was this?

Forrest glanced at the ground and kicked at the dirt. Several acorn clusters had fallen and broken open, spilling tiny glass tubes in the dirt. He bent and lifted one of the tubes. He shook it. Something rattled inside.

"What's that?" his friend, Tony, asked.

"Don't know," he answered.

The men stooped to pick up the tubes.

"What kind of tree is this?" one of them said.

An aftershock growled up the valley, causing the big oak to

waver and tremble. A shiver ran up the big trunk, and the branches shook. Dozens of acorns cascaded onto their heads to shatter on the ground causing a black cloud to erupt from the smashed tubes. The men jumped back. The tree shuddered again. The branches swayed, shaking the strange acorns to the ground by the thousands.

"Get back!" Forrest shouted. They scrambled away from the tree as an explosion of shattering glass burst through the air. A dense, black cloud lifted from the tree, hovered, and spread out like a cancer, staining the sky.

One of the men stumbled and fell, clutching at his throat.

"Run," Forrest cried. "Run!"

He sped downhill as fast as his legs would carry him. He screamed and waved at the little camp. He had to warn them. He glanced over his shoulder. The cloud continued to drift from the tree, spreading in all directions.

"Into the water," Forrest cried. "Get into the water."

Desperation filled his chest. He had to reach his family. They had sacrificed so much for so long. He couldn't let them die now.

Forrest scooped up his boy, Cedar, and grabbed his wife's hand. He plunged into the creek. The shadow of the black cloud passed overhead, whirled, and descended on them.

"Under the water," Forrest yelled. He ducked beneath the water, grabbing hold of an old root to hold himself down. He rolled over to peer up as the black cloud passed. People fell into the water. They thrashed and splashed. Faces, twisted in terror and anguish, swimming in the water all around him. His child struggled in his arms.

Terror gripped his throat. His lungs burned. They were going to drown. The black cloud seemed to go on and on. Then, the clear blue sky reappeared, and Forrest surged out of the water, gasping for breath. His limp child dangled in his arms. The bodies of his family and friends sprawled in the dirt, thrashing about in their death throes or bobbing in the gently flowing stream. Where was his wife?

A sob escaped his throat as he lay Cedar on the grass and bent over him in a desperate attempt to resuscitate him. Fevered moments passed as he performed CPR on his little boy before Cedar sucked in a rattling breath and started to cry.

Forrest held him close as his own tears of desperation slipped down his cheeks. Then he rose and staggered about, checking each of the bodies sprawled in the green grass or bobbing in the water. His wife's body was caught in a little eddy, revolving slowly in the current. He set Cedar on the bank and splashed out to her. Rolling her over and lifting her into his arms. Her eyes were black, and her face empty of life. A sob burst from him as he stumbled to the bank. He brushed the hair from her face and fell on her chest to weep. The end of the world had come.

He didn't stir until Cedar crawled over and placed his little hand on his mother's face. Then, a quiet murmur reached Forrest's ear, and he jerked upright. The great tree shivered, and a new, smaller black cloud drifted from it, heading straight for him as if it sensed his presence. He snatched up Cedar again and jumped into the creek. But the water wasn't deep enough here to cover them. The buzzing grew louder, and he spun about, searching for a place of retreat. But he was too late. The cloud was upon him, swarming around his face. Cedar cried again, and Forrest broke into a run, desperate to escape the clinging death. A metallic taste sprang into his mouth, and his eyes burned. He was going to die, just like the others.

Then the cloud was gone, drifting away on the breeze. His lungs burned, but he was still alive. Cedar wailed, and Forrest tried to calm him. How were they both still alive? He scooped water from the creek to wash their faces and rinse the metallic taste from his mouth. When he rose, he experienced the sudden realization that he would live. Whatever it was, it had tried to kill him and failed. He and Cedar would survive.

CHAPTER THIRTY-FOUR
TALLAHASSEE

THE CITY OF TALLAHASSEE blinked and vibrated around them with the buzz of human activity. A hot wind blew over the rooftops, bringing with it the briny smell of the ocean, which had crawled over the Florida peninsula and swamped everything south of Tallahassee. The city survived because it had been raised up on stilts, like New York City. The lights of the sprawling megacity stained the darkened sky. Millions of natural humans crowded into this artificial island in a desperate attempt to survive on a dying planet. A great stench rose up on the wind.

Kaiden wrinkled his nose at the unpleasant smell and glanced at the gunship behind him, where it perched on the top of the skyscraper. He questioned again what he had come to do. Did he have the right to decide whether these people lived or died? Was TAP right that the planet would be better off if it were stripped of the billions of ravenous people who devoured resources without ceasing? He knew it was really only a few who stripped the earth of its capacity to sustain life in their reckless greed. Most people were simply trying to survive as best they could. What about those people? What did they deserve? Certainly not destruction.

Willow stepped up to him. "We better get going."

Kaiden turned to her. Her face bore an expression of determined sadness. The wind blew her brown hair about her face. She was so beautiful standing with the lights of the city bursting around her body as if she were an angel. Kaiden reached out to clasp her hand.

"Is this the right thing to do?"

Willow studied him and then shook her head. "I don't know," she said. "I used to think the world could be saved if we could just destroy TAP, but now…"

"If we go in there," Kaiden said, "we could all die for nothing. And if we succeed, we could be condemning humanity to a slow, painful death."

Doubt slipped across Willow's face, but she shook her head.

"Or," she said, "we can give humanity time to correct its mistakes. Cloning may be part of the answer. I don't know. But to sit by and do nothing while Noah murders billions of innocent people makes us equally guilty. And I would rather not live than know I allowed that to happen."

Her words seemed reasonable. And yet, a nagging doubt that he was making a mistake still haunted him.

Willow stepped close to him. He could feel her presence. She peered up at him with a steady gaze. Her lips parted, and he suddenly wanted to kiss her. But it was wrong. He couldn't do that to Jade. Somehow on the flight to Tallahassee, he had come to a decision without realizing it. He did care for Willow, but he also knew that he would never be able to overcome the conflicted feelings he had for her. It might not be her fault, but the constant war of emotions he had toward her would not be silenced. He had tried. Besides, Willow was too driven by her own goals for him ever to be sure if she was being straight with him.

Jade, on the other hand, had always been transparent, honest, and loyal. She was intelligent, strong, and compassionate in a way few women were. Maybe Jade didn't want him anymore. She had never tried to show open affection for him since he had refused to kiss her. But this was wrong. Willow didn't deserve to be led to believe he felt more than he did.

Willow rose up on her toes. Her eyes glistened with the lights of the city. Her lips were alluring. Her expression was filled with longing and fear. Kaiden bent and kissed her on the cheek.

Willow blinked rapidly, and a tear escaped to slide down her face. Her lips trembled.

Kaiden squeezed her hands. "I care for you a great deal."

She sniffled. "And I care for you," she whispered.

A long pause settled between them as Kaiden struggled to know what else he should say. He shuffled his feet. Willow bit her trembling lip and wiped the tears away. Then she squeezed his hand, but the hurt never fully left her face. "We can do this," she said.

Kaiden released her hand. "You saw them slaughtering people they claimed were clones. How do we stop the massacres once we save them from The Flood?"

"I don't know. Maybe we can use the TAP records to get the laws changed and convince them to give us clones a chance."

"You think the Sons of God will ever do that?" Kaiden asked.

Willow bowed her head. "Maybe not, but we can't make our decisions based on the hatred of those who do not understand us. When will you accept that you are fully human? That *we* are human?"

Kaiden clenched and unclenched his fists. He wanted to believe her. He wanted to surrender to her acceptance of the fate forced upon them. She was like the others. They had all come to terms with it. Why couldn't he? Willow's arguments were so persuasive. She was right that he was being stupid. Those memories and emotions of the life before he had been cloned were still strong, though they were now tempered by his recent experiences. Yet, it was so hard to let go of old prejudices.

"Maybe the naturals deserve to die," he said.

"You know they don't," Willow said, "any more than we deserve what they did to us."

"I remember her, you know," Kaiden said. "The way she was before Rose died. It's like I have these two drawers full of memories in my head, and sometimes I get lost in them. But I remember her singing to me when I was scared of the noises in the night. She would hold me and rock me back and forth and just sing. I don't remember the words, but I can feel the melody. I used to play it on the violin."

"Would your past self have deserved to die?" Willow asked. "Because that's the fate that awaits billions of natural humans right now."

Kaiden bowed his head. "I know."

"My mother was all I had." Willow scanned the landscape before them. "My father was power-hungry, and he drove my mother mad. She had this little teacup she used to talk to. I think that's what kept her with it long enough to raise us. Once he finally abandoned us, she just quit trying to live."

Birch sprang out of the gunship and raced over to them with Jade trailing behind her.

"It's gone," Birch said. "California is gone. Three megacities with all those people, just gone."

"What do you mean, 'gone?'" Willow asked.

"Earthquake," Birch said. "It's all over the news."

"Wait," Kaiden said. "Didn't that guy tell us that they had shipped the nano-virus to California?"

"Yeah. He did," Jade said.

"Is there word of any massive die-off?" Kaiden asked.

Birch smirked at him. "You mean other than the few billion people who were just crushed?"

Kaiden scowled. "You know what I mean."

"Nothing yet," Jade said. She gave Willow a wary glance, and sadness crept into her eyes. Kaiden needed to explain how he felt about her. Maybe he was too late, but she had a right to know the truth.

Kaiden's wrist terminal buzzed. Another message from his mother blinked on the screen.

"They've arrived," it said. "I can't hold them much longer. Please stop us."

A painful ache burned through Kaiden's chest. His mother was pleading with him to kill her.

"Are we going to do this?" Kaiden asked.

The three women glanced at each other.

"Genocide in any form is unacceptable," Jade said, "whether it's the mass murder of clones or the mass murder of natural humans. It's just wrong."

Kaiden clenched his teeth and took a deep breath. "Then, let's go."

His conversation with Jade would have to wait.

The great, white dome of the TAP facility filled the center of Tallahassee. The files Flint discovered showed that it penetrated deep under the city through the lapping waters of the ocean into the living rock beneath. Down there in the bowels of the complex, Kaiden's mothers waited.

"We've got clearance," Flint said.

"Really?" Birch said. "I can't believe that code worked. Either our rogue Noah really is helping us, or she wants us so deep inside we can't get out."

"Let's hope she's helping," Flint said.

The gunship slipped through the hangar doors and settled onto the landing pad. Flint cut the engines.

"Hold up," the voice of the controller came over the speaker. "Your ship has a red flag on it. Where did you say you originated?"

Flint glanced at Kaiden and raised his eyebrows. "I didn't," he whispered.

"This ship is reported stolen from Ararat," the controller said. "I'm going to have to ask you to remain on board until your ship has been searched. Please have your IDs ready."

"We escaped during the battle," Flint said into the mic. "We're bringing refugees from Ararat."

"All the same," the controller said, "do not exit the craft for any reason. If you are armed, you must surrender your weapons to the security personnel."

"So much for the element of surprise," Willow said.

Kaiden peered out the window. A line of security personnel clad in black made their way toward the ship.

"This is going to get real complicated," Birch said.

Flint glanced at Kaiden. "We do have some nice-sized guns that are pointed right at the control station," he said.

Kaiden nodded. "Do it, but give us a chance to get ready. The rest of us will give them a little surprise. Then, we have to run like mad."

"Don't get too far apart, or the cloaking software won't cover us," Birch said. "It's still centralized from my WT." She glanced at Flint. "You need to extend the range on this thing or just put it on each of our WTs."

"I ran out of chips, and I'm still working on the power supply problem," he said.

"Have you got the bots ready?" Kaiden asked.

"Yep," Birch said.

"When we start shooting," Kaiden said, "light 'em up."

Flint grinned. "I love explosions."

CHAPTER THIRTY-FIVE
MY BROTHER

AS KAIDEN POSITIONED the laser cannon so that it would shoot directly through the bay doors, he suppressed a twinge of guilt. These clones were just doing their jobs. They hadn't received Willow's memories. They didn't know. But he couldn't let them stop him. Not after all they'd been through. A few lives might have to be lost to save billions.

That thought gave Kaiden pause. That was virtually the same argument Oakley had used. How had he come to this? Who was he to decide who lived and who died?

When the guards pounded on the bay door, Kaiden hesitated. He glanced at Jade, Birch, and Willow, and the other six TAP clones—Aspen, Sierra, Blaze, Basil, Pearl, and Stone—who were still with them. They could all die in here, and they all trusted him. But what choice did he have?

He nodded to Jade, who keyed in the code to open the door. It slid open to reveal a squad of security who stared in shock at the laser cannon pointed directly into their faces. The laser cannon blasted into them, and they scattered. Their clothing ignited. Men and women screamed and fell, writhing, to the floor. The stench of burnt flesh and hair filled the bay.

At the same instant, the ship's guns roared and ripped into the glass and metal of the control station.

"Go! Go!" Kaiden shouted.

Jade, Birch, and Willow leaped over the writhing guards, followed by everyone but Flint. The ship's guns rattled again. Something exploded.

"Stop playing around," Kaiden yelled into this mic as he raced after the others. "Get down here."

"You spoil all the fun," Flint said.

Kaiden reached the others as they crouched behind a loading truck while Jade set the charges on the door. A few more guards raced into the landing bay, but Kaiden, Birch, and the other six clones made short work of them. Flint dropped next to Kaiden. Billowing smoke poured out of the control station, carrying with it the caustic reek of burning plastic and hot metal. Emergency lights flashed and a siren wailed.

"I think they know you're here," Flint said. "Might want to pick up the pace a bit."

Jade raced back to them and dove behind the vehicle. The wide loading doors erupted in a spray of metal that showered the vehicle and skidded and skipped across the floor. Flint leaped up, rushed ahead of them, and disappeared into the smoke.

"Idiot," Birch called after him as the rest of the team followed him through the ragged hole where the doors had been.

The corridor beyond was empty. The emergency sirens blared more loudly in the narrow space. Flint paused in the middle of the corridor, where three other corridors converged, peering at his portable computer.

"Birch?" Kaiden said.

"I'm on it." Several nano-bots lifted from her wrist terminal and disappeared into the corridors. A blue holographic screen flickered into existence in front of her, showing the corridors in front of them.

"That's a new addition," Kaiden said, gesturing to the screen.

Birch smiled. "Makes it easier to run."

"We've got to take that corridor on the right," Flint said. "That's the quickest way to the elevators."

"How do you know that?" Willow asked.

"Because I studied the schematics," he said.

"Looks clear," Birch said, "for now."

"Is the cloaking software on?" Kaiden asked.

"Here goes," Birch said as they stepped down the corridor. "I haven't had time to improve the system much with all the fun we've been having. Eventually, you won't need to stay close to me, but for now…"

Kaiden took the lead while Jade brought up the rear. The walls and floors of the Tallahassee TAP complex were polished steel, unlike the white walls of Ararat. The pale reflections of the team on the mirror-like walls disappeared as Birch engaged the cloaking software. Like before, the software made those within its range invisible to anyone outside, but those inside could still see each other.

"That's a little freaky to see your reflection disappear like that," Flint said. "I feel like I just lost my body."

"All we need is your head," Birch said.

"Well, that hurts my feelings," Flint said.

"Will you two can it?" Jade said. "Disembodied voices defeats the whole point of using cloaking software."

"Incoming," Birch said.

The pounding of booted feet on the metal floor grew near. There was no time to dive into a side room. And they couldn't afford to get locked into a fight. Kaiden waved them to the wall. The team flattened themselves against the cold steel, keeping their weapons ready.

The security personnel rushed past them, oblivious to their presence.

"The way is clear," Birch said as the last guard rounded the corner. "The nano-bots are at the elevator."

They raced the last couple hundred yards to the elevator and crowded inside.

"Level nine," Willow said.

Flint, who stood beside the controls, glanced at Kaiden.

"That's where she'll be," Kaiden said.

When the doors opened on the ninth level, they found everything in darkness. Only the blood-red emergency lights pulsed in the corridor.

"Left," Flint said.

They pelted down the corridor, desperate to reach Noah. Kaiden knew that his mothers would know that they had come and would have guessed their purpose. But he was surprised at the lack of opposition. He had expected the elevator to freeze halfway down and trap them inside. It was too easy. If the other clones of his mother were suspicious, they wouldn't have let them come so far unless...

The nano-bots slipped ahead of them to scout the way.

"There's a squad down there," Birch shouted. But it was too late.

They skidded to a stop as bullets zipped and slapped the metal walls and floor among them. Sierra and Blaze fell. Kaiden dropped to his belly and squeezed off several bursts into the guards. Then, he rolled behind the corner and scrambled to his feet.

"I thought we were invisible," Willow said.

"They're shooting at sounds," Kaiden said.

"We can't go that way," Birch said. "The bot shows another squad on its way."

"There's another way," Flint said. "All these corridors converge on a central space that is blank on the map."

"That's where she will be," Kaiden said. "Go. I'll give you a few seconds."

The fuzzy reflection of the advancing squad shone on the polished wall. Kaiden knew the same reflection would give him away as soon as Birch was down the corridor and out of range of the software linked to the chips in his clothing. The cloaking software would no longer work. He glanced at the clones that had been shot. Sierra was dead, but Blaze was watching him with wide, pain-filled eyes. Blaze had taken at least three bullets that Kaiden could see. He wasn't going to last long.

"You and me," Kaiden said. Blaze nodded and raised his rifle.

As Birch and the others raced down the corridor, Kaiden's reflection appeared in the polished metal once he was out of range of the cloaking software. A cry rang out, and bullets slapped into the steel walls. Blaze starting firing, and Kaiden reached around the corner and fired.

Amid the deafening clamor, Kaiden heard the distant metallic bang of a grenade bouncing off the wall. It rolled past Kaiden down the corridor. Kaiden dropped to the ground and covered his head as the grenade exploded. Fragments of metal bit into his legs and back. He grimaced at the pain, but he couldn't worry about them. He had to rely on the INCR to keep him alive.

Kaiden raised his rifle. But before he could shoot, bullets zipped overhead and slammed into the guards that barreled around the corner. Kaiden glanced back but couldn't see the others who were still within the range of the cloaking software. They must still be giving him cover.

The other guards stopped and tried to poke their rifles around to get at him. Kaiden tossed his own grenade around the corner and scrambled to his feet. One glance at Blaze told Kaiden that he was dead. A large piece of metal protruded from Blaze's neck. Kaiden raced after his companions as his grenade exploded behind him, but he skidded to a stop.

The first grenade had blown a hole in the floor. He didn't have time to figure out how to get over the jagged gash in the floor. He yanked open the nearest unmarked door, glanced at his two dead companions again, and slipped inside.

He closed the door quietly, pressed what he thought was a lock, and strode into the dark room lit only with red, flashing emergency lights. Gunshots echoed in the corridor, and he figured Jade, Birch, and Willow were covering him while Flint figured out where to go.

The room was a large storage space. Row after row of shelves with boxes and equipment lined the room. A door with an exit sign flashing above it stood on the far side of the room. He broke into a run but had sped only half a dozen paces when a man stepped in front of him—a stocky, black man about seventeen years old with short-cropped curly hair and black skin—a man wearing a black security uniform carrying the same weapons Kaiden carried.

Kaiden slid to a stop. For a moment, he thought he was peering into a mirror or a highly polished wall. His senses seemed to have betrayed him. He looked on in confusion, wondering if the explosions had rattled his brain, like the one on the lunar transport.

The clone sneered. "You won't be killing our mother again," he said.

CHAPTER THIRTY-SIX
TERMINATION

"LET'S GO," Flint called.

Willow hesitated. Kaiden was still back there, somewhere. This wasn't how it was supposed to be. What if he died before she could explain everything to him?

She started back down the corridor when Birch grabbed her wrist.

"What are you doing?" she demanded.

"Kaiden," Willow gasped.

Jade grabbed her and spun her around. "You can't do him any good standing here while they shoot you," she said. She pushed Willow toward where Flint was beckoning to them.

Flint led them through a series of labs and storage rooms until they came out in another corridor. They pelted through the eerie, red lights and wailing sirens to a set of large, double doors at the end of the corridor.

To Willow's surprise, the doors weren't locked.

"It's a trap," Birch said.

"Probably," Flint said.

"Do we have a choice?" Jade said.

"What about Kaiden?" Willow asked.

They all stared at her.

"He'll make it when he can," Birch said as she pushed past them

285

and slipped inside.

Willow was the last through the door. She pulled the rifle to her shoulder even though she wasn't a good shot. The room was darker than the corridors had been. No emergency lights flashed in here, but the blue glow of dozens of holographic screens pierced the darkness. A large circular column that appeared to be another room filled the center of the space.

"Good grief," Birch whispered. "What is this?"

Machine guns exploded—little bursts of lights flashed in the darkness. The bullets zipped past, pinging and ricocheting off the walls. Flint grunted and toppled over. Pearl fell against the wall and slid to the floor, leaving a dark stain. The bullet had gone through her head. Willow's stomach lurched. They were going to die before even finding Kaiden's mother.

"So, you already know that we're clones," Kaiden said to the sneering young man who looked just like himself.

The clone raised his rifle. Kaiden tossed one of Jade's grenades and dove behind a shelf filled with boxes that bore the Tree of Life symbol. Bullets slammed into the boxes before the grenade exploded with a deafening roar. Kaiden waited, expecting to see some tiny nano-tubes spill from the boxes, but a thin, silver liquid dribbled to the floor.

Kaiden tried to avoid touching it as he worked his way around to get behind the clone. For all he knew, that silver liquid was part of The Flood—maybe some acid that would eat him alive. The clone anticipated his every move as they engaged in a weird cat-and-mouse game in the eerie shadows of the storage room.

Kaiden cursed. How does a person outsmart himself? They exchanged several bursts of gunfire before the idea came to him. If this Kaiden already knew that Noah was their mother, then maybe he had bits and pieces of the other memories. Maybe Kaiden could distract him long enough to shift things in his favor.

"How much has she told you?" Kaiden called.

"Unlike you," the clone said, "I remember my family."

"Do you remember how we died?" Kaiden shouted.

"I know how *you're* going to die," his clone replied.

"You know then," Kaiden said, "that she planned to let us die so she could clone us, don't you? Even though she knew we would rather remain dead than be cloned?" The thought hadn't occurred to him until that moment, but it made sense with everything else he had learned. Maybe he could have reconciled himself to having a new chance at life if he hadn't also known that he would be slaughtered at age twenty and reborn again. Not much of an existence.

His clone didn't say anything.

"Ah, so you *do* remember. You remember why we were opposed to cloning?" Silence. "No? Well, let me help you." Kaiden crawled to the end of the aisle and slipped into the next, trying to angle toward the door he had seen in the far wall. "The cloning program stole resources away from curing diseases," he continued, "from developing new food supplies and improving the lives of natural humans. We used to be idealistic and committed to goodness and justice. And that's why we hated her. Because she stood for selfishness, pessimism, and waste."

A bullet zipped past Kaiden's head so close that he felt the breeze against his sweating skin. He slipped a box from a shelf and crawled through to the next aisle. He needed to get to the door.

"Did you know that she cloned Rose, too?" he called. "That beautiful little girl who used to climb on our knees and squeeze our face between her chubby hands?"

Silence followed.

"Remember how much we hated her for not saving Rose? It turns out that she let Rose die too so she could test her new synaptic download and cloning process."

"Keep talking, moron," his clone said.

"And she's been using us as guinea pigs, too," Kaiden continued. The door was getting closer. "You know she's gone through several models trying to create a Kaiden just like you. One who is so devoted to TAP that he won't ask the questions every other clone has asked. She bred us to be stupid and easily controlled. I beat her at it. But you are apparently her star product—produced in a test tube to become her lap dog. To do her bidding even when it means denying your own identity."

A grenade rolled across the floor, and Kaiden dove behind another shelf of boxes as a spray of bullets ripped into the floor behind him. The grenade exploded. Boxes lifted off the shelf and scattered around him. The silver liquid spilled over his clothes, soaking into his uniform. It was warm and slick, but it didn't feel wet. Terror gripped his throat. He tried to scramble away from it, afraid that it might be dangerous, that it might simply consume him like acid. But when no pain followed, he focused on the real danger to hand.

He used the cover of the smoke and the noise of the explosion to circle back. There had to be some way to outthink his clone. There was no way he was going to escape alive, and if he did, his clone would simply follow him. This had to end now. He didn't want to kill his clone. In a strange way, it felt like suicide. But this version of himself had been too well-programmed. His mother had finally created the perfect child he'd never been able to be. Kaiden leveled his rifle at the back of the clone's head and placed his finger on the trigger. One shot with an exploding round would end this. He had to reach his mother before it was too late. But could he kill himself like this? Did he really want the added guilt of killing a clone of himself to that of having shot his own mother? He was justified, of course. It would be self-defense. Kaiden straightened and lowered the rifle. He couldn't do it. He wouldn't.

The clone spun and raised his own rifle to shoot Kaiden through the cloud of drifting smoke. Kaiden stood there. Would his clone kill him? Would he do what Kaiden could not?

Just as Kaiden's clone slammed his rifle into his shoulder and sighted down the barrel, he stiffened and cried out in sudden agony. He squeezed the trigger, and a burst of exploding shells raked across the stacks of boxes and into the ceiling as he crumpled to the floor, writhing in anguish.

Kaiden couldn't help but experience sympathetic discomfort. After all, he knew what was going through the clone's head. But this discipline episode didn't end. It kept going and going. Kaiden's stomach tightened. It was a disturbing, dreamlike experience to see himself struggling in such agony and to know that there was nothing he could do to stop it.

His wrist terminal buzzed, and he glanced down. "I've terminated him," his mother said. "Come."

A sick knot twisted Kaiden's stomach. To his mother, he would always be expendable. He approached the still-twitching body and knelt beside him. The clone's face, *his* face, was contorted in the most awful expression of torment. His body was bathed in sweat. Trickles of blood dribbled from his ears and nose.

Kaiden tried to find a pulse, but there was none. Pity and horror filled his heart. What a waste. But he had no time to ponder it. He rushed toward the door. He had to end this.

Even the Noah, who was helping him, was capable of murdering her own son. That was the true essence of his mother. Once she had determined on a course of action, nothing would stop her. She had no scruples when she pursued an agenda she thought was right. To her, the ends justified the means.

The door he had locked behind him when he entered blew open with a spray of hot metal. Kaiden spun and fired into the doorway, tossed a grenade toward it, and leaped for the exit. He raced into the corridor beyond and veered to the right. He knew from Flint's schematics that all the corridors on this level converged on a central chamber. His mother was supposed to be down there somewhere.

The emergency sirens continued to blare, and the security lights flashed. Gunfire and explosions echoed down the corridor. The guards would be following him. He passed through another room to the next corridor and knelt to balance a grenade against the door so that it wouldn't go off until someone opened the door. Then he sprinted down the corridor, ignoring the stabbing pain in his legs from the shrapnel of the first grenade, desperate to reach his friends. The INCR would have to work while he ran.

CHAPTER THIRTY-SEVEN
MOTHERS

THE SOUNDS OF battle rebounded down the hallway as Kaiden pelted through the darkness, lit only by the crimson emergency lights. He threw open the door and found himself in a dark room filled with blue holographic images and desks. The air tasted of gunpowder. To his dismay, he found his friends pinned against the wall to his right. Why didn't they have their cloaking software on?

In front of them, a squad of at least fifteen security guards fanned out in a semi-circle to protect the doorway to a large circular column that filled the center of the room. Basil's body draped over the desk. Terror for the rest of his friends burned in his chest.

A few of the security squad closest to him swung to face him, and Kaiden raised his rifle and fired directly into the flank of the semi-circle. He advanced as he fired. Guards dropped and stumbled about, apparently confused by the new assault. Half of them crumpled to the ground before the rest scattered for cover amid the maze of desks and chairs.

Jade's crouching form circled the other way around the central room. Kaiden could always count on her to see the bigger picture. Willow and Birch were firing from behind a desk. Kaiden couldn't see Flint, but Stone lay sprawled on the floor.

Caught between a three-way crossfire, the last of the guards were down within a few minutes. Jade was already at the doors to the central chamber by the time Kaiden reached her. She gave him a relieved smile and yanked on the door handles. But they were locked. So, she set charges on the door.

"Where's Flint?" Kaiden said.

"Kaiden," Willow called. Birch half-carried a stumbling Flint toward them. Even in the dim light, Kaiden could see the wet stain on his jacket. Kaiden raced to help them.

Flint tried to smile at him. "I'm trying to let those little INCR buddies do their job."

"Where are Aspen and Pearl?" Kaiden asked. They were the last of the clones that came with him from Ararat.

"Dead," Birch said. She held up her WT to show it had been hit and crushed. That would explain why they weren't using the cloaking software.

Flint scowled at Kaiden's jacket. "What have you been rolling in?"

Kaiden glanced at the silver liquid that had soaked his jacket. It was starting to lose its color, assuming the same color as his jacket. "No idea," he said.

"Get back!" Jade shouted.

They dove behind the desks as the charges blew the doors from their hinges. Jade and Birch rushed into the haze. Kaiden left Flint leaning on Willow and followed.

He found himself in a round room with a high ceiling. On the wall in front of them, a huge screen showed a map of the world dotted with thousands upon thousands of symbols of the Tree of Life. All the trees in California and the surrounding area were blinking red.

Before the screen stood three women. The one in the center was shouting at the other two.

"Mother!" Kaiden yelled. "Stop."

All three women spun as one. They were identical, though apparently different ages. Even the clothes they wore were the same. And they all wore that bright red lipstick that he found so disturbing. As they faced him, Kaiden realized that all three of them held pistols in their hands. He leveled his rifle at them.

"Please don't do this," he said. The thought of killing his mother again turned his stomach sour. Even though he now knew that they were clones, they were still human. He didn't think he could do it again.

"You're too late," the one in the middle said.

Kaiden hesitated. He knew what he had to do.

"Why trees?" Jade shouted.

The three women stared at her.

"I mean, why not rockets? Wouldn't that be more effective?"

"Rockets draw too much attention," the woman on the right said, "and they can be shot down in the outer atmosphere by any anti-missile system. The spores would be destroyed before reaching the earth." This must be the Security Mom.

"Besides," the one in the middle said. "Symbolism is important. The Tree of Life connects us back to our ancestors and grows into the future. If you're going to do something, you might as well do it with a flare, don't you think?" She was clearly the Scientist Mom.

"Please don't make me do this," Kaiden begged.

"Shoot us," the one on the left shouted. "Do it now before it's too late." Kaiden stared. This was the Loving Mom, the one that had been helping them.

The Scientist Mom in the middle raised her pistol and shot Kaiden. The bullet punched into his chest, knocking the wind out of him. He stumbled backward in shock and dismay. Willow screamed. His mother had actually shot him. Somewhere in the unconscious recesses of his soul, he had believed they would still love him—that he would be able to convince them of the madness of The Flood plan.

Kaiden regained his balance and placed a hand to his chest, expecting to find a gaping hole. But the silver liquid that had spilled on him in the lab had absorbed the bullet and held it in a silver cocoon.

"Cool," Kaiden murmured.

"Watch out!" Willow cried again. Kaiden glanced up. The Scientist Mom aimed her pistol at him again, a snarl twisting her face. Willow leaped in front of him just as the gun fired. Willow grunted and crumpled sideways. Kaiden caught her as she fell. Horror filled his chest and burned in his throat. It was hard to breathe.

Jade aimed at the woman pointing the pistol at Kaiden. It was one of the clones of his mother. She had shot one in the Genesis Room, and Kaiden had finally killed her back on level nine at TAP. Now, there were three of them, and two of them were trying to kill Kaiden. He had insisted that he be the one to kill them, but Jade saw what that had done to him back at Ararat. If he shot these three, it would tear him apart. She had done worse in the service of TAP. She would scar her own soul to save his.

Another pistol shot sounded. The Loving Mom, who had screamed at Kaiden to shoot them, tumbled backward onto a desk and slipped to the floor. The Security Mom loomed over her with a sneer.

Jade squeezed the trigger twice, and the rifle recoiled for each shot. Wham! Wham! The two remaining Noahs toppled to the floor—exploding rounds punching through their foreheads. Even if they had INCR, they couldn't survive a shot like that. Kaiden would not have to bear the pain of killing his mother again and again. Jade made sure of it.

Kaiden snapped up his rifle, but Jade was already firing. The Scientist Mom staggered with the impact of exploding rounds and collapsed. Then the Security Mom fell. Kaiden dropped his rifle and bent over Willow, fumbling with her jacket to see the wound. He had to do something. Crimson blood pumped out the hole in her throat to stain her pale white skin. A sob escaped his throat as he clamped a hand over the gaping wound. This couldn't be happening again.

Jade lowered her rifle with a grim expression.

"Birch," Kaiden shouted. "Help me!"

He used his hand to cover the hole in the other side of Willow's neck and tried to squeeze off the flow of blood, shifting to ease the pain from the wound in his own leg. The blood from Willow's neck seeped through his fingers, warm and slick.

Willow blinked up at him. She grabbed his arm and squeezed. "I'm sorry," she gurgled. "Kaiden, please forgive me." Her grip loosened. "Kaiden. It's Kaiden."

"Hang on," Kaiden said. Tears dripped from his eyes. His chest was going to explode—first his mothers and now Willow. "Please," he whispered.

Birch and Jade knelt beside him. Jade gave him a pitying frown, and Birch reached around behind Willow with a bandage in her hand to stop the flow of blood out of the exit wound. But the look she gave Kaiden told him they had been through this before with Quill.

"No," Kaiden said. He grabbed another bandage Jade held out to him and stuffed it in the wound. Willow blinked at him. Her WT buzzed like it had just finished transmitting some message, and she lay still.

The bottom fell out of Kaiden's stomach. Tears dripped from his eyes. He lunged to his feet and strode to the center of the room where his mothers' bodies lay. He was going to make certain they were finished this time for sure. But he found them all dead. Jade had shot to kill.

"Why?" Kaiden screamed. "Why?" Hot tears burned his eyes.

The blue screen above him flashed, and an old woman with white hair and bright red lipstick peered down at him from an inset box in the upper corner of the screen.

"Mother?" he said. How many more were there?

He wiped at his eyes to make sure he wasn't seeing things in his rage and horror. It was her. It was really her—not some clone. This was the mother who haunted his dreams. The one he had so longed to see. She must have been nearly eighty years old.

"Mother?" he said again.

"You're too late," she said. "The earthquake has already unleashed the virus in California. If The Flood is going to be effective, I can't wait any longer."

That's all she could say to him, after everything she had done to him? Not, *How have you been?* Not, *I'm sorry.* Not, *I love you.* Just, *You're too late.*

Her voice had grown harsh and gravelly, devoid of emotion. She had become the heartless monster he had always thought her to be.

Kaiden swallowed the knot that rose in his throat. Burning

despair flooded his chest. He let his gaze drift to the thousands of flashing red Trees of Life on the screen. His mother reached for something in front of her.

"I've sent the codes," she said.

Little trees flashed all over the world, one at a time at first and then in groups. Soon, all of the trees were pulsing red—a vibrant crimson flood sweeping the earth.

"No," Birch said.

Clearly, the Loving Mom had been wrong. His real mother had made sure her clones couldn't start The Flood individually, but she had always made sure she could. It was just like her. She had reveled in control.

"It would be cruel," his mother continued, "to condemn humanity to the slow death of a dying planet when they could all die in a matter of hours."

Kaiden stared in horror as the map of the world was lit with blinking red trees. His blood ran cold. They had failed. After everything they had sacrificed, it had been for nothing. His own mother had just unleashed the plague of the apocalypse on the world, and he had been powerless to stop her.

Flint's voice called from the doorway. "How do you know the virus won't kill clones?"

Noah stared down at them from the computer screen. "I tested the virus on myself."

Kaiden glanced down at the bodies of the clones of his mother. She had bred them and used them the same way she had used all of the clones. It was sickening. Revolting.

"I've ordered a halt to all operations against you," she said. "A new world is coming, and we need all clones to work together."

Fury surged up to strangle Kaiden. If he could have shot her at that moment, he would have done it. She was insane, a maniac, a mass murderer.

"Where's Rose?" Kaiden demanded.

His mother hesitated, deliberating. She pointed to a side door. Kaiden limped into the little room and found three terrified children cowering in a corner. They were all identical, with the same long, curly hair and pink, frilly dresses. The confusing rush of emotions left Kaiden speechless.

"Kaiden?" one of them whispered.

A knot filled his throat. Birch and Jade pushed past him and gathered the girls into their arms.

"We have to get them out of here," Kaiden said in a husky voice as they led the children from the room, trying to shield them from the site of their mothers' bodies.

He glanced up at the screen. "You're not my mother."

She cast him a grim smile with her unnaturally red lips. "I was weak," she said. "I should have let you die hating me."

"The virus is going to kill you too, isn't it?"

"Yes, but my work is done," she said. "The Flood will cleanse the earth, and my clones will soon begin to repopulate the planet and even the stars. I have given humanity a second chance."

Kaiden leveled his rifle at the screen and emptied his clip into it. It exploded in a shower of blue and orange sparks. The three little girls screamed.

"I wouldn't do that around the kids," Flint said.

Kaiden ignored him, enjoying the sight of the smoking screen that sparked and hissed. He spun around to face the others.

"We can't leave Willow here," Kaiden said. He slung his rifle around onto his back and bent to lift Willow into his arms. She was so light. He choked back the sob that tried to escape.

"What about the others?" Jade asked.

Kaiden glanced around. Short of forcing everyone to carry out a dead body, he didn't know what to do.

"I don't know," he said. "I can only carry one."

Jade and Birch collected their friends and laid them in a row with their rifles clasped in their lifeless hands. It was all they could do for them. Then Birch draped Flint's arm over her shoulder while Jade led the three little girls. As Birch and Flint stumbled through the door, a single shot sounded. Flint cried out. Birch swung her rifle around and unleashed a burst of fire into the prostrate guard who had fired at them from the ground. Then, she grabbed Flint and helped him sit down.

"Dang," Flint said through gritted teeth, "that smarts."

The little girls started whimpering, but Jade knelt to soothe them.

"You've got to quit catching every bullet they throw at you,"

Birch said.

"I'll work on that," Flint replied.

Birch wrapped a quick bandage on the new wound in Flint's thigh, and they were soon hobbling through the double doors into the empty corridor beyond. Kaiden glanced back at the smoking screen and the three crumpled forms beneath it. A deep bitterness filled his chest. It had all been for nothing. He hefted Willow in his arms and limped from the room.

As they passed through the corridors, groups of clones gathered to watch them pass. Some wore blue and white lab coats—others in black security uniforms with their weapons dangling loosely in their hands. No one tried to stop them.

Kaiden didn't care anymore. He ignored the dull ache in his legs and back from the shrapnel and gun wounds. The INCR was already repairing them, though he would have to have the metal fragments removed eventually. That pain was nothing to the horrible agony that pounded in his chest. Willow had thought she was saving his life. She hadn't known about the strange silver liquid. She had died for no reason.

The silent watching crowd marked their progress, parting for them. Some glared, and others cried. Wrist terminals broadcast the scale of the destruction sweeping the globe. Everyone knew TAP had irrevocably changed, that the world would never be the same.

They found their gunship where they had left it. The control station still belched out black smoke, and the security encircling their gunship dispersed as they neared it. Kaiden laid Willow on the floor beside the gunship. Flint collapsed to sit with his back to the landing gear. Kaiden glanced at Birch.

"You've got to get a message out to all clone stations and ships," he said, "to get as many naturals as we can to the space elevators for immediate evacuation to the space stations."

Birch hesitated. "It's too late."

"We have to save some of them." Kaiden couldn't keep the desperation out of his voice. "You and Jade take the T-60 and get as many as you can from Tallahassee."

"Kaiden—" Jade began.

"No," Kaiden said. "We can't let her kill them all. Not after..." He bowed his head over Willow's body.

"I'll send the message," Flint said. "You two get going."

Kaiden didn't raise his head to see the two women climb aboard the ship. He lifted Willow into his arms and carried her away from the ship and laid her on the ground before returning for Flint. The T-60 carrying Jade and Birch lifted into the air and shot out of the hangar with a roar of its engines. Would they be able to save anyone?

Flint began working on his computer. He called up a newsfeed in one window while he clicked away in the other. Kaiden bent close. People staggered about and collapsed into piles of writhing bodies. Close-ups showed great, black lifeless eyes and black liquid leaking from ears and noses as they thrashed in agony. No broadcasters were speaking. Only the steady stream of live images from aerial-bots from around the world showing the same gruesome scene over and over again. Kaiden turned away. How many billions would be dead before the day was over?

"I'll be back," he said to Flint.

He had no idea what they would do now or where they would go, but if that silver liquid had saved his life so easily, they might as well take some with them. If nothing else, the project gave him something to do, so he didn't have to think, so he didn't have to feel.

CHAPTER THIRTY-EIGHT
CHANGE OF PLANS

KAIDEN SET WILLOW'S computer on the table and clicked it on. Her body lay on the cushioned seat under the window with a blanket pulled up to her chin to hide the vicious wound in her neck. Flint was flying the big T-60 Python to somewhere. Kaiden didn't care where.

They had waited in Tallahassee until Flint's injuries were treated, and the INCR healed him sufficiently for him to get around. Jade and Birch had been gone for hours in their search for any surviving naturals, but the city had become a graveyard. Buildings were filled with the dead and dying. Corpses bobbed in the waters like some grotesque algae bloom. It appeared that no one was left, but the clones TAP had engineered.

All of the clones who joined Kaiden had died, and he had been forced to leave their bodies behind—Aspen, Sierra, Blaze, Basil, Pearl, Stone—all of them. They, too, had died for nothing because they followed him.

The image of Willow's face twisted in pain, and the grasp of her hand on his arm as she begged him for forgiveness still haunted him. Forgive her for what? For all the times she had concealed information from him, for taking them to Oakley, for Oakley's murder of the children? Or was she apologizing for dying without really explaining why she did what she did?

THE CLONE PARADOX

Everything he tried had gone wrong. Restoring his memories hadn't brought him any peace. He'd been forced to kill one of the clones of his mother. He failed to stop her from unleashing a horrible virus on humanity, and Willow died trying to save his life. Jade and Birch returned without finding a single natural they could evacuate to the station. After all that they had sacrificed and suffered, none of it mattered. Kaiden tried to ignore the hollow ache in his chest, but it wouldn't go away. It gnawed at him. Accused him.

For some reason, Willow's computer was already on, and when he clicked into it, a message flashed and disappeared. It looked like it had said *Sync Complete*, but that couldn't be possible. He flipped through the file folders on Willow's computer. Most of her files were password protected, so he started typing in random words that came to mind.

He tried every combination of "Oakley" and "Noah" he could think of, but they didn't work. He scrolled through the files until he found one labeled "diary." When he tried to open it, he found it was also password protected. He stared at the screen as the last words Willow said to him filtered through his mind. She had said his name twice.

Kaiden straighted and keyed in his own name. It didn't work. Then his gaze fell on the scar on his forearm where his clone number had been tattooed. He typed in "Kaiden B-22679." The computer purred and the file opened. A quick scan showed that she had kept this diary for forty years. How she had managed to do this while dying and being cloned, he couldn't guess. But, if he had kept his memories from one body to the next like she had, he might have done the same thing, just in case something went wrong.

The early pages of Willow's diary were filled with pain and despair before they evolved into careful notations of TAP operations and programs. Willow had begun scheming early on about how to escape and to find her brother. Then, she tried to work out how to get a memory to them so they would know what had happened to her. Eventually, Kaiden came across his own name. But it was years before he had ever known her.

"What's this?" Kaiden sat up straighter.

The entries were cryptic, but as Kaiden did a global search of the files for his name, his role in Willow's plans became clearer.

Was this why she begged for his forgiveness with her last breaths? Willow had identified him as the one to assist her to break free of TAP and, if necessary, bring it down two decades before he had even known her.

Then, he came across the most damning reference of all.

"I don't believe it," Kaiden whispered. He read the diary with a growing sense of invasion and horror. "What has she done?"

Kaiden jumped to his feet to pace the room. How could she do that to him?

She had started the whole thing. The rush of confused memories that had tormented him for so many weeks had all been Willow's fault. She had uploaded the memories in those few minutes he had been unconscious after the explosion on the lunar transport. Oakley had warned her that Raven was going to attack the crew, and Willow had made sure that she was on that flight to protect Kaiden. She had risked her life to save him, and then she had ruthlessly exploited the moment to awaken him to his lost life by giving him fragmentary memories.

Toward the end of her diary, Willow claimed that Noah's programming had been too effective. Kaiden wouldn't help her unless he had a good reason to question everything he knew about TAP. She had to reawaken the memory of what he had been before.

Kaiden sank into the chair again and bowed his head. This must be why he had never been able to choose Willow over Jade. In his subconscious, he had known she was using him. He had known she was the source of his pain.

What else had she done? Would he ever be able to trust the memories that clogged his brain? The memories, which he thought made him human, had, in fact, led him to murder his own mother in a futile attempt to stop her. He had allowed himself to be manipulated by two of the women he had cared about the most. Both of them had been willing to sacrifice him to achieve their goals. Willow had failed. His mother had succeeded. She had outsmarted them all in the end. Maybe Willow's goals had been less evil, and he had come to share them in the end—but she had still used him.

His mother had even managed to frustrate Kaiden's desperate attempts to save at least a few natural humans. She had been thorough. The map at TAP indicated that all the space stations had

Trees of Life of their own. So far as Kaiden knew, no natural human on earth or in space had survived the catastrophe. Their bodies lay rotting beneath the burning sun in great heaps and piles that would make all the megacities uninhabitable.

His mother had cleansed the earth of its inhabitants in one fell swoop. Her flood had destroyed millions of years of evolution and genetic diversity. Would her crop of eight to ten million clones be enough? Could they survive this final holocaust?

The last entry in Willow's diary was a photograph of Kaiden with his family. His heart raced, and tears sprang to his eyes. His mother sported a fancy, red dress, and the bright, red lipstick. His father dressed in a dark suit and flashed a big, toothy grin. Rose wore the frilly, pink dress she liked so much. Her smile showed the little dimples on her cheeks. He stood between them, gangly in his teenage skin, all legs and no muscle. Kaiden's heart ached. Tears dripped from his chin. This must have been how Willow finally understood who Kaiden was. Why hadn't she told him? She said she was unsure, and she did try to convince him not to go hunting for Noah.

The bitter irony burned in his throat. He had started down this path to find the family he had lost. And rather than finding the love and acceptance he so longed for, he'd found a woman who had already sacrificed him—not once, but many times—and who had just tried to kill him again.

He had murdered the clone of his mother to save humanity, all for nothing. How could he live with himself after what he'd done? He wasn't a monster because he was a clone. That had all been nonsense dredged up in the confusion when his identity had been stripped from him. He was a monster because he had done the unthinkable.

Voices approached. Kaiden rubbed the tears from his eyes and clicked back to the part of the diary where Willow explained what she had done to him. He might as well show it to the others. They had a right to know.

Jade entered with the three Roses in tow. She gave him a sad smile as the three girls came to sit beside him on the bench. They cast wary glances at Willow's silent prostrate form, so Jade reached to tug the blanket over Willow's face.

Each girl had changed from their dresses to the more military-style dress of TAP security. Their hair was combed back in ponytails, and they eyed him curiously. They were close in age. Without the pink dresses, he realized that they were between nine and eleven years old.

When Kaiden didn't smile back at Jade, she laid a hand on his arm. "How are you doing?"

Kaiden glanced up at her and saw the concern in her eyes. He wanted to explain to her what had happened, that he had realized how much he cared for her. But with Willow lying dead beside him and his little sisters looking on, now was not the time. Besides, after learning how Willow and his mother had used him, he wasn't feeling particularly charitable toward women in general at the moment. Did they all use men like this? He didn't think Birch did, but she had never been interested in him. He had never been a lady's man like Greyson, and now he was more convinced than ever that women were way above his pay grade.

When he didn't say anything, Jade settled down beside him and placed a cool hand on his.

"I'm sorry I had to shoot them," she said.

Kaiden glanced at her as the stab of loss punched into his chest. Tears welled up in his eyes but didn't fall.

"You did what I couldn't do," he said.

"I did what you never should have had to do," she said.

Maybe she was right. "Thanks," he said.

Jade shook her head. "That's not the kind of thing you thank someone for, but it had to be done. I wish things were different." Her gazed strayed to Willow's still form. "I'm sorry you lost Willow. I know you cared for her."

Kaiden swallowed the knot in his throat. How did he explain to her how his conflicting emotions had resolved? She probably thought he had rejected her for good. "I did—as a friend."

Jade studied him curiously.

Why was this so difficult? "I'm glad you weren't hurt," he added and reached out to take both her hands. "I'm sorry for…" He trailed off and peered at her with a desperation that boiled in his chest. Their gazes met, and Jade gave him a sad smile. She patted his hand. The Roses fidgeted, and Kaiden reluctantly drew his gaze away from Jade's beautiful dark eyes.

"How are you three?" Kaiden said. They peered at him shyly but didn't reply.

"I'm still trying to process it," Jade said. "I mean, billions of people were just murdered, and we couldn't stop it."

Kaiden grunted. "Yeah. Looks like it was all for nothing."

"You know," Jade said. "I was never opposed to cloning because I was sure we were the only real chance humanity had to survive either on this planet or in the stars somewhere." She shook her head. "But TAP wasn't giving humanity a second chance. We were just destroying them. Genetically improved doesn't mean more valuable." She glanced at the three Roses. "All those innocent children. What a waste."

Kaiden sighed, withdrew his hand, and handed her Willow's computer. "You'll want to read this."

Jade gave the computer an annoyed glance but sat back to read.

"Where are we going?" one of the Roses asked. They peered up at him shyly.

"We've got to do something about your names," Kaiden said. "I can't keep calling you all, Rose."

The girls giggled. "I always wanted to be called Jasmine," the older one said. The other two glanced at each other.

"How about Rose 1 and Rose 2?" Kaiden said.

The girls giggled again. "That's silly," the middle one said. "You can call me Lily."

"All right," Kaiden said. He glanced at the youngest. "That means you're Rose."

She smiled shyly and stepped over to hug him. He squeezed her and blinked rapidly to keep the tears from falling.

Jade clicked her tongue in annoyance. "I don't believe this."

Kaiden turned to find her gaze fixed on the computer. He gave her a sad smile. "It seems I can't trust women."

Jade scowled at him. "Don't paint us all with the same brush."

"Who's Kaiden painting?" Birch said as she stepped into the room. "His paintings would look like Picangelo."

Kaiden shook his head. "Birch," he said, "how do you manage to mix words up in your head?"

"What?" she said with wide eyes.

"It's Picasso," Jade said, "or Michelangelo. Not sure which one you were shooting for."

CHANGE OF PLANS

"Same diff," Birch said. "So, why is Kaiden painting you?" Birch wiggled her eyebrows at them. "I mean, you'd make a great model, but I'd pick someone else to do the painting if I were you."

Jasmine, Rose, and Lily giggled.

Before Kaiden could respond, Flint's voice crackled over the mic. "I've got a man on the line looking for the leader of the resistance."

"What resistance?" Kaiden asked.

"He means you," Jade said.

Kaiden groaned. "There is no resistance. What does he want?"

"How would I know, boss man?"

"All right, I'll talk to him."

"I'm putting him through," Flint said. "You're on, sir."

"Hello?"

"Yeah. This is Kaiden."

"Are you the leader of the clone resistance?"

"There is no clone resistance," Kaiden said. "There's nothing left to resist in case you haven't noticed."

"My name is Omar," the man said. "I am one of the clones Noah inserted into the government. We are sorry for what you have experienced, and we have orders from Noah to invite you to join us as we rebuild our planet."

Kaiden was stunned. "Orders?" he asked.

"Yes. Just prior to The Flood, Noah sent the Council of Clones her final orders. You and your team are to oversee global security."

Kaiden glanced at Birch and Jade. Birch raised her eyebrows. Bitterness burned his throat. His mother had planned everything. And she was still trying to control his life. Well, he was done playing her games.

"No, thanks," Kaiden said. "You should know that there are those of us who understand what's been happening. And we intend to make sure all the other clones know, as well."

"To what purpose?" Omar asked.

Anger burst in Kaiden's gut. "So you won't be able to manipulate them anymore, you murderous swine," he shouted.

"You would fight against humanity's last chance at survival just to spite your dead mother?" the man said.

"No," Kaiden snapped, "but I will fight any attempt by you or anyone else to control us. The clones have a right to be free. We've earned it."

"We seek the freedom of all clones," the man said.

"Don't play politician with me," Kaiden said. "My dad was a politician. My mother murdered billions of people because she couldn't stand what she couldn't control. And now, you ask me to help you impose your will on her lab rats? Go stuff your head in a test tube."

"You don't want us as your enemies," Omar said.

"I'm not looking for enemies," Kaiden said. "So long as you leave me alone, we won't have any problems."

Omar was silent.

"Oh, I see," Kaiden said. "This isn't about saving humanity, is it? It's about *controlling* humanity. So much for my mother's perfect, altruistic race. You're just as greedy and power-hungry as she was."

"I would advise you not to interfere," Omar said.

"You won't need me to interfere once the clones realize what you're up to. You people who lust for power never get it, do you? People, whether they're naturals or clones, don't want to be saved and controlled. They want to be liberated. No amount of genetic manipulation is ever going to strip that innate desire from the human soul."

"I will relay your refusal to the Council," Omar said.

"You do that," Kaiden said. "And, if we're lucky, you and I will never meet or speak again."

The line fell silent.

"I'm not sure he liked you," Flint said over the intercom.

Kaiden snorted.

"Well," Jade said, "I suppose that means we won't be doing guard duty anymore."

"Look," Kaiden said, "if any of you want to go join them, be my guest. I'm finished." He glanced at his three little sisters. "I have a family to care for."

He hadn't considered it until now, but that's what he needed to do. The depopulated world would need to be rebuilt. Why not do it with what family was left to him? He glanced at Jade. She had been so gentle with the girl TAP had killed when they attacked them at the cavern. And she had taken his sisters under her wing. Maybe she would help him with his sisters. He had no idea how to raise three little girls.

Birch and Jade exchanged glances.

Birch pursed her lips. "I think a vacation sounds cool," she said.

"Sign me up," Flint said.

Jade smiled and laid a hand on Kaiden's arm. Her black hair spilled over her shoulders, and her dark eyes glinted in the light of the cabin. Kaiden's gut tightened. He had always found her so attractive. He respected her. She was spunky and a good soldier. She kept a cool head under pressure, and she had always been loyal.

"I guess you have to accept that you're fully human now," Jade said. "Not many other options left."

The memory of her gentle kiss just after his memories had been restored made the heat rush into his face. It was true. His mother had seen to it that clones were the only humans left standing. "I was an idiot," he said. "It doesn't matter anymore. It never really mattered."

"That's a nice change of tune," Birch said. "I was starting to think you were going to start de-evolving into some kind of sludge. Maybe there's hope for you yet."

"I don't think de-evolving is a word," Kaiden said.

"It is," Jade said. "It's a nineteenth-century misconception of evolution because evolution cannot follow the same path twice, and it certainly doesn't travel backward. Even if some previous trait reasserts itself, it is still just the process of evolution."

Kaiden watched Jade. She had a way of simplifying things that was refreshing. Listening to their banter helped ease his sense of loss. Jade met his gaze with a steady, searching gaze of her own. She was asking him what he would do now—trying to understand his intentions.

"Where to now?" Birch asked. She patted her sidearm and batted her eyelashes at him. "We're gonna need something fun to do now that all the excitement is over."

"Colorado," Jade said. "My people came from Colorado."

Kaiden glanced at her. "I guess we don't have to go to the stars for you to find a new homeland."

Jade frowned. "I'll be returning home." She squeezed his hand. "But this time, I won't be alone."

A knot rose in Kaiden's throat. This had been the thing that had troubled Jade the most, and perhaps it was inevitable that TAP's programs would leave a person with a sense of isolation.

"You won't be alone," Kaiden said. "Ever again."

Tears glistened in Jade's eyes, and Birch sniffled.

Lily, Jasmin, and Rose stepped up to them and wrapped their arms around Kaiden and Jade. Birch joined them, and Kaiden realized that Jade had been right all along. It was our values, emotions, and relationships that made us human, that defined the family. Biology mattered, but did not determine the value of human relationships.

Kaiden tried to encircle them all in his arms as the tears slid down his cheeks. Could he create a new homeland for them? Why not? The original Noah and his three sons had colonized the world. Why shouldn't he?

The gunship banked to the left and Kaiden released them and stepped to the window. The dull brown of the rolling hill country passing underneath them was marbled with strips of blue and green, like a diseased organism. Kaiden had gone to Tallahassee to save humanity from his mother's cure for the diseased earth, and he had failed. Eight million clones were all the hope humanity had left. It would have to be enough.

Chapter Thirty-Nine
Survivors

FORREST SCRAMBLED OVER the rocky rise. Hot stones scorched his hand, though he barely felt the pain anymore. Dust sprang up to burn his parched throat. The sun blazed down with unrelenting fury. He clutched his son, Cedar, to his chest with one hand as he collapsed to the ground panting. He was no longer sweating. It was only a matter of time before he lost all cognitive ability.

Cedar moaned, and Forrest squeezed him tighter. It had been seven days since the horrible black cloud had swept over the land, slaying his family and friends. He had left their bodies to bake in the sun as he set out to find some place to hide in case the cloud returned.

He squinted down into the valley below where something glinted in the waning light of the sun. His eyes wouldn't focus because he was so dehydrated. They were still sore and gritty from the attack of the virus. He tried to blink some moisture back into them, but his eyelids clung to his eyeballs. Wrestling with the despair and the certainty of coming death, he shifted so the sun wouldn't shine directly on Cedar's face. His poor boy. Robbed of his mother, perched on death's doorstep. Forrest had given him the last of the water hours ago.

There were only two choices. He could either lay here on the ridge and die, or he could push on. To lie down might be easier, but it would sentence his son to death, as well. He couldn't do that. Not after everything they'd been through. So, he swung his legs over the stone, sat on his backside, and scooted down the rocky slope, using one hand and his feet to control his descent. He was too weak and dizzy to walk, but the promise of some shade or some water in that rocky vale drew him on.

The wild buzzing was the first thing to penetrate the dull haze of his thoughts. Then, the stench and the blurred shapes of bodies stretched out on the ground, swollen in death, materialized from the heat waves rippling over the bare land. The bodies twitched as the mass of maggots wriggled beneath the skin. A woman clung to two children. A man had fallen over them as if trying to protect them. Several more bodies trailed off toward a hovercraft with a long tarp stretched out to one side. All of them had black eyes.

Forrest crawled past them, barely giving them a glance. The burning desire for water shoved any pity from his mind. As soon as he entered the shade cast by the tarp, the temperature dropped twenty degrees. Green plants sprang from the earth beside a shallow pool of crystal clear water. Forrest set Cedar in the shade and scrambled to the water, plunging his head in.

He sucked in the cool, delicious water as fast as he could, but the water hit his stomach like a sledgehammer, and he jerked away to retch. His stomach curled into a ball of pain, and he cursed and groaned until the cramping went away, and he could straighten. Wiser now, he took small sips before resting Cedar in his lap and splashing water over his face. The boy came around, and Forrest dribbled water into his mouth. For the first time in days, he experienced the spark of hope that they might survive.

Hours later, he laid Cedar down to sleep on one of the beds in the abandoned hovercraft and went to the controls. The one nagging thought that had gnawed at him since that vicious black cloud tore the hope from his heart still hadn't been answered. Was he alone? Had anyone survived? Were he and Cedar the last humans alive?

He switched on the power, and the hum of electricity passed through the controls. Lights flashed, and a shimmering blue holograph screen popped into view. A newsfeed panned over a silent city showing heaps of bodies. Forrest stared. He had been worried about the California earthquake when, all the time, this plague had been the real threat. Where had it come from? It hadn't been a natural phenomenon. Those glass vials were manufactured.

Then a female voice came over the speaker as the image shifted to show a megacity that looked like New York City. Sleek, silver hovercraft, bearing the red image of a ship, swept across the screen.

"The new order has begun," the woman said. "The Ark Project has cleansed the earth of naturals to make way for genetically-improved humans who will give the earth time to heal."

The image of a beautiful black woman filled the screen. "This is the future of humanity—genetically engineered to be more altruistic, more environmentally conscious, more intelligent, less prone to disease, less subject to greed and self-interest. Humanity has been given a second chance."

Forrest stared at the screen. "Clones?" This Ark Project, whatever that was, had sent the disease to kill naturals so clones could replace them?

"But there are those among us who fail to recognize the last chance for humanity," the female voice said.

The image of a handsome black man with a scar on his forehead flashed onto the screen. "This clone, who calls himself Kaiden, has rebelled against TAP and seeks to undermine our efforts. He attacked two TAP installations and murdered our beloved director, Noah. He was last seen flying west and is to be seized or shot on sight."

Forrest tuned out to the rest of what she said.

He wasn't alone, but he and Cedar might be the only naturals left alive. Still, if there was a resistance to this new order, he would join it. They had slaughtered his family, but TAP would regret the fact that he had survived.

ABOUT J.W. ELLIOT

J.W. Elliot is a professional historian, martial artist, canoer, bow builder, knife maker, woodturner, and rock climber. He has a Ph.D. in Latin American and World History. He has lived in Idaho, Oklahoma, Brazil, Arizona, Portugal, and Massachusetts. He writes non-fiction works of history about the Inquisition, Columbus, and pirates. J.W. Elliot loves to travel and challenge himself in the outdoors.

Connect with J.W. Elliot online at:
www.JWElliot.com/contact-us

Books by J.W. Elliot
Available on Amazon and Audible

Archer of the Heathland
Prequel: *Intrigue*
Book I: *Deliverance*
Book II: *Betrayal*
Book III: *Vengeance*
Book IV: *Chronicles*
Book V: *Windemere*
Book VI: *Renegade*
Book VII: *Rook*

The Ark Project
Prequel: *The Harvest*
The Clone Paradox
The Covenant Protocol

Worlds of Light
Book I: *The Cleansing*
Book II: *The Rending*
Book III: *The Unmaking*

The Miserable Life of Bernie LeBaron
Somewhere in the Mist
Walls of Glass

If you have enjoyed this book, please consider leaving an honest review on Amazon and sharing on your social media sites.

Please sign up for my newsletter where you can get a free short story and more free content at: www.JWElliot.com

Thanks for your support!

J.W. Elliot

Made in the USA
Middletown, DE
15 August 2021

45339408R00187